NIGHT BLINDNESS

Susan Strecker

THOMAS DUNNE BOOKS
St. Martin's Griffin
New York

THOMAS DUNNE BOOKS.
An imprint of St. Martin's Press.

NIGHT BLINDNESS. Copyright © 2014 by Susan Strecker. All rights reserved. Printed in the United States of America. For information, address St. Martin's Press, 175 Fifth Avenue, New York, N.Y. 10010.

www.thomasdunnebooks.com
www.stmartins.com

The Library of Congress has cataloged the hardcover edition as follows:

Strecker, Susan.
    Night blindness : a novel / Susan Strecker. — First edition.
        p. cm.
    ISBN 978-1-250-04283-5 (hardcover)
    ISBN 978-1-4668-4961-7 (e-book)
    1. Life change events—Fiction.   2. Families—Fiction.   3. Self-realization in women—Fiction.   4. Friendship—Fiction.   I. Title.
    PS3619.T7448N54 2014
    813'.6—dc23   2014021148

                ISBN 978-1-250-04284-2 (trade paperback)

St. Martin's Griffin books may be purchased for educational, business, or promotional use. For information on bulk purchases, please contact the Macmillan Corporate and Premium Sales Department at 1-800-221-7945, extension 5442, or write to specialmarkets@macmillan.com.

First St. Martin's Griffin Edition: September 2015

10   9   8   7   6   5   4   3   2   1

For my mom
I love you more than you know.

The dreams always ended the same. I'd wake up startled and sweat-soaked in our Iron Road loft half a mile from the old cemetery, with Nic's arm around me. "Shhh," he'd whisper into my back. "You're okay." He'd tell me I'd been calling out "Stop, don't" in my sleep. Waking in the dark after one of those dreams made me feel like I was floating without tether, and when I stopped crying, I'd ask him to turn on the light. Only then would I fall into a black sleep. It took me years to tell him that the dreams were in part about Will, the brother I'd lost as a teenager. I'd never told him the truth that they started with Ryder Anderson, and that when I cried out in my sleep, I wasn't saying "Stop, don't," but "Don't stop."

1

I hadn't been able to drive at night since Will died. It came on suddenly after his funeral, a dull blurriness, as though swimming through water; the outlines of trees and houses appeared ethereal, dreamlike. Eventually, my parents took me to a pediatric ophthalmologist, who diagnosed me with nyctalopia, night blindness.

And here I was thirteen years later, driving into the sunset on my twenty-ninth birthday. Nic's party for me had started an hour before, and I was too far from home to get back by myself.

I pulled over. Hadley was working late at Graffiti, and he answered the phone on the seventh ring.

"I'm on Hickox, near Nic's studio," I told him.

"Where in the world have you been?" I could hear him locking the door to his gallery. "Nico has a houseful of people waiting for you."

"I had a modeling job." The truth was, the session had ended hours ago, and I'd been driving through the Sangre de Cristo Mountains near Black Canyon, trying to go home and face the crowd of artists Nic had invited over.

Hadley sighed. "He's going to be blazing mad you're not there." Hadley was from South Africa; he was always using words like *blazing* and *bloody*.

I looked out at the mountains, a deep rust in the twilight. I always felt small next to them. And all alone in the world. "I'm blind," I said. "Please?"

"I'm coming. You'll have the wind in your hair in mere moments, love."

We left my car at Nic's gallery, and I sat shotgun in Hadley's vintage Aston Martin, holding the ocotillo frame he'd made for my birthday. It was empty, just waiting for me to finish my self-portrait. "He probably hasn't even noticed I'm missing," I said.

Hadley patted my knee and lit a clove cigarette. Then he pushed his foot on the gas pedal and we were driving ninety miles an hour down those high-desert roads toward my party.

The loft was lit up like a chandelier, and when we walked up the porch steps, I could see the crowd through the window: sculptors and painters, gallery owners from Sedona, studio assistants and a few models who could have been me ten years ago, when Nic was a stranger and I was just a naked girl in his sculpture studio. Except, I thought, looking in at their tanned, pierced bodies, these girls were prettier.

"The world's come out for your birthday, love." Hadley was on his tiptoes, peering in the window. The air smelled like sage and creosote, and I wished I could disappear, walk into that cobalt sky and become one of the stars.

"They're really all Nic's friends," I said.

Hadley pushed his horn-rimmed glasses on top of his head. "Well"—he flashed me a smile—"they're good for ouzo and pot." He linked his arm through mine. "Come on, Jensen, let's do this." And we stepped into the party I'd been dreading for weeks.

"You're here." Nic threaded through his disciples, his shirttails untucked, and when he kissed me, his breath smelled like wine. "I was beginning to think you'd finally run away with Hadley." If Hadley hadn't been in love with the guy who sold me custom paints and handmade brushes, I probably would have. "I saved you a piece." Nic held up a slice of almond cake. I wondered if he'd lit the candles and who had blown them out. "And good news." He nodded to a skinny man across the room with black hair and a seventies collar. "Dante wants you next week." He took a drag from the joint he was holding. "So eat up." He pinched my belly. "He likes his girls chubby." Dante lifted his glass to me. I'd modeled for him before. His studio was freezing. He sculpted only nudes, and I'd told Nic I didn't want to do that anymore. I didn't want to model at all. But, it was easier than standing at my easel, trying to finish my terrible self-portraits. "They look haunted," Nic had told me. And he was right. It was as if my ghost were trying to emerge through a haze of earth.

"Happy birthday." Whitney, Nic's assistant, bumped hips with me as if we were friends. "Can I ask you a question?" *Can I have sex with your husband?* "Would you consider selling it?"

It took me a second to realize she was talking about the Steinway piano I was leaning against. "What? No."

She fingered a few notes. "Nic"—she blinked her peacock eyelashes at him—"says you haven't played since you bailed on Juilliard."

I took a long drag off the joint Nic had handed me, hoping the slow-motion feeling would erase the awkwardness I always felt at these gatherings. "That's not really true. . . ." The phone in the kitchen was ringing. I watched Whitney's beautiful fingers move along the keyboard. Behind her, two girls at the bar were running a spoon through the buttercream icing on my cake. "Yoo hoo." Hadley danced over in his green leather pants. "Your mama." He handed me the cordless.

"Hey," Nic called out to the room, "turn down the fucking music."

I edged over to the wall and dropped onto the cracked leather sofa. "Jamie?" My parents had already wished me a happy birthday, and my mother never called me twice in one day. "What's wrong?" I glanced at my watch. It was past midnight on the East Coast.

I patted the space next to me and Hadley plopped down. We were so low on the couch, all we could see were legs and skirts.

"Darling." Jamie's voice sounded far away. I saw her in her bedroom in Connecticut, playing with the phone cord, legs crossed, coconut moisturizer on her face. It was just like her to call in the middle of the night to tell me about a trip abroad with her models. "Can you talk?"

"Nic's having some people over for my birthday. What's up?"

Nic sat down on the other side of me and ground out his joint in a stoneware bowl I'd made in college, before I'd dropped out to be with him.

"Jensen, sweetheart, something's happened. I need you to come home." Jamie was forever telling me to get on the next plane.

"What's the matter?" Hadley was picking at his fingernail polish.

"We were at Luke's sixtieth birthday party and—" Someone put on the Beatles' "Birthday."

"Uncle Luke is sixty? Didn't he just turn fifty?" My father's best friend and I used to joke that we were psychic twins because we shared a birthday.

"Oh, honey, it's been a long time since you've been home." Hadley rolled his eyes at the phone and took a sip of wine someone had left at the table. But Jamie was right. It'd been almost two years since I'd been back to Colston, and I was suddenly homesick for the popcorn she used to cook on the stove and those old Hepburn movies we watched together. "Anyway, as we were leaving"—she hesitated just long enough for me to wonder if we'd gotten cut off—"Daddy thought he saw Will."

"Shit." My skin went cold. "Is he okay?"

"He'd had too much to drink. You know how he and Luke are when they get together. Between the two of them, they emptied a bottle of Chivas. And the valet who brought the car around was built like your brother and had those same soft eyes." She said that in the wistful way she had of talking about Will.

I tucked my knees to my chin and touched the tarnished heart on my toe ring. "Getting drunk wouldn't make him see things," I said, wishing I'd taken the call upstairs, but it was too late now.

"Oh, honey." She took one of her shivering breaths. "It wasn't just that. He wasn't himself tonight. He kept forgetting what he was saying. At first, we thought he was tipsy, but when he wouldn't stop calling out Will's name to that boy, we took him to the ER."

"The ER? What the hell?" I sat up straighter, trying to clear the fuzz from my brain. Hadley quit drinking his wine, and Nic leaned in to listen.

"Jensen." Jamie plowed over me, like she had a habit of doing. "Your father has a brain tumor."

A strange spinning sensation hit me, and I felt sick to my stomach.

"Jensen?" she asked. "Are you still there?" I could see my dad, his flyaway wheat-colored hair, how he rubbed his nose against mine and said, "Eskimo kisses, Whobaby, so you'll always be warm."

"Is he going to die?"

"We don't even know if it's malignant." Her voice was far away, almost dreamy. I wanted to strangle her for sounding so calm. She was probably giving herself a pedicure while we were talking. "We have the best surgeon, of course. You'll never believe—"

"How big is it?"

"I'm not sure."

"Ballpark it for me. Is it the size of an orange? A grape?" *Why are tumors always equated to fruit?*

"Just come home, honey. We're meeting Ryder Monday morning. You can ask him about—"

My heart stopped. "Ryder?"

"Ryder Anderson," she said. "Your brother's best friend? That's what I was trying to tell you. He's a neurosurgeon at Yale now. He's very good, a prodigy actually, and—"

"That's crazy." Hadley was pushing up against me, trying to hear Jamie's voice, and Nic had his arm around me, patting my back distractedly. I wanted everyone gone, out of my house. I needed quiet. I needed to think. "None of this makes any sense."

"I'm supposed to leave for a shoot in Brazil next week. I really need you to come home, darling."

Over the last thirteen years that I'd stayed away, Jamie had said those words a hundred times. But she'd only gotten me there every other year or so. Now I could smell the salt air in the house where I grew up, could see those ancient goalposts my father had built in the backyard, the pictures of Will and me in the foyer, and most of all, I could see my dad standing at the head of the stairs and saying, "Whobaby, come up here and give your old man a hug before I keel over from the lack of you."

"I'll be there tomorrow," I told her.

After I hung up, I realized Nic was talking, asking me questions, and Hadley was saying, "Love, I think she needs a drink."

Finally, I let Nic pull me off the couch and lead me upstairs. He sat me down on our bed and closed the door. The noise dimmed, and I stared at the ceiling, holding my tattered stuffed rabbit, Bear. I touched the space where he was missing a marble eye.

"Hey." Nic ran his thumb down my spine. "What'd Jamie do now?"

I could smell the party on his breath. "My dad's sick," I said. "He has . . ." *A brain tumor.* I stared at our wedding photo on the bed-side table, me barefoot on the beach in a flimsy, almost see-through dress with some Greek waiter as Nico's best man.

"Sick sick?" he asked.

"He has . . ." I bit the inside of my lip. The little shot of pain was an elixir. "A tumor in his brain." I didn't look at him. I felt his strong hand on my back, pulling me to him. "They're meeting the surgeon next week." Drifting up from the party a Beau Williams song, "Walk Around Heaven," was playing. *One of these mornings won't be very long. You'll look for me and I'll be gone.* "I have to go."

He smoothed my hair, and I fingered the tattooed rope around his bicep. "You don't want to wait until you find out more? I mean, it could be—"

"It's a brain tumor, Nico, not the flu." I pulled away. The sound of laughter floated up the stairs. "You should go back," I said. "Your friends are down there." I didn't want to cry in front of him. "I just need a minute."

"J.," he said. "Look at me."

I didn't want to. If I did, I might not go home. I might stay in Santa Fe in the strange, artsy world I'd disappeared into ten years before. He tipped my chin up, and there was nowhere else to look. His green eyes turned from the color of sea glass to a shade darker. "You want me to send Hadley up? He can always make you laugh."

"No, thanks."

Nic stood. I watched him walk toward the door, that casual stride that said everything would be all right. Before he turned the knob, he said, "Your old man's a tough cookie. He'll be okay."

While I waited for his footsteps to fade, I traced the birthmark on my forearm. I couldn't decide if it looked like a heart or a football. In my family, they were one and the same. When I was sure Nic was downstairs, I got up and pulled my pewter jewelry box from my top dresser drawer. Sitting on the bed, I tossed aside broken necklaces, earrings with no backs, a baby tooth, woven friendship bracelets, and my acceptance letter to Juilliard. My father's first Super Bowl ring was tucked in a corner, and I slipped it on my thumb. When I'd asked why he'd given it to me and not Will, he'd said he knew someday Will would have one of his own. At the very bottom was the worn photograph, facedown.

Lying back on the patchwork comforter, I studied the picture. Will, Ryder, and I stood three across on the overhang at Breakneck Lake the summer before Will died. Will and Ryder looked like brothers, their blond hair almost white with sun, their tanned chests newly muscled. Will was pretending to punch Ryder in the arm. I was smiling hard at the camera, the kid sister, the tagalong, my black hair wet and curly, my face so tanned that the freckles were barely noticeable. They were seventeen. They were the world. Ryder was leaning back, looking behind Will's shoulders at me. We were perfect, the three of us, so happy. Too happy. I should have known what was coming. Turning it over, I read the date. *Summer, 1996.* I stared at the numbers for a long time. Eight weeks later, Will was dead.

Finally, I put the photograph back in the box next to a foil package of birth-control pills I told Nic I took but rarely did, then stuffed pants, skirts, and shirts into my old leather duffel. I grabbed a bunch of clothes from hangers, avoiding the garment bag pushed to the far wall. Inside, pressed and hidden, was the dress I loved the most: a black vintage sheath I'd worn to Ryder Anderson's junior prom.

2

The porch light was on at my parents' house when the driver pulled in next to a black Navigator. I could barely make out the letters on the license plate. TATUM for Art Tatum, the jazz legend. It was Luke's truck. He'd had those plates for as long as I could remember. Two bumper stickers on either side of the plate read BRING OUR TROOPS HOME and 1-20-09 IT'S ABOUT TIME. Of course Luke would be a die-hard Obama fan.

Parked beside it was a dark green Audi I didn't recognize. I tipped the cabbie I'd hailed at Bradley Airport and then stood on the front lawn under the weeping willow tree my parents had planted the year Will died. In the light of the moon, its branches threw skeletonlike shadows across the yard.

The air smelled of privet hedges, and everything seemed so green compared to Santa Fe. The front door looked immense, daunting, like some kind of protector, intent on keeping me out, and I felt like running. It was strangely similar to the moment before I took off my clothes for a new sculptor, a rising panic that made me feel like I might pass out, or scream out loud for a long time without stopping.

In the foyer, I was met by photographs of Will and me. "Hello?" I set my bags on the floor. The house smelled buttery, like roasted garlic, usually comforting, except with the Navigator outside, I knew Luke was here and had been cooking, which could only mean one thing: bad news. When Will died, Luke had canceled two months of a North American tour to cook for us while we sat, silent in our grief. "I'm home." My voice sounded thready, unconvincing. I corrected myself. "I'm here." I tossed my coat on the banister. "Jamie? Dad?" Down the hall, the kitchen, with its gas burners and built-in wine racks, was dark, but the bathroom door was outlined in light. "Luke?" I took a step forward. No one answered. On the wall was a slightly crooked picture of me at six years old; I was balanced on a stack of pillows, playing Luke's baby grand. Will was standing next to me, sticking out his tongue.

The toilet flushed. A second later, the faucet ran. I heard the lock snap back. And then after thirteen years, Ryder Anderson stepped out of my parents' hall bathroom as if he'd walked out of that photograph from Breakneck Lake. "Ryder," I said. But the sound was a whisper. I could feel my heartbeat in my throat. He held the door handle tightly. I could smell him from where I stood, fresh laundry and lemon, and I almost stepped forward, almost went to him. But something kept me from it. He'd always kept his hair on the long side, but it had been cut military short, and he was wearing a monogrammed oxford shirt. In my leather sandals and cutoffs, I felt underdressed, sloppy. We stared at each other. He was taller. His hair was darker. He was still beautiful.

"Jenny," he said. His voice was low, surprisingly soft.

I wished I'd put on my silver earrings, wished at least I had on lipstick. There were snaffle bits on his loafers. I couldn't remember him in shoes like that except for prom. He'd hardly ever worn shoes when we were kids. He straightened his cuff links. I saw us on our backs on the Hamilton School field, waiting for a shooting star so we could wish for the same thing. The grandfather clock started playing Whittington chimes. He wasn't wearing a wedding band. Eleven strikes. He was so close, I could have reached out and touched his jaw. I thought of us riding double on his red ten-speed bike. He used to go no-handed while I screamed. He leaned away, against the closed door.

"It's been a long time," he said. "I—"

"There you are." Jamie appeared at the top of the stairs. And it was as if I'd never left. Her dark hair was straightened and pulled back in a low ponytail; her baby-doll dress made her look even younger. "Honey," she said in her singsong voice, "I thought I heard a car pull in." She started down the stairs. Her eyes were the color of the sky before a thunderstorm, a wild blue that made men love her. "I was just reviewing the contracts *Vogue* sent for Brazil." She hesitated, as if posing for a portrait, then kept coming with practiced elegance. "Was your flight delayed? You missed dinner," she said, as if I hadn't missed the last thirteen years of dinners. Cutting in front of Ryder, she drew me to her with her small, capable hands, and I braced myself for inspection. "Oh, darling." I could smell the Parisian perfume Mandy and I used to put on our wrists when she wasn't home. She sighed, backing up and studying me, and I felt that hope rise in me, that she would say something nice, that she would approve, but she said, "Santa Fe is still making an art hippie out of you."

"Nic did that to me a long time ago," I said quietly.

She ignored this. "At least that hot desert hasn't ruined your beautiful skin." She pressed the back of her hand to my cheek. "So." She turned to Ryder. "You've seen our little girl, all grown up."

"A sight for sore eyes." He never quit looking at me.

"She's so thin." Jamie's hand fluttered around my ribs. "If you don't have to be skinny to make a living, for goodness sake, why don't you eat? Artists' models are so lucky they're supposed to be voluptuous." She patted my hand. "Right?" I nodded, not bothering to tell her that *fat* went out with the Pre-Raphaelites. "Come." She put her perfectly manicured hand on my arm, leading me to the kitchen. "Luke made his famous coq au vin and saved a plate for you." I felt Ryder follow us. And I wanted to turn around and look at him again. I couldn't get his lips, that beautiful mouth, out of my mind.

The black granite counters were clean, and the dishes had been put away. A cast-iron skillet in the pot rack dripped onto the chopping block. Jamie opened the fridge. She looked so out of place in the kitchen. My dad or Luke did the cooking.

"Where's Daddy?" I asked.

Ryder sat at the island. He seemed so relaxed, familiar with a house he hadn't been to in over a decade.

"He and Luke drank a little too much bourbon. I put him to bed and sent Luke to the guest room."

"Is it okay for him to drink alcohol?" I glanced at Ryder, but he was watching Jamie.

"Oh, honey, we don't know what's what yet." She pulled out a casserole dish covered in aluminum foil.

"No thanks." I hadn't eaten since leaving for the airport that morning, but I wasn't hungry.

She raised her eyebrows. There was the feeling that glass was breaking all around us. "Well, then." She covered it back up. "Wine?" She pulled a bottle of white from the door. Ryder shook his head no, and even though I was dying for a drink, I did, too.

"All right." She gave Ryder a pout.

I watched her pour herself a glass.

"What's going on with Dad?"

Ryder started winding his watch. A fancy one—the kind advertised in men's magazines—that he wouldn't have been caught dead with in high school. I knew beneath that monogrammed oxford he had my father's football jersey number tattooed on his bicep. He and Will had gotten them as soon as they'd turned sixteen, and I'd run my tongue around it more times than I could count. I wanted to reach under the sleeve and touch it now, to make sure it was really him.

"Oh, honey." Jamie blew a few wispy hairs out of her eyes. "You always were one to face things head-on." She picked up her wine and glanced at Ryder. He was still winding. "I think we should wait until tomorrow to talk about Daddy." Her tone was the curt one she'd used to shut me up when I was younger. I didn't know if I wanted to slap the drink out of her hand or cry.

"I'd rather hear it now," I said, and then my cell phone rang—Nic's custom ring. I'd waited for him to call on the way over in the cab, pressing my face to the glass and watching Colston pass, so lush compared to New Mexico. I'd seen the neighborhoods I'd played in and the beaches I'd swum at, Mandy's house, Ryder's.

"I have to take this." The phone kept ringing while I walked across the kitchen. "I'll just be a minute." I could feel them watching me as I let myself out the back door and walked onto the deck. The crisp New England air ran straight through my flimsy rayon shirt. "Hey." I dropped into the love-seat glider.

"Where are you?" Nic asked.

I thought of my mother and Ryder in the kitchen, looking out at me. A thin line of smoke drifted over from the neighbor's chimney. It smelled like hickory; the same scent had been in the air the night Will died. "A quintessential fall day," my dad had said that morning. "The perfect day to win a football game."

"Home." The yard was dark. "And I can't talk long because I literally just walked in the door." I didn't dare look back at them. Instead, I studied the tilted goalposts my dad had built for Will. They were still there.

"*I'm* home," Nic said. "You're in country club kingdom. How was the flight?"

I hugged my knees, trying to keep warm. "It sucked." The yard was bordered by gardens, already in bloom. Jamie, in her designer gloves and imported straw hat, had a green thumb. It looked nothing like our front yard in Santa Fe, which was full of dirt and cacti. "This poor lady in front of me had two screaming babies."

"The only thing worse than one crying kid is two."

I chewed on my lip and traced the letters carved into the cracked wood of the glider's right arm. I was too tired to have the baby fight. I wanted one; he didn't.

"How's your dad?" he asked.

"He's in bed." On the left arm of the glider, Will had pared a line of *X*'s and *O*'s, football plays or maybe a love note. I never asked why Jamie hadn't gotten mad at him for it. I'd caught hell for my graffiti. But he was Will, and I wasn't. "Did you finish the falcon sculpture for Berlin?" I asked.

"It shipped out at five," he said. "Whitney came in around three and helped me with the wings." I heard him lighting a joint. I pictured Whitney on her back, arms spread like wings. "My usual inspiration got on a plane for preppyville." He inhaled. "So," he said, his voice tight with smoke, "are they running tests or—"

"I don't know. We're meeting with Ryder early tomorrow morning,"

"Who is this Ryder person?" He exhaled.

I fingered a hole in my shorts. My skin went hot when I thought of Ryder stepping into the hallway minutes before. I wondered if Hadley had told Nic about him. During all our hours together at the gallery, I'd told Hadley everything about my life. He knew exactly who Ryder was to me. "He was Will's friend." A familiar numbing extended into my chest.

"And now he just happens to be your father's doctor?"

"Odd, right?" I tried to keep my voice level. It was odd, so odd that I didn't even know how to talk about it. A few years ago, I'd read in my high school alumni newsletter that Ryder was a neurosurgeon. I'd logged on to Nic's Facebook account, looking for him, but none of the Ryder Andersons was him.

"Isn't he young to be a brain surgeon?"

"Jamie says he graduated early from Harvard Medical and got hired by Yale right away."

"And Jamie knows it all." I heard the music go on. Crosby, Stills & Nash's "So Begins the Task" filled the phone. *I must learn to live without you now.* "Get some sleep, sweet lady," he said, his way of telling me we were done talking. "Call me tomorrow after the appointment."

"Love you," I said. And then I held my breath, waiting.

He said what he always did. "Right back at ya, sunshine."

I put the phone on the armrest. I wasn't sure I could get up and go back into the kitchen. I wished my dad were still awake; he'd know how to make it okay. I glanced up at the second floor. The light in my parents' room was out. I wondered if my father was really sleeping, or if he was lying awake, worrying. I wanted to go up there and lie next to him. I thought maybe if I heard him breathing, if I felt him put his arm around me and say, "Whobaby, I thought you'd never come home," that scared feeling might go away.

Jamie was wrong. I didn't like to face things head-on. I was terrified of the answers to all those questions that had hounded me while I couldn't sleep on the plane. Was the tumor malignant? When would they operate? Had Ryder thought about me over the years? In the middle of a modeling session, freezing my ass off in some studio, or weaving through the Sangres on my daily run, I would try to guess what Ryder was doing right at that moment, and if, maybe, he was thinking of me. But I knew after thirteen years, he probably wasn't. I never mentioned him when I called, never asked my parents where he was, if they'd heard. And now I knew: He'd been right here all along.

Behind me, the slider opened, and I turned. "Jamie thought you might want these." Ryder was standing in the doorway, the kitchen light flooding around him, holding a red chenille throw and a cup of tea. His posture was metal rod–straight, stiff, and he looked uncomfortable. He put the wrap around my shoulders and handed me the mug. The tea smelled like peppermint. The night Will died, one of the paramedics had been chewing mint gum. I remembered thinking he was trying to cover something up.

"Where is she?"

He put his hands in his pockets. "Reviewing the contract for Brazil."

I blew on the drink. "Nothing for you?"

He checked his watch. "I'm on call. I've got to get back to the hospital soon."

"Oh." I could smell him again—springtime, starched shirts.

"Sorry for the ambush." He looked out at the goalposts. "When

your mom invited me for dinner"—he glanced at me—"I came because . . ." His voice trailed off. I watched his Adam's apple move
when he swallowed.

"Because what?" I set the tea over the graffiti on the glider.

"Because I thought you might be here." He took his hands out of
his pockets. They looked so strong. "I can't believe she didn't tell
you I was coming."

"You're forgetting the three most important things about Jamie.
One." I held up my middle finger. We both laughed. "Don't show up
for dinner without wine." I put up my index finger. "Two, tell her
she's beautiful even if she looks like death on a stick. Two and half,
she never looks like death on a stick. And three." I flicked up my ring
finger and felt Ryder's eyes on my wedding band. I quickly tucked
my hand under my leg. "You never know what you're going to get
with her."

His pager beeped, but he didn't take it out of his pocket. "You look
just the same," he said. "Except your hair . . ."

I tugged at it. "Nic likes it long." *Why did I say that?* "It needs
cutting."

"I heard you eloped."

I nodded. My face was hot.

He jiggled change in his pocket. "Where?"

"Peloponnese, near Crete." This was so awkward. "The orchids
were in bloom." I remembered how I hadn't wanted to go. It was
early 2002, and I'd been afraid of flying since 9/11, but Nic said getting over fears meant getting back on the horse. "It seemed like a
good idea at the time."

"And now?" Ryder watched me.

Steam rose from my tea. I shrugged. "I don't know." How was I
supposed to tell him about my marriage and my husband? As an
undergraduate at UC, I'd sat for Nic—my first time ever modeling.
His then studio assistant, whom, I found out later, he'd been sleeping with until he met me, said he'd pay me an enormous amount of
money to pose. At dusk, light streaming into his third-floor studio,

I'd stood naked in front of the visiting art professor everyone was talking about. Nic was thirty-two years old then, a rising star, fresh from the art scene in Berlin. While he worked, his eyes had been so intent on me, on every part of my body; I'd felt a pulsing need for him, like junkies feel the jones. I'd emerged from his studio a nine-foot angel made of rose Grecian marble. A month later, I dropped out of college to be with him in Santa Fe, but it felt wrong and awkward to tell Ryder all that. "And now is now."

"Jamie said you're modeling."

"Just for artists." I pretended to take a sip of my tea, but I couldn't stand that smell. "Not for print, like her girls." I tried to think of what to say about myself. *I pose naked for men with chisels and hammers and paint bad self-portraits.* "So," I said. "A brain surgeon." It came out sounding sarcastic.

He took the beeper out of his pocket. "That was the hospital," he said. "I'd better go."

Move, I told myself. *Hug him. Make it right.* But I didn't.

"I guess I'll see you at the appointment." He picked up his hand in a sort of wave.

"Yeah." I set my mug on top of two sets of initials on the armrest. "See you tomorrow."

The slider closed behind him. I willed myself not to turn around, in case he was still there, watching me. But as I sat there with the goalposts moaning in the breeze, I could feel him next to me, like it was yesterday, his hot breath, his hands, his mouth on the soft part of my neck below my ear.

I picked up my mug and studied the ring of condensation around the carved heart. In the middle, the initials still read *JR + RA. 4ever.*

3

Hours later, sunlight dragged me from a dream. I woke with the warmth of sex between my thighs and the leaden feeling of guilt on my chest. The pale yellow walls, piano trophies, and signed play sheets reminded me where I was. The program from Adele Marcus at Symphony Hall still hung above my whitewashed dresser. Will and my mother had been home with strep, and I'd walked in my patent leathers through the starry night with my dad. "I want to be a famous pianist," I'd told him. He smoothed my curls, frizzy with humidity. "Whobaby, you can be anything you want."

I slipped on a pair of yoga pants and went downstairs to the dark kitchen, where I made a double espresso. A leather scrapbook was lying in the breakfast nook, and I brought it to the counter. Turning the worn black card stock, I saw my dad at twenty-one in his navy blue suit, blond buzz cut, and clean-shaven face. It was 1973, the year before he got drafted, and he was holding the Heisman trophy. He was the first running back ever to win the coveted award. I took a sip of espresso and turned the page. He was in a muddy uniform, hair wet with sweat, standing next to an NBC newscaster after he'd won his fourth Super Bowl in 1980 with the Pittsburgh Steelers. He had a crooked smile, like he was trying not to laugh. Yellowed newspaper articles chronicled his tenure in the league. The last picture showed him with Chuck Noll the year he'd been named MVP and announced his retirement. When the Steelers finally won another Super Bowl in 2006, I told him I'd come home to celebrate. I never did. When they won it again last year, I didn't even bother to say I'd come back. We both knew I wouldn't.

Tucked in the back of the book was an article about Will being scouted by Notre Dame. His blond hair was curly in the picture, too long. Knowing the scout was coming, he'd promised Jamie he'd get a trim, but he'd overslept and missed the haircut. In the photo, he was wearing a Notre Dame sweatshirt I still had in Santa Fe. He died before his acceptance letter came. Thirteen years of living without him. Almost half my life spent missing him. He seemed about to come out of the picture, pinch the soft skin under my arm, and start singing Garcia's "Jenny Jenkins."

The week after he died, I'd had a constant pounding in my chest, as though my own heartbeat was taunting me. I'd wake in the morning, remembering with a stark, strange shock that he was gone. One evening, I'd had my hand on the refrigerator handle, although I hadn't been eating, and Springsteen's "Blinded by the Light" was playing. I was trying to remember who had covered it. Manfred Mann came to mind. Then suddenly I remembered Will was dead. The sun had gone down and the kitchen was dark. I couldn't see the stainless steel in front of me. The edge of my vision went black. His death had come back in a physical rush, as though someone had hit me. I must have cried out, because Jamie came running, her high heels clicking across the wood floor. "I can't see," I told her. "I can't see anything."

"Come here, baby." She smelled of expensive perfume and jewelry. It's what got her through, I would think later, making everything beautiful on the outside, even when we were falling apart on the inside.

She wrapped me in a throw and sat me on the couch, then went to the bar and fixed a little glass of brandy for me and a big whiskey for her. The light was going down outside. My father was out with Luke somewhere. She put the snifter in my hand. She'd been giving me sips of brandy forever. If the French could give their children wine with dinner, she'd told me, then she could give me a little Rémy Martin when I was sick. I closed my eyes. I didn't like being in the living room, so close to where it had happened. *Don't think of it*, I kept telling myself. *Don't.*

She stroked my hair. The glass was cool. But I didn't drink.

"Mom," I said.

She kept running her fingers through my curls.

"Mommy," I said again.

I heard her rings clink against her glass. "Yes, sweetheart?"

Her fingers caught in my hair. The slight tug was soothing, like pressure on a wound. It almost made me not want to talk again, but I said, "It's not Daddy's fault."

I heard her swallow, could smell the whiskey. "Of course it's not." She sighed the sentence, as though she'd said it but didn't believe it.

"You can't blame him." I was trying to say it quickly, before I lost my nerve.

"I don't," she said, but I'd heard them through their bedroom's thin wall. Jamie had been insisting she'd never wanted Will to play football, though it was she who put his games on the calendar at the beginning of the season, made cakes shaped like footballs, wore his jersey to games.

I opened my eyes. Even though her makeup was perfect and her hair made her appear doll-like, I knew my mother was flawed. She'd been a runway model, married at eighteen to a polo player in Argentina. She met him at a shoot and ran off with him. Her parents showed up in Buenos Aires months later, after she'd lost a baby, and took her home. My dad married her two years after that, and then she had Will ten months later. She sang us Beatles songs at bedtime and let us sleep with her when we had bad dreams. She drank a little too much and flirted with my dad's friends. She was hardworking, ran a modeling agency, taught underfed adolescents how to walk the runway with their hips out and their chins in. Still, she wasn't perfect. If anyone would understand, I remembered thinking, Jamie would.

"That boy from Hopkins didn't do it," I said carefully.

She was just about to bring her drink to her mouth, when she stopped and glanced at me. If she'd never worn makeup again, my mother still would have been beautiful. She couldn't hide it. She wore beauty and vulnerability in the same haunting way. Patting my hand, she gave a little laugh, like she did when my father called her on a third glass of wine at dinner. "He didn't do it on purpose," she said. "Will hit his head on the ground when he was tackled."

"That's not what happened." My voice sounded robotic.

She put the drink down. "What in the world?"

That same darkness crept into the sides of my eyes, and I thought I might pass out. My chest was fluttering like a bird was stuck in there, trying to escape. "Something happened—"

She leaned in quickly and put her finger to my lips. "Jenny," she said calmly, but her eyes were moving frantically, searching my face. "Your brother is dead. My Will is gone." She called him "My Will" as if he were hers alone. "Don't make this about you." Then in one swift motion, she stood and picked up her glass. I watched her move through the room and do what she did best. She left.

"Whobaby." I didn't know how long I'd been sitting there with the scrapbook in front of me. Suddenly, I noticed my father standing under the archway between the kitchen and the living room, his sweatpants hanging loosely on his hips like they always did, wearing A Will to Live T-shirt and rubbing his eyes with his bear-paw hands. He'd called me Whobaby since I was a little girl, with no good reason why. But I loved it.

"Hey, Daddy." I snapped the book shut, feeling as if I'd gotten caught snooping through his wallet.

"When did you get here?" His head was just inches from the crown molding, and he ducked through the archway when he came forward, like a cat that measures if it can fit under a chair.

"Late last night." I jumped off the stool and ran to hug him. He smelled like laundry fresh out of the dryer. He kissed the top of my head, then took a step back. "Whobaby at the homestead. Jesus

Christ Almighty, I've missed you." He took my hand and pressed our palms together, lining up our fingers. His hand was warm and so much bigger than mine. "Were you always this gorgeous, or did someone hit you with the pretty stick?" He squeezed my fingers.

"Daddy." I rolled my eyes. "I just woke up."

"Sleep okay?" he asked.

"Fine," I said. *Not at all.* "You?" Had his cerulean eyes turned a little grayer?

"Okay, considering." He started toward the coffeemaker.

"How do you feel?" I asked, following him.

He opened a few cupboards until he found the mug Will had made for him in kindergarten, a brown circle with white lines splashed across it. "Well, right now I've got a whopping hangover courtesy of the Maker's Mark Luke brought last night. He's on some goddamn health kick, but once in a while"—he put the mug on the counter—"he falls off the tofu wagon." While he poured himself coffee, I challenged the tumor to show itself, but his head was still perfect, no lumps or bumps. His color was good. He didn't look sick.

"So." He faced me, his big frame blocking the picture window. I hoped he wouldn't ask me about grandchildren, like he did every other time I talked to him, but he said, "It took a golf ball in your old man's brain to get you home."

I sipped my coffee. It was cold. "It didn't seem like Jamie was going to be able to handle this." That sounded hard, aloof, and I wished right away I could take it back despite its truth.

He took off his glasses and chewed on the arm. "How you doing? You holdin' up out there in the great art mecca of the Southwest?"

"I wish you'd visit more," I said.

"Me, too, sweetheart. Your mother has a hell of a time getting away from those runway gazelles."

Why don't you just come alone? I wanted to ask him.

He sipped his coffee. "You ever play that piano we bought you when we were out there?" This was something else he always asked.

When he and Jamie called on the phone, he sometimes said, "Play us a little something, will you?" But I would find a good excuse not to.

"Sometimes," I said, lying.

He watched me over the rim of his cup. "Ah, knowing my Who-baby, you're probably a famous Santa Fe pianist by now and too modest to tell me." Before I could answer, he said, "Nic okay?"

I had a feeling my father didn't care for Nico. "Nice shirt," I said. "How's the foundation doing?"

He touched his front, as if to remind himself what he was wearing. "It's great. The kids are amazing."

I hadn't been to A Will to Live, the charity for underprivileged kids he'd started after Will died, since I was in college.

"Warren left about a month ago, but Sid's finding his way," my dad said.

"Sid's the director now?" I felt like I'd started a book a hundred pages into it. "Not bad for a high school football coach who swears it was his idea to put peanut butter and jelly together."

My dad laughed. "I think it was *chocolate* and peanut butter. But the kids love him, and the board unanimously approved his appointment. That's never happened before."

"I'm worried about you."

He crinkled his nose at his coffee. "I know you have your doubts about Mommy because of what happened after Will—" He didn't finish. "But she takes good care of me now."

I dug my fingernails into my palm, hoping for a tiny sting, but my nails were too short. "I'm staying for as long as it takes to get you better."

"Aw, Whobaby." He touched the raised scar where his helmet strap had split his chin so long ago. He looked weathered suddenly, old and tired, my big bear of a dad. "Come here," he said. I stepped forward and leaned into him again. Outside, the red maples were in blossom. Spring was in full bloom. "It's good to have you home." He kissed my head three times. "I don't care what it took."

4

Dr. Anderson is ready for you." Ryder's receptionist had a space between his front teeth so big, I could've pushed a quarter though it. "My name is Scott, and if you follow me, I'll take you to him."

I cracked the door to the hall. "Are you coming?" I asked Jamie.

"Of course I am." She slipped her phone into her handbag and touched her finger to her mouth as though spreading lip gloss. Guilt traveled across the crease in her forehead the same way it had when I went to her apartment as a teenager and found her lover, Julian, sitting at my practice piano in his underwear. It made me wonder now whom she'd just been talking to.

My parents and I followed the skinny, perfectly dressed man down the hall. RYDER ANDERSON, M.D. was stamped on a gold plaque on the door. "Come in." Scott turned the knob. I thought of Hadley and wondered if this guy had a boyfriend. "He's waiting."

Floor-to-ceiling shelves filled with medical texts covered the walls. Ryder was standing behind a chestnut desk, wearing a white lab coat. Looking out the window behind him, I could see tiny people hurrying along York Street. New Haven was busier than I remembered, and on the way there, we'd passed two new coffee shops and a vegan luncheonette. I wanted to drive by Yale to see how different it'd become since Ryder and I had toured it.

"Thank you, Scott," Ryder said. When the door closed, he stepped forward and kissed Jamie's cheek. "Thanks again for dinner last night." She whispered something I didn't hear. When my dad shook his hand, they kept their eyes on each other a beat too long, as though some unspoken agreement passed between them. I wondered what had happened the night before, what Ryder had said to him. "Take a seat." He nodded to the two leather chairs facing the desk, and my parents sat. Jamie crossed her ankles. I stood there dumbly, leaning into my hip, easing a blister on my heel. I was in tall leather boots I'd found in my closet and a suede skirt from Santa Fe that I'd bought at some upscale shop for too much money. I felt stupid standing.

Ryder went back behind his desk. "Jenny." He looked like a wax museum rendition of himself. "In case I didn't tell you last night, it's really good to see you again." He sounded businesslike; there was no trace of the boy who'd lain naked with me and had spent more time at my house growing up than at his own. I'd been home less than a day and wondered for the millionth time what had happened to him over the past thirteen years. But then I thought of me running halfway across the country and reinventing myself in the art world. And I knew exactly what had happened. Will happened.

"She prefers Jensen now," Jamie said quickly. "Jenny's a little girl's name." Was she mocking or defending me?

"Okay," Ryder replied.

"You can call me Jenny." I wasn't sure he'd heard me; he kept flipping through my father's file. Jensen was all wrong for him. I'd ridden on the back of his ten-speed, jumped off the Breakneck cliff in my red bikini to impress him. My dad patted the space beside him, and I perched on the edge of his seat. His warm hand on my back made me want to cry. Everything about being home made me want to cry.

We all sat there watching Ryder reading the file notes. I didn't know how there could be so much information when my dad had been so healthy, but maybe I'd missed something all those years I'd barely been home. Ryder looked so grown-up and doctorly. There was something confusing about it. The last time I'd seen him, the night before I left for Andover, he'd worn ripped jeans and a sweatshirt. I'd stood at my window, watching him get out of his car in the rain. Jamie knocked on my door and said, "Sweetheart, please come down for a minute." But I wouldn't. I stayed in my room until I saw his headlights come on and heard his car leaving. Now I watched his hands: a surgeon's hands—capable but gentle. It was weird to think they'd touched me. Nic had hangnails, calluses, sculptor's hands. I wondered if Ryder ever thought about that first night at Hamilton field, my lips on his neck, his hands on my hips.

He glanced first at Jamie and then at my father. "I'm going to tell you what I see," he said carefully. "And then what I think we should do." Jamie's pretty satin shoe bounced up and down. "The MRI shows a tumor growing near the base of the brain, pressing on the pons." I felt myself go very still. Beside me, my father didn't seem to be breathing. "A meningioma." Ryder's eyes were unreadable, his lips had gone pale, but his voice was calm. I stared at a half-hull replica of an America's Cup sailboat above his desk and imagined grinding winches instead of thinking about what a meningioma might be.

"Malignant?" my dad asked quietly, as though he were saying the name of someone who had passed away. Jamie sucked in her breath.

Ryder dropped his eyes. "Yes, but the survival rate is very good." When he glanced up again, he looked smug, and I wanted to slap him.

"Well, goddamn," my dad said, squeezing my shoulder. "I knew this was nothing to worry about."

Ryder held up his hand. "But the location of the tumor concerns me. The pons is in the pneumotaxic center, which controls respiration, breathing." The words *malignant meningioma* were going around and around in my head. My boots were buttery soft. They'd cost $350 at the York Street Bootery thirteen years ago. *Malignant.* I'd stolen them, walked right out of the store wearing them, my ballet flats in my bag. *Malignant.* After Will died, I'd gone into stores, made myself invisible, and had taken things. *Malignant. Malignant. Malignant.*

"So, what's the treatment plan?" my dad asked in that hearty, fake voice he used when someone had just said something awkward.

"We have a few options." Ryder clicked his pen. "Usually, we'd go in and take the mass out, then repeat the MRI to see if there's a need for radiation. But this tumor is in the rostral area of the brain, a place we don't like to operate. I'd rather shrink it with radiation and then do another scan to see where we stand." He was watching my father in an intense way that made me think they were peers, equals. Where was the boy who said he'd wear shorts to work and give his patients lollipops? Ever since I could remember, Ryder had wanted to be a pediatrician who made kids' tummy aches feel better. Not a brain surgeon operating on adults who were probably going to die anyway. "If necessary, I'll go in and remove what's left of the tumor after radiation."

"But normally you'd do surgery first," I said. *Normally.*

Ryder's smile was somehow comforting and condescending all at once. "Yes, normally I'd operate right away. But *normally* a meningioma would be in the temporal lobe, away from all the important stuff. So I'd like to see if we can radiate the area daily for eight weeks and then repeat the scan. Meanwhile"—he shifted his gaze to my father—"I don't want you driving or doing anything even remotely risky. Just lay low while we work on this thing."

If Will were here, it'd be so much easier, I realized. We'd get coffee somewhere, talk about what we were going to do. He'd kept us all together, a hinge of humor and invincibility that made sure we didn't fall apart.

"No driving for eight weeks?" Jamie blinked quickly. She never cried, and I silently dared her to cry now, dared her to steal this moment. But she wrapped her fingers around my dad's. "I'm supposed to leave for San Paulo in five days."

Is this why she'd wanted me to come home? To take care of my dad so she didn't have to? "I've got it, Jamie," I said coldly.

"Well." She used her hurt little girl voice. "I just mean . . ." She looked at Ryder. "Do you think I should go or . . ."

"Of course you should go," my dad said. "I've got Jensen here." He squeezed my shoulder again.

"But Jensen can't drive at night," Jamie said. "She can't see in the dark anymore."

"Oh, right." My father tousled my hair while I sat there wanting to punch her in the head. "Well, I have Luke and Sid and . . ." His voice trailed off.

"We'll take care of him," I said, sitting back against my dad. "Go." I crossed my arms over my chest. "Just go."

"Jamie, if I were you," Ryder said, setting the chart down, keeping eye contact with her, "I'd stick around. Nothing is ever sure in a case like this." The room felt charged, tense. She took a package of tissues out of her pocketbook.

"My beautiful girls," my dad said. "This is good news. I could have been given my walking papers today." I listened for an edge of sarcasm in his voice, but he was smiling, really smiling. "I feel like skydiving!"

Ryder cleared his throat. "Slow down, Sterling. Your prognosis is excellent. You'll probably outlive us all. But I want you to rest. There's no need to kill yourself jumping out of a perfectly good airplane." He flipped through his calendar book. "I've already scheduled an appointment for you with the radiation oncologist. In the meantime, if the blood tests tell us anything different, I'll let you know. Questions?"

My mind was in a freeze. I had a feeling Ryder hadn't told us the whole truth. I wanted him to guarantee that the tumor would shrink with radiation. That it didn't matter if it was malignant. That waiting on surgery was the right thing to do. I definitely didn't want to hear about skydiving. "Is there anything we should be doing now?" I asked.

"Just sit chilly until your appointment with Dr. Novak next Monday."

"Monday?" I tried to keep the irritation out of my voice. "Can't we see him before then?"

Ryder held my eyes. "Were you planning on going somewhere?" We stared at each other.

"I'm sure Ryder did the best he could making the appointment," Jamie murmured.

"I'm right here," Ryder said evenly, "if anything happens between now and then. Dr. Novak can tell you a lot more about what's going to happen from here on in. But educate yourselves as much as possible, so you know what questions to ask. The Internet can be a great resource, but sometimes the good ol' library is more reliable. If you do use the Internet, don't panic if you come across confusing or scary information. Just ask. I'm always available." He sounded like a stranger, a walking textbook on how to be cordial to your patients.

"So, you're not going to be the one treating him?" I asked.

"I'm a surgeon, Jenny. I operate. Dr. Novak will be in charge of radiating the affected area. When that treatment has been completed, we'll do another MRI and then—"

"I know. Then you'll decide if surgery is necessary." I felt like I'd been slapped. "But basically we'll be working with Novak?"

"Don't worry. Dale is the best there is. Sterling"—he looked at my dad—"you'll be in great hands. And I'll be here the whole time. We'll get through this together."

The room fell silent.

My dad shifted in his seat to face me. "Well, sweetheart, your mother and I have to head to Peter Doherty's office. We should leave now if we're going to drop you at home first."

"Attorney Doherty? Why?" I asked.

He put his glasses back on. "Just routine . . . stuff."

Routine? What could possibly be routine now? And then it hit me: his will. He was settling his estate.

. . .

"What in the world did Ryder look like?" Hadley asked. His South African accent sounded even more pronounced, which probably meant he'd had too much wine the night before.

I stood in the foyer, not wanting to enter the living room. Familiar, I wanted to tell Hadley. So familiar that I hadn't been able to stop thinking about him. But instead I said, "He looks like a Brooks Brothers ad. All ironed shirts and monogrammed cuffs, the poster boy for grown-ups." Sunlight was streaming through the windows, lighting up the dark wood of the piano.

"Well, love, we are grown-ups now, aren't we?" The phone was all echoey because he had me on speaker while he flipped through proofs.

"Yeah, I guess." *Too grown-up to work with kids,* I thought.

"That's the problem with these boys—they don't stay eighteen forever." I wished I were there, lounging on the velvet couch in Hadley's West Palace gallery, drinking a latte from the Cowgirl Café while he tried to find the hottest up-and-coming photographer. "Is he married or gay, and what in heaven's name has he been doing since he was curled around your tiny finger?"

"He's not wearing a ring. You didn't tell Nico, did you?"

"These lips are sealed. I mean in terms of talking; otherwise, love, they're wide open. Oh, I have to go." He sounded fluttery. "His royal highness is calling, and if I don't jack him off with phone sex, I'll never hear the end of it."

"You haven't broken up with him yet? It's so unlike you to hold on to the clingy ones."

"Send me the Brooks Brothers boy, and I just might. Ta-ta." The line went dead.

I held my phone in my hand and studied the hearth, remembering Jamie on her knees with a bucket and a sponge, a week after Will died, though there never was a stain. She'd been talking to herself. I hadn't tried to hear what she was saying. I'd backed away, frightened to see my mother like that, her hair falling limply around her face. A few days later, I came home and found shiny black marble had replaced the flagstone hearth. All these years later, no one had ever asked why she had it replaced.

Now I thought I should go upstairs, put on a pair of shorts, and run the seven-mile loop along the beach out toward Luke's, run away this sick feeling that was coming over me. Or I should put the stereo on loud, smoke the weed I'd stupidly stuffed in my suitcase, and set up the art supplies I'd packed, so I could start painting again.

But I walked into the living room and sat at the piano. My father had bought it for me when I was six years old, after I'd played "Joy to the World" by ear at Sid's Christmas party. Everyone in the room had gone quiet, and my dad and Luke had crowded around me, asking where I'd learned it. I told them I'd heard it on the radio.

Luke had sat next to me. "Can you do it again?" I remembered feeling scared, not sure if I had done something good or bad. He watched my hands as I played. Everyone applauded. He asked what other songs I knew. I told him whatever I heard on the record player.

The piano smelled like lemon furniture polish. Claude Debussy's "Reverie" was still propped on the music stand, the notes trailing across the page. I could hear it as I read the lines, could feel the way the piece spoke, a dramatic rise and fall, as though two people were slipping over each other. I had never played it for anyone. I'd sat in front of the keys at Will's funeral and stared at the pages until someone—my father, I think—led me away.

I thought of those pianos I used to pass in the music building at the University of Colorado on my way back from modeling for Nic. They sat in single rooms, waiting, obedient and patient, and I used to feel as though I'd betrayed every one of them. At the same time, I'd felt an incredible, almost visceral pull that reminded me what it was like to fall in love.

I hadn't played this piano in more than a decade. The keys were slick beneath my fingertips. Closing my eyes, I waited for muscle memory to take over. If I could play something, anything, maybe I could break that thick glass that separated me from my feelings. I pressed a few keys, but they were singular sounds in the quiet room, and "Reverie" was nowhere to be found. I opened my eyes and reached to bring the top down.

"She exists," I heard a voice say. Luke was watching me, rings on every finger, dreadlocks down to his elbows, smiling his big white smile.

"There you are," I said.

"Where else would I be, baby girl? That guest bedroom drugged me." He ran his hand over his dreads. "I slept till about thirty minutes ago, when your father called to whip up a surprise for his best girl." He took up the whole room when he crossed it.

"What is it?"

He put his huge arms around me. "I ain't telling his secrets, but it's shiny and red." He lifted me up, twirling me around, so the living room was a blur. Finally, he set me down, and we sat on the bench. I was laughing.

"You eating out there in the high desert?" he asked.

I nodded.

"Well, it's all going down your hollow leg." He lifted the backfall. "I didn't know you'd started playing again."

"I haven't." I leaned against his shoulder. "You heard me; I lost it." He smelled like musk.

"You're trying too hard." He rested his hand on mine and placed it on the keys. I snapped it away.

"I don't remember 'Reverie,' Uncle Luke."

He tapped my chest below my collarbone. "Your brain might not, but your body does. It's in there somewhere." He used to call me his "prodigy," his "rising star," and I had that sinking feeling, as he put my hand down and I pressed haltingly on the keys, that I'd disappointed him.

"Close your eyes," he said. The first verse came out stilted; then the grandfather clock struck twelve, and I remembered the second verse was in the same key as those chimes. At the beginning, my fingers felt stiff, cramped, but after that first refrain, they started moving, like water. I wasn't sure where they were on the keys, only that I was hitting the right ones.

And then I was the vibration of hammer hitting string; I was existing both inside and outside myself. My body leaned into the music. I heard the two voices, their melancholy so beautiful, it made me want to cry. The crescendo of the song came, and I played drunkenly, my fingers moving furiously. The playing loosened something in me that had been mashed down, way down, and I could breathe. The secret choking in my chest was, for one brilliant, beautiful moment, gone. And then my fingers tripped over the keys, they missed a note, and I stopped. My hands wouldn't play anymore.

Luke put his arm around me. We didn't speak for a long time. Finally, he said, "Why'd you quit?"

Outside, a breeze made the weeping willow appear to be dancing, slowly, sadly. I didn't answer. I felt that thing shutting down inside me again, that slanting edge that built itself instantly when someone asked questions. Luke took his arm away and fingered the keys lightly, pushing against me a little. He was playing an old Harry Chapin song. His handmade silver bracelets glinted in the sunlight. "You're afraid," he said while he played. He'd segued to Buffalo Springfield's "For What It's Worth."

"I am not."

"You *are* afraid. You're afraid to feel anything." It was like this with Luke; he skipped the small talk and went deep.

I watched his fingers running effortlessly over the keys. I wanted that again. I used to play in my sleep, in my dreams. "How do you know that?"

"I can read your spirit." He transitioned to "Yesterday."

"I'm not afraid to feel something," I said. The sun glinted against his thumb ring. "I'm afraid because I don't."

He was playing a different version, slower than the original, more melancholy. "How long are you staying?"

I'd like to see if we can radiate the area daily for eight weeks. "Two months," I said.

"I know this is a lot to throw at you a day into it," he said over the music, "but you've got a choice to make here. Either tell your old uncle what you've been locking up so tight all these years or I'm going to make you play it out." I watched his hands, felt the fireplace behind me. I heard Will's voice coming out of the dark: *What the fuck are you doing to my sister?* "Things left to boil too long," Luke said now, "always combust."

5

Three days later, I was driving my father around in a red 1966 Alfa Romeo 1600 Spider Duetto he'd borrowed. It was supposedly the one they'd used in *The Graduate,* my favorite movie. My hands held that shiny wooden steering wheel while the radio played an oldies station out of New Haven. He sat next to me, his wheat-colored hair blowing with the wind. It was just like him to call up a gazillion people he'd known since his football days until he found this car. After Will died, he'd bought a '57 Porsche 356, and whenever I came home from Andover, he'd knock on my door. "Wanna go for a drive, Whobaby?" Hungover, not really wanting to see anyone, I'd realize on those quiet rides how far I'd slipped from the honor roll, piano star girl, so far that my father probably had a hard time recognizing me, barefoot, my wild hair wrapped in woven string, tiny bells on my ankles, smelling of pot.

It was a warm day, warm enough that I was wearing a red sundress I'd found in my closet and flip-flops I'd bought at the Colston drugstore the day before. It was incredibly humid, so green compared to the high desert, my eyes could barely get used to it. In the passenger's seat, my dad sat smiling, tapping his fingers on the window in time to the music. I thought it was unfair when sick people looked healthy, like God was playing a trick. Not wanting to break our sweet silence to ask where we were going, I just drove the roads along Long Island Sound. I had the feeling I used to get as a kid, that just being near my father made me lucky. The forsythia and crocuses were blooming, the gammagrass was blowing sideways in the wind, and the air smelled of lilacs and salt. I drove north on Route 1 past antique shops and boutiques, lush marshes and sea-worn boats, places we'd water-skied as kids, docks where Mandy and I had set up portable radios and gotten tan, summer ice-cream stands, and the beach where Will had worked as a lifeguard the summer he was fifteen. We also passed the farmhouse where I'd gone to parties when I was home from Andover, the eyes of my old classmates telling me they were sorry but also glad it wasn't their brother. We did cocaine off the butcher-block table and drank tequila out of dummy-locked liquor cabinets. I secretly hoped Ryder would come home from Yale and show up at those parties. But he never did. Instead, I would end up kissing some boy I didn't care about, giving him a fake number, and then sleeping at Mandy's until three the next day.

"How was it?" my father asked. We were stopped at a red light in Madison, and he took off his cap to smooth his hair. "Seeing Ryder again."

"Weird." I watched a group of high school kids sprawled on the town green. One of the boys was on his stomach next to a girl on her back. The night before, I'd been rummaging through Jamie's desk in the living room, looking for a pad of paper, when I found a manila envelope. A stack of Mother's Day cards was inside. I recognized Ryder's handwriting right away. He'd sent one every year since Will had died. My hands were shaking when I shoved them back in the desk.

"His parents retired and moved to Florida," my dad said. "Did he tell you that?"

"No." It made sense. His mother had been forty-three when she had him. His father was even older. They'd shared an obstetrics practice.

"Damn good at what he does," my dad was saying. The light changed, and he put his hat back on.

When we were zooming down Route 1 again, I asked, "How long have you been back in touch with him?" I hadn't known I would ask it, but it came back to me now how familiar he'd been with the kitchen, the way he'd brought me tea, and how he'd been with my parents in his office—the intimacy the three of them shared.

"He's been coming by the house for a while."

A faint ringing sounded in my ears. "How long?"

He didn't answer for a minute. I switched gears, gaining speed on the straightaway, waiting for him to tell me to slow down. "Long time," he finally said. "Almost five years."

Madison's historic neighborhoods passed in a blur. I'd been in Berlin five years ago, installing Nico's exhibit, "Nightingale," in a new museum there. "Why didn't you tell me?" I could hear the hurt in my voice.

He shifted in his seat. "Your mother and I didn't want to upset you." A cold, horrible feeling washed over me that maybe Ryder had confessed what we'd done. "I know how hard it was for you after Will. They were so much alike. I worried you wouldn't want to see him." He stared out his window.

He was right. I might have half-hoped Ryder would come to the farmhouse all those summer nights and during Christmas breaks, but I would have been scared out of my mind if he had. He knew me only as the girl who didn't drink, never broke curfew. He'd have been mortified to see what I'd turned into. I downshifted, slowing for traffic around Hammonasset Beach.

"He asked about you." He tapped his fingers on the window. "I told him you were married, happy, still my best girl." He put his hat on backward, and he could have been Will, twenty years from now, if he'd lived. "Painting up a storm, about to be the next Georgia O'Keeffe out there in Santa Fe."

Above us a banner waved on the I-95 overpass: WELCOME HOME SERGEANT KINNEY, WE MISSED YOU! I thought of some soldier making his way home from Iraq to this idyllic town, I thought of Ryder at my parents' kitchen table, hearing I was happily married, and I felt like I might scream.

"Aw, Whobaby." My dad put his hand over mine on the gearshift. "I'm sorry I didn't tell you. It's just been nice having him around. Your mother's gone so much, and it's like . . ." His voice faded. But I knew what he was going to say: *like having part of Will back again.*

We drove along the coast, past beach houses, churches, and harbors, my father's palm over my hand the whole time. It was good of Ryder to come by. They needed that. Ryder had been like a second son to my father. He and Will had worshiped my dad. Ryder's own parents were too old, too stiff to be any fun, and he'd spent most of his time at our house. The three of us were always together. He wasn't great at football like Will, but he loved playing in the backyard while I kept score and made lemonade.

It was my fault, I knew. They needed *someone* to visit them. At Andover, I'd made it home for holidays. But after I went to UCB, I'd been terrible at keeping in touch. I'd been home maybe six times since I graduated. I tried to make up for it by sending my parents presents I knew they'd love. I'd scour antique shops and flea markets when I was on tour with Nic. In Venice, I'd found a candid, never published photograph of Dorian Leigh, the original supermodel. And last year in Cheltenham, England, I'd come across a leather football helmet worn by Bill Hewitt, one of the best NFL players of the 1930s.

When I got married, even those Sunday conversations we'd made a habit of in boarding school stopped. I hated those calls. It sounded like my dad's voice had lost its backbone, and it made me feel like the plates of the earth were shifting beneath me. He'd tell me how long it had been since he'd seen Will, recalling the number of days, as though keeping track might bring him back. Inane things ran through my mind while we talked: Will had left his history homework in my room that day; he'd asked me whether I thought Eileen Williams would go to homecoming with him. He and Ryder finally showed me how to drive a stick; they'd taught me all the words to the Stones' "Sympathy for the Devil." *I miss his laugh*, I'd wanted to say while I sat on my narrow bed at Andover. But I just hung on the phone, trying to keep up my end of the conversation and sifting through that shoe box I dragged with me wherever I went. In it were Will's high school ring, which he'd left on the sill in the kitchen; ticket stubs from an Oasis concert he and Ryder and I had gone to; the dried daisies they'd swiped from the neighbor's yard on my fifteenth birthday; notes he'd tacked on my door: *J—Mandy called. Call that crazy girl baaaaack! Jenny—I took the VW to Titer's bash. Get your ass over there! Meet R and me at Breakneck if Jamie'll let you have the car. Waterskiing!* The shoe box also held the condom—the one Ryder and I had never used. As the paramedics were strapping Will to the backboard, I saw its silver corner under the couch and slipped it in my pocket.

It was grounding, sorting through that shoe box while we talked, breathing the musty smell of my closet, like a bizarre time capsule. Almost everything in it was a piece of history from the three of us. I'd taken it with me to college in Colorado, but after I'd moved in with Nic, it'd gotten lost.

I didn't want to let go of my grief. Without it, I would have disappeared. Sometimes, going through my days, I'd forget about Will for a moment, and then feel a sharp panic when he'd come back to me. I deserved to remember what I'd done every second of every day. So, when I still woke at night to the weight of what Ryder and I did, and the physical pressure of remembering made me gasp for air, something in me didn't mind so much. It made me know I was alive.

"Earth to Whobaby," my dad said now.

I squeezed his hand. "I'm here, Daddy."

We were stopped at a red light again near the Westbrook town line, his skin sun-kissed from the drive. "Thinking, thinking, my bright shining star, always thinking." He beamed over at me as if that tumor weren't ticking away like a clock. My dad still thought I was the straight-A student I'd been before Will died, when he used to pin my report cards on the refrigerator next to newspaper clip-pings about Will. "My Whobaby's going to be somebody someday," he used to say. "You watch."

I wondered what he thought when my Andover and UCB report cards arrived. In prep school and then in college, I sat for hours in a hidden carrel in the library, a little stoned, trying to read about the French Revolution or the astronomy of Copernicus. I usually found myself at Hanky's bar, shooting pool, or, later, in Nic's studio, lis-tening to Van Morrison and trying to get that self-portrait to be somebody else. What Ryder and I had done, Will's death, eclipsed every other thing that came after it.

We'd driven all the back roads and were almost to the Baldwin Bridge when my dad asked if I was hungry. I felt flushed from wind and sun, and the constant drone of the road had made me sleepy. I didn't care if we stopped for lunch or if I ever ate again. I wanted desperately to go back in time, to spend every weekend of my life riding around like this with him. I wanted to keep driving forever.

6

"I can't believe you're here." Mandy looked even more beautiful than she had when we were teenagers, her blond hair swept up in a loose twist. I couldn't believe I was there, either, sitting across from her at Liv's, a lily of the valley bouquet between us, the diamond pendant around her neck throwing rainbows all over the restaurant. "How's my second papa doing?" Mandy never held it against me that I rarely called or e-mailed and almost never came back to visit.

"He's okay." I felt like crying. Liv's was noisy for late afternoon in the middle of the week, and no one would have noticed if I had cried, but there was no reason to. "Overwhelmingly favorable odds," Ryder had said. It was great news, my dad's prognosis, but I knew no matter how many little red cars my father borrowed for us, I still couldn't make myself believe it. "They think radiation will get it." Mandy put her hand over mine. I studied her big hoop earrings, I remembered now she'd bought them at the plaza when she'd come to Santa Fe.

Her eyes filled with tears. "Damn." She picked up her napkin and dabbed at them. "Of course he'll be fine, right?" The end of her nose was bright red, like it was when she cried. "It's just he's larger than life, you know?" She shook her head. "I'm such a cow. You're supposed to be crying on my shoulder, not the other way around." I loved her for crying. I loved that she could traipse through the rain forests of Ecuador with baby anacondas draped around her like scarves, photographing for *National Geographic* and having one-night stands with award-winning cameramen, and still come to lunch with me, hold my hand, and cry about my father.

Just like Mandy, she kept right on talking, filling the space between us before it could turn to silence. "I already look fatally ugly, and now I have to cry on top of it." She tucked a loose strand of hair behind her ear. "In the past thirty-six hours, I've been on a riverboat, a rickshaw thing pulled by some hairy animal with horns, two planes, and a town car from Bradley driven by a guy who farted the whole way, and well . . ." She put her fingers to her lips. "I *need* a mojito." She whistled at a cute waiter across the room.

"Mand, he's not a dog," I whispered.

She gave him a flirty smile. "It's so good to see you, J.J."

Everything Mandy had wanted to do, like cut class to get high or give blow jobs to the boys at the neighboring Catholic school, I'd been hesitant about, and she'd started every sentence with, "Jesus, Jenny, it's only a joint." Or "Jesus, Jenny, it's just a cock in your mouth." Eventually, she started calling me J.J., a constant reminder of how uncool I was compared to her. That all changed after Will died, and then I was the first one to drop acid, run off to boarding school in the middle of the academic year, and quit college to be with my art professor.

"What can I get you lovely ladies today?" The waiter's words came out lazily. I thought of Nic, except this guy probably wasn't old enough to drink.

Mandy touched his hand. "We'll have a couple of mojitos, please, D.J.," she said, reading his name tag. "And why don't you order one for yourself."

His cheeks colored. "Ma'am, we're not allowed to drink on the job."

She leaned forward. Her green silk shirt brought out the emerald color of her eyes. "How long are we going to have to sit here and drink until your shift ends?"

He glanced at a silver clock above the bar. "Um, about two hours. Do you want anything to eat?"

"We need a little time to decide," I said.

He walked away, swaggering, as if he knew we were watching. "Every time I come here, I want to snog that boy," Mandy told me. She checked her reflection in her knife and then raised her eyes to me and whispered, "I need need need to hear about Ryder." Her eyes were bright, like when we were teenagers and she suggested we play strip poker with the neighborhood boys. "And Nic." She said his name like an afterthought. "But mostly Ryder. Is he still in love with you?"

"Mand." I sipped my water. "That was a long time ago."

"Oh, honey," she said. "That doesn't matter. I know you better than anyone, and I know you have something to tell me."

I took a deep breath. "Okay, I'm going to talk, but you can't ask any questions."

She scrunched up her nose. "Why?"

"Because I'm not ready to answer them."

"Okay," she said. "I get it."

"Promise?"

"Scout's fucking honor."

"He's Ryder, but he's not. He's all serious now, with a buzz cut and monogrammed oxford shirts. He hasn't even shaken my hand since I've been back."

She let out the breath she'd been holding. "That's what you had to tell me?"

D.J. came back and put our drinks down. He hesitated before leaving, as though wanting Mandy's attention, but she plucked a mint sprig out of her glass and waited for me to speak. I realized too late that I was going to have to drink a lot to handle the smell of mint. "And?" she said when he left.

"I can't stop thinking about him." I spoke quickly so I wouldn't quit talking. "I don't know if he hates me or loves me or what, but I feel like I'm fifteen all over again." Mandy was the only one who'd known how crazy in love Ryder and I had been, and now she looked like she was going to explode. She took a huge sip of her drink and started to speak, but I said, "You promised."

"Okay, fine. It's just that—" She stirred her cocktail with her pointer finger.

"What?" My stomach felt weak. I didn't know if it was from the mint, hunger, or finally talking about Ryder.

"I always knew he'd be the one to make you come home." She whispered it, like she didn't know if she really wanted to say it.

"Mandy, my dad has a brain tumor."

"Oh, I know that. I just, well . . . he'll make you stay."

"Subject change, subject change." My hands were sweaty from what I'd told her. "I'm serious. I want to talk about something else. Tell me about the married filmmaker."

"Hmm, Philip Philip Philip. I finally met his wife. She found me in his address book. We met while I was in Paris on a layover."

D.J. appeared again. "How's the first round, ladies?"

"Almost as delicious as you," Mandy told him.

"We need menus," I said.

We watched him weave between the round tables. "That boy is edible," she said.

"Wifey?" I prompted.

"We went back to their place to talk." She ran her finger around the rim of her glass, then licked it. "Philip was home when we got there. So . . ."

I stared at her. "You didn't?"

She emptied her drink. "I hadn't had a threesome since you came to visit me at Columbia." She flashed her pretty teeth at me.

"What was that guy's name?"

"Timmy. Whenever I see him in the city, he tells me how sexy you were when you played the piano at that cigar bar. Remember we sang 'Born to Run'?"

"Oh God," I groaned.

D.J. came back with two menus. "Thank you." I could hear the soft slur in my voice. "Maybe we should eat something."

"We'll have the shrimp satay and caprese salad," she told him. She shoved the menus across the table so he'd leave, then leaned in and whispered, "But that's not what I wanted to tell you." She took a sip of her drink. "I want to have a baby."

I spit out my mojito. "A human baby?"

She nodded. "I was fucking Philip and wifey, and they had pictures of their kids everywhere and their finger-painted artwork, and I just, you know, I'm ready for it. The husband, the spit-up, a house with, you know, food in the fridge." She ate the mint leaf off my plate and a tiny fleck of green stuck to her glossed lips. "And I'm not getting any younger."

"Mand, we're not even thirty."

"I know, but don't you remember our master plan?"

We'd sat in her blue bedroom with those Jane Goodall prints on the wall and made a pact about being married with babies by the time we were thirty. "It was just a silly dream," I told her. "We were fifteen."

"And now we're not."

I sat there, stunned. Of all the people I knew, Mandy was the last girl I thought would want a baby. She was so . . . free. "But you're allergic to serious." She'd been the new girl at school our sophomore year. I existed mostly in the world of Will and Ryder, but she was so easy to chat with when we had study hall together or when I saw her at lunch. After Will died, she was the only person I talked to.

I'd almost convinced myself that just because my wild single friend didn't want a baby, neither did I. As if reading my thoughts, she eyed my belly, which felt concave. "I'm surprised Nic hasn't knocked you up yet."

Nic's lazy drawl echoed in my head: *We can't fuck on the counter with a kid staring at us.* "You know he doesn't want kids."

"That's a red flag."

I groaned again. "Mand—"

"No, I'm just saying." She put up her hands in defense. She sort of hated Nic for taking me away to Greece and marrying me and then hiding me away in Santa Fe. "Don't you ever think about it?" she asked. When I didn't answer, she said, "J.J.?"

"Actually, this thing with my dad has gotten me thinking." Mandy's green eyes went wide. "We don't have all the time in the world."

"You know what I think—" She put her chin in her hands.

"I know what you're going to say, and it's bullshit. 'Everything happens for a reason'—that's what the minister said at Will's funeral, and it made me want to throw up."

"Suit yourself, J.J. But you'll see."

My phone rang, and I dug in my handbag for it. "It's Ryder," I told her. "Let me make sure my dad's all right."

"He's fine," Ryder immediately said when I answered.

"Mandy's back from Madagascar," I told him. I twisted my wedding band. "We're at Liv's"—I smiled at her—"and we're a little drunk."

"Same as it ever was." I could hear the laugh in his voice. "I just got off. There's a band playing at Bar tonight."

I covered the phone and whispered this to Mandy. She crossed her arms over her chest. "I just got you to myself, and now he's going to steal you away?" And then louder: "No fucking way, Ryder."

"I think that's a negative," I told him.

"Okay, Miss Jenny." He sounded a little sad. I was, too.

"Sorry," I said, and before I could keep the words from falling out of my mouth, I added, "I'll call you later." I hung up and tossed the phone back in my bag.

D.J. set our plates in front of us. "Anything else?"

"We're fine," Mandy told him. When he was gone, she leaned across the table. "You're going to call him later?"

I closed my eyes. "Hang on, I'm still trying to picture you in sweatpants with baby poo on your sleeve." I opened my eyes. "Mandy, I love Nic." I picked up my fork.

She twirled a few hairs around her finger and watched me. "The same way you loved Ryder?"

Typical Mandy, just lay it right out. "Look how well that turned out." I slid a shrimp off the skewer.

"Oh, girl." She picked up her own fork. "If you hadn't run away to boarding school, he would have loved you until eternity ended. After you left, he used to follow me around Hamilton, asking if I'd heard from you. I almost couldn't wait for him to graduate"—she winked at me—"except he was so cute." I watched her drizzle olive oil on a tomato.

After that day I'd tried to tell Jamie what we'd done, I swore I'd never tell anyone about Will. And then I'd taken off for Andover without explanation. But now, a little drunk, sitting across from Mandy in that old restaurant where we used to go on our birthdays and double dates, I watched her toss a shrimp tail on her bread plate and suddenly wondered why not. Why hadn't I told her? Maybe Mandy, who slept with married men and their wives and hung out with crocodiles in the Amazon, would understand, and then she'd know why I could never be with Ryder again. Because if I was with him, every night I would lie awake thinking about what we'd done to Will, and every morning I would get up having to face it again.

D.J. came toward us, holding a small round tray above his head. On it were two shots with gold flakes floating in them.

"Goldschläger," he said, his hair over his eyes like a teenager. "Good news," he told Mandy. "I got off early. If you want me, I'm all yours."

Her mouth opened in an O. "Actually, you'll get off later." She said those things without even trying. Everything, even his ears, turned red. As he walked away, she said, "Oh shit, and I told you to blow off Ryder." She put her napkin on the table and turned toward the wait station. "I'm going to tell him to forget it."

"God no." I pulled at her arm so she'd sit. "Go forth and start a family." I giggled. "He's good mating material."

"Oh, bite me," she said. "I know how to let a boy down." She started to get up again. "I've been doing it since grade school."

"Please," I said. "I'm too drunk to stay out anyway."

"You could come with us."

"No way." I was done with threesomes the night we played with poor Timmy. "Take Boy Wonder home, have a ball." I took a sip of the shot. Cinnamon. "Are you ovulating?"

She rolled her eyes. "How will you get home?"

"Cab," I said. "I love cabs. There aren't any in New Mexico. None that I'll get in alone anyway."

She picked up her shot.

"One, two, three," I said, and we downed them.

I was in a lovely drunken glow, as if I were watching myself from the ceiling. Ryder's voice kept coming back to me as if no time had passed, as if I'd never married the art professor and was now in the business of modeling nude for whoever would have me.

"I'm so glad you're home," Mandy said. "Even if it is for a shitty reason. We're going to have so much fun."

D.J. came back wearing faded jeans and a tight black T-shirt. He gave Mandy a hunky smile.

"Where's the check?" I asked him. I couldn't quite control my tongue.

"On the house," he told me.

Outside, I stood on the sidewalk and took my phone out of my bag. "Hey," I said when Ryder answered. "Will you come get me?"

The next thing I knew, I was sitting at East Rock Park with my feet dangling over the stone wall. Far below, the lights of New Haven spread out like stars. Ryder had his arm around me, and I was leaning against him. The sky had gone an inky black, and clouds shifted across the moon, but it all looked unfocused, blurry. Not because I was drunk, but because of my night blindness.

"Do you remember?" he was asking me. A hundred feet above us, the Soldiers' and Sailors' Monument was a fuzzy outline. The year before Will died, Ryder and I had climbed the eighty-seven steps to the top. It was the first time he told me he loved me.

"I remember this." I made a peace sign and put my fingers over my heart. It'd been our secret code, our silent *I love you*. Whenever Will went to the bathroom while the three of us were watching a movie or when we were at his football games, Ryder and I would sign back and forth.

He smiled and picked his hand up like he might do it back, then stopped. "I had a patient once who was a sign-language translator. I actually asked her if that's how you say 'I love you.'"

I wanted to tell him that wasn't the only thing I remembered. As if reading my mind he said, "I remember everything." He was watching me.

I put my hand back in his jacket pocket. I'd put on the coat when we parked, soft, camel hair, not something he would have ever worn when we were kids. It was about seven sizes too big, and while we'd walked, arm and arm, up the steep slope to the top, I'd felt around in the pockets. I didn't know what I wanted to find, but all I got was a crumpled wrapper.

"Jenny, look at me," he said now.

I glanced at him, but his eyes were too intense. I made myself look away, at the monument. I knew that below it, carved in stone, were the cardinal virtues. I'd learned about them in ethics class: prudence, justice, temperance, and courage. I was exercising none of them.

"Tell me what you think about us," he said.

"There is no us." There was something frightening about Ryder. He was still the same boy who had taught me how to skip stones at Breakneck Lake, but with his sport jacket and banker haircut, it was like he was trying to be someone else. Or maybe he was and I just wanted him to be like he was before. Even the way he walked was controlled; everything was safe. Ironic as it was, the fact that he was safe scared the shit out of me. I tried to find my way to standing but lost my balance.

"Are you going somewhere?" he asked.

"I need to get home. My parents are going to wonder—"

"I called them."

"You what?"

"Why are you doing this?" He watched me.

"Doing what?"

"Avoiding, Jenny."

I gave up trying to stand and lay back on the wall. My head felt thick. "I'm not avoiding." I thought of Luke on the piano bench. *You're afraid.* If I rolled left, I'd topple to the city below. I could feel Ryder's eyes on me.

"It sure feels like you are," he said. "Escaping to boarding school, eloping to Greece." I'd hardly ever heard Ryder angry; he'd always been laid-back, rarely in a bad mood. Now his voice sounded stilted, wrong, not rising, but getting lower. "Coming home in your flowy skirts and your long hair and calling me only when you're drunk."

The back of my throat tasted acidic. I remembered rolling down the window in his Audi on the way to East Rock, leaning my head out for fresh air. "And you're trying to save people who can't be saved," I said. "It doesn't take a brain surgeon to figure out why you chose that career." This struck me as so funny or so terrifying, I started laughing. But underneath was a sliver of desperation; something inside me was screaming.

"How come you never wrote to me?" I heard him ask.

I quit laughing and opened my eyes. I felt light-headed, like I might blow away. The sky was deep purple and charcoal gray, and it kept moving. "It's not like you wrote to me," I said. "And all those years coming to see my parents, you never asked them for my phone number?"

"Your dad told me about Nic." He said it evenly, like he was trying to keep something out of his voice. "I wasn't about to fuck that up for you. And you made it crystal clear you didn't want to talk to me."

I thought of Ryder, standing at my bedroom door a few nights before I left for Andover, his face pale, his eyes dark. "If I promise we'll never tell your parents, will you stay?" His voice had been shaking.

"Who let you in?" It was a ridiculous question; he'd been coming to the house forever. In the corner was a box of photographs and notes from him. Will's football jerseys, clothes, and posters were stacked neatly in the garage. My parents had stripped our house of Will. And I had removed all evidence of Ryder from my room.

He came in and closed the door. "Why are you running away?" He was wearing a sweatshirt I'd brought back for him from Florida. "We need each other."

I picked up a Doors CD he had given me and winged it against the wall like a Frisbee. The plastic case cracked in two. "You need another girlfriend," I told him. "That's what you need."

I remembered the quick, sharp pain when he'd grabbed my wrist. "We didn't do anything wrong." His voice was low, vicious. "Will overreacted."

"You're hurting me." I tugged my arm free. I could feel tears coming, hot and ready. I turned back to straighten the rest of the CDs so they all faced the same way. It was suddenly very important to me that they were lined up right.

"Jenny." I didn't answer. "Jenny, talk to me." But I couldn't. "Jenny, goddamn it, I love you." I kept stacking the discs in perfect order until he left.

A plane passing overhead startled me out of the memory. Ryder was watching me. "I just want to know." He'd nicked himself shaving, and in the moonlight, he looked so fresh-faced. He'd always had a little scruff before. "What do you think about when you lie awake at night under that big Santa Fe sky?"

The question surprised me and my answer slipped out without my wanting it to. "I never stop thinking about what we did."

He quit blinking. Quit moving altogether. "It was an accident." He said it as if I were a child, like he was telling me not to go in the road, not to touch a hot stove.

"Accident or not"—I studied the tassels on his loafers—"it was our fault."

We stayed that way for a long time, Ryder looking at the city he'd never left and me lying on the stone wall, watching his back. I thought maybe we'd stay there until the sun came up, but after a while he said, "Let's go."

We didn't talk the whole way home.

7

When I made my way up the attic stairs to paint the next morning, my head felt stuffed with cotton, and my limbs were sandbags. My father had renovated it when we were kids and made a play space for Will and me. But since I'd been up there last, the front of the room had filled with Christmas decorations. I had to step around garlands and wreaths to reach the back, where there was a bathroom and sink.

Nic thought holidays were pedestrian. Instead of celebrating with a tree and presents, we went up to Angel Fire for Christmas, where Hadley and a bunch of friends shared a house. Nic hosted a Greek dinner that lasted till the New Year. People skied and ate and screwed, lounging around the house, playing ukuleles, talking about art, drinking mushroom tea and smoking herb. As I threaded my way past homemade clay angels and the ancient pinecone ornaments I'd made in elementary school, I pictured my parents—my dad in a wool hat, Jamie in her cashmere gloves—venturing to the Christmas tree farm in Chester to cut down their evergreen, just the two of them. It made my heart feel like lead.

The sun had risen bright and swollen and was shining through the attic windows, throwing short shadows across the wood floor.

The slanted eaves and hidden corners made me think of Will. We used to play up here for hours. Across from the tiny bathroom, the wooden easel was where I remembered it, an old-fashioned kind with a double-masted H frame and a child's crayon marks across it. I touched its smooth ash wood and bent down to slide open the little drawer. A few stiff watercolor brushes were still in there. It wasn't the steel Italian easel Nic had bought me for my birthday, but it would do.

I put my art bag on the floor and pulled out my new sabeline brush kit and some charcoal. Nic had wrapped up five of my self-portraits, the ones he said were best, and packed them in my bag before I left, telling me it was time to finish something. Every time I worked on one of these pieces, it felt like my hands were rebelling. I knew what they really wanted to do was play piano. I wanted to remind Nic that before I'd dropped out of UCB for him, I'd finished everything. I'd gotten perfect grades and was on the student council and taught piano lessons to kids in the New Haven projects for free.

I used steel clamps to fasten an unfinished canvas to the easel and got out the paints. My phone rang as I was mixing up the blues. "Hey there," I said.

"Why didn't you call me back last night?" Nic asked.

"Sorry. I was out with Mandy. I haven't seen her since I've been home." I stared at that fleck of light in the portrait's eyes.

"Didn't you get my messages?"

"I got home late." I thought maybe if I painted over that piece of light, they might become my eyes. They were so close, but not quite right.

"Hadley said he tried to get you, too." A strange alliance seemed to have formed between my husband and my friend since I'd been gone.

"Hadley texts so much, his thumbs are going to fall off," I said.

"That doesn't explain where you were."

"Jesus, Nico, I'm sorry. I've been doing a lot of research and trying to keep my family together. It was nice to go out for a couple drinks and forget about everything for a little while."

He sighed. "Let's not fall apart because your old man is." The room darkened, and I moved to the window. I saw Nic in those sexy jeans with the patch on the ass. Clouds had covered the sun, and I could just make out the outline of the old goalposts in the northwest corner of the backyard.

"He's not trying to fall apart, Nico." I used to lie out there with Ryder and Will, staring at a clear sky.

"How's he doing?"

Paint was stiffening on the brushes; in Santa Fe, they would have been bone-dry by now. "Nothing's changed since we talked yesterday. We're waiting for his blood work to come back."

"Did you decide how long you're staying?"

When I walked by Nic that first time, I knew the guest professor was watching me, knew he could see the outline of my legs through my sheer skirt. It was rumored he slept with his students. "Look at her," he'd said to no one. "Sad and beautiful." I'd kept walking, as though I hadn't heard, my face burning. I'd wanted so badly to stop, turn around, go to him. It'd been so long since I'd cared if a man had noticed me. "It's not like I have to rush back to the café," I said now. "Hadley said his gallery assistant can fill in until I get back."

"Your job is not to serve people coffee at Hadley's gallery. You're a model." He sounded anxious.

I left the window and wandered over to the Victorian dollhouse that my father had hired an architect to build. "That's not really a job," I said. "It's just standing around naked for some rich guys who think they're sculptors. Getting the right amount of foam on a latte, now, that's a job."

"Well, Dante is a serious artist, and he needs you to model for him." Nic sucked in his breath. "His show is in October." The dollhouse was Tudor in style. It opened in the front so all the rooms were exposed. "He needs his model—"

"Eight weeks," I said, interrupting him.

He was quiet. The numbness arrived. It started as a faint ringing in my ears and then widened, like a diaphanous curtain, spreading through my limbs. I sat cross-legged in front of the dollhouse. I hated making Nico mad. "Jamie has to work, and my dad can't drive." We were supposed to spend the summer in Greece, looking for a house. He'd been talking about moving there for years.

"I can't be without you," he told me, as plainly as if he were talking about oxygen.

I put the mother in the bedroom, in front of the tiny vanity with the real mirror. It was odd that Nic got like this when I left. He brought beautiful models to the studio, stripped them of their clothes, and molded marble replicas of them. Ever since we made love that first time, he said I was too real to be his model anymore. "I see you in every woman," he'd told me.

"Did you hear me?" he asked.

I picked the plastic father off the living room floor and propped him in the orange plaid recliner. I suddenly wanted to get off the phone so I could dust the floors and windows and use the tiny hand vacuum to clean the rugs. "Don't tell anyone I play this with you," Will had said. He'd stopped arranging the dining room one afternoon, his mouth serious, his blue eyes going back and forth on mine. I was eight, and he was not quite ten. "I won't," I told him. I remembered the importance of that secret, how loyal I'd made myself to it.

"It's only two months," I said to Nic. "Just until he's out of the woods." The rotary phone on the wall by the bathroom rang. "Let me call you back," I told him; "that's the house line. We're supposed to get labs back today."

"Just answer it," he said. "I'll hang on."

The old yellow phone hung outside the tiny bathroom, and I managed to grab it before the answering machine picked up.

"Jamie," Ryder said.

My stomach lifted into my throat at the sound of his voice, just like it used to when I was fifteen. "Ryder," I said. "It's Jenny."

"Oh. Jenny." I still hadn't gotten used to hearing anyone call me that, but I liked the way he said it, almost singing my name. "I keep expecting you to sound like a teenager."

"Yeah," I said. "I know." I thought about calling him from Liv's the night before. "Did the blood work come back?" I could tell he was at the hospital, because a doctor was being paged in the background.

"Yes, nothing alarming there. We'll proceed as planned. Radiation first, then, if need be, surgery." His voice was flat, professional, not Ryder's at all.

I suddenly wished it was last night again, under the stars, his camel hair coat around me, signing *I love you*. "Is that a good thing?"

He didn't answer. I tried to think of something to say about the night before, but I didn't know what.

"We should talk about it with your parents."

"Ryder, it's me, Jenny. You can tell me." I could hear more voices in the background. "Listen, I'm sorry about last night. I was drunk, and I shouldn't have called you. It's just—"

"Let's stick to the plan. Radiation, then we'll see where we are." His voice was businesslike. "Tell your father to give me a call. I've got to go; I'm getting paged."

The line clicked off. I stood there with the phone in my hand, hating him for hanging up so soon. And then I remembered Nic. I put the receiver back and picked up my cell. "Sorry, Nico." He didn't answer. I thought he'd gotten tired of waiting, but the display said we were still connected. "You there?"

Nic never said anything when he was mad; he just simmered, like water that wouldn't boil. Days could go by, the silence between us like a hard wall neither of us would reach through. Sometimes I wished we would fight, yell at each other. Silence was so infuriating, and lonely, but I was also grateful for it. I thought if we fought, I might say things I would regret.

"He calls you Jenny?" His voice was cold.

"What?" I sat in front of the dollhouse again. The father had fallen off the plaid chair. "Everyone called me Jenny when I was a kid." The floor was covered in contact paper that looked like hardwood, peeling at the edges.

"And now they don't. Remember when I introduced you at the 'Nightingale' exhibit as Jenny? You screamed at me when we got back to the hotel that your name is Jensen. Not Jenny. Not Jen. Jensen." I'd told him Jensen was an adult's name. What I hadn't said was that Jenny belonged to Ryder.

"Jesus, what's the big deal?" But I knew exactly what the big deal was. One word had cracked open my past. "It's just a name."

"One that you'd never let me use, but some old boyfriend from preppyville still gets to."

"Did Hadley tell you?" I knew right away I shouldn't have said it.

His breath caught in his throat. "No," he said. "I can hear it in your voice."

"It was a long time ago." I saw now that the dollhouse was all wrong. The living room couch was in the kitchen and the bathtub was in the attic, as if another child, a ghost, had come and played with it while I was gone.

"And what about last night?"

I didn't have the energy to explain. "Nothing happened."

"J.," he said quietly. "You're making me crazy."

I laughed, a harsh, mean sound. "If I didn't know any better, I'd think you were jealous. I thought you didn't believe in that. Jealousy coming from the guy who always used to say monogamy and monotony were interchangeable."

"That was before we were married. And have I ever once acted on it? Is there anyone I want more than you?"

"You've ruined me for every other woman," he'd said when I'd asked him a few years before if he'd been with anyone else. His voice got louder now. "I'm just feeling a little blindsided by all this, you being away for the summer, hanging out with your old boyfriend."

"There's nothing going on between Ryder and me, if that's what you're worried about."

"But you're staying for eight weeks?"

The familiar panic rose. Since I'd dropped out of college, I'd surrendered to Nico. Modeling and working at the café aside, my job was to be his wife, traveling from country to country with his exhibits, getting lost in his world, belonging to him. He was all I'd known for so long. But it was different now. I was different.

"Why don't you come out here?" I asked. If I didn't have Nic, what did I have? I wanted to tell him I'd be on the next plane. "Now that your falcon exhibit is done, can't you get away for a little while? My parents would love to see you." I didn't know if that was true, but I had to say something. *Understand,* I pleaded with him in my mind. *Understand.*

"All right," he finally said, surprising me. "I have that show in a few weeks at Lazelle in New York. I'll come before it starts."

"It's still you and me, Nico," I said quietly. "We're not going anywhere." But I had that unsettled feeling I got when I lied.

8

On Monday evening, I found my father in his office, going through art therapists' résumés for A Will to Live. "You ready?" I asked him.

He crumpled a page and threw it across the room at the wastebasket. It hit the rim and went in. "Are we going out dancing?"

"Nice try. Tonight is all about Dr. Novak."

"The radiation doc?"

"The one and only."

"I'd much rather boogie." He shimmied in his chair. "Let me make some quick notes on this one." He held up a résumé on cream-colored paper. "She might be a keeper."

"Dad." The old grandfather clock in the foyer chimed six times. "Your appointment is in fifteen minutes, Mom's already outside."

He put a sticky note on it. "All right." He sighed. "Let's go."

I drove the fifteen minutes to Yale–New Haven Hospital. Jamie sat in back; my father traced shapes on the passenger window. He had been doing things like that lately, and it made me think of a child daydreaming.

There were no pictures in Dr. Novak's waiting room. The furniture was expensive leather, but when I sat, it was stiff and uncomfortable. I leaned back against the hard chair and tried to ignore Jamie, who was madly texting someone.

I closed my eyes. I saw the self-portrait I'd been working on that afternoon in the attic. The eyes still weren't right and my cheeks were too dark in the painting, as though I were stuck in shadow. And my strange almost smile made me look like I'd murdered someone.

My phone vibrated with a text from Hadley. *What did you do to Nico? He's a nightmare.* Instead of writing back the truth—that I was staying for the summer—I studied the sage paint and crown molding. I bet Dr. Novak, whoever he was, finished everything he did. He'd never leave incomplete self-portraits lying around in the attic. *He's constipated,* I typed. My father picked up a copy of *Architectural Digest.* And just when my phone vibrated with another text from Hadley, which said, *I can take care of that,* a woman in a tight black skirt and high heels I wouldn't be able to survive two steps in came through the waiting room door. She stood in the threshold, taking us in. "You must be the famous Sterling Reilly," she said.

My dad's eyebrows shot up.

"I'm Dale Novak." She put out her hand. *Dr. Novak?* She was supposed to be old and fat and a he. Instead, she was perfect in a way that was both glamorous and boring.

My father glanced at Jamie. "Very pleased to meet you," he said.

Jamie quit texting and put her phone in her bag. "What a surprise. We thought you were a man." Leave it to Jamie.

"Why don't you follow me," Dale Novak said.

She led us through a corridor with recessed lighting, and I caught up to my dad.

"He's a girl," I whispered.

"A very pretty one," he whispered back.

"As you may know," she said as we walked, "I'm not accepting new patients." She stopped in front of a closed door and faced us. I never would have been able to pull off red lipstick if I'd had her chestnut hair, but it looked good on her. "But, I couldn't say no to Dr. Anderson." *Oh Jesus.*

Her office was all windows, and New Haven spread out below us. I knew East Rock, where Ryder and I had gone, wasn't too far away, but I couldn't see anything beyond the street lights on Howard Avenue. There was a computer on her desk but nothing else.

"Please," she said, "make yourselves comfortable." We sat in stiff chairs that were the same as the ones in her waiting room, and I immediately felt my back start to ache like it did when I modeled. My blouse was a little see-through, and I'd spattered some paint on the new designer jeans I'd bought with Mandy yesterday after dropping my dad off at A Will to Live. I felt childish in front of Dr. Dale Novak, with her tailored black blazer and expensive pumps.

She leaned against her desk and gave us a recap of just how overqualified she was to be treating a mere mortal. Thin in that sturdy way of never ever missing a day at the gym, she seemed scheduled, disciplined, and completely unspontaneous. "The next eight weeks, we will be working very closely together, so it's imperative that you're comfortable with me." She leaned away from her desk and touched my father's hand. "Would it be helpful to start with an overview of exactly how the radiation process works?"

I glanced at Jamie, who had one hand in her purse and seemed to be trying to read something on her phone. "All I need to know is that Ryder thinks you're the best radiation oncologist around," my father was saying. "That's good enough for me."

Dale Novak told him what to expect anyway. She detailed what would happen in the radiation room and how often he'd be coming and what the side effects might be. I could hear my phone vibrating and thought of the gossip Hadley was probably texting. Everybody in Santa Fe hung out at his gallery's café. While she talked deliberately, like those computerized voices on telephones, I pulled a small notebook from my bag and made notes. I'd come prepared to ask four pages of questions to a fat, balding guy with mustard stains on his lab coat. I hadn't been ready for her to be so pretty, and tall. And pretty. I wondered how many cases Ryder referred to her. I could see them lingering over cappuccinos, discussing treatment plans. It

made me feel slightly sick to think of my old boyfriend with someone as perfect and as pretty as Dr. Dale Novak.

"Questions?" She clasped her hands together and looked at my
parents.

"Um," I said, feeling invisible, "when we met with Ryder last week,
he encouraged us to educate ourselves as much as we can about the
disease. So, I've been doing some research on alternative treatments."
Surgery always comes first. "What do you think about vitamin C
injections, laetrile, shark cartilage, and Essiac?"

Dr. Novak stretched her fingers across the desk. I wanted her to
be wearing a ring. I wanted her to belong to someone. But her beautiful hands were bare. "Conventional medicine takes precedence,
but if we find a homeopathic treatment that isn't contraindicated,
then we can proceed with caution."

"Okay." I sat back in my seat and tried to hide my nails. Luke
was right: I needed a manicure. "But there have been clinical trials
with these so—"

"*Clinical trial* is a loose term." Her smile was patronizing.
"B-seventeen is harmless, and while it has popped up in a few underground journals, there's nothing to support its claim that it re-
tards the growth of cancer cells." I put an asterisk next to it on my
list. "C injections, from what I've read, are most beneficial when
given immediately before surgery. Shark cartilage, however, is showing real promise as an alternative complement." I put a big star in my
book, but she nixed my enthusiasm with a quick wave of her hand.
"But its taste, from what I'm told, is horrific."

I'd read the same thing online. "Can't he just take the capsules?"

"I've done quite a bit of research myself on these kinds of treatments." Her voice was low. "First, I don't like to toy with things
that aren't regulated, and none of this has been FDA-approved yet."
She went on to tell us about the importance of placebos and double
blind studies. All this talk of research reminded me of high school,
and how Ryder and I had spent hours on the fourth floor of the
Colston Library, where the town history books were kept. No one

went up there, ever, and he would come up behind me, kissing my neck, lightly at first, then harder, almost biting, while I protested because I had to study. He got good grades without trying; he could afford to screw off. I studied hard, reading about the American Revolution or Jung's theory of the collective unconscious while he seduced me to the point where I couldn't say no.

The ache to be with him back then was constant, and I remembered not knowing how much longer I could hide what we were doing. The stacks were the perfect place to be alone together, to let him take off my clothes without being discovered. In a way, I'd wanted to be found out. He and Will were my best friends, and I hated hiding something from my brother that made me so happy.

Once at Andover and twice at UCB, I'd fucked boys in the library, though I rarely dated anyone. "Ice queen," they called me in boarding school. To my surprise, that made boys crazy for me. Sometimes I couldn't get those days with Ryder out of my mind, so I'd draw a guy into those lonely research stacks. Closing my eyes, I'd smell the dust and old leather and think of Ryder. But they weren't Ryder. He and I had that thing that was hard to put into words, that wild, hot spark.

Dr. Dale Novak was still talking. "You're a big, strong man," she was saying to my dad. "I bet you could still play with the best of them." She made like she was throwing a football, and he pantomimed catching it. I couldn't figure out if they were flirting or getting ready to scrimmage. "Anyway, based on his stature and size, he'd have to take about sixty of those shark pills a day," she said to me, and I realized they'd been talking about his weight in relation to the shark cartilage. I felt myself slide down in my seat. "Essiac," she said, "doesn't sound familiar. But I'd be happy to check into it if you'd like." Her voice was perky, in a fake way.

I checked it on my list. "Well, I've read that radiation can be more taxing on the body than surgery. It just seems like if we're going to go this route, which is pretty unconventional from what I can tell"—I could feel my mother staring at me—"it might be a good idea to support him with alternatives. I have a list of supplements he's on if you want it."

"You must forgive Jensen." Jamie leaned forward in her seat. "She gets something in her head, and well"—she laughed nervously—"there's no stopping her. She's the genius in the family and very precocious."

"Oh"—Dale turned to me—"are you in medicine, too?"

Jamie cut in before I could answer. "She could have been a doctor. She could have been anything. But now, Jensen is a"—she stumbled a little—"a painter and she models for artists. She's married to Nico Ledakis? The sculptor? He has shows all over the world, Berlin, Paris, Cairo, Crete." It occurred to me that Jamie must have been feeling ashamed of me, her daughter, who had accomplished nothing and had no framed diplomas. "She was a prodigy." She perched on the end of her seat. "At the piano?" She was talking quickly, to no one really. "She's a very good artist now and, well, who knows . . ." Her voice trailed off. "But she's definitely not a small-town girl." I hadn't bothered to tell Jamie that I did more waitressing than modeling.

No one said anything. My father was staring at the ground.

"Well," Dr. Novak finally said, ignoring Jamie's soliloquy. "A list of supplements is fine. You can bring it to the first appointment." She checked her watch. "If there aren't any more questions, my secretary, Alison, will give you a call in the morning to set a schedule. And," she said to me, "please feel free to e-mail me any other questions. Even the silly ones."

Even the silly ones? Bitch. She touched my shoulder as we were leaving her office. "I think this is wonderful." She motioned to my notebook. "Your dad is lucky you're here."

I mumbled "Thank you" and hurried down the hall because I thought I might cry. I was sure no one had felt lucky to have me around in years.

We rode the elevator in silence. "Well, she seems capable," my dad said when the doors opened on the ground floor.

Jamie was checking her phone again. "And about as warm as an Alaskan salmon," she said, surprising me.

My dad laughed.

"I'm starving," I said miserably. Dr. Dale Novak was so skinny, she made me hungry.

"Me, too," Jamie said, which shocked me even more. Whomever she'd been texting all the time seemed to be keeping her in a good mood.

We stepped out of the hospital into the evening air, and suddenly Ryder popped around the corner, holding a brown paper bag. I had the sudden, foolish thought that he'd brought me a present. The three of us stared at him. The way he looked back at me, as if I were the only one there, made me catch my breath. He was dressed in a white T-shirt and worn jeans, just like the old days. Beneath the short cotton sleeve, I saw the end of the number 18 on his upper arm. So the homage to my dad's jersey number was still there.

"Ryder." My dad clapped him on the back. "What a wonderful surprise."

"Who's hungry?" He glanced at me nervously. We still hadn't talked about that night at East Rock. "I'm in the mood for fried clams and corn on the cob. Anyone up for the Seafood Shack?"

"Atta boy," my father said. "That's my kind of food."

"That would be lovely." Jamie took Ryder's elbow.

"I figured you'd have some questions after meeting Dale," he said.

My father and I fell in step behind them. "I have one," I called out. "How come you didn't tell us she was a woman?"

"Aw shit," my dad said, stuffing his hands in his pockets. "Is there an escape hatch anywhere?"

I smacked his stomach.

"She's very bright," Jamie said.

"Even if she does have a boy's name," I yelled above the noise of a passing truck.

"Dale can be a girl's name," Ryder called back.

I pulled on my dad's arm, until we were walking four across on the sidewalk. "Name one girl Dale."

"Dale Bieberman." Ryder stuck out his tongue at me.

"She's not a real person," I shot back.

Jamie whispered in Ryder's ear. "Dale Evans." He pumped his fist in the air.

"Traitor," I called to Jamie.

My father started laughing, and then we were all laughing, walking along York Street in the hot spring air, daffodils all around us, about to eat seafood fresh from the Atlantic Ocean. With my father alive and seemingly well, it was hard to give a shit about Dale Novak.

The Seafood Shack was full, and it smelled like melting butter and oysters. Everyone was sitting around picnic tables, drinking beer out of coolers, while a band set up on an old stage. TABULA RASA, the sign said, AMERICAN SOUL AND ROCK AND ROLL. I took a pretzel from the bowl on the table and licked off the salt.

A pretty teenager whose hair was the same dark red as her nails read us the specials. Ryder brought out a bottle of Chardonnay and a few Stella lagers from the paper bag he'd been carrying. He set a Dixie cup in front of Jamie and filled it with wine.

Condensation ran in tiny rivulets down my bottle. But I didn't drink. After that night at Liv's, I wanted to be clear-headed around him.

"Really," Ryder said. "What did you think of Dale?"

I waited for someone else to answer. Jamie was putting on a good act, like my dad was the only guy in the world. With her arm draped on his leg and her head resting on his shoulder, she actually appeared content and could have passed for someone who really loved her husband and had never done him wrong.

My dad leaned across the table. "You recommended her. That's good enough for me." That salty smell the warm breeze blew off the marsh made me feel drunk, and I kept my mouth shut.

When the waitress came back, we ordered baskets of clams, onion rings, shrimp, scallops, everything fried. The band started playing a bluegrass version of "Twist and Shout," with banjos and fiddles. "What I wonder," my father said, "is what Dr. Novak thinks of us. Susie Notetaker over here interviewed her like an FBI agent."

I held up my hands. "If she's going to shoot laser beams at your head, I'd like to ask a few questions first."

People started filling the grassy space in front of the band.

"It was more like the Spanish Inquisition," Jamie said.

Before I could defend myself again, the waitress came back with our lobster-tip appetizers and then our entrées.

We tied plastic bibs around our necks and dug in.

"Well, what did you think?" Ryder watched me, and I realized it was really important to him, what I thought of Dale. When we were kids, even before we started dating, he'd wanted my opinion. On the afternoon of his and Will's eighth-grade dance, he brought over three ties and asked me to choose. I picked the ugly one with bright green stripes because even then I hadn't wanted any other girls to like him the way I did.

I pictured her framed diplomas from Northwestern and UPenn on the wall. "I think she's probably a really good doctor," I finally said.

My father started telling a story about driving from Philly to the Jersey shore with his brothers to get seafood when he was growing up. He'd been the second-youngest of nine boys in an Irish-Italian neighborhood in north Philly, where they never had enough of anything. "I got really lucky," he liked telling people when they saw his wall of trophies. "The old man in the sky gave me the gift of playing ball, and it brought me every goddamn thing I ever wanted." And then he'd beam like an eight-year-old. "Otherwise, I'd be pumping gas in Fishtown." He was always tipping toll collectors and handing car wash attendants an extra ten. Whenever we ate out, he acted like he'd won the lottery, buying drinks for everyone, tipping the chef, leaving an extra hundred on the table.

The clams were divine, and the shrimp popped in my mouth. Seafood in Santa Fe was terrible, frozen and stale. Hadley always pretended he had food poisoning the next day and stayed in bed.

While I ate, I watched the skinny piano player sitting on that old wooden bench, banging on the keyboard. He was hunched over and had awful hand position, but somehow he played beautifully.

Before we were halfway through our meals, my father ordered more food and reminded us that the first time I'd ever had lobster, I ate so much, I threw up. He and Ryder talked about the Colts and the Cowboys, and Jamie named the players she thought were handsome. I ate everything on my plate and stabbed at bits of Ryder's clams. I couldn't remember the last time I'd eaten that much, and had felt so happy and relaxed.

"Come on." Jamie tugged at my dad's hand. "I can't stand it when a good band plays a great song and I'm not dancing." I watched them join other couples in front of the stage. In her Italian heels, Jamie was almost mouth-to-mouth with my father. An inch apart, gazing at each other like nothing else existed and the whole world was theirs, they started to dance. Jamie's fresh white skirt twirled. She was never tottery in heels, and my dad was still sure on his feet, smooth. I felt myself sinking into that feeling I used to have when I was little, that everything would be all right.

Ryder leaned into me. "Did any of that dancing rub off on you?"

"I can hold my own." I was a sophomore when we went to his junior prom, convincing everyone we were just friends. Will had made it clear that I was off-limits to Ryder, that our dating would ruin the trio. But in that tight black sheath, with his hands on my hips, I hadn't cared if anyone knew.

"Prove it."

I followed him to the edge of the grass, where a few teenagers were slow-dancing to fast music. We stood for a second facing each other. So what if I had paint stains on my jeans and my shirt was a little see-through? Now that we were away from Dale Novak, I felt prettier, smarter. I pushed my palms against his, and he spun me away, then tightened his grip and pulled me back. I had no idea what steps we were doing, but somehow I followed. Those early dance lessons Jamie had made me take had paid off. We jigged and spun as if we'd been dancing together for years. The song ended with our backs pressed together, our hands clasped, and we were both breathing hard. I could feel sweat running between my breasts, and I was sure my shirt was now completely see-through.

The band started a slow song that began with a piano solo. My back still to Ryder's, I watched the piano player close his eyes, his hands finding their way across the keys. "Mind if I cut in?" I heard my father ask. His face was red from exertion, and I was glad it was a slow song. He started the four-step waltz he'd taught me as a kid. I'd put my feet on his and he would dance me around the living room, saying "One, two, three, four. One, two, three, four." The teenagers around us held on to one another's waists. Doing a formal dance step with my dad felt old-fashioned and sweet.

"I love having you home again, Whobaby." He'd told me this about twenty times a day in the week and a half that I'd been home, and it made me feel both happy and so guilty, I thought I might poison myself.

"And I love being here." I stumbled and stepped on his toe. "Sorry. I'm not exactly good with the classics."

"Aw, sweetheart, you're perfect." He'd also said this a lot, but it was always tentative, as though he were afraid of jinxing it. As if one day, poof, I'd disappear back to the Southwest. He drew me to him, resting his cheek on the top of my head. "My good girl is home again."

We danced around and around the grass while the waitstaff lit tiki lamps and the piano player closed his eyes and did another solo.

Jamie and Ryder twirled by as the song ended, and my dad reached for her. "Come on, good-lookin'. Let's show these kids how it's done."

"How it's done?" Ryder asked, grabbing me around the waist, his fingers snaking under my shirt, gripping me as though I might disappear if he let go. "Jenny, I think we've been challenged."

The four of us stood among other couples, waiting for the music to begin. "Put your hands on my shoulders." He grabbed my hips, hard. "When I count to three, I want you to jump."

The song was a Stray Cats cover with a fast rhythm. "Three." He tossed me in the air. I had to put my legs around his waist to keep from falling. We spun once, and I slid through his grasp. I swung my feet to his left and then his right, and he hooted, and laughed out loud. The small of his back was sweating. His hand felt hard and sure on my spine. The tiki lights blurred, and I was breathlessly happy.

By the time the song was over, my father's silver-blond hair was windblown and he was laughing. "You won." Ryder held out his hand and my dad shook it. "In your age group." My dad snatched his hand back, but he was still laughing.

They had brought us strawberry shortcake while we were gone, or maybe my father had ordered it without our noticing. The strawberries tasted just picked and the cream was real and the cake underneath soft and moist from the fruit. "I always feel like a little girl when I eat strawberry shortcake," Jamie said between mouthfuls. I couldn't believe she was eating it.

My father kissed her on the nose. It had gotten completely dark, but everything around us was golden-hued and bright under the torch-lit lamps. Above us were those same stars Ryder used to point out as we'd lie together on the football field the summer before my junior year—the harp in Lyra's constellation and the head of the bear in Ursa Major. I knew they were there, but I couldn't see them well anymore.

My dad was smiling at Jamie, and he had a little dab of strawberry on his chin. She was talking in her girlish voice about drinking too much Chardonnay and how she'd have to play hooky so we could see the seals at Clam Beach the next day.

For one stolen, fleeting moment, the guilt washed away. It was as though I'd entered a dream where Will's death wasn't my fault. There they were, my family: Ryder, my mom, and my dad. Will was missing, but his death was what it should have been, a sad, pure thing. I heard myself saying I would go to Clam Beach with them, and Ryder said he'd love to see Jamie in knee-high rubber boots.

The feeling stayed like the lingering taste of a really good dessert. But I knew about feelings like that; as much as I wanted to bottle them up for safekeeping, something always came along that was much stronger and would shatter them all to pieces.

9

I sat at the dining room table, rereading an article I'd found on meningiomas. All the websites said the same thing: "The recommended course of treatment is surgical resection, followed by radiation." Ryder had seemed so sure in his office that doing radiation first was the right thing to do, but now I wondered. He'd told me to do my own research. And everything I'd read said to operate first.

"Whobaby, turn off that damn computer," my dad yelled from the kitchen. "And come see what Luke's cooking up for us." I bookmarked the page, closed the laptop, and hopped up.

In the kitchen, Luke was unloading green tea, krill oil, and kale from a reusable grocery bag. Other unfamiliar leafy greens and pinkish tofu were scattered on the counters. "You're not going to make us eat this, are you?" I pointed at a squishy mound of seitan.

"Luke's starting me on a macrobio-whatever diet tomorrow." My dad pulled a cherry tomato from the vine and popped it in his mouth. "But tonight, we gorge ourselves on caviar."

"Everyone's whispering about his tumor," Luke said. "Might as well bring it out into the open and throw a party for it."

My father put his arm around me. "And you, our youngest musical genius, will be our D.J." He twirled me around the kitchen and dipped me to the floor. "We need theme songs," he said when he let me go. "You know, 'Gravedigger,' 'The End.' Stuff like that."

"Dad!" I turned to Luke. "Tell him he's not dying."

"Don't forget 'Funeral for a Friend.'" Luke unloaded chocolate-covered strawberries from Tatiana's, the same bakery that had delivered a cake in the shape of a football to Will's sixteenth-birthday party.

"Only you two would think this is funny." I dug through a junk drawer for a pen and pad.

"Maybe you'll even get to meet Starflower," my dad said. "Luke's new honey." He whispered loudly, "She has purple hair and smells like patchouli." He put a hunk of red cabbage on his head.

Luke batted away the vegetable. "She doesn't have purple hair, and she's not new; it's just that Jensen hasn't been home in a hundred years." He winked at me. "Anyway, she's at a Tantric retreat."

"A what?" Women moved in and out of Luke's life like water. They'd make an occasional appearance at dinner. It was only when the next one arrived that I'd realize the last one was gone.

"It's an ancient practice that concentrates on enhancing sexual experiences," Luke told me.

I put my hands over my ears. "La la la," I said loudly. "I can't hear you."

"'Don't Fear the Reaper.'" My father pointed to the pad. "Put that on there."

After they took off for the liquor store and I heard the garage door close behind them, I looked at my playlist. "Late for the Sky," Luke had added, and "Stairway to Heaven." I felt so sad, I had to sit down on the kitchen floor. I stayed there for a long time, my dad's voice ringing in the room, the kitchen clock ticking on the wall.

Two hours later, I heard a car door close in the driveway. I was pulling lemons, Parmesan cheese, and garlic from the fridge, and my cell phone was ringing. "What are you up to?" I asked Nic when I answered my phone.

"Oh, nothing." He sounded sad. "Trying to shake off the ache of missing you." I thought of the sun coming in the skylights this time of day in the house. Since we'd moved in together, almost nine years before, we'd never gone this long without each other. "I feel like I've been ditched at the prom," he told me.

"You didn't even go to your prom."

He laughed. "I would have if you were my date."

More people started arriving, and I heard Jamie's heels clicking down the hall.

"My parents are having a few people over." I drizzled olive oil into a ramekin and listened to the party move into the living room. The doorbell chimed. "Are you going out to sushi without me?"

"Hell no," he said. "And listen to Hadley go on about his upcoming tour? I frankly do not know who he is expecting to find in east bum fuck Latvia or Estonia."

I'd forgotten all about Hadley's trip. "Oh, Hadley could find a good photographer in the Mongolian desert." I could hear the plink of piano keys, and I knew he was sitting at that Steinway I never played.

"Who's coming over?" he asked.

"People I haven't seen for a thousand years."

"How's your old man?"

"Well, he still has a brain tumor."

"If you love me, you'll shoot me before I get old."

That was so Nico. "I actually just read that brain tumors can happen at any age." I could see Jamie through the arched doorway, holding court in the living room with Sid and his assistant coaches. I hadn't seen him since I'd been home. He'd been the defensive coordinator when Will played for Hamilton and had helped my dad start A Will to Live after the accident. All the players he coached and the kids at the foundation loved him because he was a great storyteller, talking quickly and with his hands. He was probably telling Jamie and the group how he'd discovered Springsteen as a scratchy-voiced kid singing in a bar in Asbury Park. Or maybe he'd moved on to how he'd invented fire, or the wheel. The doorbell rang again. "I gotta go. This place is a madhouse. I love you."

In the foyer by the grandfather clock, I straightened the lone photo of Nic and me at our wedding. We were standing on a beach, my gauzy white dress and my hair blowing in the wind. I was barefoot, laughing, and Nic was holding an empty bottle of ouzo. I remembered that light-headed feeling, the shock of flying to Greece and getting married without telling anyone but Hadley, who'd driven us to the airport. The doorbell rang again.

Ryder was standing in the threshold in jeans and a lightweight sweater the same color as his eyes. I hadn't seen him since that night at the Seafood Shack.

"Someone told me there's a party here tonight." He held out a bottle of wine.

I stepped toward him to take it, and he leaned in like he might kiss me. "Someone told me the same thing," I said.

"Well, you can put your glad face on now." He grinned. "I'm here." I wanted to tell him I was happier than I should have been to see him, but I couldn't get the words out. He put both hands over his heart and staggered. I punched his arm. I was fifteen again, catching him watching me in my red bikini at Breakneck Lake, the week before he'd shown up at my house when he knew my parents and Will wouldn't be home.

He half-punched me back. "You've got that look in your eye."

"Which one?" I tucked my hair behind my ear.

He closed the door. "The one where you stick your tongue in the side of your mouth." A strand of hair fell over my eyes, and when he pushed it back, my skin chilled. "And try not to say what you're really thinking."

I was glad more people were arriving, because I didn't know what to say. Sid's wife came in and practically knocked me over, she was so happy to see me. Next came a slew of Jamie's photographers, a handful of models, and the whole board of directors from A Will to Live. As I showed them the bar, I thought it strange how happy everyone was to be at a party for a guy with a brain tumor. It wasn't something I'd celebrate, but that was my dad. He needed his friends to know he was okay. That he was going to beat this thing.

By the time I saw Ryder again, he was in the living room, sandwiched between a couple of Jamie's models, who'd probably found out he was a doctor and were trying to marry him.

Around nine, Mandy came through the back door in skintight black jeans and a see-through button-down blouse. She could have been one of my mother's runway girls. Some hot Latino guy was following her. "Antonio," she said to him, "meet my very best sister, Jensen." Mandy had an older brother and two younger sisters, but she always said that.

He kissed my hand. "So lovely to meet you." His accent was divine.

"He owns the estancia in Uruguay where we did a bird-watching shoot," she told me, and I had a flash of her, pregnant and happy, with little Antonios running around.

"He's very pretty," I whispered when I hugged her. She smelled of champagne.

"And very married," she whispered back.

Before I could say anything else, my father and Luke stormed the foyer, calling her name and bear-hugging her. Mandy screamed and jumped up and down and called them both "Daddy-O," then explained to Antonio that it had been a million years since she'd seen them.

"Antonio," my dad said when she introduced him, "*Usted es un hombre muy guapo.*" Whatever that meant. Then he did some sort of flamenco dance.

Luke clapped poor Antonio on the back and blatantly stared at his wedding ring. "*No hablo Español,* my friend." It was a lie; Luke spoke five languages, including Portuguese and Spanish. "But I think this translates: Don't mess with our Mandy."

I tried to give them stern looks, but I had to excuse myself. Nicole, from two houses down, stumbled in behind her Afghan dog. They both had long noses and frizzy red hair. I was going to tell her we didn't really want a dog inside, Jamie was allergic, but the house began to fill with people I barely remembered from the Colston Country Club and my father's time at ESPN, Jamie's makeup artists and scouts, people I hadn't seen since Will's funeral. My cheeks ached from smiling.

Jamie was standing at the piano, touching Ed Kane's shoulder. He was an old-time sportswriter for the *New Haven Register* and had been in the stands the night of Will's accident. Behind her, Luke was playing "Red Red Wine." Mandy lounged beside him, singing along, clearly a little drunk, Antonio nowhere in sight. I watched Jamie laugh, her hand on Ed's arm. *Still the same flirty Jamie,* I thought.

My dad came in from the kitchen, cupping his hands around his mouth. "Back off, Ed," he yelled. "She's mine."

Jamie turned, surprised, her high, sculpted cheekbones pink from too much wine. "Oh, honey, you know I am." She blew my father a kiss, and when she caught me standing in the doorway, she called over. "Jensen, darling, I was just telling the boys how you play piano." She came twirling over to me.

Ryder had appeared, holding a beer, his short hair a little messy. He had the happy, glassy look of drink in his eyes that I remembered from when we were teenagers.

"Jamie, you know I don't play anymore," I said. I'd taken a pair of earth-colored linen pants from her closet. They were cool on my skin, and I was glad I'd dressed up.

"You're kidding, right?" Ryder glanced at the piano, the way he used to stare at organic-chemistry problems. Maybe if he looked long enough, they'd make sense. "Why? You were so good. That's all you ever wanted to do."

"You know why," I told him quietly.

Without music, the room grew quiet. Luke called out, "Come over here and give your father a song, baby girl." My dad started clapping, and Ed Kane put his fingers to his lips and whistled. I could feel people gathering behind me. Luke had told me that one way or another he was going to get me to start playing again.

I walked toward the piano. Luke surrendered his seat, and Mandy gave me a big kiss on the cheek. "Oh goodie," she said. "Just like old times."

I sat on the padded bench. The room had gone quiet. Mandy set her elbows on the guide rail, her chin in her hands, and waited for me. I could feel people watching; all of them had known me as Sterling's piano prodigy daughter. They were all expecting me to play. And why shouldn't I? Why couldn't I play again? The room felt still, as though someone had just died, or was about to. "If you wait much longer," Mandy whispered, "someone is going to turn on that terrible playlist again." I chewed my lip, trying to think of something I might remember. The piano used to be my religion. Now it felt as foreign as a lost language.

Then I remembered, during our breaks from studying for finals sophomore year, Mandy and I used to sit on this same bench, and I'd play Crosby, Stills & Nash's "Got It Made" while she sang along. She'd just scored highest on the PSATs, and I'd bested seven hundred other players to win the PianoArts North American Piano Competition and the chance to play with the Milwaukee Symphony Orchestra, one of the best in the country. We had it made, and we knew it. " 'Got It Made,'" I said. She gave me a thumbs-up.

As soon as she started singing, the chords came back to me. The music was stored in my hands. I looked down at them in amazement; they coordinated without my say-so, as if they'd been waiting, patiently, for this chance. I closed my eyes and felt myself fall into the rhythm as though gravity had given way and I was floating. The party disappeared, my father's brain tumor, Ryder's surprise when he found out I'd quit. The refrain melted an ache I wasn't even aware I was holding on to. I vaguely heard the doorbell ringing, people cheering, Luke saying, quietly, behind me, "You got it going on, girl, that's right," and just when I was about to transition into Billy Joel's "This Is the Time," I felt a ripple of panic spread through the room, and I realized Mandy had stopped singing. I opened my eyes.

A crowd had formed by the couch. In the spaces between the people, I could see my father sitting with his head between his knees, his hair disheveled, his feet pigeon-toed. Ryder was kneeling beside him. I pushed my way over. His eyes were filmy, and he was covered in a thin sheen of sweat.

"I'm fine." He was wiping his glasses on his shirt, his breath labored. "Just got a little nauseous."

I sat on the arm of the couch and took his hand; his fingers were cold, clammy. Ryder pulled a penlight from his pocket and flashed it in my dad's eyes. Worry lines wrinkled Ryder's forehead. He placed his fingers on my dad's wrist. "Your pupils are dilating and your pulse is strong. Have you been eating?"

My father's voice was hoarse. "Sometimes I don't feel like it."

I squeezed his hand, trying to recall if he'd finished his cereal and grapefruit that morning. "Dad, you need to tell someone when you don't feel well."

"It's okay, Jenny. Lack of appetite is normal." Ryder stuck the flashlight back in his pocket. I tried to imagine Nic ever carrying a penlight.

"Could you get Sid for me?" my father asked, searching the room feverishly. "We were discussing why the flea-flicker play needs to be retired." He took off his glasses and chewed on the arm. "I know I know why; I just can't find the words."

Cold fear exploded in my stomach. Sid had left over an hour ago, and my father had been practicing the flea flicker all his life. "That's easy." I tried to keep my voice steady. "It's too risky. If the defense isn't tricked into thinking you're setting up a running play, the quarterback ends up on his ass."

My dad patted my hand, his eyes searching my face. "You're my good girl, Jensen."

Ryder caught my eye, but I didn't smile.

The party broke up after that. Jamie put my father to bed, and people started filing out. Luke drove Mandy home because Antonio had brought her there in his rental car, and she had no idea where he'd gone. "I think your dad and I might have scared him off," Luke whispered to me.

To avoid good-byes, I escaped to the kitchen to deal with dirty dishes. I needed to think about something other than the fact that my father was disappearing in front of me, and I'd been hiding out in Santa Fe with Nic. Out of the corner of my eye, I saw Ryder come through the archway. Taking a dish towel from the oven handle, he stood beside me and dried a serving bowl. "What the fuck was that?" I asked.

He kept drying. "Just part of the disease. He's going to forget stuff."

I felt like smashing the plate against the sink. "Stop telling me what you think I want to hear." I turned off the water.

He quit drying. "What the hell does that mean?"

"I think you're holding out on us." I took a paper towel from the roll and dried my hands furiously. "I think he's sicker than you're letting on. And maybe Jamie is willing to be in denial." I wadded up the paper towel and threw it in the trash. "But I'm not." I had a feeling of pushing a boulder over a deep precipice, but I kept going. "Just like you told me to, I've been reading up on this," I said, "and I know you're doing something risky."

He looked as though he were deciding something. "Santa Fe made you hard," he said. "You know that? You don't trust anyone."

"Oh, so all the research is wrong, and you're right? Every article I've read says that resecting the tumor immediately will give him the best chance of survival."

"You're reading guidelines, general practices. Most meningiomas aren't so close to the pneumotaxic center. They usually grow in one of the temporal lobes, just under the dura. Removing those tumors is a cakewalk. Your dad's is not following the norm. I have to treat his specific illness, not what the disease usually does." His face was set like stone. "I love that man like a father. You think I'd do anything." He spit out the words. "Anything, to hurt him?"

Out the kitchen window, I could see the deck, where people had left half-finished beers and cocktail napkins.

"Andrew Benning," he said. "He's a neuro in my practice. I encourage all my patients to get second opinions so that when they're on my operating table, they have one hundred percent faith in me. I would have given you his name before now, but I didn't think you'd want anyone else." He threw the dish towel on the counter.

"What do you want me to think? First you tell us that a well-informed patient is the best patient. And then you go rogue with his treatment." I folded the towel he'd thrown, draped it over the oven handle. "I'm still trying to get used to your being a brain surgeon, to even being back here."

"I'm not the one who left. And if you'd wanted to find me, all you had to do was look, but you didn't look, Jensen." He took a step back. I saw his neck was bright red, like it used to get when he was angry. "You hid out instead." He looked like he was going to say something more, but then he turned around and I watched him walk out of the kitchen and down the hall. I let myself out onto the deck. Standing at the railing, I half-expected him to come back, to come after me. But eventually I heard a car door shut and an engine start, and I knew he was gone.

Upstairs, the light was off in my parents' bedroom. Because of the dark, I couldn't see much beyond the sea of blooming yellow forsythia bordering the fence. The night smelled of the lamb Luke had cooked on the grill. I could feel a headache starting at the base of my neck.

I'd been faking it all night. The only thing that had felt real was when I'd been playing the piano, but just when the groove hit, reality had come crashing back. It was the way life rolled. Maybe I was home, eating chocolate cake and taking drives in convertibles, but my father was sick. He was probably dying. And we needed a second opinion. We needed to talk to someone who would tell us the truth. Because right now, we were all standing in quicksand, and I was the only one who could feel we were sinking.

10

I never called Dr. Andrew Benning for a second opinion. I kept his number on my bureau, but it felt like a sacrilege. And somehow I was too busy. My life took on a rhythm, driving my dad to radiation and spending time with him while Jamie worked, messing up self-portraits in the attic while he napped, running on Hammonasset Beach at dusk with Mandy when she was home from photo shoots, and playing piano with Luke three times a week.

I could now play *Islamay*, the Oriental fantasy by Balakirev; *Gaspard de la Nuit*, by Maurice Ravel; a *Petrushka* transcription by Stravinsky; and Rachmaninoff's Piano Sonata no. 2, 1913 edition. I also played Springsteen's "Racing in the Street." I'd started to learn it as a present for Ryder's eighteenth birthday, but then I'd left for Andover. I didn't try "Reverie" again.

My dad's illness and something about being in Colston made me organized, focused. I was the keeper of his radiation schedule and secretly recorded his headaches and any other strange behavior. I made sure we had an emergency supply of his medicine in the car. While Jamie was at work, I stocked the fridge with the food Luke recommended: organic, gluten-free, high-protein, low-fat. I spent hours at the Yale library researching meningiomas, studying recent dissertations from neuroscientists, and reading about the workings of the medulla and pons. Hadley was a vitamin junkie, and I had him investigating different supplements. Then I figured out which ones would interact with my dad's meds. I organized it all in a hanging file in the kitchen, beneath the phone books.

Most of what I read, I didn't share with anyone. I didn't ask Dale or Ryder about it, but I wanted to know everything about this disease. And doing the research made me feel needed and smart. I had a purpose, and whether it came from guilt or some feral instinct to save my dad, I was still doing some good. In Santa Fe, I was so far from the girl I'd been. I modeled for the people Nic chose for me and gossiped with Hadley about all the galleries downtown closing because the economy was in the toilet. And I went on tour with Nic. But I wasn't organized like I had been. I'd forget to pull bills out of the wire basket in the kitchen and pay them on time. I never balanced the checkbook or made our bed. I usually had to sift through a pile of laundry to find a pair of socks. Since I did my job naked, it hardly mattered, except when I helped Hadley out at the café.

But here I was different. I was on the ball. I'd been one person, and then I wasn't. Now I was someone completely different. In Colston, I was back to my old straight-A self, the good girl my father could count on. The Jensen I'd created with Nic, the numb, unfeeling version of myself, was fading.

Despite his brain tumor, which made him forget everyday things and gave him horrible headaches, my dad was in high spirits. Sometimes I caught him in his office, holding his head in his hands, or I'd see him trying desperately to think of a word, but mostly he was up early, knocking on my door, asking what I had planned for the day, saying he wanted to play hooky from the foundation, and asking if I was game.

During those long June days, I sometimes got that feeling I'd had at the Seafood Shack, that everything was okay. Piecing together my favorite Elton John and Ella Fitzgerald songs on the piano, swimming at Shoal's Beach in a black bikini I'd bought in town, I could almost trick myself into believing that life had rewound. I'd never given up a full ride to Juilliard or hitchhiked to San Francisco to see the Dead, never dropped acid or slept with my art teacher, never posed nude for sculptors in Santa Fe or gotten so drunk at the Cowgirl Café I let a *bruja* tattoo a nightingale on each ankle. That had all been a long, outrageous dream, and now I was back where I belonged.

After the Alfa Romeo, my dad rented two more sports cars, a green Triumph Spitfire and a Porsche Carrera, which we took down the Merritt at 5:00 A.M. all the way to the New York border so he could feel the speed on the straightaways. He wanted to go zip lining, too, but Dale Novak nixed it. He shrugged when she told him. "Well, then let's buy some water skis for Luke's Whaler," he said.

"Dad . . ."

"What?" he asked innocently.

Instead, we took the Whaler down the Connecticut River, dropped the anchor between Essex and Hadlyme, and Mandy and I swam near Nutt Island while he and Luke fished. The current was so strong, twice Luke had to throw us a line so we could get back to the boat. I was glad we weren't water-skiing. While we tanned on the bow of *Charmer,* I thought about Ryder and wondered what he'd been doing. But we were deep into radiation with Dale, and I didn't have an excuse to call him. He was the surgeon. His part was on hold until after radiation ended.

On an overcast day at the end of the June, when the humid, still air of July was starting to creep in, my dad took me to North Cove Outfitters and bought us matching yellow Wellies. We went clamming like we used to when Will and I were little, filled an old Benjamin Moore bucket to the top, and called Luke on our way home. Jamie was just back from signing a new girl from Moscow, and the four of us spent the night on the deck, eating fresh seafood, drinking Chardonnay, and squirting each other with lemons.

On nights like those, Jamie seemed settled, almost peaceful. She relaxed into the glider with my father, leaning against him, her eyes blinking lazily, not unhappy or restless like she used to get. Sometimes it felt like I'd dreamed that span of time when she had her apartment and a lover on the side. Except I knew her. I still had the clear memory of how she'd been after Will died, spending nights at the brownstone with God knows who. As though strangers could take away her hurt better than her own family, or what was left of it.

"I interviewed that list of acupuncturists you gave us," I said. Luke and I were sitting on the railing, watching fireflies. "And if you're willing to be a pincushion," I told my dad, "I think they can help your headaches."

"Give this girl a task, and she gets it done yesterday," he said.

I smiled at him and wriggled my nose. But being home again, being a gold-star student, clamming, driving fast cars, and dozing on the Whaler couldn't change what my hours of research on the Internet and in the Yale Medical Library had told me. A meningioma was still a brain tumor. We couldn't lose our vigilance; we couldn't turn our backs on it, not even for a second. I'd read everything I could find on my father's condition, could recite statistics to anyone who asked, and there were still plenty of people with meningiomas who didn't survive.

11

"What color do you think the freaky receptionist's fingernails will be today?" I turned in to the hospital parking garage, and the Lexus's headlights went on without my having to push any buttons. I wasn't used to a car that gave me directions, warmed my ass, and created playlists on the stereo. I felt like I was driving a servant. I missed Sabrina, the '87 Saab convertible I'd inherited from Hadley, with the crank windows and cloth seats. It'd been six weeks since I'd put the top down and driven fast through those desert mountains, past tabletop mesas and the edges of the Rio Grande, Dave Matthews blaring.

My father didn't answer. When I glanced over, he was groping at the air, his mouth open, his tongue resting on his bottom lip. I'd seen that look in his eyes a million times before when he was going through playbooks or watching film, concentrating, as if he could just *think* hard enough, he'd understand.

When I turned in to the parking space, he surprised me by reaching over and touching my face, tracing it the way a blind person might, running his fingers over my jaw as though to conjure missing words. Cold prickled my spine. I turned off the ignition. "I'm Jensen," I said. "Remember? Rhymes with Benson. Your high school football coach." The books I'd read had suggested making up games to help him remember the things we never thought he'd forget. Our street, North Parker, sounded a little like fourth quarter. When he couldn't think of a word, I'd quote his favorite TV show, " 'Mnemonics for five hundred, Alex.' "

He waved at me as though I were being silly. "Of course," he said. Instantly normal again, as though nothing had happened, he unclipped his seat belt.

I pulled my leather backpack off the seat. "Hang on a sec," I said, opening my notebook.

"Are you ever going to tell me what you write in that thing?" He leaned across the console.

"Just stuff I don't want to forget." He seemed satisfied with my half-truth, and I waited for him to climb out of the car. When his door closed, I scribbled *June 30th—forgot my name again.* It was the third time in six days.

In Dale's office, we stood at the front desk, waiting for the receptionist who'd checked us in five days a week for the last three weeks. "Name?" she asked.

Really? "Sterling Reilly," I told her as patiently as I could.

She ran a Smurf-colored fingernail down an appointment book. "Oh, there you are," she said cheerily. "You get the day off. Dr. Novak had an emergency and said your treatment can wait until tomorrow." The phone rang, and she slid the partition closed.

I glanced at the wall clock. "She could have called."

My dad hooked his arm through mine. "Do you know what this means?" He winked at me. "Caller's Island."

"Oh jeez," I groaned.

"Come on, you loved it as a kid."

We stepped into the elevator, and I pushed the button. "That was before I realized their roller coasters are held up by a couple of rusty nails."

My dad loved Caller's Island, a tiny amusement park near Taft Airport, with rattling rides and paint-chipped carousel horses. Right up until Will died, the four of us, plus Ryder, would pile in the car for the forty-minute trip east, where we ate cotton candy and rode the looping roller coasters. Weathered carnies conned us into playing games we never won, promising oversize stuffed animals if we could just pop the balloon with an old dart.

My dad was staring up at the elevator numbers like a little boy. I felt bad for him. Dale had said no to spending too much time at the foundation during radiation, and I was forever telling him he couldn't drink a beer or eat a cookie and that waterskiing was out of the question. Jamie worked so much that I'd had to turn into the bad cop, the unfun parent.

"Okay," I said.

His face split into a grin.

"Just this once," I told him, even though I thought it was a terrible idea.

We stood in front of the wooden roller coaster, Caller's Island's main attraction. There had been an accident on I-95, and it had taken us a hellish hour to go six exits. I'd forgotten my sunglasses, and I had to put my hand up like a visor and squint. Looming past the ticket booth stood the double-loop roller coaster, its paint now faded to the color of the sky. "Are you sure about this? Dale said you should be taking it easy."

He stood with his back to the sun, trying to block it from my eyes. He'd insisted we get fried dough with powdered sugar, and he had a telltale trail of it down his front. "I didn't hear you telling me to be careful when we were flying around Hamburg Cove last weekend." I set my fried dough on a picnic table next to the carousel and sat down. He sat next to me. "And don't go getting a guilty conscience and fess up to Luke about our treats today." He wiped his mouth on his sleeve. TLA was crudely etched into the table next to two pairs of initials. *True love always. Trouble lies ahead.*

He balanced his sunglasses on his forehead. "Come on, be my good girl, go on the roller coaster with your old man."

A man and his German shepherd service dog sat at the table next to us. My father had no idea how not good I was. The dog stretched out and laid its head on the man's foot. "Doesn't he remind you of Bailey?" My dad nodded at the dog.

"Bailey?"

"Our old dog. The one Will begged us to adopt from the shelter."

"Dad," I said, my heart racing, "we've never had a dog. Jamie's allergic."

He took off his glasses and stuck the arm in his ear. "Goddamn." He shook his head as if to clear it. "I guess my excuse for getting you home is acting up."

I looked at the squint lines around his eyes and the twitch in his bottom lip. A swarm of families went by, toddlers in strollers, kids holding giant pretzels. After they passed, I asked, "Are you worried? Does it make you scared?"

He waved away a yellow jacket buzzing around my uneaten fry bread. "Everything's a trade-off. When I entered the draft, I wanted to play for the 49ers or the Raiders, get as far away from Philly as I could. But the Steelers picked me up. I was pissed off at the time, but if I'd gone to San Fran or Oakland, I never would've met Luke. His college roommate was our backup punter. My last year playing, Luke introduced me to your mom at a VIP party before the Super Bowl. Everything happens for a reason, Whobaby. And don't you ever forget it."

I stared down at the yellow jackets circling my food. After we'd buried Will, the priest had said the same thing, and I'd stayed there under the granddaddy maple, trying to think of a good reason why I was in the Edgehill Cemetery, putting flowers on my brother's casket. Finally, Ryder had taken my hand and led me away, holding me against him so I wouldn't fall. We didn't care anymore who saw us together. It was Will who had forbidden it, and after he died, it hardly mattered.

I got up. "Well, if we're going to do it, it might as well be now." I threw the soggy dough in a nearby garbage can. There was a brand-new metal roller coaster beyond the Ferris wheel, but my dad had insisted on the old wooden one. He still had pictures of Will, Ryder, and me crammed in one car, mouths open, arms up. When the wind blew, it made a low, moaning noise like the goalposts in our back-yard. "What if you fall out and bonk your head?" I asked him while we walked toward it.

"Maybe it will knock the tumor out through my mouth." He tousled my hair. "Ever think of that?"

I handed two tickets to a teenaged kid who might have been asleep if not for the fact that he was reciting the rules. "Keep your arms inside at all times. No standing. Do not raise the safety bar until the ride has ended."

My father folded the rest of our tickets like an accordion and stuffed them in his front pocket. "Ready?"

I couldn't shake the feeling that we shouldn't be doing this. That somehow flying upside down was not the right thing for a man with cancer.

We found a blue two-seater and pulled the safety bar over our laps. People were filling the cars around us. I leaned back. The air smelled of popcorn and sugar. Under the peeling blue was a layer of yellow paint, and I picked at it with my fingernail, wondering how old this thing was.

"So what's happening with those piano lessons?" my father asked while we waited. "You working on a concerto for your old man?"

Before I could answer, the carnival music started, an odd mix of cymbals and saxophone, and the train of cars lurched forward. Kids behind us started screaming. "If they do that the whole time," my dad said, talking close to my ear, "maybe they'll blow out my ear-drum and the tumor will come flying out."

The ride picked up speed, and then the car felt like it had dropped off the track as we headed straight down. For a few seconds, we were free-falling. I tried to watch my dad, but it was hard to focus.

Just as we finished the first loop, I saw he had raised his hands over his head, and he was laughing so hard, his eyes had disappeared. While we started the slow crawl up the second loop, the people waiting in line got smaller. I held on to the side of the car. We dropped off another time, and I felt myself laughing hysterically when we went upside down.

Finally, we slowed to a stop, and our safety bar unlocked. My elastic band had slipped, and my hair was wrapped around my neck. I combed it with my fingers. My dad tucked in his striped polo shirt, but he stayed in his seat. The robotic teenager was coming toward us, shooing people off the ride. "Dad, come on."

He held up two tickets. "One more time," he said to the bored worker. I sat back in the seat. "One more crazy, screaming time," he said, almost to himself.

When we finally dismounted the ride, the world seemed tilted wrong on its axis. We had to hold on to each other, and as we headed off the hot tarmac, I felt like I was walking sideways, and all the rides and games were slanted at odd angles.

"Okay," I said, touching his hair. "What did this get you?" He cocked his head, as if he didn't understand what I was asking. "You said before that everything's a trade-off. What did a brain tumor get you?"

He sat heavily at a picnic table. Taking off his glasses, he chewed on the end, squinting in the hot sun. "You," he said. "This old broken brain brought you back to me."

And then his eyelids fluttered and his pupils disappeared. His eyes rolled into his head.

"Dad?" I sat next to him. "Dad?" I said frantically.

But he slumped against me, unconscious.

12

I tried to follow the ambulance to Yale, but I lost it on the I-91 interchange, and by the time I parked and got to the main entrance, the woman at the nurses' station said they'd taken my dad upstairs. "Dr. Novak will be here as soon as she can."

I sat on one of those plastic ER waiting room chairs in that code red atmosphere and left messages for Jamie and Luke while berating myself for taking my father on a fucking roller coaster. Hadley kept calling, yapping about some new photographer he was going to bring over from Hungary. I felt as if Santa Fe, with its willowware blue skies and its hundred galleries, were on another planet. I couldn't stop seeing my father's eyes rolling up in his head. It didn't make any sense. He seemed to be doing so well, always ready to water-ski or ride up and down the Merritt Parkway like a maniac.

"Jensen." I saw the red pumps first, and then Dale was standing over me. Her lips were tight, and it made me think she was going to give me bad news. When I stood, her eyes took me in the same way the shrink at boarding school used to, as if she expected me to talk first. Finally, she said, "Your dad had a vasovagal episode." She said it slowly, breaking down each syllable.

"Any guesses what caused his blood pressure to drop?" I might as well have said, *I know what vasovagal means, you dumb cow.* I loved the Internet.

She straightened her necklace so a tiny gold stethoscope faced front. "Most likely, he's dehydrated and run down from the radiation." Her pumps looked brand-new. I thought it was odd, a doctor wearing red pumps, but that was Dale—something about her was a little off. "We'll give him some fluids overnight and see how he is tomorrow. I'm off for thirty-six hours, but I'll check on him from home. Dr. Weiss is on call until I get back."

I should have thanked her, but I had an overwhelming desire to punch her in the head. It was guilt, I knew; it was the feeling that she could somehow tell I had just taken my dad on a double-loop roller coaster. Twice. I'd fed him fried dough and cream soda in the hot sun, and for the entire month I had been riding in sports cars with him, when I should have been putting him to bed with a cold pack on his head. But he was persuasive. He was fun. And Dale probably did not understand fun.

"He's in room two thirty-six," she said, touching my arm in an unexpectedly kind way. When she moved aside, I saw him, or someone who looked just like him, the ER doctor from the night Will died. He was standing at the nurses' station, writing on a chart, and when our eyes met, he hesitated before turning away. It took me a minute to recognize him, and later I would not really know if it was him or not. He still had the full beard, but his face had the puttied look of people who don't age well. And then he was gone, down the hall.

I pushed open the door to my dad's room. The shades were pulled and a vinyl couch, cracked and worn, was under the window. "Hey, Dad." I sat on the edge of his bed. "Do you feel okay?" His eyes were unfocused, cloudy. I rested my palm on his forehead. He jumped at my touch, then settled, his eyelids fluttering like a child fighting sleep. I felt his body relax as he drifted off. The door opened and a nurse came in. She had spiky blond hair.

"I'm Lusana," she said. "What happened here?"

"I'm not sure." *I took him on a roller coaster and probably killed him.*

"I need access to this side of the bed." She rolled a metal cart over.

Feeling the hot sting of tears, I turned away, pulled my phone out of my pocket, and stood at the window. Outside, shadows from the hospital stretched across the street. I didn't wait for Jamie to say hello. "Didn't you get my messages?" The nurse tucked the blanket around my dad's feet.

"She needs more liner on her bottom lip," Jamie said into the background. "Not too shiny, people. Jensen"—her voice was softer now—"what happened, darling? I saw you called, but we were in the middle of the shoot with the Moscow girl, and I—"

"Daddy passed out earlier. He's in the hospital."

I heard her gasp, and a male voice in the background asked if she was okay. "Close the door," she said to someone. The nurse pressed a few buttons on a monitor. "Is he okay?"

I don't fucking know. "I think so."

"My God, how did it happen?"

Lusana left. I sat on the cracked couch and tucked my knees to my chin. "We were at Caller's Island, riding the roller coaster, and—"

"You what? Jensen." She said my name like she was trying to wipe off a stain.

"The ride didn't do it." I couldn't keep the defensiveness out of my voice. "And anyway, he's been begging me to go for weeks."

"Piers," she said, as if I weren't on the line. "I have to go. Something's happened to Sterling." I could hear her calling to her photographer. "Alkalina can step down now. She was magnificent."

"Don't bother coming tonight." I glanced at the bed. "Daddy's sleeping."

"Oh, sweetheart, I'm coming."

"Don't. It'll be a hassle after visiting hours. Just come in the morning. Dale said it was his blood pressure, that it can happen during radiation."

"If you think—" But before she could finish, I said, "Can you bring his supplements and meds with you in the morning?"

"Oh, honey." She sounded strung out by the request. "There are so many. Do I bring all of them or—"

"They're dated and sorted in plastic bags in the pantry." When I closed my eyes, my lids stung. "Just grab the bunch marked for this week."

"Oh, Jensen, what on earth would we do without you? Tell your father I love him."

After we hung up, an orderly rolled in a cot stacked with linens and pillows and told me Dr. Novak had said I was welcome to stay the night. I was glad I didn't have to sleep on the couch, since it was about three feet too short. When he left, I lay on the cot, pulled the papery blanket to my shoulders, and studied my father. His breathing was even, the skin around his eyes relaxed, and the monitor lights seemed to be traveling in a calm trajectory. I thought of him at the kitchen table that morning, putting checks in the donation envelopes that came from various organizations asking for money. Jamie said he'd been giving away money like mad since the economy had gone downhill. But I wondered if, being close to death, you start to understand what is really important. It was quiet in there, and I felt suddenly drowsy from the sun and from worrying and from that long race to the hospital.

I dreamed I was with Ryder on the baseball field, where we used to go to kiss on weekend nights. In the dream, we were in the dugouts. The bleachers were full of people, and we were trying to hide from them. I could feel Ryder's lips; he was kissing my neck, trying to soothe me, but I was panicked someone would see us. I couldn't get loose. I patted my thighs and realized I was missing my legs— they were just stumps. But when I opened my mouth to tell him to find them, nothing came out. I woke in semidarkness, and it took me a minute to understand I'd been asleep. The cold terror of the dream was still with me.

The room was quiet except for the monitors. I could hear the soft rhythm of my father's breathing. I thought of the first time I'd ever kissed Ryder. Late August, right before sophomore year, alone in the house, watching some Tom Hanks movie on HBO. Will had gone out with Eva Sibley, and my parents had driven to Yankee Stadium. When Ryder showed up, I was embarrassed that I was by myself on a Saturday night, but he seemed to know I was there alone and asked me to go for a drive. We'd headed up to Hamilton the back way, skirting town, not talking. Something was already screaming between us.

A bootleg of the Phish show he'd been to the summer before was playing, and when we stopped at the baseball diamond "Swept Away" was on. He said he liked to go there at night, when no one was around. It was the first time I'd been out alone with him, and he talked about how much he wanted to be a pediatrician. He loved kids, and kids loved him.

He was the only boy I knew who baby-sat, and I usually teased him about it, but while we walked out to the middle of the field, I felt that charge between us. It had been so intense that summer, I'd sometimes checked the mirror to see if I had visibly changed. He hadn't been able to keep his hands off me since school ended, tickling me in the kitchen, pretending to want the candy bar I was eating so he could grab my wrist, tackling me in the yard when we played football. His hot breath made my heart beat faster; his touch did something frightening to my pulse.

He'd had a blanket in the trunk of his mom's Peugeot. "Stargazing," he'd said when he laid it out on the empty field. Back then, before Will died, I could actually see in the dark, could see every star clearly. He kicked off his shoes. I remembered the tan marks from where he'd worn flip-flops all season. The late summer honeysuckle was still blooming. The stars were out by the thousands, and even as we lay there on our backs and he said the constellations aloud, their names ringing with a kind of poetry, "Pegasus and Lynx, Sextans and Tucana," I'd known it would happen, but when he lifted up on his elbow and I saw Ryder Anderson, the boy I'd known since I was nine years old, above me, felt his lips on mine, it was as though someone had shocked me. I couldn't reckon myself with that wild girl who rose up inside, asking for more, wanting him. I felt drunk from the smell of clover and cut grass, his mouth and his hands. And then my shirt was off, and Ryder was on top of me, trying to catch his breath. When I told him I couldn't, not then, not yet, he stopped, and for one ugly second, I worried that maybe he didn't want me. But he kissed me gently on the lips and whispered that I was worth waiting for. "A hundred years," he said.

After that first kiss, I couldn't stop replaying that night in my mind. I kept waiting for the phone to ring, couldn't quit wondering how we could keep it a secret from everyone, most of all Will, who had made Ryder promise he'd never date me. "Never my sister, man. Anyone but her." Even then I didn't understand what Will's problem was. His sister and his best friend should have made him happy. It'd always been the three of us. But maybe if Ryder and I were suddenly a couple, he'd feel left out.

My dad was calling for me. I pushed off the scratchy blanket, slid off the cot, and sat next to him. "Hey, Dad." In the thick glow from the lights outside, his skin was gray. I reached over to feel his forehead, but he batted my hand away.

"Where's the dog?" he asked irritably.

"What dog?"

"The goddamn dog." He pushed himself up and slapped around the table until he found his glasses. "Help me off the couch and get me a flashlight."

Fuck. "Dad," I said as evenly as I could. "You're in the hospital." I straightened his glasses. "Your blood pressure was too low."

"Take a look around." He swung his legs to the floor. "Are there trophy cases in hospitals?" He made a sweeping motion with his arm. "Now get me his leash." I'd never heard him use that voice before.

When I reached over to find the nurse's call button, he swiped my hand away and grabbed a water bottle off the bedside table, rip-ping the IV out of his arm. He still had a running back's physique, all muscle, no fat. "Dad!" But then he was flying across the room in that little johnny, and the door slammed shut behind him.

Outside, I found him shuffling down the brightly lit hallway, aiming the water bottle like a flashlight. "Bailey," he was yelling, frantically. "Bailey!"

The nurses at the station were in action, and a doctor who looked about fifteen was calling out, "We need a restraint out here, stat."

"Bailey?" he kept calling.

"We'll find him in the morning." I had finally gotten a hold of his hand, but he turned on me with a strange, almost violent expression. A sheet of fear sliced through me, and then he did something that in all my years of knowing my father, he had never done: He pushed me. I fell sideways, but when I tried to get my footing, I stumbled on a crash cart and smacked my head, hard, while I was going down. Tiny bursts of light exploded in my eyes.

"Bailey!"

When I got my vision back, I saw the young doctor leaning over me. "You're bleeding," he said.

I touched my forehead. It was warm and sticky. I pointed down the hall. "Can you just get my dad? He's hallucinating." My father was zigzagging toward the elevators, his johnny open, so the world could see his backside. Lusana was following him with a wheelchair, and two fat men in scrubs were trying to hold him.

"Don't hurt him," I called, but my voice was thin.

"Calm down there, buddy. You're all right." One of them put his arms around him in a bear hug. Lusana pushed the wheelchair under him and, surprisingly, my dad went limp, slumping like an old man.

I tried to stand, but my balance was all wrong and blood was running down the side of my face, so I sat against the cool concrete wall and watched them wheel him down the hall toward his room. The doctor opened the door, and they all went inside. I wanted to get up, but my legs were too sluggish. I closed my eyes and thought of that dream where my legs were stumps. Someone came on the intercom, and when I opened my eyes, another nurse was running past me into his room.

After a while, the doctor came out with a cold, wet towel. "Put this on the laceration and press hard." He smelled like rubbing alcohol.

I took the towel. "I'm fine." I closed my eyes, waiting for my stomach to settle. "What's happening with my dad?" My head hurt when I pressed on it.

"The nurses are with him, and his doctor will be along momentarily. You're not fine." My head throbbed with the pressure. "You'll probably need sutures."

"Okay," I said. "Okay." I felt like asking him if he was old enough to drive.

After a few minutes, he managed to get me up and lead me to a small room with two couches and a kitchenette, where I lay on a vinyl love seat. "I'm in the middle of rounds, but as soon as I can, I'll stitch your head. In the meantime, don't get up."

I lay on the couch with my knees draped over the armrest and held the soaked cloth to my forehead. If I could just sleep, I thought the pain would subside, but it was so bright in that room; the lights hurt my eyes even when I closed them. Minutes later, the door squeaked open.

"Jenny." Ryder was standing over me with a surgical mask around his neck. He took the towel off my head, and his eyes searched the wound. "What the hell happened?"

"Bar fight," I said lamely. "You should see the other guy." A clock on the microwave said it was just after one in the morning.

The boy doctor came back, carrying a plastic caddy. "Dr. Anderson," he said. "This young lady took a spill in the corridor."

"I'll take it from here." Ryder took the supplies from him and slipped on a pair of latex gloves. Neither of them moved. "Really, Jeff." He sounded annoyed. "You can go." The door closed. "Residents," he said impatiently. He never would have used that tone if he were a pediatrician.

When I tried to sit up, he gently pushed my shoulders back, and I watched him fill a bottle. "Saline." He squirted it at my head; I jerked away. He waited until I stopped moving, then sprayed again.

"Something's wrong with my dad."

"He's sedated now. I'm sorry I couldn't get here sooner, I've been in the OR with the victim of a motorcycle accident." The dream came back to me, how we'd been in that dugout, his lips on mine. He untied his mask, set it beside him, then filled a small syringe and flicked it with his finger. "This is going to sting." The hot pain immediately faded, and my head started to tingle.

A month after Nic and I moved in together, I came home one night burning with fever. He ran a cool tub and sat with me as I shivered in the water. He'd put me to bed, and all night whenever I woke from a sweaty, disoriented sleep, I would find him next to me. I was so thirsty, but too weak to move. I'd wanted to wake him, ask him to bring me water. But I was afraid he'd be annoyed. So I shivered and dozed until morning, when my fever broke and I could get my own drink.

"You don't have to do this." I poked my forehead above my left eye. It was already numb. "Doogie Howser could have handled it."

He laughed. "Twenty-nine and still gets carded." He threaded a needle, a miniature version of what I used to repair buttons. "Close your eyes and try to relax." He sat motionless until I did. Every few seconds, I felt his hands lightly brush against my cheek. He was so close, I could smell his deodorant, could feel his breath on my forehead while he stitched. The rhythm of him working, tugging gently on the thread, two quick pulls, then the pressure of the needle, was almost hypnotizing.

"Why aren't you a pediatrician?" I asked. "You used to want that." I opened my eyes.

"Shut them," he said sternly. "Believe me, you do not want to see a needle coming at you like this." He waited a few seconds, and then I felt a gentle tugging. He worked without answering me. Finally, he said, "Okay, you can open." He snipped a few ends with a tiny pair of scissors. I patted at my head to find the stitches, but I couldn't feel anything. He drew my wrist away. "Don't touch it, unless you want a scar." When he tossed the gloves in the trash, I saw they were covered in blood. He grabbed a square bandage and a roll of white tape from the caddy. "I do good work," he said, positioning the gauze over the cut and securing it with tape. "Give it a week; the stitches will dissolve, and no one will ever know."

"How many?" I asked.

"Seven." I stared at a bunch of dying daisies crammed in a cheap plastic vase. Their stems were crooked and the petals were browning, as if someone had broken their hearts. "Are you going to tell me what really happened?" He handed me a wet wipe.

"When you tell me why you're not a pediatrician. It's all you ever wanted."

"Are you going to tell me why you quit the piano? It's all *you* ever wanted."

He used to ask me to play while he and Will were studying, said it helped him relax. "Piano's not the only thing I ever wanted," I said quietly.

He glanced at me, those dark eyes soft for a moment, and then he took the wipe from me and threw it in the trash. "You're going to need some clean clothes." I pulled at my blood-covered shirt. He went through a few cabinets until he found a stack of pink scrubs. "Medium's all we've got." He tossed me a top and pants.

They looked big enough for two of me. "Thanks."

"No one uses the lounge this time of night, but just in case." He locked the door. "After you clean up, we'll check on your dad."

I went to the sink and ran hot water over a paper towel, squirted soap on it, and wiped blood off my face and neck. Then I took the scrubs to the other side of the room and pulled off my clothes. I could hear Ryder behind me, tapping on his phone. Stitching those sutures, he'd been so close to me, I'd felt my breath quicken and would have sworn his had gone screwy, too. Standing in my bra and underwear, I turned just slightly so I could glance at him, then turned away. He looked up, and then, just as fast, he dropped his eyes. But he'd seen me. That was the thing about Ryder. He was the only one who'd ever really seen me. I wrapped the drawstring around my waist, tying it tightly so the pants wouldn't fall down, then slipped the scrub top over my head.

The halls were quiet as we walked to my dad's room. I wondered where the Ryder was who listened to Phish, who wore flip-flops year-round, who loved kids. My father was sleeping on his side. Ryder picked up the chart at the end of the bed and flipped through a few pages. "He hit the pharmaceutical trifecta: He's on a sedative, a sleep aid, and an antipsychotic." The chart clanged softly against the metal rail when he put it back. "He'll be out till noon."

I sank onto the cot; I just wanted to sleep. "Why did he suddenly go crazy?"

Ryder straightened an IV line and pressed a button on the monitor. "Depending on where the tumor is, it's not uncommon for brain cancer patients to experience psychotic episodes." He sat on the arm of the couch and rubbed his hand over his face.

"If he's medicated up the wazoo, is it safe for me to go to sleep?"

"Kind of. You can sleep for only about an hour at a time."

"What?" I lay back on the cot. "Why?"

He came over and stood above me. "Did you lose consciousness?"

I shook my head. "I don't think so."

"See stars?"

"Yes." I closed my eyes.

"Nauseous?"

"Fuck." I opened them. "A concussion?"

"Yep."

I closed my eyes again. And then I felt him smoothing the covers over my shoulders; it gave me a lazy feeling. I was having a hard time staying awake. He flicked off the lights and sat on the couch. "I'll wake you up every hour."

I rolled over and tried to see him in the darkness. "That's ridiculous," I said. "The nurse can do it; you should go home."

"I'm here anyway."

I heard Ryder's voice and felt his breath in my ear. "Jenny, open your eyes." I thought I was dreaming and wanted it to last a little while longer. "Jenny." I felt his fingertips on my cheek. I never wanted to wake up. "Get up or I'll lick you."

I opened my eyes and in the dim light saw Ryder leaning over me, his fingers tracing the outline of the bandage on my forehead. I tried to sit up, but my head throbbed. "Did you just say you were going to lick me?" I sat up enough to see my dad sleeping on his side, one arm flung off the bed.

"Don't you remember? You used to tell me—"

"To help me with my chemistry or I'd lick you."

"And to share my Pop-Tarts or you'd lick me. And to choose songs for your recitals or you'd lick me." He pulled a penlight out of his breast pocket and held open each of my eyelids while he gauged how my pupils reacted.

"That was the beginning of it for me." It was easier to talk in the near darkness. "The beginning of us. I actually had visions of licking you, tasting the salt of your skin. And then you and Will starting teasing me because I went through that growth spurt and ate more than most girls. But I have to tell you: I loved the attention."

"You ate more than most football teams." He smiled as he held up a finger for me to follow with my eyes. "You were known to eat entire pizzas by yourself."

I felt my cheeks color. "Let's be fair here. They were small pizzas. But, yes, I could eat. Will used to say that he'd never have to worry about you going for a girl who could put away seven hot dogs during one episode of *Seinfeld*. But, I secretly thought that would have made you like me more."

"It did," he whispered. "I liked you for so long before that night at the baseball field. But I just couldn't betray Will . . . right up until I did."

"We loved each other. That's not betrayal." My dad shifted restlessly. "Is he going to wake up?" He told me no, so I kept talking. "Why do you think Will was so against us dating?"

"Because we were always together. The three of us. He was afraid if we were a couple that we'd eventually break up and then things would be weird. He was just trying to keep the band together. How's that for irony?"

Laughing hurt my head. "Did he tell you that?"

"Yep. About a week before the accident."

"You talked to him about us? Why didn't you tell me?"

My father rolled onto his back and mumbled something in his sleep. Ryder waited a few seconds before he spoke. "Because I lied to him, Jenny."

"About what?"

"Us. He caught me signing the peace symbol to you at the jazzfest on the New Haven Green. And I flat out lied. I told him that he was drunk and didn't see anything. I sat on the grass across from Richter's Pub and told my best friend that I wasn't screwing around with his little sister."

My stomach hurt. "That's why he got so mad that night." I heard Will yelling at Ryder about all the other girls he'd been with. It was so unlike him to take shots at anyone or to get angry like that. "All this time, I've never understood what set him off."

"I'm sorry I never told you."

"It doesn't matter now." I'd meant it to be kind, but it came out accusatory. "Am I okay to go back to sleep? I'm really tired."

He didn't say anything more and we sat in the dark for a long time, until finally I lay down and went back to sleep.

· · ·

Ryder woke me three more times before dawn, asking my middle name, my date of birth, the town I lived in, and how many fingers I had. We didn't talk again about Will.

In the morning, light filtered around the window shade, my father was gone, and Ryder was reading a sailing magazine on the couch. I thought of those *Madman* comics he used to collect. "Where is he?" I sat up. My mouth felt like I'd slept with a sock in it.

"Radiology." He tossed the magazine aside and got up. "He'll be back in an hour or so. "How's your head?"

I touched the bandage. It was squishy with blood. "Hurts."

Four Styrofoam coffee cups were scattered on the floor. His eyes were bloodshot. "You look as bad as I feel." I lay back down. "I'm so tired."

He pulled the covers over my shoulders. "I hear ya, sister. Between you and the motorcycle guy, I was running back and forth all night."

I patted the space behind me, not sure if I was dreaming. "You can sleep here," I mumbled. "There's plenty of room." And then I was gone again.

I dreamed I was at the beach, watching lemmings scramble up the dunes. They gathered at the top of a cliff and, one after another, jumped, disappearing into the ocean. My father was one of them. He was perched on the ledge when I woke.

"Morning, sunshine." It was Nic's voice. I opened one eye and saw him standing in the doorway, holding a bouquet of stargazer lilies in front of him like an offering. I thought maybe I was still dreaming, but I could feel the weight of Ryder's arm on my shoulder.

"Nic?" My pillow was wet with drool, and it hurt to move my head.

He came in the room and glanced from the empty bed to me. And then he looked behind me, at Ryder. "What the hell?" he said quietly.

I pushed myself up, but my head was spinning, and my limbs were suddenly cold. I watched him start to back up. "Gallery Lazelle is this weekend? Oh God, I forgot." I started to get up, but I felt weighted to the cot. "Stop, please."

But he kept going, reaching for the door handle, tossing the flowers in the trash. Before he opened it, I saw how he was looking at me. It was the same as when I'd finally told him, two years after we'd been married, that I'd had a brother, a brother named Will, who'd died. He'd looked at me like he had never seen me before.

13

"Please," I said to the skinny attendant in the Plexiglas booth. "My dad was rushed here by ambulance yesterday." I caught a glimpse of myself in the rearview. The bandage on my head had slid down and the threads stuck up like tiny antennae. "I didn't get a ticket when I came in."

"Honey." He leaned his scrappy arms on the windowsill. "I sit in this booth nine hours a day, five days a week, people watching." His T-shirt read, I USED TO HAVE A HANDLE ON LIFE, BUT IT BROKE. "And I know you got bigger worries than paying some stupid ticket." When he smiled, I saw he was missing a bottom tooth. "You're all set." The digital display flashed a big yellow zero.

This felt like a glorious act of kindness. When I waved, he was already pressing a button on the screen and signaling me on. The yellow gate rose above my car.

I drove the back roads into Milford, then took Merwin Avenue along the beachfront, the radio on high, trying not to think about the expression on Nic's face. I hadn't run after him. I couldn't in those huge hospital clothes, and anyway, my head was throbbing and I was exhausted. *How could I have forgotten he was coming to-*

day? I wondered. After he'd slammed the door, Ryder had lifted up on his elbow. "That was bad," he'd said.

"I have to go." I'd scrabbled around on the floor, looking for my clothes. "Damn it, where's Jamie?"

"Don't worry. I'll stay and wait for your dad until she gets here. Just go." And then Jamie breezed through the door, throwing her Barbour coat over a chair, saying it was raining so hard, the old railroad bridge was already flooding, and Ryder jumped up and sat on the couch, trying to pat down his hair. "Where's Sterling?" she asked.

"Radiology," Ryder replied.

I was sitting on the side of the cot, holding my head.

She startled when she saw me. "Oh, sweetheart, I just saw Nic. He was in such a rush, I hardly had chance to say hello. What a nice, um"—she smiled briefly and glanced at Ryder—"surprise. I gave Nic my extra house key just in case he wants to go home or . . ." Her voice trailed off, and no one said anything else until finally she told me I should go home and get some rest. I got up, dressed again in my bloody clothes, and left before she could ask what had happened to my head.

I drove around in the rain for twenty minutes before I parked across the street from Cambridge, Jamie's brownstone. I hadn't been there in years. The elaborately carved doorway and its enormous acanthus leaf brackets still seemed to be collaborating with her need for space, her constant wish to be away from us after Will died.

Since I'd been home, Luke had been urging me to practice there because, he said, it had the best piano. But I had found a thousand reasons not to, avoiding the brownstone at all costs. And then a day ago, before I'd taken my dad in for radiation, Luke had called. "Tomorrow we're going to play that Steinway." His voice was serious, the way it had been when he took me to lunch at Cuomo's before I left for Andover and told me that the things you run from in life hunt you down, trap you in a lifestyle of running, until your feet forget how to form roots. "Be at Cambridge tomorrow or else."

I'd been running along the sound when he'd called, and I'd stopped. "Or else what?" I'd watched a butter-colored yawl take down its sails.

"Or else I'm sending you to a great therapist I know."

I'd given him a scoffing laugh. "And I know how effective *they* are," I'd said, but something had risen in me, a panicked feeling that maybe Luke did have that much power, that maybe he could make me go.

When we acquired it, the Steinway was worth over $65,000. Before Jamie bought the brownstone, Sylvia Winters, a ninety-year-old opera singer who'd been famous in her day, had owned it. Her kids were happy to sell the piano with the place if we paid a little more. When Luke first saw it, he almost fainted. It was a Model M in a Louis XV scalloped case with ivory keys, and it had been fully restored, new soundboard and bridges, a rebronzed harp, new agrafes, pin locks, strings, tuning pins, hammer shanks and leathers. Luke sent a tuner every six months to work on it, and now my hands were itching to play it, but I'd thought coming here would remind me too much of that time right after Will died. Jamie'd told us she needed the apartment because she thought redoing it would help keep her mind occupied. And, she said, my father and I should be spared her grief.

Trying to avoid the puddles, I walked up the marble steps and worked the key in the lock. Jamie had given me a spare when Luke said he wanted to practice here. The door swung open easily. That white carpeting was as bright as the first time I'd been there. On the wall was that same Victorian mirror, and on my left, a half flight of stairs, leading to the master bedroom. Directly across from me was the piano. Without thinking, I took a muddy step toward it, but then I realized my mistake and pulled off my sandals. I stripped in the middle of the hall and carried my clothes upstairs.

The master bedroom was all white and clean, with a big fluffy bed under a wide window overlooking a brick courtyard. I wished I could lie down on it, but instead I went into the bathroom, also white, turned on the hot water, and peeled the bandage from my head. In the shower, I sat on the marble bench. The water was too hot to sit under, really, but I stayed there all the same, watching my skin get red. I kept thinking of Nic walking in with those flowers, of Ryder's warm body against my back, and then for some reason I thought about the day I'd auditioned for the Vienna Conservatory's summer program. It was the December after Will died, and I hadn't played since before his funeral. I sat at the piano on the stage, in front of Monsieur Mercier and a recruiter from Vienna. "An honor," he had said, "that I give you because you are, my dear, a rising talent." His pointy nose and even pointier chin smelled of coffee and curdled cream. He didn't say anything about how I'd missed weeks of lessons.

It had been a chance to go to Vienna for the summer, get a jump on Juilliard. Monsieur Mercier knew the recruiter and though he was mostly auditioning at high schools that focused on the arts, the tall, aging man had agreed to hear me play.

Schubert's Impromptu no. 2 in A-flat had been propped against the stand. It should've been six minutes of sheer beauty, except that, as I sat there, the black notes turned to hieroglyphics. I couldn't fathom what they meant to my hands. Sweat trickled down my belly. Monsieur Mercier cleared his throat. "Jenny, is something wrong?" The auditorium swelled with silence; my hands felt hot on my lap. I knew this was important, my ticket out. I could go to Austria, leave them all: the guilt I felt with Ryder, my cheating mother, my broken father. But then I rose and walked off the stage without saying anything. In the parking lot outside, where the wind cut through my silk wrap, I called Jamie to come get me.

We'd stopped at Cambridge on the way home. She never asked how the audition went, and I stood in her front hall, replaying it again and again in my head, shame rising like a hot blast in my chest. When she went upstairs, I wandered around the living room, arms crossed, taking in the couch, the glass table, the silk lamp shades. I hated that she could form a private life all her own, leaving my father and me marooned in the house where Will had died. When I walked into the kitchen, I saw a note on the counter: *Thanks for everything, darling. You are sensual, amazing, my miracle. Call me, J.* The rage had made it hard to breathe. I'd left, sat waiting for her on the steps outside.

"Let's go," she'd said breezily when she came out, not asking why I was sitting on the stoop in the freezing cold, not giving me that threshold to a fight. I'd been silent on the way home. The streets were slick with the sleet that had begun to fall, and Jamie hummed beside me, a Christmas carol, so that by the time we reached North Parker, I couldn't keep my mouth shut.

"You know what?" I told her. "You're a bitch." The words were acidic, and they shattered something between us. A tiny fissure occurred in the humming, before she continued on as though I'd said nothing at all. As she kept driving down North Parker, I felt stunned, almost awed. But when I glanced at her, every muscle in her face was strained, as though she was trying desperately to keep the world at bay. She was blinking, very fast, but even that couldn't stop the tears coursing down her cheeks.

I turned the shower off now and stood in front of her mirror, dripping. I was glad it was steamed up and I couldn't see myself. It didn't escape me that my husband had just run out on me because he thought I was cheating, and here I was, where Jamie had brought her boyfriends.

I saw them once, when I was home from Andover. It was a few days before Easter, and Jamie was walking down the street arm and arm with Julian, one of the agents she worked with in New York, whom we'd known forever, a pretty man with gray eyes and long lashes. He was holding on to her, looking at her like he might devour her top to bottom, and I had ducked into the Yale Art Gallery. Afterwards, I'd gone straight to Luke's. He didn't seem surprised to see me. "Is my mother fucking Julian?"

His expression never changed. "She might be."

"Does my dad know?"

He watched me for a while, then nodded. "He knows. Come on in, baby girl. Let me fix you a snack." But I'd left Luke's and gone to Mandy's, where I drank so much rum while her parents were at a party, I threw up.

I took a pair of shorts and a T-shirt from a drawer of clothes Jamie kept there for emergencies only, as if she might get trapped inside the place she had bought to escape. Her shorts were loose in the waist, and I knew I was doing it again, not eating, as though food were an ingratiating, needy friend who offered things I didn't want. It wasn't helping that I ran so much, beating the pavement until those endorphins kicked in.

Downstairs, the retro-style couch curved like a white semicolon in the middle of the room, and above it, hanging on the wall, was a series of photographs of Will and me as toddlers at Three Rivers Stadium. I wore my dad's Steelers Jersey like a dress and Will clutched a football with determination, a glimpse of the player he'd become. Jamie's cameraman had taken them, and they were startlingly lifelike. I pictured how Julian must have felt when he used to come here with Jamie, sitting at the glass table, surrounded by her children and worrying my father might show up and break his face.

My dad must have known about her lover. How could he not? I wondered why he hadn't beaten the shit out of him. "She says she's not like me. She wants to talk about Will all the time. And I can't, Whobaby. It hurts too much," he told me one night, sitting at the kitchen table after dinner when it was just the two of us. Jamie was at her apartment. She was always there, then. And then he'd cried. He cried so hard, the table shook, and saliva came out his mouth. I stood watching from the kitchen island. I didn't go to him. If I did, it would all be real: Will would really be dead, my mother would really be gone, and my father would slowly be falling apart.

I leafed through the music on the Steinway now. I wanted to play something vicious, something so hard-core and energetic that it would make my fingers burn. I thought of a Candlebox song called

"Far Behind." I wasn't at all sure I could do it without Luke and his metronome clicking off arpeggiated chords.

A key clicked in the lock, and Luke walked through the arched entryway. He stopped when he saw me. He was wearing black sunglasses and a silk sarong with animal prints on it. "Baby girl?" He took off his Ray-Bans. He wore sunglasses, no matter what the weather. "I wasn't sure you'd come."

"Yeah," I said. "I'm here."

A silver hoop gleamed in his ear. "So you are." His voice was filled with wonder, and pride. I watched him bend down and unbuckle his leather sandals, lining them neatly against the bright white walls of the foyer. He stared at my muddy footprints. "Get me a dustpan, Jamie'll never let us practice here again if we stain her carpet."

I went into the kitchen and opened the pantry. When I came out, I gave him a broom. The animals on his sarong were antelopes.

"So." He watched me kneel down. "Why's my favorite girl on the lam?" He rubbed his nose where the diamond stud usually was. The piercing had left a tiny pockmark in his skin. "I was just at the hospital. We've all been wondering where you raced off to."

I started brushing up the mud. "Is my dad okay?"

"He's fine. They've got it under control, and I'm glad you aren't rotting from worry in that hospital room. I think my Jensen might be coming back to herself, keeping her appointment with old Luke and all." He gave me that huge white smile and squatted next to me. "So, you sleeping with Ryder?"

I felt my face heat up. "Jesus Christ, why would you ask me that?"

"Ah, it was Jamie who took the wild guess."

"Figures." He held the dustpan down so I could sweep the dirt into it. "She thinks I'd do to Nic what she did to my dad?"

He didn't answer; his brown eyes were steady on mine. "Which was what?" he asked.

I quit brushing the dirt and stared at him. "She hid out here, saying she wanted to spare us her grief, and then she fucked Julian and God knows who else and—"

"And maybe it was a relief to your daddy." He stared at me with those steady eyes. "Maybe he didn't want to share his grief, either. Maybe he wanted to know someone was taking care of your mother."

"She should have been there for him." But I remembered what my dad had said about Jamie's wanting to talk about Will and his not being able to yet.

"Aw, baby girl, that's the bitch of losing someone you love. It's different for everyone."

The counselor at Andover had said the same thing. Then she'd rattled off a statistic I still remembered. Seventy-five percent of couples don't stay together after they lose a child.

"Well." I swallowed the lump rising in my throat. "I'm not sleeping with Ryder, okay?" I threw down the brush and sat on my butt. The mud wasn't dry yet, and I was making the carpet worse.

Luke sat on the step above me and put his hands between his knees. "Tell your old uncle what's up." He said it slowly, testing each word.

I hugged myself, suddenly cold. "Daddy's really okay?"

He nodded. "He's going to be just fine."

"I was so scared," I told him. "He was just sitting there at Caller's Island, and then his eyes rolled back and his mouth was open and . . ." I shook my head trying to clear it of that terrible image. "And then the ticket guy called an ambulance, shouting questions at me, and I was answering them, but I was thinking, you know, Uncle Luke, I was thinking how many things I haven't told my father that I need to tell him."

"What do you need to say?" he asked quietly.

I thought of my dad in the hospital bed, his eyelids fluttering, thought of him running helter-skelter down that hallway, calling for a lost dog we never had. "Everything is my fault," I said. That numbness started in my feet and rose.

Luke got off the steps and sat on the floor with me, holding my hands tightly in his. His cell phone rang, but he didn't answer it. I could smell his musk scent. We sat there in the foyer, rain pinging against the windows. My head throbbed. If I could tell Luke about the night Will died, he might be able to help me explain it to my dad, help me repair everything I'd broken.

"What's eating you alive, baby girl?" He squeezed my hands. "Tell your old uncle Luke."

He'd been asking me that since I left for Andover. I wiped my nose with the back of my hand. The words were coming up, a breaking wave. I took a shaking breath. "That night. The night that—" But I felt a cold fist in my stomach. I thought of Jamie on the couch when I'd tried to tell her, when she hadn't listened. And then it was gone: that one second I thought I could tell the truth. Trying to get it back was like swimming from the bottom of the ocean with a boulder tied to my ankle. I just wanted to be gone. "I have to go," I said. The apartment smelled wrong, and all those pictures, the dirty white rug, Luke and me with a dustpan in front of us, thirteen years of lying to everyone I loved.

"Hey, hey, not so fast." Luke was reaching for my elbow, but I was already on my feet. "What's going on?"

I whirled around, snatching away my arm. "You want me to tell you what's going on?" I asked. "I fucked everything up; that's what's going on."

And then I opened the door and ran down the steps and across the street barefoot, not looking out for traffic. When I made it to the other side, I slid into that slippery leather seat and pulled out fast. Without stopping at the red light, I turned right and raced down Ferry Street, past the harbor, to Island Avenue and back onto the main road. It was getting dark, my eyes were having a hard time adjusting, and the rain was coming down hard, the onslaught of headlights blinding me. I saw the domes of black umbrellas where people were standing in front of Willoghby's, waiting for a table. Legion merged with Route 1, and I headed to Plains Creek. I needed to talk about it, and the only person I could talk to was Ryder. I called him, first his cell, but it was off, and then his house, which went to voice mail.

The rain was coming down so hard, my wipers couldn't slap it back fast enough. I raced through yellow lights, the speedometer hitting seventy. The wind tossed leaves and branches across the windshield. I needed him to hold me. I needed the old Ryder, not the doctor, but the one with the number 18 tattooed on his arm, the one who never wore a collar, even to prom, the one who hit Whiffle balls to the neighborhood kids and who kissed me in the library carrels when we should have been studying. The voice in the car was telling me my seat belt was off. "Shut up," I yelled at it. I pushed redial over and over. Maybe the wind had knocked out his service. Half a lifetime ago, I never would have called before going to his house.

I turned onto McKinnon Avenue, a couple of streets over from North Parker; it led to the ocean. My father had said Ryder had kept his parents' house when they retired to Sarasota. The road smelled of privet hedges; the trees arched from the rain and made a canopy over the car. I was squinting in the dark. I was fifteen again, holding his hand over the gearshift, while he sang "Sugar Magnolia" to me, fresh with our secret, the first one, the one that seemed so benign now: that Will should never know about us.

A black BMW sedan was parked on the street in front of his house. Ryder never would have driven a car like that when we were young. He had falling-apart MGs with Dead stickers on the back. Pulling into his driveway, I checked my reflection in the rearview mirror. My face was streaked with tears and the black-and-blue bruise on my forehead had traveled to my eye. But there was nothing I could do about it, so I opened the car door and stepped into the pouring rain, running across the lawn and up his front steps.

The porch was dark, but a light was on in the front hall, and I knocked on the oak door. My clothes were soaked through. I knocked again, harder. Cupping my hand around my eyes, I peered in the window. A standing lamp near the fireplace lit up the room's new muted earth tones. He'd put in French doors leading to the terrace. The floor was covered in a Persian carpet I'd never seen before.

And then I noticed them. In front of the green sectional, thrown off carelessly, one of them at an odd angle to the other, was a pair of red heels. I stood there, trying to make sense of them. Maybe his parents were visiting and those were his mom's. But no one's mother would wear shoes like that. Plus, his parents were older. His mother must have been seventy-five by now. The stairs were dark, and the fact that he was with someone dawned on me like ice exploding in my gut. I turned my back against the door. I felt a strange light-headedness, a feeling that this wasn't really happening. A car drove by and put on its blinker. I had to get out of there before someone saw me waiting on his stoop, wet and pathetic. I ran down the steps, trying to jump over puddles. As I passed the BMW, I saw the license plate: NOVKMD. I thought of Dale Novak in the emergency room. Those red pumps.

I slammed my door, and a light went on upstairs. I put the car in reverse and backed out as fast as I could. Hot humiliation burned my face. Ryder'd let me think Dale was a man, he'd wanted so badly to know what we thought of her, and the two of them were always walking down the hall together, as if they'd come from the same place. I wanted to go back, to bang on the front door and scream at him that he'd lied, that I hated him. I'd been home for almost two months, and he hadn't told me there was someone else. Some sick perversion kicked in, and I wanted, more than ever, or maybe now I was just admitting it to myself, to be the one upstairs with him.

At the light on the corner of Water and Reardon, I scrolled through my phone list to call Mandy, but while it was ringing, I remembered she was off somewhere, chronicling the lives of hedgehogs or some small animal that immediately ditched its mate as soon as it found a more attractive one. "Monogamy is so unnatural, even rodents know it," she'd said as I lay on her bed, watching her toss hiking boots and sunscreen into the same rolling suitcase she'd taken to college. "Oops, sorry, J.J." I was sensitive about my mother and Julian, even now. "I'm right, though. Aren't I?" Yeah, Mandy was righter than she knew.

I hadn't driven at night since high school, and now I tried to navigate as best I could, keeping my eyes on the immediate lines of the road. Where was the Ryder I had grown up with? The one with the rusted-out convertible who loved the Dead and surfed the Watch Hill waves in hurricane season—sure he wanted to be a pediatrician, even though he hardly ever cracked a book and he didn't like people who took themselves too seriously, like Dale. I was about to call Hadley, when I realized he would probably tell one of the sculptors or gallery hags, who would tell someone else, who would eventually tell Nic. I threw my phone in the seat. *Fucking Ryder.* The light changed, and I turned right, toward home.

14

By the time I got back to North Parker, the house was dark. I went through the back slider, wiping my feet so that Jamie wouldn't bitch at me for tracking in mud, and headed upstairs. I wondered where Nic had gone, and I had a horrible feeling he might have gotten on a plane. I thought of calling Hadley and making up an excuse, just so I could talk to someone. But I wouldn't be able to hide the truth from him. Plus, I didn't think Hadley was good at real live feelings. He was good at parties, at sex talk, and making me laugh, but I didn't know if he could handle the whole truth. And he definitely wouldn't be able to keep it to himself.

I stripped in the hallway, tossing Jamie's clothes in the wicker hamper. I was sticky and cold from the rain, and I wanted to take another shower. Standing under the hot water, I let my head hang like a rag doll, trying not to think of those red shoes in Ryder's living room.

When I turned off the water and stepped out, Nic was leaning against the bathroom counter. I caught my breath. "You scared me."

He gave me a half smile. "You finally made it home." He was wearing a rumpled, clay-stained oxford shirt, and he smelled of pot.

I reached for a raspberry bath towel, but he grabbed it first and held it up for me to step into it. "I didn't think anyone was home. How did you get here?"

He put his arms around me. "Taxi." I remembered how my father used to wrap me in a towel when I got out of the pool as a kid. "I was on the upstairs deck."

The deck off Will's room. We didn't do that. We didn't go in there—ever. There was something both annoying and comforting about Nic's not knowing this. I checked my forehead in the mirror. The bruise had spread across my right eye.

Nic watched my reflection. I thought he'd ask about my face, but he said, "I see you've redecorated your bedroom."

I squeezed water out of my hair into the sink. "I thought the INXS posters were a little outdated."

"The butterfly comforter's gone, too."

"How do you even remember that?"

"I remember everything about you." He caught my eye in the mirror.

I watched him. His goatee needed a trim, and he looked thinner, tired. He reached around me and opened the towel. The water hadn't dried on my body, and I felt instantly chilled. Turning me around, he took me by the hips and kissed me. I held on to his thick hair. "It took me a long time to find you, J." His green eyes were turning gray while we stood there. "That day I saw you coming across the quad, even before I knew who you were, even before I thought of asking you to model for me, I knew you were going to change my world."

I studied his mouth. It was that same beautiful burgundy. When he pulled me to him, my stitches throbbed. "I forgot you were coming today. And then my dad passed out at the roller coaster. And it's been so crazy . . ."

He picked up my hand and kissed the fingertips. "I've missed you."

"What you think you saw doesn't exist," I said.

He turned my palm over and kissed the soft middle. "Then you won't care if I kick his ass, just for the hell of it."

I watched him kiss my wrist. "Well, nothing happened, but you were the one who said we should have an open marriage."

He gave a short laugh. He was still holding my hand. "That was a long time ago, J. Before we were even married."

I could feel a fight rising in me. I knew it was about the red shoes. I faced the mirror and picked up my hairbrush. He leaned against the wall. I could see him in the mirror, watching me under those heavy lids. "You know you are the only one, whatever I said in the beginning."

I raised my eyebrows. "Do I?"

He rolled his eyes. "Jesus Christ."

"See?" I whirled around, with the hairbrush raised. "You can be jealous, but I can't."

He had that knowing smirk on his face. I put the brush down and started for the door. But before I could turn the knob, he grabbed my waist and put his lips on my ear. I could feel his warm, soft mouth on my throat. "I'm crazy without you." He kissed my neck. "I don't care about Ryder or who slept on that fucking cot."

Sex was the best antidote. We could just fuck it out, instead of trying to fight it out. Ryder had moved on, and so had I. "He's like a brother to me," I said while he kissed me. "You know that, right?"

But even as Nic picked me up like a bride and carried me to my childhood bed, even as he placed me down and threw that crimson towel aside, I knew I was lying.

I was flipping through the Yellow Pages for take-out menus when Luke came through the slider in tight, shimmery pants, carrying a gigantic picnic basket. "Well hellfire," he said to Nic. "He exists."

"How you doing?" Nic went around the island. "It's been a while."

Luke nodded. "Too long." He put the basket on the counter, shook Nic's hand and patted his back. "You taking good care of my girl?" He came over and hugged me.

I felt like a petulant child. "I'm okay, Uncle Luke."

"I'm always here," he said quietly. In a louder voice, he said, "Now, let's eat some chicken tagine and drink some wine."

While Nic was getting the plates and glasses, I called Jamie. "I just got back to Daddy's room, and he's sleeping like a baby," she said.

"*Back* to Daddy's room? Where were you?" I asked.

She ignored me. "Listen, Dr. Novak called, said your father might be able to go home tomorrow."

"Great." I had a clawing, claustrophobic feeling that I'd never get away from Dale. "When he wakes up, tell him I love him and that I'll see him in the morning."

"Will do, sweetheart."

"Thanks Mom."

She said good-bye without making her usual huffing noise when I accidentally called her "Mom."

Hours after Nic fell asleep, I lay next to him, watching the shadows the oak tree outside my bedroom window made on the wall. It was odd having him in my childhood room, especially since some nights I went to sleep feeling like I'd gone on some hallucinogenic trip to Santa Fe to be an artist's wife and now I was back in my own skin. But Nic's coming here had merged the two worlds in a disturbing way. And we had fucked it all right out of us: the hospital room, that almost fight in the bathroom, Ryder. We were good at being in bed. We knew well how to pleasure ourselves through each other. We barely talked during sex, but reverted to some place inside that held instinct and need, an ancient place I couldn't quite name, but it felt like an escape. Nic let me drop my history; he believed in the power of silence.

The first spring I knew him, when he'd sculpted me, I'd seen it there—plain as my mouth and eyebrows and cheeks—my grief, that guilt and shame. An almost belligerent look of solitude. He seemed to accept it without inquiry, married it, and never asked questions. Except what I was learning now was that Nic wasn't accepting it, like I had thought; he was denying it. He didn't care why I never brought up Connecticut. And the problem was, now I wanted to start talking.

15

When Nic and I came down to the kitchen the next morning, Luke had already brought my father home from the hospital, and Jamie had a pot of coffee brewing and was scrambling a dozen eggs. "You're just in time." She wore a simple pink warm-up suit and hadn't brushed her hair. "I'm no Luke, but I think I did okay." She scraped the eggs onto plates and set them at the breakfast bar with slices of rye toast.

"Thanks, Jamie." We sat at the counter in front of a vase of flowers. I could read the card from where I sat. Sid and his wife. "Where's Daddy?"

"Went straight to bed," Luke said, coming in from the living room.

"Dale wants him to rest," Jamie said. "Now eat up."

Thunderclouds moved across the windows while we ate, and by the time we'd cleared the breakfast dishes, the sky had darkened to the color of charcoal and rain splattered the windows.

"Challenge you to a game of Scrabble," Luke said to me.

"Or we could watch my old Audrey Hepburn movies," Jamie offered. For one fleeting moment, I wanted to see if the old-fashioned popcorn maker was still in the pantry, make a buttery bowl of fat and salt, and curl up with my mom.

"We can do both." Luke poured another cup of coffee.

"I'm on Nic's team." Jamie put her arm through Nic's.

"Former straight-A student and songwriter against sculptor and model agent." Nic made a face. "We get a handicap advantage."

Jamie's cell phone rang, and she lunged for it like only she could, fierce and quick, but still poised. "Well, hello there," she said. "Hold on one second, my dear." She eased open the slider, and I watched her step onto the deck in bare feet, pressing herself against the side of the house, ducking from the rain as she talked. The thick glass muffled her voice.

"Come on, kiddo." Luke was watching me. "Let's get the board."

I tried to keep my voice even. "What's with the secret call?"

Nic followed me to the living room. "Maybe she's starting a charity to donate all her shoes to the needy." He massaged my neck while we walked.

I rolled my eyes. "Somehow, I don't think homeless people need four hundred pairs of stilettos."

"No one needs stilettos." Luke took the Scrabble board from the cupboard by the television. "But you ladies sure look good in them." He walked on the balls of his feet to the coffee table, his hand on his hip, his dreads swooshing rhythmically.

I plopped down on the couch. "You pick the letters," I told Luke. Nic sat next to me. "You'll have to choose for my mother."

Jamie came in, droplets of rain on her velour sweatshirt, the color high on her cheeks. "Did I miss anything?" She sat next to Nic and squeezed his arm excitedly. "Are we winning yet?"

It was both soothing and aggravating, I thought as Luke scooped seven letters out of the canvas bag, how whenever I came home, almost everything stayed exactly the same.

By the time my dad appeared at the top of the stairs Friday night, he'd slept almost ten hours. His hair was messy and his eyes were bright from sleep. "It lives," he announced. "And it's hungry."

We all jumped up. We'd been drinking the last of the wine from dinner. "Welcome back, Daddy." I gave him my arm and helped him down the stairs.

"You're just in time for some grilled tuna," Luke said.

We crowded the kitchen table to watch him eat. "What the hell happened to me?" He licked a drop of lemon off his hand. "I feel like Rip van Winkle."

I gave him a napkin. "You slept," I said. "Something you should try more often."

He glanced at me and stopped chewing. "What?" I asked.

He put down his fork and pushed back my hair. I felt his thumb on my cut. It had turned an ugly bluish yellow over the past few days. "What's with the stitches?" His tone was caught between worry and impatience. I thought of him running down the hall, searching for an imaginary dog. "Jensen?"

The table went quiet. Finally, Jamie said, "Really, Sterling" in her dreamy, careless way. "You've been asleep for a dog's year. Less talking, more eating." Glancing at my mother, then back at me, he speared a grilled kiwi with his fork and popped it in his mouth. "That's my good man." Jamie touched his face. She seemed so in love with him, it boggled my mind. "You need to get your strength back," she said, and kissed him tenderly on the mouth.

"Nic," my father said after he finished eating and we were sitting in the living room, drinking coffee. "It's good to see you."

Nic was in the armchair by the piano, wearing a half-buttoned linen shirt, a turquoise ring on his thumb, his skin brown from the sun. He looked somehow wrong in our house.

"Jensen's been worried about you," he told my dad. "And so have I."

My dad studied the middle distance between them and nodded. "I'm sorry we've stolen her away." He glanced at me. "Jamie says you're on your way to New York."

"Gallery Lazelle is showing my work again," he said. "The exhibit opens right after the Fourth."

Suddenly, my dad got that happy little-boy look I knew too well. "The Fourth of July!" he said. "I almost forgot." He loved Independence Day; it gave him a reason to buy illegal fireworks and set them off on Luke's boat. "What are we doing for the Fourth this year? I want to have a party."

"Dad," I groaned, and Luke said, "Here we go again."

My father rubbed his hands together as if he were plotting. "Jensen, call Mandy and tell her to get her pretty self here for dinner on the Fourth. And invite Ryder, too. There'll be s'mores and fireworks for everyone!" I deliberately looked down, not letting Nic catch my eye at the mention of Ryder's name.

On Saturday night, Nic and I drove to Madison and had dinner with my parents at The Wharf. Afterwards, we left our shoes on the seawall and walked out to the sandbar. My parents held hands. Nic said the bright blue pieces of sea glass Jamie found reminded him of Greece. The night before, he'd asked again about moving there. And again I'd told him I couldn't even think about it while I was taking care of my dad.

While we sat on the breakwater to watch the sunset, my dad asked if I remembered him reading Saint-Exupery's *The Little Prince* when I was a kid. He kissed the top of Jamie's head. At odd times like these, the memory of those red pumps in Ryder's living room refused to leave me alone.

Luke showed up on the Fourth with coolers of lobsters, oysters, and shrimp. Behind him trailed a woman he introduced as Starflower. "Oh, honey." She hugged me and touched my hair. "You're just as beautiful and ethereal as Luke said." She had long black ringlets, a nose stud, and beads coiled around her neck. I liked her immediately.

Jamie was out somewhere doing one of her vague errands, but the rest of us took Luke's marching orders and shucked corn, sliced tomatoes, marinated steak, and unwrapped mozzarella.

"What else needs to be done?" I asked him.

He handed me four bottles of wine. "Go outside and put one on each corner of the table to keep that cloth down."

Just as I was setting the last one on the farthest corner, I heard, "Sister, check out what I got for us tonight." Mandy was coming across the yard with a big cardboard box in her arms. FIREWORKS was stamped across the side in block letters.

"Are those legal in Connecticut?" Nic came out the slider, holding a platter of chilled shrimp.

"Jesus," Mandy said. "You haul contraband across state lines for your friends and this is the reception you get?" She cocked her hip. "Hi, Nic."

He gave her a quick smile. "Hello, Mandy." I watched him put the shrimp on the table. Mandy and Nic had never liked each other. It had been torture when she'd come out to Santa Fe. "You joining us for dinner?" he asked.

"Of course. I practically live here." She was wearing white jeans and a loose silk top that made her look ravenously beautiful. "J.J.," she said in a conspiratorial whisper. "Philip has an extra ticket to his film premier, just for you. We're going to Paris." But before I could answer, Starflower came out, holding a tray of oysters on the half shell, and I introduced her to Mandy, and then Luke came out with the lobster tips and made a huge deal over her, and my father arrived with bread and salad and hugged her until her feet came off the deck.

Jamie came home about a minute before we were going to eat. Although I'd left a message for Ryder, he hadn't shown up.

"Who's uncorking the wine?" Luke asked when we were seated around the picnic table. The wind lifted the edges of the cloth, and Mandy traded one of her sandals for a bottle of Chardonnay. Within seconds, she had opened it and was filling our glasses. She took off her other shoe and put her feet up on the railing. Her legs were tanned and seemed longer than when she'd left to photograph the polygamist hedgehogs. "To Sterling, my second daddy and everyone's hero."

We ate to the music of silverware clinking on plates and tree frogs peeping their songs out back. I was facing the lawn, a sea of dark green in the fading light. My dad had taught me to catch butterflies out there with a net so soft, it wouldn't hurt their wings. Will had taught me to throw a football. Mandy had showed me how to smoke a cigarette, keeping it downwind so that my clothes wouldn't smell. And the summer I was sixteen, on a patchwork blanket tucked behind the side yard's stand of pine trees, Ryder had put his mouth between my legs and given me my first orgasm.

As if on cue, the slider opened and Ryder was standing there.

I wiped butter off my chin and started to get up, but Mandy put her hand on my knee.

Ryder grinned down at her. "Hey, kiddo."

She had to stand on her tippy toes to hug him. "Hey, brother." This is what Mandy had always called Ryder.

Jamie patted her lips with her napkin. "My goodness," she said, turning in her seat. "I was worried you wouldn't come."

I saw Nic studying his plate.

"I'm sorry I'm late. The hospital was busy tonight." Ryder shifted from one foot to the other.

"Grab a chair from the kitchen," Luke said to him. "There's plenty of food. You know me, always cooking for a crowd."

My dad got up. "Let me get you one, old boy."

Ryder followed my father inside. We all kept eating. No one spoke. We abandoned the discussion we'd been having about how sixteen networks were planning on televising Michael Jackson's funeral in a few days, but Farrah Fawcett, who'd died the same day, barely got a mention in the paper. I didn't look at Nic. Mandy sat down and pinched me under the table, I'd sent her the world's longest e-mail about driving to Ryder's house and seeing Dale's red shoes on his floor. And she'd written back two sentences: *Red heels don't mean squat. He's yours if you want him.* When Ryder and my dad came out with a simple wooden chair from the breakfast nook, Nic stood up and extended his hand. "Nico Ledakis, Jensen's husband." His voice was crisp, free of his usual lazy drawl.

Ryder put the chair down. "Ryder Anderson. Sterling's surgeon." I watched them shake. "You're a lucky man." He wasn't smiling.

"No doubt." I felt Nic put his hand on my back, a rare show of public affection.

"And this"—Luke held up his wineglass—"is Starflower." Luke smiled at her as if he'd made her himself.

Ryder put out his hand. "Pleased to meet you." She ignored it and kissed his cheek. "You're a real healer," she said.

"Take it from Starflower," Luke said, happily chomping on his salad. "She can see straight through a person."

My father told Starflower he'd known Ryder since he was a little baseball player. "Reminded me of Nolan Ryan. Course his parents were intent on him becoming a doctor, and it's a good thing." *Pediatrician,* I thought. He was supposed to work with kids.

Nic sat back with his wine while this was said, as if he wasn't listening. The twilight sky had gone from brilliant pink to an indigo black, and we heard the New Haven fireworks before we saw them. My dad stood up. "To the roof," he said.

"Oh, honey," Jamie said. "It will collapse." But she was already up, her wine in hand, and we followed them inside, traipsing through the front hall, up the stairs to their bedroom, where my dad opened the tall south-side window, and we piled onto the flat roof above his office. I was first. Ryder was last. We sat in a row with our legs over the edge, watching the bursts of color explode and trickle down the sky. I could hear Ryder and Mandy laughing. Nic put his arm around me and held me tightly around the waist. "Happy Independence Day, beautiful wife," he whispered, but another round burst in the air, and whatever I would have answered was lost.

Ryder left after the fireworks ended. Mandy wanted to go out on Luke's boat to set hers off, but he promised her we'd do it soon, and she went home instead. My father and Luke went to the office to show Starflower pictures from when they were younger. I could hear Jamie rattling around in the kitchen.

"I'm beat," Nic said. We were standing at the bottom of the stairs. He'd been like the new kid at school all night, hands in his pockets, not really talking to anyone, so out of his element. In Santa Fe, he was royalty, holding court in his custom cowboy boots, gallery owners and art dealers draping themselves on him like jewelry. "You coming up?"

"I should help Jamie," I told him. I walked down the hallway, grabbed a beer from the kitchen, and let myself onto the back deck. Instead of clearing the picnic table, I sat on the glider, watching smaller fireworks pop randomly in the sky. When they lit up, I could see everything clearly, just for a moment.

After a while, the slider opened, and Jamie came out and sat next to me. I could smell Chardonnay and her party perfume. I tried to peel the label off my beer bottle, but it split down the middle and all that was left was Ma Ha. "Do you ever get scared?" I could hear her breathing next to me. "About Daddy?" A quick burst of light startled the sky to the east and I saw that the grass was long. It was unlike her not to have everything perfect for company.

"Sometimes." She moved the glider with her foot. I took a sip of beer; its coldness floated out of the top like fog. "But I pray," she said.

I was surprised. "Really?"

She shrugged. "It can't hurt."

My eyelids felt hot. I thought about that night in the waiting room, before that doctor came out to tell us about Will. "It can hurt to hope," I said. "When you have hope and then nothing gets better, it makes it even worse."

She rocked the swing. "Praying isn't hope," she said. "It's gratitude. Luke taught me that." I watched her dab her mouth with her cocktail napkin. She was one of those women who could look elegant blowing her nose. "You should talk to Luke, sweetheart. People pay good money to get his spiritual advice."

I leaned back against the glider and let myself be rocked. "Since when?"

She moved a strand of hair from my face. "Goodness, since forever. He's a wonderful caretaker. But you have such a hard time letting anyone take care of you." I watched her twist her engagement ring around her finger. I thought of her mother's ring, waiting for me in a safe-deposit box, a platinum band with an emerald-cut diamond she'd gotten from some heir of the Getty family who'd died before he married her.

"Nic takes care of me," I said.

"I suppose he does." She leaned back with me, both of us taking in the sky. The cloud cover of the night before was gone, and the sheer number of stars was dizzying. I couldn't see them individually, but the sky seemed wrapped in a blanket of light. Jamie kept pushing the swing, and the rhythm made me drowsy. "It's just nice to feel like there's something greater than us in our lives."

After Will died, Luke had bought me a bunch of books on ghosts, reincarnation, and near-death experiences. They told amazing stories of euphoria and light. Death as one big cocaine trip. I knew he'd given them to me to help me find some kind of peace, but they just made me lonelier. Mandy had flipped through them one night when my parents were out and we were smoking pot in my bedroom and listening to Neil Young. "Maybe you could actually talk to Will," she had said. And of course, Mandy, being Mandy, had found some psychic in Mystic. But when we got to the house, a small brick cape in a nice neighborhood, I turned around. "Where are you going?" she'd asked me.

"I changed my mind," I'd told her. I didn't want to give the psychic a piece of Will's clothing or my palm. If she were the real thing, she would have known exactly what I'd done.

Now I traced Ryder's initials etched into the glider's arm. I'd carved them as a kind of rebellious announcement. Behind us, I heard the slider open. My father came out wearing a Yankees hat backward and carrying a glass of water with lime. "Ah," he said. "Here are my girls." He scooted next to me, resting his arm on the glider. "Luke and Starflower said to say good-bye."

I leaned against him. Jamie put her hand up on the back of the glider to meet his, and we sat there, the three of us, the only family we had left, twenty yards from those old goalposts, lit up by fireworks, silhouetted in the dark like a living ghost.

16

A sign posted by the entrance of the Morse Reading Room in Yale's Medical Library said drinks had to be in covered containers. The librarian had the dissertation on hold for me when I arrived. I set it down next to my double espresso in one of the wooden cubicles, kicked off my flip-flops, stuck my earbuds in, and turned on my iPod. The dissertation was about a miscarriage drug from the fifties, thalidomide, which was possibly making a comeback to treat malignant tumors.

I sat there, trying to make sense of the medical jargon and smoothing my bitten nails with a file I'd snagged from Jamie's bathroom. No one, including my father, seemed concerned about his overnight stay at the hospital, but if Ryder had operated first, I wondered if this would have happened. "The ischemia that created the devastating deformities in fetuses is hoped to trigger the cessation of blood flow to cancerous masses, thus causing necrosis of malignant cells," I read. It went on from there, and after four or five pages, I glanced at my computer. I had only an hour before I was supposed to meet my family at the football game on North Square, A Will to Live versus the Salvation Army. The dissertation was too many pages to copy. Unless I swiped it from the library, I wasn't going to have time to figure out what the hell it was saying.

Someone touched my shoulder. I smelled the perfume first: flowery and expensive. Dale Novak was staring down at me. I wanted to shoot myself. I'm pretty sure she said, "Jensen, how nice to see you." But all I heard was, *Ha-ha. I'm sleeping with your old boyfriend.* I took my earbuds out. Her auburn hair was in a tight, perfect bun.

"Hello," I said. I'd read a book the summer before about a teenager with Asperger's syndrome who didn't understand pleasantries and said only what he meant. *Fuck you, Dale. We hate each other.* She peered over my shoulder at what I was reading, and I covered it with my elbow.

"Doing some research?" she asked. I'd seen her in here once before, and she'd barely nodded, so I was surprised she was even talking to me.

Instead of answering, I said, "Nice ring." She was wearing a cluster of diamonds in the shape of a flower. I thought of my grandmother's engagement ring in Jamie's safe-deposit box.

She glanced at her hand. She had a perfect pale pink manicure. "Thanks." She started to say something else but then stopped and flashed that nauseating closed-mouth smile. I wondered if she and Ryder ever had quickies in the library.

"Listen," I said. "I have a question for you."

"It's actually my day off, if you can believe that." She held up her watch. "I was just about to head out." Her impatience made me think of the summer Jamie tried to teach me how to ride a bike. "Just pedal faster," she'd said, "and you won't fall off." "What can I do for you?" Dale said.

Move to Alaska. "Radiation isn't even halfway done," I said. "I still don't understand why my dad got so sick."

She started to explain about dehydration and radiation being cumulative, all the same bullshit she'd said in the hospital.

"But," I said, interrupting her, "shouldn't you have seen this coming?" I was all out of graciousness. "I mean, you are the one treating him."

Heat flashed across her face. "Obviously, if I had, I would have done something. I'm sure Dr. Anderson told you that every case is different."

"My father is a person," I said. "Not a case. And by the way, Dr. Anderson was at my sweet sixteen, so I think you can refer to him as Ryder." God, I was turning into a jealous bitch.

"Fine." She had a clipped, cutting tone. "*Ryder* decided it was best to alter the typical treatment protocol. So he's the one you want to talk to."

"He told me he discussed the decision to do radiation first with you." There was nothing I hated more than someone who wouldn't take responsibility. "And that you agreed it was best."

Suddenly, I got the awful feeling that she'd agreed with Ryder only because she was in love with him. What if she knew the plan wasn't right but had never said anything? What if my dad was about to die because she didn't want to contradict Ryder? She looked back at me, and I thought I saw a stiffening around her eyes. "We need to treat the patient in the current situation."

"All right, then, what route do you propose we take, going forward?"

The librarian glared at us from her desk, silently told us to shut up, and went back to reading. Dale crossed her arms. "That's an excellent question, one we should discuss with your parents and also . . ." She glanced down, as if she could see right through my elbows to the dissertation. "Dr. Anderson should be present. We'll have some big decisions to make in the coming weeks, and it will be important that we make them as a team."

"I'm the one taking care of him." I'd meant for my tone to be businesslike, but I couldn't get the *fuck you* out of it.

"Technically I can't discuss your dad's case without his being present. So you should call the office to schedule a sit-down."

NIGHT BLINDNESS · 139

My head felt like it was about to split open. "Good enough." I started gathering papers. "Have a nice day."

"We didn't even come close to winning," I said to Nic later that afternoon when I was kicking off my muddy sneakers. "You should have played." I tried to ignore that his lips didn't have any give when I kissed him. I wondered if he was mad I'd been gone all day. He was sitting on a stool at the kitchen counter, watching Luke brush dirt off his elbows.

"I could have used another blocker," Luke told him.

Jamie came in next, her hair falling out of its ponytail, and her hot pink warm-up suit had grass stains on the knees. "Without Sterling, we got annihilated."

My dad patted her butt. "We would have done better with Nic on the team," he said. It was the first time my father had sat out on A Will to Live staff football game, and we got killed, but whenever I saw him in that lawn chair on the sidelines, he was smiling and clapping.

"Maybe next time." Nic wasn't a sports fan. When I first met him, I'd been surprised he'd never heard of my dad, hadn't known the story of Will. His idea of exercise was using a chisel and rasp to sculpt a hunk of marble.

Luke peeled off his sweatshirt. "I need a beer," he said.

"I want one, too," my father called from the doorway to the deck.

"No way," Luke and I replied together.

"Well," my dad said meekly, "at least a ginger ale."

Luke grabbed a bunch of drinks from the fridge. "You guys coming'?" he asked.

I was about to trail after them to the deck, when Nic grabbed my arm. "Can I talk to you?"

"We'll be out in a sec," I yelled.

"Suit yourself," Jamie called. "I'm making old-fashioneds in a few minutes."

They filed out to the deck, and I followed Nic through the

kitchen, down the hall, and into the formal living room. We never really used it, except as a way to get to my father's office. I sat on the uncomfortable couch, with Nic across from me in the white wing chair, which I was terrified he'd get paint on. He put his elbows on his knees and leaned forward. I was sweaty and hot, and I wanted a beer, or anything cold to drink. My phone beeped. Mandy had some secret boy she was meeting and she'd texted me to guess. *Who?* I'd write. *Guess,* she'd write back.

"I'm going to Crete," Nic said.

I'd just started to take off my socks, and I stopped. "When?"

"In a few weeks." He watched me.

I rolled my socks in a ball. "I thought with everything going on . . ." I threw them into the hall. "That we'd wait."

"We've been talking about moving there for four years. We've had this trip planned for months." Above his head was the Heisman my dad had won at Notre Dame. The little gold man was running with his hand out. That's what I felt like doing, blocking out what I knew was coming. "Everything's paid for," he said. "And my cousin spent a lot of time researching houses. My family's expecting us for six weeks." The first time we'd visited Demetri, his cousin, we'd gotten so drunk on homemade Kotsifali that Nico asked me to marry him, and we'd eloped on the beach.

"But that's the rest of the summer."

"Greece isn't the Third World." He tented his hands like he did when he was trying to convince me to try new things, like goat-hair paintbrushes or modeling in front of an art collective. "You can fly home if you need to."

"It's a fifteen-hour plane ride."

"We've been planning this all year, J. I've been waiting for you to bring it up," he said. "Every phone call, I tried not to push you, but I assumed we'd still go." I'd been foolish to think he would put off this trip. Nic never dropped anything. "It's the perfect time to buy a house there; with their financial crisis, real estate is rock bottom. It'd be stupid to cancel, and I want you to come. You've been gone a long time, J."

This was the point in our arguments where I usually got quiet and swallowed what I wanted to say because Nic was so sure of what he wanted that he made me believe I wanted it, too. Those crooked goalposts seemed to be watching us. I could hear Luke talking and Jamie laughing. She was saying she wanted to rinse off, and my father was telling her to use the outdoor shower, promising Luke wouldn't peek. Our silence felt like a tight wire.

"I thought he was almost done with treatment," he finally said.

"Halfway . . ."

"Jamie and Luke are here. He has a ton of friends."

A pulse was beating in my neck. "So you want me to leave him?" I could hardly believe this.

"I didn't say that."

"You didn't have to."

He held his breath. He always held his breath when he was deciding what to say. I waited for the soft hiss that meant he was letting it out. "I talked to Luke when you were at the library this morning. And he said they still think your dad will fully recover, that he'd be fine if you left for a few weeks." I didn't move.

"If you're going to take the summer off, why do we have to go to Greece? Can't you be here with me?"

"What are you staying here for?" He sounded exasperated, as if he were trying to show me that one plus one equaled two and I just wasn't getting it. "What would we do here? Live in your childhood bedroom? Sort your father's pills? Follow Ryder around?"

Those were mean words. We didn't fight like this. He stood and went to the window. "What the hell are you holding on to here? Twenty-nine-year-olds do not come home and live with their parents. Especially not if they're married."

I wanted to throw the doorstop at him. It was a heavy wrought-iron cricket that someone had given my dad at the tumor party. It was supposed to bring good luck. "Oh yeah," I said to him. "And only the weak hold on to things from their past." I kept my eyes on the cricket. "Isn't that what you always say? But since I never, ever come home, I don't know what the hell you're talking about. My father has a fucking brain tumor. I'm not here for fun."

Nic paced from the marble fireplace to the door and back again. "You're the one with the boxes of letters you won't throw away and the dreams you won't tell me about." I wondered if I'd ever said Ryder's name out loud during those dreams.

"Well, what about *your* family, Nic? You want to move to Greece. Isn't that holding on to the past? You're so quick to want me to move across the world to be with your family, but you've never given mine a chance."

He stopped where he was in front of the door, his green eyes on mine. "I don't belong here," he said, his voice flat. "Your fancy house and your model mother and football father and that brother who walked on water."

Fuck you, I wanted to scream. I tried to numb out when rage hit. It had been harder to do since I'd been home. Everything was welling up, the guilt, the sadness. Why didn't I want to leave? Why wasn't I trying to escape to Greece? I stared at the paint on his jeans. In Santa Fe, everything was easier. We wandered through our days without fighting; we slept and fucked and went to parties. I didn't play piano anymore and I took off my clothes for sculptors. It was easy to keep everything stamped down, hidden. "What happened to us?" I whispered.

He turned his back on me and held on to the door jamb. "I don't know. Something's different."

I was silent. I was afraid he would turn around and touch me if I said anything tender, and I didn't want that.

"I know your father's sick." He sat in the wing chair, his hands on the armrests. "But you're treading water. And something keeps dragging you down." His shirt was untucked, and I could see his hard brown stomach through the open fabric. I had the quick, visceral thought that another woman would love him better.

The summer I started middle school, I got caught in the waves on Martha's Vineyard; an undertow sucked me sideways along the coast. Whenever I tried to surface, it would pull me back and flip me over, until I didn't know whether I was faceup or facedown. Finally, I stopped struggling, stopped feeling the sting of salt in my throat, the pressure of water in my lungs. I didn't think about trying to get air. I was struck by the blue of the water, the tiny ground shells moving around me. Later, I learned drowning survivors say the moments before they lost consciousness were the most peaceful of their lives.

It was Will who saved me. He got to me before the lifeguard. That night, he told me my body had been limp, tangled around him like seaweed, and he'd been scared. Sometimes in Santa Fe, I lay awake while Nic slept, thinking about that day. If Will hadn't gotten to me before I drowned, he'd still be alive.

Jamie appeared in the doorway, wearing a white linen cover-up. Her hair was wet, and I knew she'd used the outdoor shower. "You don't know what you kids are missing," she said. "I'm making old-fashioneds. Come and get them."

As I watched her walk away, I realized that I finally did know what I was missing: waterskiing off of Luke's Boston Whaler, sailing that old Sunfish my father bought me when I was twelve, sleeping under the Christmas tree because I loved the smell of pine, sledding down Barker's Hill on the Radio Flyer, pretending my hairbrush was a microphone and singing Beach Boys tunes, banging songs out on the piano while Luke played the tambourine. I was missing my childhood. And now that my father was sick, I was trying to bring it back.

Nic was waiting for me to answer. In his untucked oxford and stained jeans, he was still hoping I'd quit taking care of my dad and go to Greece. Of course he thought I'd go. I was the hippie girl who'd dropped out of school for her art professor, dropped her clothes for famous sculptors, dropped everything to fly to Crete and get married on a beach. I looked down at the flying nightingales on both my ankles and wondered how I could make him understand. I had to stay. I needed to find that other, happy girl I'd lost along the way.

17

Nic was in New York, and Mandy and I were in Bottega on Chapel Street. She was trying to cram her feet into a pair of gold kidskin heels that were on sale for three hundred dollars. I zipped a pair of camel boots up my calf and tried not to think about how a baby cow had to live in a box to get the leather that soft. She walked a small circle around me. Her heels hung over the backs. "Can I get away with it?" She clomped to the three-way mirror. I hobbled with her and put my foot up like a flamingo. In my Daisy Duke shorts, the boot made me look like a hooker. "Shit," she said. "These are so cute. Maybe I can cut off my toes." We sat side by side on the bench, taking off the shoes. The sandal straps left red marks on the tops of her feet.

"J.J." She put her arm around me. She smelled powdery, like rose petals ground up and thrown in a bath. "I've kept my mouth shut since that day at Liv's. But I can't take the suspense. You have two men stupidly in love with you. Will you please just pick one? Or"— she flashed me a full-mouth smile—"I'll do it for you."

It was one of those days that even air-conditioned places felt stifling hot. I fanned myself with the top of a shoe box. I was still tired from staying up until 3:00 A.M. the night before with Nic, who'd

nd your to Greece. Begging was not something he'd
" an come back from Crete whenever you need
here are flights all the time." But I never con-

the se-
d know beautiful doctor girlfriend?" I asked Mandy.
." She lifted the top off a box with grass green
lipping Every time I thought of Nico on a plane to
didn't eeling in my chest. "Do you think I can wear
strange t month while I'm photographing mountain
en with
know ndy. She decided she was going to be a photo-
werful, the Frances Benjamin Johnston exhibit at the
high school and had never gotten derailed. I,
What's so far off the track, I couldn't even see it any-
like I lum ankle boot. I hadn't worn anything that
et Nic. I put it on my lap. "Why am I buying
land."
"What d. "Everyone in Paris wears boots year-round."
landys nt idea I was going to fly to France for Philip's
weekend. "On me. Just for three days," she'd
Will's gine the conversation with Nic: *Sorry I didn't*
. Why *m just going to jump across the pond to watch*
me in *chman.*
joint, to Paris," I told her.
sun- king about Ryder," she said.
it. " hing to talk about."

he got up and turned to view the sandals from the
end or no, he's still in love with you. Even if he's doing
ression of a military man, all starched shirts and shiny
an, where is the Ryder with the tattoo and the long hair?"
lerk came back and squatted down with a few more boxes.
t him help her into a pair of sequined party shoes.
he'd gone, she walked to the three-way again, turning
ar in silver sandals. "I never understood why you guys just

didn't fess up to everyone. Will would have come around, a
family would have been thrilled. It's not too late, you know.

"*Thrilled* is an old-lady word," I told her.

"I'm mature." She stood back so she had a long view of
quins. "I look like a Persian concubine." Only Mandy woul
what a Persian concubine looked like.

Bending down, I gathered the cones of tissue paper, s
them back in the random shoes we'd left on the floor. "W
come clean because Will didn't want us together." I had that
shaky feeling I had gotten at Jamie's brownstone when I'd be
Luke, the truth bubbling up from a wellspring I didn't ever
was there. Since I'd been home, the urge to tell had been po
persistent.

Mandy cocked her hip at me and crinkled her forehead. "
wrong, J.J.?" I dropped the tissue paper I was holding. I fel
was going to cry. "J.J.?"

My voice sounded strange and far away. "It was my fault, N

She kicked off her heels and picked them up by their straps.
was?" Behind her, the three-way mirror showed a hundred M
at different angles. "What are you talking about?"

I felt the hard ridges of the shoe box dig into my chest. "
accident . . ." I stopped. Mandy flicked her hair out of her face
was I doing this in downtown New Haven, after she'd visited
Santa Fe and we'd lain in the downstairs hammock, smoking a
our legs entangled, Nic in bed, telling each other stories unti
rise. I could have told her then, but I hadn't ever considered
wasn't an accident," I said now.

She sat on the bench next to me. "What wasn't?" She said i
slowly.

Glancing over her shoulder, I saw the salesclerk in the ha
section, showing a pocketbook to some fat lady. "It was us."
cold. "Ryder and me."

"What?" She laughed a little. Cello music came out the spe
around us, one of the Mozart sonatas I used to love to play o

piano. "What are you talking about?" I could smell her sweet breath. She never held it against me when I didn't call. Whenever she picked up the phone, even if we hadn't talked for six months and she had left messages five different times, she acted like I was the best person in the world. "I've missed you J.J.!" she'd say, and I knew I never had to ask forgiveness from her. And then, in the middle of a high-end boutique on Chapel Street on the second Tuesday in July, I told Mandy the whole story.

It happened during the seventh football game of the season, the year I turned sixteen. The night Hamilton played Hopkins, the air smelled like cedar and hickory smoke. Ryder and I were sharing a box of soggy popcorn. My parents were in back of us. It was the fourth quarter. Hamilton was winning thirty-one to seventeen. Will had thrown for 236 yards. He was one play away from breaking the school record. We were stamping our feet on the aluminum bleachers, and it sounded like thunder. An old Queen song was blaring through the loudspeakers. I leaned back against my dad's legs.

"They're going to win," he said. "Why are they pushing him?" My father chewed on the arm of his glasses, intense, like he was when he watched football with Will or spent hours in his office studying film for ESPN. I watched the offensive coordinator hide his face with the clipboard so that the Hopkins's coach couldn't read his lips. "What the hell are they doing?" my dad said. "Coach should be setting up an Izzy, not a damn Ozzy. Will's the quarterback. Just let him throw for one more down."

I watched Will set up his team for a running play. His blue-and-white uniform was muddy. "I bet he sets up to run, then fakes to pass," I said to Ryder.

He pretended to brush something off my shoulder and ran his fingers through my hair. "What'll you bet?" he whispered. But my dad looked over at us, and Ryder let my hair go. It felt thick and heavy down my back.

As the play clock counted down on the scoreboard, I whispered, "I'll bet you a blow job on the living room couch. Tonight."

Ryder raised his eyebrows and gave me a huge smile. He was wearing an old Steelers sweatshirt of my father's, and his hair was long and curly. It was still warm out; he had on the rope huaraches Jamie had brought back from Mexico.

Out on the field, the center hiked the ball to Will, and I watched him dance in place, looking for an open receiver. My father cupped his hands around his mouth. "Throw it, Will." The numbers on the scoreboard ticked. I knew the coach didn't like him handling the ball for more than five seconds, and I watched him jig backward, trying to find a wide receiver.

Then I saw him: Hopkins's biggest defensive end, a six-foot-six kid who must have weighed three hundred pounds. He plowed through two of Hamilton's tackles, coming right at Will. Everyone in the stands seemed to stand up at once and yell Will's name, but the kid came too fast, and just as Will turned, the player leaped off the ground and sailed through the air like a flying stone wall. His helmet landed in the middle of Will's chest.

The thump of Will's body hitting the ground with three hundred pounds of muscle and bone on top of him silenced the field. The cheerleaders stopped jumping. The music quit playing. Coaches from both teams threw off their headphones. The kid rolled off Will, clutching his head. Will lay on his back, unmoving. The coaches ran to the line of scrimmage.

Ryder leaped to his feet, cupping his mouth with his hands. "Will," he yelled. "Will." His voice echoed against the night sky. Two medics ran over from a waiting ambulance and moved the coaches away. One of them knelt down to unstrap Will's helmet, and the other pulled out a neck brace. Will's body was still. Ryder was muttering "No no no," grabbing at his hair, holding his head in his hands. And then the players formed a circle around Will, their arms stretching across one another's shoulders like braided rope. Before I could ask him what he was doing, Ryder was taking the bleachers two at a time.

My father's face was white and still.

"Is he all right?" I asked. He didn't answer. Jamie had her hand to her mouth, her gaze fixed on the circle of boys around Will. When I turned back, the medics were dragging a gurney across the field. Ryder was running alongside it.

"He'll be fine," I heard my father say. "That kid's tougher than nails."

I watched them lift the stretcher into the chute and through the double doors of the ambulance.

"Let's go." My dad's voice was gruff. "We'll follow in the car." People stepped aside as we came. I watched the ambulance speed off the field, leaving deep tire tracks in the grass.

When we got to the chain-link fence separating the grandstands from the field, Ryder was coming toward us. He reached through and touched my fingers. "He's conscious. He says his head hurts. But he's okay."

The ER waiting area was packed. The lights were too bright. Ryder and I had to stand while we waited for my parents to come out. Sirens whined outside. There'd been some kind of bus accident, the loudspeaker calling for doctors. People were streaming in and out. The nurse was curt and stressed when I asked about Will.

"What if he's not all right?" I asked Ryder.

He leaned against the wall, his eyes closed. "He'll be fine." His shirt was stained with sweat. "He's just a show-off."

I tried to laugh, but nothing came out.

It seemed like a long time before Jamie pushed through the doors. I couldn't read her eyes because they were puffy, her makeup smeared from crying, but when my dad appeared behind her, I knew Will was okay, because the color was back in his face and he was smiling. "He just got out of the MRI machine. He's getting dressed now." He put his arm around Jamie. "He has a concussion, but he's fine. We can leave in a few minutes."

"A concussion?" I asked.

He cleared his throat. "It's a brain bruise. Sounds worse than it is." Jamie put her head on his shoulder. "The doctor said he'll have to take a week or two off from playing, but that's it."

The doors swung open, and Will appeared in a wheelchair with a pretty nurse behind him. He was wearing a plastic hospital bracelet and had a blanket on his lap. "It's alive," Ryder said.

Jamie tried to smooth down his hair. "We're going to sign you out, baby." She bent down and kissed him. "Thank God you're okay."

As soon as they walked away, Will hopped out of the wheelchair. "Man, it's a zoo back there," he said. "Ten bucks says I'll be back to practice by Monday." He put out his hand to Ryder.

"Never bet against a madman," Ryder said.

"You scared the shit out of us," I told him.

Will covered his heart with his hand and let his neck hang as if broken, his eyes rolling in his head. I punched him on the shoulder. It irritated me that we'd all been so worried, the whole school was terrified, Jamie was a mess, my father drove down the highway going a hundred miles an hour, and now he was making jokes. "Quit it," I told him.

At home, Jamie made Will put a bag of ice on his head, and then he and Ryder went up to his room to do whatever boys did when they hung out, and I stayed in the living room, eating Twizzlers, watching *Pretty Woman*, and pretending I wasn't waiting for Ryder to come downstairs. Finally, I heard Will's television go off.

"You mind if I bail?" I heard Ryder say.

"You going to Hotch's tomorrow to watch the game?" It was Will's voice.

"I was thinking about it."

"I'll pick you up," Will said. "We'll take the convertible."

"Don't die on me in your sleep," Ryder told him.

"Bite me," I heard Will say back.

Then the door clicked. I'd turned the lights out, and moonlight filtered through the window in the living room. When Ryder reached the foyer, I said his name. He walked over and knelt by the couch. I wrapped my legs around him. "Hey," I said.

"Hey." He kissed me softly. He tasted like M&M's. I held on to his belt loops and kissed him harder. He pulled away. "What if they wake up?" he whispered, looking at the ceiling. But I couldn't stop myself. I touched his belt buckle and heard him moan softly; his hand went up my shirt. "Jenny," he whispered. He was breathing hard. "We can't."

Ryder had made me promise we wouldn't mess around in my house; he was so afraid Will, or my father, would catch us. Our house was his refuge away from his stiff, hard-driving parents, and I knew to lose it would mean to lose everything. "What if Will comes down?" But I was starving for him, and for one dizzying moment, I couldn't remember why we didn't want Will to know about us. He was Ryder. Everyone loved him. If Will could have him for a best friend, why couldn't I have him for a boyfriend?

"Yes, we can." My voice was edged with defiance. I kept kissing him, and then the chocolate taste was gone, and it was his taste in my mouth. I could taste his neck and throat, his hands, his fingers. I felt him lift me up and lower me onto the couch. I couldn't breathe; I didn't want to. He was taking off his T-shirt, and I was kissing his chest. His fingers were undoing my buttons, quickly, frantically, and I was taking off my shirt. I couldn't get enough of him. I had a flash, a quick white lightning realization that I didn't want to be a virgin anymore. I was tired of being the good girl. His naked body was on top of mine, heavy and hot and hard. *Why not?* I thought. I'd been thinking that a lot lately, when we were in his backseat, or when he managed to sneak me into his house so his strict parents wouldn't know. *Why shouldn't we?* Some part of me thought if he took away my virginity, he wouldn't go to college next year and time would stand still. I opened my eyes, the moonlight came across our bodies, and I felt myself moving with him like water, something I couldn't stop. This would be my first time, here, in the place we said we'd never do it, under this roof, with my brother and my parents sleeping upstairs. Time seemed to fly and melt, and then something hit the wall like a gunshot and the light went on.

Will was standing by the piano, staring down at us. For a moment, no one moved. Ryder and I blinked against the light. Will was wearing blue pajama bottoms and a Hamilton football T-shirt. And then, all at once, Ryder was up, grabbing for his pants, and Will was coming across the living room at him. "You son of a bitch, what the fuck are you doing to my sister?" I knew the look on his face, the one he got before he went ballistic on the field. "I almost dropped dead tonight—"

"Will—" I was trying desperately to put my shirt back on.

"—and you're down here nailing my little sister."

Ryder was backing up, pulling on his jeans. The coffee table was between them. "Hey, c'mon." He put his hand up to ward off Will. "It's not what it looks like."

"Then what the fuck is it?"

"I love her," Ryder said.

"Yeah?" Will's eyes narrowed. "Yeah? You love her? The way you loved Caroline Rhodes and Elle Johnstone and Candace McPhee?"

I was trying to get my jeans on. "Will!" I couldn't believe he was acting as if I were just any other girl. "Stop it." How dare he come down here and ruin this one thing I had that he didn't. "Get out," I heard myself telling him.

He whirled around. "What did you say?" He'd never looked at me like that, a combination of scorn and hatred, as though I'd stolen something from a child. It took the words right out of me. Slowly, he walked toward Ryder.

"She—" Ryder started to say, but Will punched him hard, and Ryder doubled over.

I was up, running at Will. I pushed all my weight at him. "Leave us alone." His arm went up to fend me off, but he was off-kilter. I watched him stumble back. It wasn't like Will to lose his balance, and just as he was falling, something in me awakened, something fierce that had been there, maybe, since childhood, since Will was the one everybody loved, the boy wonder, my dad's favorite, Jamie's pet. I went for him again, just as he was trying to gain his equilibrium. I pushed him hard, and this time I saw his eyes do something odd, flutter like they were going to roll back. His body twisted at an awkward angle, and he fell backward onto the hearth. He never tried to break his fall with his hands. He lay there unmoving.

"Will." Ryder was standing by the piano. The room was silent. A slice of moonlight fell across Will's face. "Will, come on."

Will didn't move.

"Get up," I said to him, but he didn't. "I didn't hit you that hard."

Ryder came over and squatted beside him. "Hey," he said, touching Will's arm. "Quit playing." But Will's body was heavy, limp.

Ryder knelt down and put his ear to Will's mouth, and almost immediately he said, "Call nine one one." He was so calm, his voice so steady, it scared the shit out of me. "He's not breathing."

And then I couldn't really see. Everything was a blur; nothing would come into focus. "I didn't hit him that hard," I said.

"Jenny." Ryder was tilting Will's head back and opening his mouth to start CPR. "Call nine one one," he said again. "Hurry up."

I made my way to the end table. Grabbing the phone off its cradle, I tried to dial. The TV clock read 12:37. I heard Ryder blowing air into Will's mouth. "Dad," I screamed while the phone rang. "Daddy."

The operator asked the nature of the emergency. "My brother's not breathing." What was I supposed to say? "We need an ambulance." I heard my father's door open upstairs, his running feet in the hall above. "Forty-one forty-one North Parker Lane, Colston. Please hurry. Oh God, please hurry."

My dad came flying down the stairs, his robe following him like a pair of lopsided wings. "What the hell happened?"

"Daddy—" But he ran right past me to the fireplace and knelt down. He started chest compressions while Ryder continued mouth-to-mouth resuscitation.

"Do you know what caused him to stop breathing?" the operator was asking. *I didn't hit him that hard.* "Oh please," I was saying. "He's still not breathing."

"What happened?" my dad was yelling at me.

I was crying so hard, I couldn't see. I was still trying to snap up my jeans.

"Go wake up your mother," he said. But somehow, I never did.

The doorbell was ringing, and a man's voice was yelling through the front door. "This is Colston Fire Rescue responding to a report of a nonbreathing individual at this address."

When I opened the door, two men rushed in, and before they got to the living room, the taller one had unpacked a portable defibrillator. "How long has he been down?"

The same digital flashed 12:44. "Seven minutes," I said.

Something passed between the paramedics. The shorter, heavier man, who smelled like mint, spoke into a radio on his shoulder. "Dispatch, this is unit one oh six. We have a ten-fifty-four." He rubbed silver paddles together, and the other medic turned a dial on the machine. "Clear," he yelled.

"This is not happening," I heard myself say. "This is not happening." Where was Jamie? I couldn't go upstairs; I couldn't move. Will's chest rose off the floor and slapped down. He lay perfectly still. They shocked him again. He didn't move. My head felt very light, like it might float away. But my body was so heavy.

The radio crackled with static. "Unit one oh six, this is Dispatch. What's your status?"

The taller medic dropped the paddles. "Patient is still down. We're eight minutes out." He turned to my dad. "You can follow us to the hospital. Yale is closest."

The four of us got in the car. Jamie rode in the passenger seat, her hair still in its tie and her face cream only partially wiped off. "What the hell happened?" My father's face seemed huge, distorted in the rearview mirror.

Ryder spoke. "I—"

"Did everything he could," I said, interrupting Ryder and grabbing his hand in the dark backseat. All our Thanksgivings playing touch football in the backyard came back to me. The boys were only allowed to pull ribbons from the girls' belts, but we could tackle. I'd hit Will much harder than I had in the living room. It was just a stupid little shove that shouldn't even have unbalanced him. "Ryder and I were watching TV, and Will came down to get a drink." I swallowed. Had they noticed the TV wasn't on? "He just . . ." I felt like I was going to be sick. "Collapsed." Ryder's hand felt hot in mine; he was squeezing my fingers hard.

Ryder started to talk, but I cut him off again. "Will just fell down. And he was lying there, not moving, not breathing. Ryder did CPR and told me to call nine one one."

My mother turned to us; her eyes were clear and her mouth was a thin, tight line. I thought she knew we were lying. She put her hand over the seat, and for a second, I thought she was going to slap me, but she patted Ryder's other hand, which was resting on her seat back. "Thank you," she said to him, "thank you, darling." She turned to my dad. "Sweetheart," she said in that tone she used when she was trying to calm him down. "He'll be fine."

My father flinched. "I was there when Chuck Hughes died during the Detroit-Chicago game in '71," he said in a hard, distant voice. "A ten-fifty-four is a probable dead body."

We left the car double-parked and stumbled into the ER. The same front-desk clerk from earlier in the night said Dr. Griffith was waiting for us. When we went through the double doors, a man with a thick beard was writing something on a clipboard. "Dr. Griffith?" my father asked. "Where's my son?" Will had talked on the way home from the hospital about the ER doc who'd looked him over after the game.

"Please, come into my office and have a seat," Griffith told us. His

southern accent surprised me, and he had the shifty eyes of someone who couldn't hold still. When he motioned to a bank of chairs
against the wall, we all stayed standing. He cleared his throat; a thin
scar the shape of a sickle ran from his right eyebrow to his ear. He
put the clipboard down. "Your son wasn't breathing when the paramedics left your house." I hated him then, the hardness in his eyes,
how just three hours later, he'd apparently forgotten Will's name.

"Will," my dad said. "His name is Will."

Dr. Griffith picked up a box of tissues and offered them to my
mom, but she didn't take one. He held the box like a shield. "We
think it was a subdural hematoma."

"What do you mean you *think*?" My father took off his glasses
and rubbed his eyes.

"That would be consistent with a head injury. But we won't know
for certain . . ."

My dad dropped his glasses. His movements were awkward,
abrupt; he appeared not to be aware of what he was doing.

Jamie started toward the door. "I need to see my son," she said,
trying to push past Griffith. "Where is he?"

Griffith blocked her, and my father took her in his arms. "Let the
doctor finish."

I'd backed myself into the corner under a wall-mounted TV, as
far away from everyone as I could get. Ryder stood dumbly in the
center of the room, his shirt untucked, his belt on upside down.

Dr. Griffith cleared his throat. "A subdural hematoma occurs
when there's a hard impact to a person's head." He paused and
looked at each of us. His eyes were the same color as Will's, a bright,
piercing blue. "Basically, the brain bleeds into the dura, the protec-
tive wrapper that surrounds—"

My father slumped. "Just tell us how he is."

I thought I was going to scream. Something was coming for me,
something dark that didn't have a name.

"We did everything we could for Will." The doctor's pager beeped.
He reached for his belt and turned it off.

Jamie gripped my father's hand. "What's happened to him?" she said tightly. "What happened to my Will?"

"Mrs. Reilly." Griffith sucked in his breath and blew it out as he spoke. "I am so sorry."

"No." She rocked back like she might lunge at him, but her legs gave. My dad caught her. I wondered how many people that doctor had seen collapsing, people whose lives had been normal, happy before they'd walked in. Gently, my dad helped her to a chair. I knew I should tell them that Will didn't collapse, that he'd smacked his head on the slate because I'd pushed him, but I didn't hit him that hard.

"But, but, we were just here. You said he was fine." My mother's voice was accusing; my father was trying to help her sit. She was pointing at the doctor, her voice shrill and terrifying, "You said—"

Griffith's voice sounded tinny. "Will's neurological exam was normal. He shouldn't have had any complications." He looked from my mom to my dad. "Are you sure he didn't hit his head again later on in the night?"

"He passed out." I was surprised to hear my voice. "One second he was standing there and the next he was on the floor." Every time I told that lie, it felt a little more like the truth. I could feel Ryder watching me.

I kept my eyes on Griffith, as steady as I could. I took in his beard, his scar. His pager beeped again. "That's what it said in the paramedics' report." He pulled it off his belt and read the message, then slipped it in his pocket.

"But why didn't this hematoma show up on the MRI you did earlier?" my father asked.

Dr. Griffith's eyes jotted right; he moved from one leg to another, as if agitated. "All I can tell you is that the brain is a delicate organ. Sometimes a devastating injury can present as nothing at all." I saw a thin line of sweat at his temple.

"Would an autopsy show what actually happened?" my father asked.

"You will not butcher my beautiful boy." Jamie began to cry.

Whenever I thought about this night, I knew this would be when the fissure between my parents began. Neither would know how to deal with the other's grief. My dad put his arm around her and tried to hold her up. But Jamie had gone stiff. "I forbid you to touch him," she said.

We stood there, listening to her cry, and I thought back to the spring before, when I'd been on that back road heading home from the dugouts with Ryder, hearing that unmistakable thud and seeing the body in my headlights. I'd expected the doe to run into the woods, but she stayed still, watching her fawn. When I got out of the car, I realized she was making a sound I'd never heard before, a devastated bleating that made me wish I could speak her language. It was dark. I hadn't had time to swerve, or brake. When I bent down to see if the fawn was breathing, the doe came closer and hit my shoulder hard with her head. I fell back, startled. That deer stared at me with a dark look in her eyes until I got back in my car and drove away.

While Jamie cried, I thought about that deer and how I'd never called Animal Control, how I'd gotten in my in my car and left that doe, red from the taillights, retreating in the rearview mirror.

When I stopped talking, I was still sitting in Bottega, but I was in their posh bathroom. Mandy had given the clerk her credit card and, taking my hand, had led me to the ladies' room where I'd sat on the toilet seat and finished telling the story. She'd stood next to me without letting go of my hand. It was the first time I had ever said it aloud, and I was shaking hard.

Mandy sat down on the floor next to me. "Oh my God, J.J." She was still holding my hand. "You poor thing."

The clerk knocked on the door and asked if everything was okay. "We're fine," Mandy called to him. And then she took me by the arm as though I were frail and old, and we went into the brightly lit store, where I watched her sign the receipt and take our bags.

Outside the sky had gone from a sallow blue to an angry gray. The air smelled like wet cement and hot oil. We sat on a bench to the left of the door. As cars passed us, I saw my warped face in their windows.

"That doesn't mean anything," Mandy was saying in her quick, certain voice. "The doctor said he got a concussion when that Hopkins kid hit him."

I felt like I was going to throw up. "No, Mand." It was important that she get this. Now that I had finally told, she had to understand. I spoke slowly, as though talking to someone from another country. "The ER doctor asked us three times if Will hit his head after the game." It had started to drizzle and my hair was wet, plastered to my forehead. "I couldn't tell them what happened." I wiped it out of my eyes. "I just couldn't."

That was the part of the story I hated most. I had lied. I hadn't lied as a child. "Her face is too goddamn honest," my father used to tell his friends. "Will's the fiction teller." After that night, though, I found lying easy. I'd lied to guys about my phone number, my name, told them I was available. I'd lied to my parents about my grades, about Nic, and I'd lied to Nic about my dreams.

A little girl crossed Chapel Street in a pink raincoat, holding a Barbie in one hand and her mother's fingers in the other. I had the hideous feeling a car was going to come around the corner and hit her while we sat there watching. "I told that doctor nothing happened." I felt a raindrop hit my bare neck and slide down my back. "I have dreams that the emergency room doctor comes to our house and tells my parents the truth." Everything was itchy, the band of my denim shorts, my underwear hem, the T-shirt, my hair down my back. "I could tell he didn't believe me." It started to rain harder, but we just sat there. "Sometimes I think I see him. In the health food store in Santa Fe. Behind me at a red light. And since I've been home and back at Yale, I sometimes think he's going to come for me. He's going to show up on my parents' doorstep and tell them what I did. He must have figured it out by now."

"J.J.," Mandy said. The traffic sent up spray that almost hit our legs. "No matter what happened that night, it was an accident; you didn't do it on purpose."

I stared at an open sewer hole down the street with bright orange sawhorses surrounding it. That it had been an accident hardly mattered. Mandy put her arm around me and laid her head on my shoulder. We watched the traffic pass. Customers went in and out of stores; I could feel their eyes on us. "Tell your parents," she finally said. "You'll feel so much better."

"I tried once to tell my mom."

"Yeah, well, that's Jamie. Tell your dad."

"He'll die hating me."

"He's not dying." Her mascara had left two black rims below her bottom lashes. "And he couldn't hate you if he tried."

I watched people hurrying past, huddling under umbrellas, car wipers frantically beating back rain. My hands felt like deadweights at my sides. "You're the only person in the world who knows."

"You never told Nic?" I could hear the surprise in her voice. I shook my head. "Oh, J.J.," she whispered. "You poor, poor thing."

I put my face in my hands and sobbed. I cried for Will and for my dad; I cried for everything I'd lost and would lose and for how different my life could have been, how different I wanted it to be. The rain came down harder, sideways, slanting rain that soaked our clothes through, but we didn't move, we just sat there, side by side on the bench, our new shoes in boxes at our feet, while I cried and cried.

18

After I told Mandy, I went around in a daze. I didn't know if I felt relief or if something inside had disconnected. My mirrors felt like windows looking out at a crowded street. I didn't see my reflection, just the image of someone who looked vaguely familiar, like a girl I used to know in grade school but whose name I had long since forgotten.

At odd moments, I felt as though I would open my mouth and tell my father what had happened, like when we were sitting at the drive-through prescription window downtown or at the grocery store buying asparagus. Things with Jamie felt even more strained. My urge to confess was constant, but she was off-limits. After she hadn't listened to me when I tried to tell her in high school, I couldn't do it now, and I was so angry at her for that.

In early August, I took Jamie to drop off her car at the dealership. On the way home, we stopped at her agency. It was three blocks from the hospital where I'd been taking my dad for radiation five days a week all summer and I hadn't been there once since I'd been home. The elevator doors opened, and as we got closer to the studio, I heard Piers, her photographer, pleading in his Italian accent with a model to look more desperate.

He was heroin-skinny as ever, black hair back in that same pony-tail, camera around his neck, looking up at a six-foot teenager in a bathing suit. The overhead lights made the place feel like an oven. Covering the walls were black-and-white photos of all the girls Jamie and Piers had discovered. Four fans were blowing the model's blond hair everywhere. "Poutier." Piers frowned, showing her what he meant. He just looked constipated. "I need hopeless." The girl stuck out her bottom lip. He spun in a small circle and smiled when he saw me. "*Bella*." He put his arm around my shoulders. "Just look like this one. Damaged and beautiful." He released me and kissed Jamie on the cheek. "You take tiny break," he said to the relieved girl. She studied me for a moment before disappearing into the break room.

Jamie handed Piers a portfolio. He tucked it under his arm and said to me, "It's been ages, darling, congratulations on your father's"—he searched for the word; he'd been in the United States thirty years, and he was still searching for words—"recovery."

"He's not recovered, Piers," I said. "He has a brain tumor."

He put his hand over his mouth, and I felt bad for being mean. He'd always been kind, brought homemade taffy for Will and me when we were little and Jamie brought us to shoots. "Yes, but it is okay?" He tilted his head. "I thought—" Then he saw another model appear from the back. "Janel," he called over his shoulder, "you are mine in T minus two." He tapped his watch. "So, Ukraine's port-folio, it is perfect, no?" He looked at Jamie. "She's a gold mine." He put his thumb and forefinger together to indicate money. "Okay." He clapped his hands. "Ta."

"My God, Jensen," Jamie said while we were getting into the el-evator. "Do you always have to be so full of doom and gloom? Weren't you listening when Ryder said the odds—"

"Are overwhelmingly in our favor." I pushed the button for the ground floor. "There are still risks," I told her. "I've been research-ing at the medical library, and there are a boatload of reasons not to relax about this." What did she *think* I did all day?

She sighed. "You're so much better at this than I am."

"Better at what? Reading?"

"Taking care of Daddy." She took a small pill out of her pants pocket and swallowed it without water. "I could move out today, and he probably wouldn't even notice."

There she went again, playing martyr so she could escape. "Dad needs you." The elevator doors opened. "He loves you." We stepped out into the palatial lobby. "More than he should." In my flip-flops, I could walk quicker than she could in her stilettos.

Her heels clicked behind me. She was almost running to keep up. "What are you saying?" The doorman opened the doors for us. She stopped on the sidewalk. "Jensen?"

It was one of those days when it was too hot to argue, almost too hot to speak. The streets were empty. I looked at her in that perfect silk dress. "You left him behind after Will died."

Confusion crossed her face. "I know that was hard for you." She took a step forward. "But you don't understand what it was like—"

"What don't I understand?" I could feel sweat rolling down my stomach. "Losing someone I loved? Feeling like if I tried hard enough I could stop breathing?"

We stood in front of the building with her name in gold letters on the side and stared at each other. She was blinking very fast. "I'm sorry, honey," she finally said. "I'm just not good at this part."

"Then go back to your fucking brownstone." I started toward the car.

I could hear her heels in back of me. "That's not fair," she said.

"Could you hurry up?" I asked. "I'm going to be late to take Daddy to the foundation."

Jamie and I didn't speak the whole way home, and when I dropped her off at the house, she only said, "I'll get your father." I stared straight ahead, waiting for my dad to get in the car and berate me for fighting with her. Whenever Jamie and I fought, she got my dad to lick her tears. It drove me crazy.

But she must not have said anything, because while I drove up

Route 1 to A Will to Live, he only told me about the boat he and Luke had been thinking about buying: a 1938 catamaran with hand-made sails. He hated the name *Miss Majestic,* but it was bad luck to change it. Finally, he laid his head back, closed his eyes, and by the time I pulled into the foundation, he was snoring.

I parked in his reserved space and turned off the ignition. He was so vulnerable, slumped against the door, his mouth slightly open. Ryder said he'd tire easily, and in the past few weeks his eyelids had gotten heavy whenever we drove farther than the center of Colston. He hadn't rented a fun car in ages. When we went out on Luke's boat, he stayed quiet, watching the waves. I tried not to think of it as a bad sign. If I let it, everything seemed like an omen. A WILL TO LIVE was ornately painted on the sign beside the vast front door of the Victorian home turned center for kids.

My dad had decided to start the foundation a month after Will's funeral. He'd been sitting at the breakfast nook, his hair greasy, as if he hadn't washed it in days. He hadn't gone back to work for ESPN, and I had a feeling he never would. He'd been sitting there staring at absolutely nothing. It was this stare, among other things, that had motivated me to fill out the application for Andover. That morning, though, the stare broke, and he glanced at my mom. "Let's build something," he said. "For kids."

Jamie was sitting at the counter, drinking black coffee in her robe, beautiful in her messiness. "What kind of something?" She flipped the page in her magazine.

It was a windy November day, and the goalposts appeared isolated and lonely. "We'll build someplace where kids can play," he said. The *New Haven Register* was sitting on his place mat. 17-YEAR-OLD KILLED AT EDGERTON PARK. "And we'll name it after Will."

Ten months later, I'd come back from Andover and stood between Jamie and Luke while my father cut the huge red ribbon and dedicated the facility to Will. It was this building that got him showered and dressed again.

At the reception, I'd scanned the crowd for Ryder. Jamie had casually mentioned, when I'd come down to breakfast in a shapeless pink dress, that his mother was planning to attend. I'd run back upstairs and changed into a clingy black skirt and sleeveless silk top. But as my high heels sank into the freshly laid sod, I saw neither Ryder nor Mrs. Anderson.

"Hey, Daddy," I said now, gently shaking his arm. "Wake up sleepyhead."

The waiting room of A Will to Live was where the parlor used to be. Newspaper clippings, report cards, school photos, and candids of the kids who'd passed through the center covered the walls. A woman with cropped gray hair came out of the front office and hugged my dad. "Sterling." She was smiling as if she were a child and he had fixed her broken toy. "I didn't think you were coming in today. Everyone's already in the boardroom." Jamie and I had made him late with our fight.

My dad held on to her hand. "Danielle is the best office manager you'll ever meet," he told me. "If not for her, I wouldn't know what day it was. This is my daughter." I could hear the swell of pride in the word *daughter*.

"Oh, Jensen." She held out her hand. "Your dad talks about you all the time." I felt bad that it had been years since I'd been there. I hadn't been able to make myself come back east alone, and Nico so rarely was willing to travel with me. "Would either of you like some coffee?" she asked.

My dad whispered loudly in her ear. "The home guard has me drinking some green tea slop with soy milk."

"So that explains the odd things in the fridge. I'll go brew some lawn clippings right now." As she turned to leave, she patted my hand. "So nice to meet you, Jensen. Welcome home."

"Make yourself comfortable," my dad told me. "This should only take an hour." When he opened the meeting room door, a cacophony of voices rose like a cheer, and I wondered, vaguely, what it would feel like to be loved like that.

It was quiet at the center. I wandered through the arched door-ways and over the shiny wood floors, touching unworking fire-places. Along the mantels, I found scribbled sweet notes to my dad. I thought how some of the kids who came here had seen him more than I had in past years. I headed to the rec room to check out the new Ping-Pong table Sid had told me about, and when I opened the door, someone yelled "duck," but it was too late. A ball bounced off my head, and a little girl with skin the color of creamy coffee bolted from the table, saying, "Sorry, ma'am, sorry." She had a speech im-pairment, and it came out *sah-wee*.

"Here you go." I handed the ball to her.

She eyed me suspiciously. "Thank you, ma'am." Her dress had HELLO KITTY on the pockets. "You look like the lady in the picture on Mr. Sterling's desk."

"Is she beautiful?" I flipped my hair, but she missed the joke.

"She looks like you," she said impatiently, as though I'd commit-ted a crime.

I glanced around, wondering who was taking care of this child. I felt a little awkward around kids; they were so unabashed, so un-ashamed of who they were. "I'm Jensen. Mr. Sterling is my dad."

"My name is Alexandria." She tapped the paddle against her thigh. "Does that mean Miss Jamie is your mama?"

My skirt was too short to be bending down, but I did it anyway, tucking the material between my legs. "You know my mom?"

"She's my favorite grown-up."

"You're kidding." I thought about Jamie and me arguing on the sidewalk by her building. *But you don't understand what it was like—*

"What grade are you in?" I asked.

"I'll be in first grade. *Fuwst gwade.* She touched her hair, pulling at the ribbon woven into her braids. "I know how to spell thirty-two words," she said proudly. "Miss Jamie helps me." I imagined my mother examining her fingernails and saying, *Manicure, darling. M-A-N-I-C-U-R-E.*

The girl swayed back and forth. I had the urgent wish to hold her miniature warm body against mine. "What's your favorite word to spell?"

"I just learned it. L-O-V-E." Her whole face broke out into a grin. She was missing a top tooth.

"Alexandria of Prettytown." My dad's voice called from the doorway. "What's up, my beautiful girl?"

She dropped her paddle and ran into his arms. He raised her in the air, hugging her, as if it were no strain at all. "Mr. Sterling, Mr. Sterling." *Mista Stuh-wing. Mista Stuh-wing.* She flung her arms around his neck.

I got up from the squatting position, my quads burning. "That was quick," I said.

He looked embarrassed. "Bathroom break."

Alexandria seemed braver in my father's arms. She had almond-shaped eyes that widened when she spoke. "Can I come play with the dollhouse in your attic again?"

He glanced at me. "Well now, first things first. How did your talk go today?"

"Good," she said. "The lady gave me a lollipop." I wondered what meeting they were talking about. "Miss Jamie said I could redecorate the dollhouse and play dress-up."

My dad laughed nervously. "Whatever your little heart desires."

Danielle came in, running her fingers through her short hair. "Goodness." She took the girl from my father. "I was looking all over for you."

A Will to Live kids never came to our house, it was a rule the board of directors had laid down. "Boundaries need to be set," Jamie had told me once. "Or your father would let them all live with us."

Alexandria leaned out from Danielle's arms and gave my father a peck on the cheek. "Bye-bye," she said before Danielle took her away.

My dad smoothed his hair. "Back to work." He grinned at me, and I watched him walk out the door and down the hall toward the boardroom.

"Didn't you need to go to the bathroom?" I called after him.

"Oh," he said. "Right." He turned around and started up the other hall.

"Dad," I said.

He raised his eyebrows.

"Has Alexandria been to our house?"

He cleared his throat. "Well," he said. "She's . . . Her parents died in a house fire and . . ." His voice trailed off. "Just once or twice." And then he turned abruptly toward the bathroom.

I sat on one of those big exercise balls next to the Ping-Pong table. It made me feel slightly sick, imagining Jamie teaching Alexandria all those words. I couldn't identify the feeling at first. I thought of Jamie and the beautiful little girl having a tea party and getting their toes painted. I saw them doing all the things that she and I had never done together. Slowly, it came to me that I was jealous. Jealous of a six-year-old orphan girl.

19

I woke to rain slapping against my window and the fight I'd had with Jamie on my mind. Days later, her words were still buzzing in my head: *But you don't understand what it was like*—Fuck her. I knew exactly what it was like.

I ran a brush through my hair, put it in a ponytail, and made my way down to the foyer, skipping the one stair that creaked. Stepping off the porch, I saw lightning traveling across the tree line, a deadly game of connect the dots. The sun hadn't risen yet, and I knew better than to run in weather like this, but I had to shake the murderous feeling I got when Jamie and I fought. Somewhere in me, I thought it had something to do with what I'd told Mandy, but I was too mad to puzzle it out.

Walking down the driveway, I turned my iPod as loud as it would go and, not bothering to warm up, went at the pavement in a full run. I wasn't sure what time it was, but with the rain, it still felt like the middle of the night, and my eyes had a tough time adjusting to the dim light. At the end of North Parker, I turned left onto Brook Hill, also known as "Heartbreak Hill," a mile climb that would eventually turn into Overlook Drive and level off. Will and I used to run this route during preseason for field hockey and football.

He'd run backward to see if I could catch him. Or he'd run ahead and hide behind someone's hedges and then yell "Gotcha" when he jumped out to scare me. I missed how he'd made everything a game—the clown faces when I was on the phone, how he used to stick green beans in his nose at the dinner table, and how he'd climb the old oak tree instead of coming in through the front door.

Except that he used to pretend, too, that he was dying. He'd make me count how long he could stay underwater at the country club pool, and then he'd stay there so long, unmoving, that I'd get scared. I'd be just about to scream, when he'd pop up. Sometimes, as I tried to get him up in the morning, he'd act like he'd died in his sleep. I'd thought about it that night, when he hit his head. I'd thought about it during the funeral and for a lot of years afterward.

No one was out. I thought about that spring I dropped out of college and went on the road with Nic, when the streets were quiet like this and we'd drive for hours to the next gallery. I finally understood why no boy had ever meant more than just sex. Their need terrified me. Nic didn't have that clawing want. He adored me, but I felt like he could do without me. The slow tenderness in his lovemaking was innate, or maybe he'd learned it from all those Tantric books. "His mother loved him," Mandy had said when I told her. "Men whose mothers love them are always confident in bed."

Three-quarters of the way up the hill, my lungs felt like fire, and I was ready to lie in the street and drink from a puddle. The sky had lightened to the color of nickel, and when I could see the bright green street sign, I started walking and took my pulse. Sweat dripped down my face while I counted, and I moved aside so the car behind me could pass. But it kept following me.

A scare crept up in me, and I suddenly wanted to get past Overlook Drive, to McKinnon, where there were houses, so I started jogging again. The car stayed behind, and I ran faster, my sneakers slapping the wet pavement. Finally, I got up my nerve and glanced back.

It was Luke's Navigator. He drove up and leaned across the console. "Somebody chasing you?"

"Jesus Christ." I didn't know if I wanted to hug him or hurt him. "You scared me."

"You're going to drown." He held up a tray of coffee with a little white bag crammed in the middle. "Get in; you and the coffee are getting cold."

"Lucibello's is open this early?"

"Yeah. Starflower wanted a chocolate croissant. Even I can't make them as tasty as those Italians."

The rain picked up, and his wipers slapped faster. I ran in place to keep warm. "Will you make me my favorite egg and cheese sandwich?"

"I'll make you a cooked goose if you'll just come on."

A crack of thunder sounded to the north, and I ran around the car, squealing, and got in. He called Starflower to say we were on our way. In five minutes, we were sitting in front of his old farmhouse.

I hadn't been to Luke's in a million years. His doormat still said NICE UNDERWEAR, and the kitchen smelled of oranges. Starflower was standing at the counter in front of a juicer, her hair tied back in a paisley bandanna.

"Thanks for letting me intrude on your breakfast," I told her.

She smiled and poured me a glass of orange juice. "This will rehydrate you." She was wearing some kind of caftan and long dangly earrings. "I started a bath and put lavender mineral salts in to help with your sore quads. I left some sweats on the basin."

Taking the juice, I closed the bathroom door and peeled off my wet clothes. I wondered how she could possibly know my quads hurt. The small bathroom was filled with steam, and the lavender, good for my muscles or not, smelled great. I studied the purple velour jogging suit. I was pretty sure 1976 wanted it back.

Back in the kitchen, I sat at a chair that had been carved out of a wine barrel, and Luke put an egg sandwich on my plate. "I'm so glad this is one of her eating days," he said to Starflower, who was cleaning out the juicer.

I stuck out my tongue at him. But when I bit into the sandwich, I almost spit it out. "I think a piece of wrapper got left on the cheese," I said.

Luke laughed. "That's what soy cheese tastes like."

I picked it out of my teeth. "They make real cheese, you know."

"Now you get a feel for what your old man's been going through," he told me, "following Starflower's curing diet." I'd forgotten that she was the reason we knew what to feed my father, how to make his system alkaline so it could kick out the disease. "She doesn't let us have any dairy in the house—bad for you. Course"—he winked at her—"she gets to eat a chocolate croissant."

She threw some orange rinds in the compost bucket. "Don't tell my secrets," she said. "A girl has to have her indulgences."

"Thank you for breakfast." Plastic cheese or not, I was starving, and I wanted them to know how happy I was to be there.

Luke rapped my elbow with his fork. "Are you going to tell Uncle Luke how your old man really is? I only got half a story when I was at Pilot's Point Marina with him last week."

Starflower dried her hands. "I'm going to get dressed. Kisses to both of you." At the banister, she stopped and pulled on one of her ringlets. "Don't worry about your mother," she told me. "She will have forgotten all about your fight by the time you get home today." Then she disappeared upstairs.

I sat there with my mouth open; Luke put his arm around me. "Isn't she amazing? She's the only person I've ever known who really does see with her third eye."

I mopped up some yolk with my sandwich and told him my dad had spent Saturday afternoon teaching Sid's eldest grandson how to hike a football. And a few days before that, two of his brothers had road-tripped up from Philly, and they'd gone to the Seafood Shack and then to a drive-in. He didn't get in until two A.M. "He gets tired, but he seems happy." Luke was squinting at me. I sipped my tea. "Except that I know brain tumors can be deadly . . ."

"You need to knock it off with the negative energy." He took a croissant from the bag and cut it in two. "The one lesson that keeps smacking me on the head"—he tapped his dreads—"is that anything, and I do mean anything, is possible. A hundred years ago, folks died from chicken pox. Now people are living with one kidney and titanium knees and animal valves in their hearts. It's okay to have hope, Jensen." He popped a piece of pastry in his mouth.

"But what if—"

He interrupted me. "But what if belief is as strong a medicine as science? People walk across red-hot coals and mothers, even yours"—he lifted my chin so I had to meet his eyes—"pick up cars to save their children. The human body is a goddamn miracle."

The rain had stopped, and a thin stream of sunlight came through the window and lit up the funky kitchen with its slate countertops and cupola.

"Can I tell you something really awful?" I heard the shower running upstairs and thought how unlike Luke it was to be playing house with a woman. "I love having this time with my dad."

He laughed his deep baritone laugh. "Since when is that a bad thing?"

"I'm here to take care of him. This was supposed to be hard."

"That's God's way of fucking with you. There's beauty in the damnedest places. Come here, let me show you something."

"Are we going out?" I asked. "Because people might mistake me for Jimi Hendrix."

He laughed again. "Nah, just down the hall."

He led me to a small room off the den. Beads hung from the jamb and soft sax music was coming from overhead speakers. A couch sat across from an armchair, and bookshelves lined the walls. *The Power of Now; When Things Fall Apart; Zen Mind, Beginner's Mind.* "My sanctuary," he said. "Where I sit with people who need a little guidance." I stood at the threshold. "You don't need to stand there like you got called to the principal's office."

I sat on the end of the couch. The woven Indian rug felt good under my bare feet. "This isn't really my scene. God and I aren't exactly on speaking terms."

He settled in the armchair. "Lovers' quarrel?"

The sound of the fountain next to me made me want to take a nap. "I'm waiting for Him to answer a few questions," I said. "But I don't even know who He is."

"Ah, what does it matter? Maybe He's a white light or an essence; maybe He's the sun. There's some kind of force out there, and you might as well pray to it, because data proves prayer works." He had the voice of a good teacher, kind, but not patronizing. "I bet He could handle your questions."

"I don't think He wants to hear from me," I told him. "You and my father think I'm some kind of angel, but—"

"God doesn't give a fuck. He still loves me, and you should have seen me and your daddy when we were young and had too much money. We did things you'd think God would have sacrificed us on a stone slab for—drove drunk, took other people's prescription drugs, slept around with groupies, crashed our cars, stayed up until the sun rose, and then did it all again the next night. Anything to help us run away."

This surprised me. "What was my dad running from?"

"Growing up poor. Both of us. It made us feel like we didn't deserve the money and talent and luck." I imagined my father and Luke snorting lines of cocaine off a hooker's belly. "Your dad found Jamie, and then they had Will and you, so he quit screwing around. When I was messed up, I couldn't play piano at all, so I quit because of that. It was simple. We found purposes greater than ourselves."

"So that's what you preach to my parents to make them so . . ." I couldn't think of the right word. "Okay with this."

"I don't preach." He reached out his big hand and patted my knee. "I help people reframe their beliefs, so life doesn't feel so hard. The first thing is to know what you can and can't control."

"Oh yeah?" His hands were so square and substantial; they'd picked me up and brushed me off as many times as my own parents' had. "What can we control?"

"Well, we can tell the truth."

The truth. Ever since I'd told Mandy about Will, I'd been thinking about telling my father, but the *what ifs* were hounding me. What if he hated me? What good would that do? "What if it's too hard?"

"Your mother used to say that." He got up, lit a candle, and gently waved it like a wand. It smelled like jasmine.

I leaned back on the couch. "What'd you do for her?"

He secured the candle in a holder shaped like a half-moon. "I helped her learn how to comfort herself." He sat down again. "She was finding comfort in all sorts of things before that."

"How do you know she's not anymore?"

"Rule number one," he said, "in action. Can you control Jamie?"

"Hardly."

He nodded. "Then don't worry about it."

"It's that simple?"

"Pretty much."

"Okay, I can't control 'Why us? Why my dad? Why Will?' So I just shouldn't think about it?"

His mouth turned up like he was going to laugh, but he didn't. "Horrible things happen. We can't know why. And if our faith has to be tested to lead us to believe in something greater than ourselves, so be it."

I leaned back and let my eyes close. I thought of Will dying, my father in the hospital, Ryder loving someone else. "That's so fucked-up."

"Can you control whether it's fucked-up or not?"

I didn't say anything. I just thought about my dad standing in the kitchen the night before, drinking a glass of carrot juice. When he put it down, he'd had an orange mustache above his top lip, little boy–style. And I'd been afraid, sitting there across from him, that if I told him what had happened, all his innocence would drain out and he'd never look like a little boy again.

. . .

Luke dropped me at home. When I walked through the back door, Jamie was at the breakfast table in her satin robe, studying the pages of a fashion magazine. It was already past noon. "How did this girl get a job?" She held up an ad for Revlon lipstick, as though we hadn't had a fight, which is exactly how she ended fights, just blowing through them as if they'd never happened. The model had one stilettoed foot resting on an ottoman, blowing out candles on a cake with wine-colored lips. The cake reminded me that Will's birthday was the next week. Jamie had planned his parties herself, throwing him bashes at the carousel park down the street, waterskiing parties, beach bashes where Luke cooked lobster over a fire pit. I walked in and took the magazine, studying the underfed teenager before handing it back to her.

"Cankles," I said, although I probably could have touched my thumb and middle finger around her ankle.

"Exactly," she said. "I had the perfect girl for this ad, and they chose *her*."

I walked to the counter and put on some coffee. I was still wearing Starflower's ugly purple sweatsuit, but Jamie hadn't noticed. "Want some?" I held up the pot.

"No, honey. Diuretics dry your skin." The canary diamond on her hand flashed while she flipped the pages. I wondered if Julian had been intimidated by a piece of jewelry that cost as much as a car. Standing there holding a package of Starbucks dark roast, I blurted out, "Are you sleeping with someone again?"

"Now this girl is flawless." She held up an ad for mascara, as if she hadn't heard me. A woman with blunt bangs and smoky eyes stared past the camera. "But Elite signed her before I had the chance."

"Just tell me who he is." I dumped a scoop of coffee in the maker. "I won't tell Dad."

She turned the pages like she was mad at them. "I'm sure I don't know what you're talking about."

I put the measuring cup on the counter. "You're always taking secret calls and running off on vague errands. What am I supposed to think?"

She let out a long breath. "I love you, Jensen, but stay out of this. You don't know what you're talking about."

"Then tell me." I wanted to slap her.

"You know what?" She got up and brought her teacup to the counter, putting it down so hard, I thought it might crack. "You're living in the past. That was a very specific period in our lives. Your father and I needed time apart. Grief"—her eyes filled with sudden tears—"is not uniform. Everyone goes through it in their own way. I wanted to talk to Daddy about it, about Will. More than anything else, I wanted . . . I needed your father to help me live without Will. But he couldn't. I needed to remember Will. And your father just wanted to shut down." She looked past me at the slider. "Things are different now." She turned back to the table and flipped the magazine closed.

"Exactly how are things different? Now Daddy just goes along with whatever you feel like doing?"

"Stop it." She sat in her chair and glared at me. The veins in her neck stood out. "I'm the one who's been here." Her voice was low and furious. "The one who knew something was wrong, that he wasn't the same. I'm the one who had to live with it. Trying to decide what to do. Not daring to call you because every time I did, it was as if we were some horrible burden on you." I stood at the counter, not moving. "And now you suddenly decide to come home with your brains and your research, painting in the attic and playing piano with Luke and making me feel like an idiot for who I am." She picked up the magazine but didn't open it. "I have done the best I can." She looked up at me. "I am not perfect. Show me one person in the world who knows how to act when their child dies." She studied me with a hard glare. "I am the one who has been here day in and day out with your father, eating meals with him and brushing my teeth next to him, sleeping in a bed with him night after night, and I have loved that man the best I know how. So don't you dare come here and make me feel bad for how I live. I was the one who was still here when he was ready to talk again. To live again. It was me, Jensen. Not you. You're the one who left. You walked out on our family. Not me."

We stood in the kitchen with the hot, still air around us. I saw then the faint lines around her eyes, the draw on the sides of her mouth. I saw that my mother would also die someday. I thought of what Luke had said that day in her apartment. That maybe her seeking shelter somewhere else, with someone else, made it easier for both of my parents. And now, after listening to her talk, I realized my dad had hurt her, too. "I'm sorry," I said.

She nodded curtly. And then she picked up her breakfast plate and set it in the sink. "Nic called from Greece early this morning," she said in an entirely different voice. "Apparently, he couldn't get you on your cell. He's going to some remote island and isn't sure when he'll be able to call again." She took her gardening gloves from the counter and opened the slider. I watched her walk out onto the deck. She closed the slider and stood with her back to me. She was past middle age, a woman who had worked hard and been married a long time. And I felt something I'd never really felt for Jamie. I felt respect.

20

After the rain, a heat wave hit, and even in my skimpy sundress and flip-flops, I felt as if I were going to melt. Hot air hung above the driveway and the low-tide marshes smelled like they were cooking. It was Friday night, and my parents were on a double date with Starflower and Luke. Mandy was in the darkroom. If my father hadn't had a brain tumor, and Nic hadn't gone to Greece, I'd be in Santa Fe, meeting him and Hadley at Hapa on the square for sushi. "Raw fish," Hadley used to tell us, "should only be used for bait." But we'd convinced him. And it had become a Friday-night ritual. When I called Hadley to say hey, he told me he was in Sedona at the opening of a fusion restaurant. "They just put ecstasy in my drink. Wish me luck." I felt so far away from him, for a minute I wanted to cry.

I waited for the garage door to open and then backed out. It would be dark soon, and I knew I shouldn't be driving. But I hated being alone in the house. If I painted in the attic, sometimes I was okay, but lately it had been too hot to paint. Since the summer began, I'd started four more self-portraits and finished none. I took a left out of our road, then two rights toward New Haven. When my parents went out, I usually drove to Jamie's brownstone and banged out music I hadn't played in years. Those lessons with Luke were reminding me how to get my groove back.

There were three ways I could get to Route 1 and avoid Hamilton. It was so hard to pass the school where Will, Ryder, and I had been inseparable. Lately, I'd been going by it anyway, as though testing myself. Now I found myself drawn to it, rolling down the sloping driveway, past the academic buildings, to the athletic fields. I could feel them, those steel bleachers, that empty field. Just as I was almost past the parking lot, Ryder's ringtone sounded in my purse. It was the Velvet Underground song he used to sing to me when we were kids.

I pulled over. "Hey," I said.

"Are you avoiding me?"

"It's not like you've been calling me." I put the car in park, and the breeze coming through the window stopped. Sweat gathered between my breasts.

"But you're mad, aren't you?"

There was no point in bullshitting him. "I don't want to talk about it on the phone." I wiped my forehead with the back of my hand.

"Where are you?"

"Hamilton Field."

He was quiet for a moment, then said, "I'll be there in five." He hung up.

I watched the backlight on my cell go dark and then drove into the empty parking lot. I hadn't seen Ryder since he'd stopped by during that Fourth of July picnic. Radiation had gotten back on track without any problems, and there'd been no reason to see him. Except I thought about him all the time and wondered why, if he'd been coming to my parents' house for years, he hadn't been stopping by since I'd been home.

I surprised myself by getting out of the car and walking toward the football field. That familiar melancholy hit me sideways. I felt it settling in my solar plexus, making me vaguely sick. The field was dotted with dandelions and buttercups, and the yard lines were faded. I opened the little gate and walked in. Then I sat on the first bleacher and waited. I thought about how I'd finally told Mandy and wondered if Ryder had ever told anyone.

It didn't take him long. I heard his car crunching the gravel, his door slammed, and I turned and watched him come through the gate. He bent down and picked a buttercup. He was wearing a white T-shirt, and his short hair was damp. He sat next to me. He smelled good and clean. He held the flower under my chin. "Yup," he said. He was tanner than the last time I'd seen him. "She likes butter."

"I love butter." I took the flower from him, picked the petals off one by one. His arm was cool against mine. Neither of us said anything for a while. The tree frogs had started in, and two low-flying bats circled the field. "Are you engaged?" I asked. His flip-flops were leather; it was comforting to see him in something other than expensive loafers. "To Dale?"

He took a breath in. "We were once."

I saw her car in your driveway, I wanted to say, *her shoes in your living room. I had to imagine her in your bed.* "She's wearing a ring," I said, remembering the one she'd had on at the library. A dog was barking frantically in the distance.

"We're dating again," he said. "She wants to get married."

"You were with her before?" I thought of those red heels. "And then broke up?"

He stared across the field at the tree line. "I cheated on her."

That shocked me. Even though girls had loved him, Ryder had been so loyal. "Who was it?"

"Some girl at a conference." He pulled at a fraying bit of leather on his flip-flop. "I was getting a name badge, and she was across the room. The place was packed. She had your same hair, and she was wearing a dress like you wear, sort of swingy at the bottom." He shrugged. "And she had the same shoulder blades, a little too thin, muscular." He was speaking in an odd monotone. "I'd thought I'd seen you a million times, but this time..." He ran his fingers through his hair. It was a tiny bit longer and curling with the humidity. "I got out of line. She was standing like you do, too, with her hip out, holding her hair up. And then she turned around." He quit talking.

I tore the petals off the flower. "And you were with her?"

"She was just a girl in my bed in the morning." He said it in that same dry, cold voice he used to tell us medical information.

"How'd Dale find out?"

"I told her." He sounded surprised I had asked. "It was easier than pretending there wasn't something missing."

"She took you back?"

He nodded.

"When?"

"The first night you got here." I remembered the tea he'd brought to the deck, our initials on the arm of the glider. "I operated on one of her patients last year, and she died that night. She had two little boys. Dale was a mess."

"What was wrong with her?"

"She was just crying. Really sad—"

"No," I told him. "What happened to the mother?"

I knew the answer before he said it, the way he turned to me but stared over my shoulder at the trees. "Brain tumor."

A siren sounded in the distance. I thought of my parents out with Luke and Starflower and tried to gauge which way the ambulance was headed. "Do you love her?" I asked.

He reached down between the bleachers and picked a dead dandelion. "Not as much as I loved you, if that's what you're asking."

"Loved?"

"Stop it." He tossed the weed onto the field. "You're married."

The scoreboard said HAVE A GREA SUMMER; the *t* had fallen off. "Nic's in Greece." I said it so quietly, I didn't know if he'd heard me. Lately, I'd had the strange feeling I'd invented Nic.

"Without you?" His hands rested on the knees of his jeans. They seemed so mature, like someone's father's hands.

"He's house hunting. We're supposed to move there." Sprinklers went on in the field. I felt a fine spray mist my legs. It felt good. "We've been talking about it for years." I pulled my hair off my neck.

He glanced at me. "Is that what you want?"

It'd been so long since anyone had asked me that. "No." He nodded as though that were the most normal thing in the world.

"Is it nice?" I asked. "Living in your parents' house?"

"Yeah, but sometimes I'm embarrassed as hell about it." His voice was relaxed, and he grinned.

"Why?"

His shoulder brushed mine. "I don't know. When they left, we rented it out for a while because I thought it was lame wanting to move back to Colston. But I couldn't stand having someone else living in it. And then I got the job at Yale. But when I was renovating, I had this fucked-up feeling I was trying to redo something about my past." He squinted at me.

My breathing went screwy. He was so close, all I would have had to do was lean in and our lips would have touched. That was what I remembered most about him, how soft his lips were. "I want to see the inside of it." The sprinklers stuttered and turned. I could feel the heat from him. Everything in me pulsed. I needed him to kiss me.

"I don't care if you're married," he said quietly. "I don't give a shit about him."

I stared at the collar of his shirt, the curly hairs. *Did losing Will fuck up your life?* I wanted to ask. *Do you even know who you are now?* The sprinklers shut off, and the night went eerily quiet. Out in the field, again, was that circle of football players; I could see the ambulance, the stretcher, a younger Ryder running beside it. I didn't want to feel guilty anymore.

"It's always been you." His voice was almost a whisper.

A breeze kicked up, and I saw now that thunderheads had gathered to the north. I pressed myself into him, put my head against his clean white shirt, and listened to his steady heartbeat. "We need to tell my parents," I said. "We have to tell them about Will."

I felt his hand go up to my neck. It felt good. "Now?" How many times had he tried to get me to tell before I went to Andover? "Your dad still has a couple more weeks of radiation." I felt his lips on my head. He touched my waist. It was crazy, how hard my heart was beating. "I don't think we should do anything now that could set him back." I could hear the doctor in his voice. I hated it.

The wind picked up. I could feel other hot, sticky places where my sweat had dried. *If I could only take off my clothes and lie in the grass with him,* I thought. "My life hasn't made sense since that night," I whispered. I buried my face in his neck. He smelled like my childhood, like summer and hope. "I lost everything," I told him. "And I want it back."

21

My dad and I waited until the carousel closed for the night before walking the block to the park. I carried the picnic basket, heavy with sparkling water and crab salad sandwiches. Will would have been thirty-one today. Thirteen years of silently singing "Happy Birthday" to him, thirteen years of thinking about this place, of remembering the cherry red carousel horse and the smell of steamed lobster in the barbecue pit, waterskiing off Luke's boat, setting off illegal fireworks.

We walked across the parking lot. The blacktop had sprouted weeds, and beer cans littered the grass. My dad slipped through a break in the chain link, and I followed. We walked down the overgrown grassy slope to the beach. The horses watched us, mid-gallop, their eyes open, bits in their mouths. They seemed smaller than they had when we were kids, chipped and worn.

On Will's seventeenth birthday, I'd ridden the cherry red horse while Ryder watched me from the pier. Our plan had been for me to sneak out after the party ended, he'd be waiting for me, and we'd come back, climb the seventy-four stone steps to the lighthouse, and lay his sleeping bag down in the tower. But Will had wanted Ryder to stay and watch *King Kong* when we got home, and Ryder and I had sat there, separated by Will, who never fell asleep. Finally, I'd drifted off on the sectional with the mad thought that Will had known our plan, and ruined it.

My dad spread out the checkerboard blanket. His hair had thinned a bit around the radiation site. "Do you come here every year?" I almost didn't want to know.

"Try to," he said. He rested on his knees, the water lapping against the beach. "Last year, there were a bunch of kids horsing around." He smoothed one of the blanket's corners. "So I just stayed in the car."

I thought about being in Santa Fe with Nic, not telling him it was Will's birthday. Not calling home. I watched the tide come in and retreat. The air had been still and thick like this that last year, and I could still see Will standing on the yellow horse's back, going around on the carousel, balancing like a rodeo star while Jamie shrieked from the side. Later, he'd sung "Happy Birthday" to himself when Jamie brought out the cake, his arm around Ryder, a little drunk on Gosling's and ginger beer. They'd been eating Life Savers like crazy, trying to hide it from our parents. He'd laid his head on Jamie's shoulder after he'd blown the candles out. "If my wish comes true, I'm going big-time."

She knew he was drunk—she must have—but she just kissed him on the head. "Of course you are, sweetheart," she'd said.

I hadn't wanted to come to the park, but my father told me Jamie couldn't bear to be here, and I didn't want him to be alone. He'd been acting odd lately, forgetting things, falling asleep at the dinner table, not being able to keep his head up when we watched movies at night.

"The sunsets here are spectacular," he said, shaking the sand off his flip-flops. But we'd come too late for the sunset, and the sky over the harbor was clouding over, already losing its deep magentas to dark violets and maroons. I looked out at the breakwater, where they said ships used to get tangled in the rocks before the lighthouse was built. "You're a good girl, coming here with your old man." He'd said that a bunch of times already, and it made me feel guiltier.

"I always remember that lighthouse on his birthday," I said.

"And you send forget-me-nots to his grave." He watched me dig a piece of conch shell out of the sand.

"How'd you know?"

He smiled. "I know my Jensen. Quiet about the good she does."

"He used to make tuba noises with these," I said, holding up the half shell. "The whole ones." I passed the piece to him, and he turned it around in his fingers.

"He was good at stuff like that," he said. "Remember the duck call he used to do?"

"I hated that sound," I said meanly. I could feel my father staring at me, and I pushed my feet into the sand, burying my toes. "Sorry," I said. "I'm ugly. Sometimes I say ugly things."

He shook his head. "You're not ugly."

Heat lightning lit up the rail around the lighthouse. "I am." Thunder followed several seconds later. I could hear the belligerence in my voice, could feel the anger rising. "I'm not what you think." I suddenly felt claustrophobic, being with my dad, who ignored that I'd fucked everything up, called me his "good girl" even though I'd hardly been home in thirteen years. Now with only one more week of radiation left, I'd be back in Santa Fe before we knew it, never having told him the truth.

"Well," he said, "if that old wives' tale is true, we only have about ten minutes until the storm hits. What do you say we eat?"

His shirt had a line of sweat down the middle. He reached over and opened the picnic basket.

"You know the night Will died?" I dug my fingernails into my leg. "Remember that ER doctor kept asking if he'd had another accident after the game?" I felt a drop of rain on my neck.

My dad took his glasses off and stuck the arm in his ear. "Sure, of course I remember."

"He did, Daddy." A seagull called, a desperate sound.

He blinked at me. "An accident?"

I nodded.

He paused, as if trying to remember the words. "What kind of accident?"

I felt like I had when I used to get those awful fevers as a kid: My skin was hot, but my insides were cold. My voice came out as though I were talking in a foreign language. "Will hit his head on the fireplace." I said it very quickly. The words floated between us, vulgar and obscene. My father opened his mouth. I felt as though I were shrinking. "Will told Ryder not to date me, but we . . ." How could I explain it? How could I tell him I'd been about to have sex with Ryder, and that Will had come down and I'd pushed him so hard, he'd hit his head a second time? How could I say all that and not make it sordid and horrible? "Will came down, and Ryder and I were on the couch. We were . . . together; it was nothing bad. Will got mad, and he came at Ryder—"

"Jensen." My father laughed, a short, odd bark. "You're not making sense."

I spoke quickly. "I didn't tell you until now because I was scared; I was afraid you wouldn't love me anymore." I realized I was crying.

He stared at me. His face had changed to carven stone. It was a look I'd seen before, but it had never, ever been directed at me. "Tell me what happened," he said.

The waves were bigger now, slamming against the beach. "That's why I went to boarding school." Another roll of thunder hit. "Because I couldn't stand for you to see me after what I'd done."

"What"—his voice was rigid—"did you do?"

I swallowed. I had to speak loudly because of the waves, because of the thunder. It was raining harder now and I felt it on the back of my neck, on my head. It occurred to me it had been raining the day I told Mandy, too, as though the sky were commiserating, crying. "When Will found Ryder and me on the couch, he hit Ryder. He was threatening him, so I pushed him, and then I pushed him again. I was mad; he—"

But my father cut me off. "What happened to him? What happened to Will?"

Oh Jesus. Why? Why had I started to tell him? I couldn't stop now; the words were running all over themselves. "He stumbled backward. And his head hit the hearth. He wasn't breathing, so we called nine one one and . . ." I told him I didn't mean to; I must have said it a hundred times. "It was an accident," I said. I was cold, shivering. "Will was so mad, he hit Ryder." I realized I was blaming him. Blaming my dead brother. "Daddy," I said. "Please . . . I didn't mean it . . . I shouldn't have told you."

But my dad did what I'd been hoping he wouldn't do: He stood up. He walked backward a few steps, then stopped. "That must have been terrible for you." His voice was choked, as though he were holding something back, an entire city. "Keeping this to yourself all this time."

"I'm sorry, Daddy." I was still kneeling on the beach. "Please, I don't know why I told you like this—"

But his words ran right over me. "I'm glad you did." And then he put his pointer finger up as though he was going to say one more thing, but he never did. He just turned and walked away, past the carousel, up the grassy slope, small and hunched, his blond hair windblown, his feet sinking into the damp sod.

And then he found that little break in the chain-link fence and went through it, leaving me alone on the beach with that wet picnic basket and those horses in mid-flight, their eyes wide open.

22

J.J. Why are you here?" Mandy rolled down the passenger window. She was wearing her hair in two long braids. Her T-shirt read TELL YOUR BOYFRIEND TO QUIT CALLING ME.

I put the picnic basket in the back of her Touareg and got in the car, my arms crossed in front of me. I was shivering, but I didn't feel cold. She pulled out. "Where am I taking you?"

"I can't go home," I told her.

"Okay." She dragged the word out several syllables. She smelled like the silver iodide she used to emulsify film. "Let's go to my place."

I glanced back at the lighthouse, blinking in the dark. Hours before, it had seemed cozy, welcoming; now it was a warning signal.

"Is it your dad?" she asked.

I nodded.

"Is he okay?"

I didn't answer.

"J.J., you're scaring me."

But I told her I didn't want to talk about it, and Mandy, being Mandy, just turned on the radio and let me sit there like a ghost in the car.

At her apartment, she led me through the hallway, which was covered in African masks and Balinese art, and plopped me down on the overstuffed couch. I was shivering and couldn't seem to do anything but stare at that row of little matryoshka dolls she'd brought home from Kaliningrad. Each figurine was smaller than the one before. I counted thirteen, an unlucky number. The last was half the size of my pinkie. I heard Mandy taking the glass top off the decanter at the antique tea caddy she called her bar. "Here." She handed me a glass of something that might have been brandy. A tapestry hung against a back wall. She'd sent an identical one to me in Santa Fe after she'd been shooting okapi and white rhino in the Congo.

She took a sip of the brandy. "What the hell is going on?"

"I told him."

Her eyes widened. "Your dad?"

I nodded.

"Just now?" Her windows were open, and it smelled misty and wet. I could see the New Haven Green sprawled out below us. "What did he say?"

I was completely numb. I couldn't feel anything. I tried wriggling my toes. "He just"—I shrugged—"walked away."

"Jesus. What did you tell him? I mean . . ."

"I told him Will came downstairs that night and found Ryder and me on the couch, and I pushed him, and he hit his head." I wanted to tell him that I hadn't hit Will that hard. That I didn't think I was strong enough to knock him down. I couldn't believe I'd told him on Will's birthday. I couldn't stop seeing him going through the chain link. "And then he left."

"J.J." Mandy put her brandy glass on the table. "You're ringing."

The Velvet Underground song was playing. Ryder. I held my phone, staring at it. "What if my dad went over to Ryder's with a shotgun?"

She grabbed the phone from me and pressed the green answer button. "Your dad is a Democrat." She handed it to me. "He's anti-firearms."

I gulped the drink. It burned going down. "Hey, Ryder." I tried to sound like I wasn't falling apart.

"Jenny." His voice was tight. "You need to get to the hospital right now."

"The hospital?"

Mandy scooted over to listen, and I held the phone between us. "Your dad's had a seizure." He had the same flat, slightly patronizing tone he used when I'd overheard him talking to patients, his Mr. Rogers voice. "And he's unconscious."

Mandy was already shoving her feet in a pair of sandals. "I'll drive."

When we got to her car, she put me into the passenger's side. "I'm not drunk, Mand. I can do it." But I slunk down in the seat and let her strap me in. "I never should have told him," I said. She didn't answer. She just patted my arm and shut the door. I watched her run to the driver's side. I wanted to take it back, all of it.

Mandy talked loudly and quickly as she drove, too fast, toward the hospital. "Listen, this didn't happen because you told him. You know things like that don't happen. You don't have a seizure because you're surprised. He probably—" But her voice became just noise, I couldn't really hear the words. Restaurants zipped by, all-night gas stations, grocery stores. Luke was full of shit. There was no relief in telling the truth. I thought of my dad at the roller coaster that day, of his eyes rolling back. I wondered if he'd been alone after he left the beach.

Stopped at the red light on Howard and York, Mandy banged the steering wheel. "Hurry up." She honked at a group of kids crossing in front of the car; the girls had on bathing suit tops, and the boys' shirts were untucked. They were laughing, walking in that careless way of people who have their whole lives ahead of them and nothing to regret. As soon as the last one got an inch past her bumper, Mandy pushed down on the gas and sped through the light.

In the ER, she grabbed my hand and dragged me to a balding doctor who was reading a chart. "Sterling Reilly," she said.

The doctor closed the file and took off his rimless glasses. "Through the double doors, take a left." He sized me up. "Room one thirteen."

Mandy pulled me down the hall and around the corner, and just as we got there, Dale came out of the room. "Jensen," she said.

"What happened? Is Ryder here?"

"He got called away." She was standing in front of the door like a linebacker, defending it. She glanced at Mandy.

"She's my best friend," I said.

Dale raised her eyebrows. "Why don't you have a seat?" She nodded to a folding chair across the hall. I sat on the edge of it, and Dale stayed standing. Mandy hung back, reading a bulletin board.

"What happened?" I asked. My clothes were sandy and dirty, and I was still shivering.

"Your father is very sick. He's lost consciousness." She pushed her hair behind her ear. She was wearing ladybug earrings, which reminded me of a child's jewelry box. "His temperature is almost a hundred and four, and your mother said the seizure lasted several minutes. We're not sure what caused it." I touched the fray of my jean shorts. I hated Jamie for being with him when I wasn't. "Jenny," she said.

"It's Jensen," I told her.

"But Ryder . . ."

"He's the only one."

"Okay, Jensen." She seemed to draw up into herself. "Has he been acting strange lately?"

"Define *strange*." I felt cut off from myself. "Is it strange that he can't think of words like *yogurt* and *chair*? And that he goes from sitting at the kitchen table, talking about our plans for the weekend, to crying uncontrollably for no reason?"

"Aphasia is part of the disease. I'm talking about new symptoms. Anything you can tell me could help."

At dinner the night before, Luke had asked my dad to pass the tofu steaks, but he couldn't make his fingers connect to the platter. "He's been grabbing at the air, like he's trying to catch something."

Her back stiffened. "How often?"

I could tell by the tone of her voice that something was wrong. "I don't know, a few times a day for the last three days."

"He could have been having an aura," she said. Jesus, now she sounded like Luke. "It's a prelude to a seizure," she explained.

I felt a wash of relief. Maybe it wasn't because I'd told. "If I'd known what it was," I said, "I would have brought him in. I just thought we were so close to the end of radiation, he must be getting better."

She ignored this. "We need to get him to radiology as soon as possible." She held her breath for a moment. She was infuriatingly calm. "We'll run a series of tests." She continued in her level voice. *Stop it,* I wanted to scream at her. "And then we'll have a clearer idea of what stressed his system."

I knew exactly what had stressed his system. "Luke is with your mother at the cafeteria. She was very upset, and I asked him to take her out of the room. I'll check in again soon." She walked purposefully down the hall.

"I'm going in," I told Mandy.

When I pushed open his door, the room was dark and quiet. It smelled like ammonia. My dad was completely still, his face pale and waxy. His eyes were closed. I thought of what Dale had said: *Your father is very sick.* Leaning over the metal rail, I put my lips to his forehead just like he'd done to me a thousand times when I was a kid. He was really hot. Putting my ear against his thin hospital gown, I could hear him breathing.

I stayed like that for a long time, watching the lights go up and down on the screen above us, listening to that steady, hypnotizing heartbeat. Finally, I raised my head and pushed the lever that lowered the safety bar. I lay next to him. He didn't move when I wrapped my hand around his belly and put my head on his shoulder. His mouth was open a little, and I could hear a whistling sound through his nose when he exhaled. "Hey, Dad," I said. Beyond him, the window shade was up. On the street below, cars sped through green lights; people stood at the corner of York and Legion, waiting to cross. I didn't think any of them could have known pain like this. Very softly, I touched his cheek, his wiry blond eyebrows, and the tiny veins in his lids. "I'm sorry," I whispered.

Lying there next to him, half-falling off the bed, listening to the beeps of his vitals, I knew I shouldn't have been so stupid as to think people lived forever. I should have come home when he asked, shouldn't have missed a single holiday, should have gone on all those trips to California when he'd invited me. I should have had him out to Santa Fe every chance I got, stayed up late playing gin rummy, like we used to. Now I would have done anything to save him—cut off my arm, blinded myself, given up every single year I'd spent in New Mexico, every vacation to Greece. I should have sat there on the carousel beach, eating the crab salad sandwiches in the rain, remembering Will, instead of believing for some reason it was a good idea to tell the truth.

23

My father slept through that night and into the next day and the one after that, until I lost track of the hours and eventually the days. The light drained out of his face, as though I were looking at a stranger. I replayed how he'd stepped away from me as if his bones had been put together wrong. I felt that adrenaline burst of regret every time I thought about it.

Dale and Ryder came and went. I hadn't really talked to Ryder since the night at Hamilton, when we'd almost kissed. Every time he came into the room, he was brusque, businesslike, as though somehow he knew that I'd told. I commanded myself to take him aside and let him know what had happened, but then I couldn't do it. I just sat in that room hour after hour, not speaking.

I wanted Nic. He had a way of dismissing things. He knew how to brush things away and to make like everything would be fine. He didn't allow vulnerability or doubt. He believed things turned out how they were supposed to. And his stance on the past was not to think about it. "What's done is done," he liked to say. "Life happens in the moment." I needed to hear that right now. I needed to feel that the past was small, insignificant. That nothing from before could have done this to my father.

I called Nic again and again, listening to the staticky ring. It seemed like no one had answering machines in Greece. I thought he must be in Chania by now, strolling down those cobblestone streets, perusing whitewashed houses with Realtors. He'd be swimming in turquoise waters next to topless European women. He believed that soon my dad's radiation would be done and we'd be meeting back in Santa Fe. I put the phone on the windowsill and pulled at the jeans Mandy had brought in for me. I'd already spilled hospital coffee on them, and Jamie had gone to get me another cup.

From the stiff, cracked couch, I watched my dad. His face shone with a thin sheen of sweat, which made me think of the dead. The room was very still. Everything smelled like antiseptic and brand-new rubber. I leaned back on the couch, closed my eyes, and listened to the wall clock tick. I felt dirty, unloved, and selfish. All this time my father had been sick, I'd been begging God, or whomever, to keep him healthy, but now I was half glad for this fever that wouldn't go away. It kept us from having to talk about what I'd done.

Jamie came through the door, holding a cardboard tray of drinks. "I ran into Dale and Ryder," she said. "They want to do another MRI to compare to the one they did when he first got here."

Dale and Ryder. Ryder and Dale. It sounded like the beginning of a nursery rhyme. She put the drinks on the table and wedged herself on the side of the bed. I watched her stroke my dad's cheek tenderly. He didn't stir. She'd been the same way with Will, comforted him through bruised ribs and lost games. She'd nurtured him in a way she hadn't been able to do with me.

"I'm going to brush my teeth," I said. But before I could, the door opened and a chubby nurse rolled in a wheelchair and parked it by the bed. Jamie stood up and lowered the rail while the nurse removed the IV line from his port. "Time to go for a ride, Mr. Reilly," the nurse said in a voice so perky it made me want to smother her.

She put a pulse ox on his finger. My dad opened his eyes, taking in the room. He was usually only awake long enough to eat a couple

bites of food and to go to the bathroom; and then he was often sus-
picious of us. He thought we were impersonating his family. He
hadn't recognized me in days. Now he couldn't seem to focus. I
went to the side of his bed. "Hey, Daddy."

"Ma'am"—his voice cracked—"could you tell the cruise director
I ordered the salmon?"

The nurse straightened his IV line. Her name tag said KATI, with
a tiny heart above the *i*. "That happens with fevers." As if I didn't
know that by now. "You're in the hospital, Mr. Reilly." Her words
were too loud, too slow. She slipped the monitor off his left index
finger. "We need to take you down the hall." She helped him up. "To
take some pictures."

He sat there, his knees bare, pulling at his hands. "Daddy," I said.
"They're going to do a scan of your head."

He seemed to take that as a cue and stood. He'd been obedient,
the peacekeeper among his brothers. We lowered him into the chair.
Dale appeared and propped open the door with her foot. "He's still
really hot," I told her.

"I'll order some more acetaminophen," she said. "But right now,
we have to get him to radiology."

"Where's that?" Jamie ran a hand through her hair.

"Third floor."

The nurse turned the chair around.

"Wait," Jamie said. "I'm going with him."

"You'll have to stay in the waiting area," Kati told her.

Jamie came up behind the nurse and slid her out of the way. "I
don't care," she said. "He's my husband." I watched them leave the
room.

Half an hour later, Ryder came in. He was wearing blue scrubs
and had circles under his eyes. I sat up on the couch.

"Hey," I said.

"The scan is clean." There was no inflection in his voice, no clue
as to what he was thinking, but I got the feeling something was really wrong.

"What do you mean? The tumor's gone?" I couldn't believe it. "But he's not done with radiation."

He nodded. His face was tight, sculpted from wax.

"Isn't that good news?" I asked.

The chubby nurse rolled in the wheelchair. My dad was sleeping in it. His chin had drooped to his chest—so undignified, I wanted to cry. Jamie and Dale came in behind them. Dale was holding a clipboard. She was forever clutching clipboards and writing things on charts.

"No tumor," I said to Ryder, "is what we were after. It's what we want. Right?"

Dale glanced at Ryder, and then she dropped the clipboard on the table with a loud clang. No one moved. She seemed angry. "The mass is no longer present," she said, "so this seizure wasn't caused by new tumor growth, which means we don't know why it happened." She crossed her arms over her chest. I felt that horrible panic return.

I watched Jamie help the nurse move my father from the wheelchair to the bed. I heard her cooing to him. "That's my boy," she said.

My stomach was up in my throat. *Tell Ryder*, I told myself. *Tell him what you did.* "What now?" I asked.

"I believe he's hyponatremic," Dale said.

"What does that mean?"

"His sodium levels are low. He was dehydrated when he got here," Ryder said. "So we put him on a wide-open IV saline drip. But saline can dilute the body's intravascular sodium. Unfortunately, people with brain disorders are particularly sensitive to changes in sodium levels. In extreme cases, it can cause disorientation. We believe that's what's going on here." We all looked at my dad, who had not been coherent for more than a minute or two since the seizure. My mother leaned over him and kissed his cheek. The nurse released the wheelchair brake with her foot and left. "Reintroducing sodium too fast can have devastating neurological implications. So we'll add a slow drip and see if we can get Sterling to join the land of the living," Ryder told the room.

In high school, I swore Ryder could read my mind. He'd scratch the unreachable place under my shoulder blade before I even knew it itched, and he was always finishing my sentences or climbing up the oak tree to my window on nights when I silently prayed he'd come. Now I stared at him, I didn't want to ask him why, if it was only sodium, my dad had this enormous fever. I just wanted him to promise me my father would be okay. "Try not to worry. It's probably an infection we haven't tested for yet." He glanced at Dale and then back to me. "It won't last forever."

24

Jamie and I took turns staying at the hospital. At night, I crammed myself on the cold leathery couch in the corner, but I could never sleep. Even though the tumor was gone, my father's fever still wouldn't break. He wasn't eating, and his collarbone stuck out like a boomerang.

We were having another heat wave, but inside his room it was cool and dark. IVs pumped saline, meds, and liquid nutrients into his body. Only Jamie could get him to open his mouth for a spoonful of chocolate pudding or a bite of banana once in a while. Watching her feed him, wiping the sides of his mouth, coaxing him with songs and childish noises, I kept thinking of what she'd said to me in the kitchen. I was beginning to realize that she wasn't alone in what had happened between her and my father after Will died.

Dale came in and out, blaming infection, contamination, viruses, anything but the radiation. Specialists were called, and they tested him for everything from malaria to AIDS. I asked a team of fellows visiting from the UK if they thought my dad had been shooting up in the jungle. No one thought it was funny. I stayed by his bedside every day. Vigilance didn't reverse the guilt, but it held it at bay.

In my notebook, I tracked the number of words he spoke and his temperature, whether his sleep seemed restless or peaceful.

On the eighth morning, I walked out of the bathroom, to find a male nurse at the sink, filling a pink plastic tub with water. Jamie had kicked off her high heels and was helping my dad out of his johnny.

"Time for his bath," the nurse said to me. He resembled Hadley, with his high cheekbones and his soft blond hair, and I realized then that Hadley had left on his European tour and that I'd never gotten to say good-bye. "You might want to get a cup of coffee." He looked me up and down. "Or a double cheeseburger—with bacon."

"Yes, sweetheart." Jamie stood up. "You need a break."

I told her I'd go home and water her garden. I drove back to Colston in ninety-degree heat. We used the house only as a locker room now, a place to shower and change clothes. Wandering through the rooms felt strange, as if the house were holding a secret that swirled with the dust cones in the living room.

I went into the hall bathroom, splashed my face with water, and stared at myself in the mirror. My skin was gray from not being outside, and my rib cage was poking out at an awful angle. When Will died, I'd done the same thing. Food was abhorrent. The smell of it had made me feel like I was going to vomit. I remembered pushing it around my plate, and Jamie watching me with eagle eyes. "You don't have any weight to lose, sweetheart," she'd say in her quick, hard voice. Both my pediatrician and an ophthalmologist had told me that malnutrition could have caused my night blindness, but I didn't care. One of my favorite things to do with Will and Ryder had been to sneak onto the golf course at the Colston Country Club or lie on the fifty-yard line at the Hamilton High School field and watch the stars. I'd wanted to tell those stupid doctors that since Will was dead and I'd lost Ryder, it hardly mattered that I could no longer see at night.

Along the south side of the house, I went to work watering Jamie's garden. The storm on Will's birthday hadn't given us much rain, and we'd had eight days of heat. I watched the water stream over her water lilies. They were wilted now, ready to die. "Peace and new life," she'd told me one day after I'd been back a month. I was sunning myself on a lawn chair, and she was weeding. "And those"— she pointed to the magnolias—"mean perseverance." I'd watched her hands moving deftly, pulling weeds. "I planted them right after Luke started counseling me," she'd said.

I watered quickly, facing away from the sun, trying to hurry so I could get back to my dad. All those years my mother had been muddling through, getting by, and what had happened to make her come around? "I helped her learn how to comfort herself," Luke had told me that day at his house. I stopped watering and touched the leaves. *Peace and new life.* I thought of my father going through that break in the chain link, thought of him lying there in the hospital bed day after day. And no one could figure out why. I looked at the lilies again. *Peace and new life.*

Jamie kept repeating, almost chantlike, that my dad would pull through, said he'd be fine. I felt sweat trickling between my shoulder blades. But she didn't know what I'd done. A slight breeze kicked up, and I could smell the earth. I'd been hiding out half my life. And the one time I faced what had happened, the one time I told the truth and things didn't go right, I'd started hiding again. I dropped the watering can. I had to tell Ryder that I'd told my father. No matter the consequences. And if I didn't do it right then, I might lose my nerve.

It took me twenty minutes to shower and change clothes, and then I was back at the hospital, waiting in Ryder's reception area.

Scott slid open the glass partition. "I'm sorry. He's on the phone. Damn insurance companies. They're going to put us all out of—"

"It's an emergency."

"Sorry." He lisped and shrugged his shoulders in an exaggerated way. "He can see you tomorrow at ten." He ran his finger down his appointment book, then added, "As long as his morning surgery is done by then." I saw his tongue worry that fat space between his teeth.

"Please, Scott." I found myself moving past him toward Ryder's office. "This is really important."

"Miss Reilly." Scott was practically shouting at me as I went down the hall, and I felt bad, ignoring him, but I couldn't help it. Ryder's door was closed, but I turned the knob.

"Miss Reilly," Scott called again. He was probably in love with Ryder, too. Who wasn't? "Stop," he called.

Ryder's head jerked up when I walked in his office. "I'll have to call you back," he said into the phone. I wondered if it was Dale. "No," he said into the mouthpiece. "I can't talk now."

Scott blew into the room behind me, but before he could speak, Ryder said, "She's fine." The door shut behind me.

Ryder stared at me. "Jenny? I'm glad you're here. I'm sorry I haven't seen you. It's just after that night at Hamilton when we . . . I just thought maybe we could both use some—"

"I told him," I said.

He blinked. "Told who, what?"

On the street below his window, midday traffic was scurrying along York. "My dad. I told him. I know you told me not to, that stress isn't good for him. But I had to." I said it quickly, without pausing to breathe. "I did what you told me not to, and here we are."

He pressed a black button on the phone, and a red light came on. "Scott, tell my next patient it might be a while." The light faded. "Jenny, the disease did this. Not you."

I slumped in the leather chair across from his desk, feeling weak suddenly, almost faint. "You don't know that," I said. *Please,* I thought, *make this not my fault. Make something, anything, not my fault.*

He came around the desk and squatted in front of me. "You didn't do this," he said firmly.

I watched him. "I did."

"No, you didn't."

"I told him, Ryder." I sounded like a child.

"It's all right." He put his hand on my knee. "Telling him didn't cause a seizure and a one-hundred-and-four-degree temperature for a week."

"Eight days," I said.

He nodded and gave me a sad smile. "Right, eight days."

"Ryder. I had to tell. I felt so . . ." There were tiny winches on the sailboat above his desk, books lining the walls, and diplomas framed and displayed. "Guilty."

He watched me.

I said it again.

"I know," he said quietly.

"But you told me you never felt guilty. You said—"

He slapped his hand on the arm of the chair. "Why do you think I took your father on as a patient?" I looked up at him. "To save him. To take it all back." His brown eyes were moist. "As a physician, I'm not supposed to take friends on as patients, but when your dad got sick, as fucked-up as this is"—he ran his hand through his hair—"I thought, *Here's my chance. Here's my chance to make up for what I did.* I thought, *Here's my chance at . . .*" He looked around the room, as if searching for the correct word.

"Redemption," I said for him.

"And what I said at East Rock was a lie." I felt his hand get firmer on my knee. "Will is the reason I'm a brain surgeon. It's why I broke my back getting through medical school in such a short time, why I'm constantly trying to cure people who are most likely going to die anyway." For the first time, I noticed circles under his eyes, worry lines on his forehead. "It's my whole fucking life. All I do is try to prove myself. I work all the time. I hardly sleep. I haven't been out to eat since I went with you to the Seafood Shack. I never visit my parents." I saw him on Will's handlebars when they were thirteen, grinning at me when they rode by the yard. "Every single day, I think about it. I don't want anyone to sleep with me, because I dream about it. I can't get a hold of myself." He took in a big breath. "Do you know how crazy this is making me? Something's wrong with your dad, and I can't figure out what. What if I screw this up, too? I have to"—he turned in his chair—"cure him." I felt a deep, almost exhausting relief wash over me. I wasn't alone. Ryder understood. I wanted to touch his face. I remembered the quick, hot feeling in my body when I was with him.

"It's all right," I told him quietly. I thought about my mother cheating, how much I'd hated her for it in high school. But now I was starting to understand. My parents had to be alone in their grief to be able to come back together. Being there with Ryder, feeling what I was feeling, I knew I'd been unfair to Jamie all those years. "It's okay." I felt myself move forward in the chair, felt myself reach over, and before I decided to do it, I was kissing him, kissing Ryder Anderson. And he was kissing me back; he was murmuring, "Jesus, Jenny." I heard him try to catch his breath. He said my name again. My fingers went to the buttons of his oxford shirt, his smooth skin. I thought maybe I would die from that urgency, from that hot, sure thing that bound him to me. It didn't feel horrible anymore to be alive. It felt so right. And then the intercom sputtered. Scott said his name, and Ryder jerked away from me.

25

I didn't talk about kissing Ryder. I didn't text Hadley, and I didn't tell Mandy or Luke. My dad's parents had passed away long ago, but Jamie's mother came and went. She flew in from Venice, Florida, a teetering old woman with bright red lipstick, an inch of powder on her face, and spindly legs. She talked too loudly and still pinched my cheeks. Like her daughter, she was a former beauty queen. Now she lived in a simple cape-style home a mile from the beach with a poodle and a man who loved her. Jamie was in a foul mood for the four days she was there, and then my father's brothers showed up, the whole pack of them, and stayed at the house for two days, eating up all the food and snoring and farting in their sleep, and Jamie really started to unravel. One day, she wore her bedroom slippers to the hospital. "Oh," she said when I pointed them out. "It was too much trouble to change." Her nails were breaking, and I could see gray roots starting in her part. Sometimes she didn't put on lipstick all day.

Mandy texted daily from Paris. *Any change?* she'd write. *No,* I'd write back. Hadley must have been busy on his tour, interviewing Latvian photographers or something, because I rarely heard from him. I kept calling Nic and got a couple of scratchy, broken calls back, but the connection was bad, and I couldn't tell if he could hear what I was saying.

Luke came every day, but he didn't tell stories anymore. He sat with his hands between his knees and his eyes closed, and I knew he was praying to whatever God had claimed him. When Ryder came, he tried too hard to be all business. There was something electric between us I couldn't name. We tried not to look at each other.

But as the days passed, and they were no closer to figuring out what was wrong with my dad, I sat vigil at his bedside and started to feel that kissing Ryder was like those mirages lost travelers have, where they see water in the desert moments before they die of dehydration.

I was in the cafeteria when I saw Dr. Griffith a second time, getting a coffee from the machine late one morning. When I turned around, he was standing there, watching me. We stared at each other. I remembered the night Will died, how we'd waited for him to tell us everything was going to be all right. That same sickle-shaped scar was standing out in bas relief now, and I saw his thick eyebrows twitching. "Are you sure he didn't hit his head again later on in the night?" he had asked. "Dr. Griffith," I heard myself saying now. "I'm Jensen. Jensen Reilly." I stepped forward, and saw recognition in his eyes. "Sterling Reilly's daughter." His swarthy skin flushed a deep red.

He came at me like he was going to shake my hand, then veered off to glance at the other people in the room. His eyes darted from one person to the next, as if he'd just shoplifted. Without speaking, he turned quickly and disappeared through the swinging doors.

When I got back upstairs, I sat on the couch while my dad slept and thought about how Griffith had been standing there in the middle of the cafeteria, as though he'd followed me there. As though he'd been watching me, waiting for me. And again I had that strange feeling that maybe it wasn't Griffith I'd seen. Maybe my mind was playing tricks on me. The door opened and Luke was standing there wearing a Hendrix T-shirt. He glanced at my father, who was sleeping, as usual, and then at me. "You need to get out," he told me.

"I went home yesterday to change."

"No." He walked across the room and gave me his hand. I could smell the sandalwood lotion he used when he played piano. "I mean out out. I have something to show you."

I let go of his smooth skin and sat on the end of my dad's bed. "How long will this take?"

He rolled his eyes. "Jesus, girl, your uncle Luke's not flying you to Spain. Come on."

Jamie had gone downstairs to get food with Sid and his wife, and I knew as long as they were here, Jamie wouldn't miss me.

We went in Luke's Navigator. It felt weird not to get on the highway to Colston right away. Just like every other time I'd been out, I envied the people bustling along the streets, so unconcerned. Their fathers weren't dying. We went out South Frontage and took a right onto Church Street. "I've lost count of the days," I said.

"Give Him time," Luke told me.

"If you mean the big Him, He better be coming up with a way to pull a cure out of His divine ass." He laughed, a quick, sad noise.

I watched Yale's Tudor dorm buildings pass. Back in high school, Ryder had talked about applying there, to stay close. I tried not to think about him.

"Don't you even want to guess?" We were passing the New Haven Green. I had no idea where he was taking me. "My T-shirt gives it away."

"Hendrix?"

He jiggled in his seat. "He played there, too."

"Played where?"

Luke grinned that famous smile. "Where you are going to play today. Right now."

A glimmer of excitement I hadn't felt in I didn't know how long sparked inside me.

"Holy shit. Luke?"

He nodded, his dreads bouncing.

I didn't want to say it aloud, in case I was wrong. But, sure enough, when we got to Woolsey Hall, Luke parked the Navigator in front of the Roman columns framing the door. This was where I used to see myself when I was a kid on Luke's piano bench, when he would say, "Picture yourself famous, baby girl, visualize." I'd imagine my parents in the audience under that beautiful round dome. Will and Ryder, too.

Luke took a key from his dash. "I reminded an old friend of a favor." He tossed the key in the air and caught it. "It's now or never, little Mozart."

Three students were sitting on the benches outside, smoking, and as they watched Luke work the key in Woolsey Hall's lock, I felt inflated, larger than life. "You ready?" he asked before he opened the door.

Inside, the place was silent. The only word I could think of as I stood under the vast ceiling was *holy*. The arched windows were shot through with an incredible light, which bounced off the ceiling's gold filigree. When I gazed up at the frescoes, I felt Luke's hand on the small of my back. "Yes, angel," he whispered, "God exists." He slipped his hand into mine and led me forward, our footsteps echoing in the huge space. My dad had held my hand like that, one night long ago. I was eight and Claude Frank, Seymour Lipkin, Christopher O'Reilly, and Jody Gelbogis DeSalvo had been playing here. I'd gotten to stay up past my bedtime, and my dad had worn a white silk scarf. He'd bought us front-row seats. I knew now, twenty years later, that my father didn't understand or care about piano concerts. He had done it just for me.

"I'll sit in Mr. Taft's seat." Luke took a wide seat in the front row. "You go on." I took one step and stopped. "Go on. Show me what I taught you."

The 1884 Alma-Tadema Steinway sat on the stage. Rumor had it that it had been bought at auction for more than a million dollars.

The walk to it felt endless. Luke appeared tiny in the front row. He sat with his hands folded in his lap. His patience reminded me of my kindergarten teacher, Miss Rettig, who used to kneel beside me while I worked on the *y* at the end of my name.

As soon as I sat down, I could feel them, those haunting ghosts people talked about whenever they mentioned Woolsey Hall. Luke had told me once they were melancholic spirits who played the organ in the middle of the night—wandering melodic phantoms. My hands moved lightly across the keys, fingering them restlessly. It took a while before they began to press down, to really move. I didn't play what I'd been practicing with Luke, the old Springsteen tunes or those Beatles songs that came so easily and brought back such acute nostalgia. I played something I hadn't remembered learning, Schumann's "Pleading Child" in D major. My fingers moved like wind, remembering; they flew across the keyboard as though ordered by a higher force. It hit me somewhere deep, the playing, and I almost started weeping. Except, it seemed, my hands were doing that for me.

When I finished, I stared at my fingers. Luke was silent, but I could feel him waiting. It seemed he was holding his breath.

"I kissed Ryder." The words echoed across the hall.

"Is that why you played so beautifully?"

"You liked it?" My voice was almost lost in the huge hall. "Did I do the right thing?"

He raised his eyebrows. "Kissing Ryder?"

"Marrying Nico." My fingers played with the keys, but no sound came out. I thought of the day that Nic had slipped the thin gold band on my ring finger. "I was only twenty-one," I said.

"None of us are static, Jensen." Luke pushed forward in his seat and put his elbows on his knees.

"What do you mean?"

"Change is our nature. We're made of water; water conducts energy, and energy is constantly shifting. What you felt back then isn't necessarily what's right today."

I watched him. He seemed perfect in that enormous space. "I'm afraid," I said.

"Fear," he told me, "is just resistance to the unknown."

This little lecture, delivered in Luke's reassuring, easygoing voice, made me feel better. But I said, "Until death do us part."

"Death can mean a lot of things," he shot back.

I didn't want to talk anymore. I wanted to play the piano. I wanted to play until my fingers bled. That's what I did. I played pieces that must have been living in my cells, songs whose names I couldn't remember, my feet moving on the brass pedals, my fingers liquid. I played hard and sometimes very fast, played until my knuckles rebelled, my hands stiffened, and my back hurt from sitting on that bench.

When I finally finished, the light had shifted. Luke was still sitting in William Howard Taft's oversized seat, tears running down his cheeks.

26

When I got back to the hospital, a man in blue clogs with a bunch of pens stuffed in his breast pocket was standing by my dad's bed. "I'm Dr. Waller." His name didn't sound familiar, but lately there'd been a constant stream of men and women with clipboards and white coats. They had a seeming inability to smile. "Infectious diseases." His accent sounded Australian.

"Jensen Reilly." I offered my hand. "Sterling's daughter." We shook. "I thought they already ruled out all the scary stuff."

"Well, we need to keep at it until we have an answer." The monitor near the top of the bed beeped, and he reached up and pressed a few buttons until the machine quieted. My dad never moved.

"Have you ever seen anything like this before?" I asked.

I wanted him to reassure me, but he dropped his eyes. "It's unusual for a fever not to respond to meds, even if only temporarily." He hung the chart on the metal hook at the foot of the bed. "There's a saying in the medical profession. 'When you hear hoofbeats—'"

"'Think horses,'" I said, finishing for him, "'not zebras.'" By now, I knew all the jargon.

"That's right." His smile was a little crooked. "We're all out of horses, so I guess I'm the zebra guy." He checked his watch. "I'm going to borrow him for about thirty minutes to examine him."

It took a second for me to understand he was asking me to leave. "I'll run down to get something to eat." I touched my dad's foot. "I hope you can find out what's wrong."

"Demetri and I went to Corfu," Nico told me as soon as he picked up. I was standing at the vending machines, trying to decide what to get. "I didn't get your messages until we got back." His voice sounded echoey and unfamiliar.

My phone beeped. Low battery. "Did you have a nice vacation?" I asked. I'd forgotten my charger at the house.

"Come on, J.," he said. "I went for us."

I chose a bag of pretzels, even though I was never hungry any-more. "Find any girls to paint on the nude beaches?" The bag dropped down. My phone beeped again.

"Jensen," he said, then stopped. I heard him take a deep breath. "How is he?"

Confused. Terrified. Dying. "It's been several weeks, and he still has a high fever." I slid down the wall and sat on the dirty floor with my pretzels. "When he comes to, which isn't very often, he has no idea where he is."

"Did the tumor grow or . . ."

"They don't know, okay?" I snapped. "No one fucking knows. He won't wake up, and all these supposed experts poke and prod him and stick needles in his arm, and he looks like a fucking refu-gee." My phone beeped again. "So ask me something easy, Nico, okay?"

"J., I'm coming," he said. His voice was calm, sure. This is what I loved about him. "My flight leaves in—" And then my phone beeped in my ear and went dead.

I stuffed it in my pocket and slid down the wall to sit on the floor. I let my mind go numb, I didn't want to think about Nic or

Greece. I didn't want to think about anything. I stared into space and just let myself do nothing. I don't know how long I sat there before I walked back to my dad's room with the bag of pretzels. Waller was gone.

"Will?" my father said as soon as I walked in. "Will?" He squinted at me. "Is that you?" His words were garbled. "Will?" He tried to sit up in bed.

"Dad." I shook him by the arm. "It's me, Jensen. You were dreaming."

He reached for his glasses. "I can't see." His voice was panicked. "I can't goddamn see."

I gently pulled his glasses away from his face and turned them right side up, slipping the arms over his ears. "Is that better?"

He stared at me. In the dim light, he seemed so much older. "Who are you?"

"Jenny." I thought he might recognize that name. "Your daughter."

"My daughter?" This seemed to panic him more. He pulled the sheets up to his chest. "What did you do with Will?" He reached for me, patting my face, pressing too hard. "Is that you, Will?"

My skin went cold. The monitor above his shoulder said his temperature was 105. I reached for the call button, but he threw up all over both of us. "I'm sorry." His voice was scared.

"It's okay." The vomit smell was medicinal, almost sweet from the glucose running through the tubes to his veins.

"I have to go to the bathroom," he said, and I immediately smelled urine. I lowered the bed rail, threw the covers off, and managed to get his feet over the side. Then I used all my weight to leverage him to a standing position. He wobbled for several seconds then grabbed the IV pole to steady himself. At first, I wasn't sure I could get him to the bathroom, but he was lighter than I expected. I thought about the dead dove Nic and I had found in a fallen nest last spring, how it almost felt like nothing when I put it in my palm. "We can do this," I told him.

He started to cry.

The bathroom was a few feet away, but it felt like a mile. Diarrhea puddled on the floor between his legs. I guided him around it. "Take small steps and don't let go of the pole."

But the walk to the bathroom took forever, and by the time I got him lowered onto the toilet, we were both exhausted. I curled his hand around the railing. Then I took off my sweatshirt, threw it in a corner, grabbed the trash can from under the sink, and placed it between his knees. "Will?" He waved his arms like a blind person; then he threw up again.

I turned on the shower, untied the strings of his gown, and wrestled his arms out of the holes. I was too scared to disconnect his IV, so I left his johnny hanging off his arm. I tried to pull his glasses off, but he pushed my hand away and held fast to them. I checked the water. It was lukewarm. "Dad," I told him. "I'm going to try to get you into the shower." I pried his fingers loose and helped him across the tiny bathroom, finally managing to lower him onto the handicap seat. Leaning his head against the wall, he closed his eyes. I went to work, squirting soap out of the dispenser onto a plastic loofah. As I made sudsy circles around his chest and arms, water seeped into my clothes and soaked my hair, and the vomit fell off him onto the shower floor.

The door swung open, and the nurse on duty poked her head in. "What's happened here?" Her eyes were wide with alarm.

"He's vomiting." I worried then that I shouldn't have moved him. "And his fever's gotten worse."

She put her hand through the water and turned the knob. Cold hit me like ice. I jumped back. "Sorry, we need to get his temperature down now. How many times did he throw up?"

"Three."

"Why didn't you call me?"

"I was all alone," I told her. My father's face was flushed, and he was sweating. "I didn't know what to do."

"You did fine," she said, her voice neither compassionate nor hostile. She unhooked his IV and tossed his gown in the corner. "Just keep him under the cold water, and I'll call the doctor and get someone to clean up. Can you handle this for now?"

"I don't think I—" But she was gone.

I moved farther down my dad's belly, soaping away the vomit, shivering in the cold. His eyes were wide open now, and he looked scared. "Hey, are you okay?" I asked him. He didn't answer. I felt like crying. I wanted to tell my dad about this. I wanted to call him on the phone and tell him I'd had a dream that he was really sick and that I'd had to get in the shower with him after he threw up on me, that I'd had to soap his bare body just as if he were a child. I wanted him to call me Whobaby and tell me how sorry he was for me. He didn't seem like the same person, this thin, naked man.

"Will?" he said again.

I stopped washing him. "Yeah?"

His eyes were still distant, but they got peaceful, like he'd slept a long time and had awakened satisfied.

"Jensen?" The nurse poked her head in again. "I brought help."

My father squinted at her and then at me. "Who?" he asked.

I watched him. "I'm Will," I said to her. "Sterling's son."

She drew the curtain back and reached in to turn off the shower. "Yes, you are," she said. She had a fresh johnny and two towels draped over her arm. "And what a handsome son you have, Mr. Reilly." She stepped in. "Let's get you up and at 'em." She toweled him off expertly while I stood there shivering in my wet clothes. She slipped his arms through the new gown and tied it in back. "You'll be fine, won't you, Mr. Reilly."

But I didn't think he'd ever be fine again.

When we got back to the room, the sheets had been changed and the floor was clean, but I could smell vomit beneath the antiseptic. "Can you lie down, Mr. Reilly?" the nurse asked.

My father's breathing was quick and labored. She managed to get him on the bed and pull his legs onto the mattress. I took off his glasses and dried them while she tucked the new sheet around him.

She had two syringes in her pocket, and she put them between her teeth. Pulling on one, she left the cap in her mouth and inserted the needle into the port below his elbow. "Phenergan for nausea." She did the same thing with the other. "And lorazepam to help him sleep." He seemed to drift off before she even got the second shot in, but his breathing was still labored, and his skin was jumping all over the place.

While she hooked him back up to the monitors, I stood there in my dripping clothes with a towel around my neck, watching him. The vein on his head was raised like a lightning strike. It beat a one-two rhythm, and once in a while a muscle in his cheek would twitch. I thought of the card tricks he used to teach me on the back deck while Jamie was doing the dishes and Will was at practice. The secret was having superfast moves.

The door opened, and Ryder came in. He was dressed in wrinkled brick red scrubs. A surgical mask hung around his neck. "A spiked fever and vomiting," the nurse said. She told him what medicines she had given him.

Ryder picked up my father's hand and took his pulse. He did that more than he checked the monitors, and there was something humane and reassuring about it. "He might be hemorrhaging." I didn't know if he was talking to the nurse or to me. A little louder, he said, "Hey, Sterling, my good man, what happened here?" But his voice wasn't cheerful or happy.

"What does that mean, hemorrhaging?" I asked.

"It's not good." His jaw flexed. "I need you to wait outside."

"Jesus, Ryder, why? What's the—"

But two nurses came in as if they'd been beckoned by some silent whistle, and he said something to them I couldn't hear. They went to work, unlocking the rails of the bed and gathering the plastic tubing that tethered my dad to his IVs. "Wait in the hall," Ryder told me. "Please."

I didn't move. A yellowish liquid dripped from the IV bag into my dad's veins. I counted the drips. "But he's had a fever for a couple of weeks," I said. "Why is he hemorrhaging now?"

"Please," the nurse said to me irritably. I waited for Ryder to say something more, and when he didn't, I let myself out.

In the hall, the cinder-block wall was cold and smooth on my back. *I'm not ready,* I kept saying in my head. *I'm not ready.* Finally, I got myself together and went to the nurses' station. "Can I call my mom?" I asked an older woman behind the desk. "I forgot my charger at home."

"Come back to the hospital as soon as you can," I told Jamie when she answered. "And call Luke."

I waited by his door, watching nurses run in and out, listening to their murmured voices. Ryder came out once, but he kept his back to me. He disappeared down the hall. A minute later, I heard a doctor being paged on the intercom. Ryder came back down the corridor. "Sorry for the wait," he said to me before he went back in the room.

Finally, Jamie rushed in, wearing old leggings and a zip-up hoodie she never wore out of the house. "What happened?" Right away, she started for the door.

"You can't go in there."

She jigged in place, like she was hopped up on pills. Her pupils were huge and her voice was too quick. "What in the world are you talking about? Of course—"

I put my hand on the door. "Ryder's in there with a shitload of nurses, and we have to stay out of the way."

She slumped against the wall. "I shouldn't have left him today." She glanced at the clock above me. It was just past eight. "I knew something bad was going to happen," she said, as though I had denied it. "There was something different in his eyes." Her face was bone white, and her movements were too quick, jerky. She was very sleep-deprived. It scared me to see her like that.

Two nurses went into his room, and then a doctor I'd never seen before, followed by an orderly pushing a gurney. "What are they doing?" Jamie put her hand over her heart.

"I'm here now." Luke was jogging down the hall in jeans and a Muddy Waters T-shirt. He went right to my mother and hugged her, and then he put out his other arm, and I fell into it. While we stood there, it occurred to me that everything Ryder and Dale had told us was bullshit. A clean scan didn't mean anything. Weeks of poisoning him with radiation had done nothing but make him sick. For all my willing and wishing and hoping and, thanks to Luke, praying, my dad might be dead before sunrise.

I knew I wouldn't be okay if something happened to him. I didn't know what would happen exactly, but I wouldn't make it. I thought I should tell someone this, but I had no one to tell. I leaned against Luke in my wet clothes and felt his chest pushing air in and out of his lungs. For the first time in my whole stupid life, I saw how breathing was a miracle.

A minute later, the door opened. Ryder's face was impermeable as stone. "We're taking him to intensive care," he said. "His organs are failing."

By the time they let us into the ICU, it was the middle of the night. Frontage Street was as quiet as I'd ever seen it. There was nothing comforting or quiet about this part of the hospital. Machines and monitors beeped and blinked constantly. Ryder was still in his scrubs, and he stood on the other side of the bed, holding my father's chart. "Medically speaking, we've done everything we can. He's medicated and shouldn't be in any pain. Now it's up to him." He looked at his watch. "I've got to run upstairs, but I told the nurses to page me if anything happens."

"Thank you, sweetheart," Jamie said.

"Don't thank me yet," Ryder told her. He squeezed the IV bag. "I haven't done a goddamn thing."

When he left, I went to my dad. With tubes up his nose, he didn't look like himself. His mouth was slightly open. He was pale, spent, and small. I took his hand. When I was a kid, I used to run my finger over his calluses, pinch them between my nails. "Does that hurt?" I'd ask. "Nope," he'd say. "Can't hurt me." Now his palm was smooth and soft. When I kissed him on the cheek, he smelled clean, almost powdery. I could hear Jamie behind me, crying softly. I pushed the hair from his forehead and ran my finger over a scar between his eyebrows. "It's okay," I told him. "You can go to Will." I wanted to scream, *Don't die. Don't you fucking die on me.* I felt like I was choking. "Go home to Will if you need to." I said it as peacefully as I could. Behind me, I heard Luke's voice. "I got Ryder's message that we could come in now. I've been in the chapel," he said. "I'll give him last rites."

"Can you do that?" I asked. *He can't die.*

"Faith is faith. This will just make his journey a little easier if he has to go." I watched Luke pull a small prayer book from his back pocket. He stood next to the bed and began speaking in an ancient language. He talked for a long time. Then he leaned close to my father's face and whispered in his ear. He brushed his lips across his mouth. My dad didn't move; he stayed very, very still, while those machines teased us with their maddening monotony, as though everything were just fine.

27

After Jamie and Luke had spent hours watching my dad lying unconscious, Ryder convinced them to lie down in the on-call room. Then he'd told the ICU nurses to let me stay with my dad. Just before dawn, I drifted off, cramped at an awful angle on a cold vinyl couch. When I woke, my head felt as if it were nailed to the cushion.

"Jensen?"

I opened my eyes.

"Jensen?"

My heart quit beating. I was almost afraid to look.

"What in God's name are you doing here?"

Slowly, I unfolded myself and turned, to find my father sitting up in bed. His skin was a healthy color, and he was struggling to put his glasses on straight. "Daddy?" I untangled my legs. "But I thought you . . ." I couldn't finish the sentence because I was crying. "All the doctors said . . ."

"Aw, Whobaby. Come here." I ran to him and hugged him. He smelled like medicine and rubbing alcohol, but he also smelled, unmistakably, like my father. "You're not going to get rid of me that easily." He kissed my head. "Your old man's still kicking." I watched him finger one of the stickers on his chest where the wires were attached.

"But you were so sick last night." I wiped my nose on my sleeve. "And Ryder came and gave you morphine, and—" I didn't know how much I should say.

He patted my hand. "Where's your mother?"

"Stay here." I grabbed Luke's cell phone from the bedside table. "I'll find her." I was worried if I let him out of my sight, he'd disappear. "Don't move."

"Where am I gonna go?" He blew me a kiss.

I almost ran into a black-haired nurse pushing a machine on wheels. "No cell phones in here," she said.

"My dad's better," I told her, calling my mother anyway.

The nurse abandoned the machine and ran to the room. "Mr. Reilly," I heard her say. "Good morning."

Jamie's ringtone sounded from down the hall. "Mom," I yelled. She and Luke were walking toward me. "He's back," I told them, shutting off the phone. "Daddy's back." Then I saw Ryder come through the double doors at a jog.

Back in the room, we crowded around my dad's bed. "Do you remember anything from last night?" I asked.

"Everything, Whobaby." He reached up and mussed my hair. "Even the part where you told me I could go . . ." He hesitated.

"In that case." I squeezed his fingers. "I have to ask what Luke whispered in your ear."

"He asked me to telepath where he'd left his keys."

Luke let out a belly laugh. He was always losing his keys.

"No, really," I said. "What did he say?"

"He said if it came to it, he'd take care of my girls."

There was a knock on the door; then it opened. Dr. Waller came in, wearing those same blue rubber clogs. "Welcome back, Mr. Reilly." He arranged the pens in his lab coat pocket, his big black eyes swimming behind thick glasses.

"Thank you, sir," my father said.

Dr. Waller stepped into the middle of the room. "Well, I'm fairly certain I know what caused the fever." We all held our breath. "And"—he smiled—"we can make sure it doesn't happen again."

Without thinking, I hugged him. He was a head taller than I was, and I ended up kissing his shoulder. I stepped away, a little mortified, but he didn't seem to notice.

"Keppra," he said, as if I'd never mauled him, "the antiseizure drug."

I almost jumped up and down. "Is there another one you can put him on? And why now? He's been on it for months."

"Hold up, Whobaby," my dad said. "Let the poor man speak."

"When you got sick last night," Dr. Waller said, taking the chart from the end of the bed, "Dr. Anderson"—he nodded to Ryder—"upped your morphine for pain control." He capped his pen. "But to prevent adverse side effects, he took you off everything else. It's common with end-stage patients." *End stage.* I felt disconnected, weak. "Keppra builds up in a person's system over time." When he took off his glasses, Waller's eyes appeared minuscule, like a mole's. He cleaned the lenses on his lab coat. "It's the only thing that makes sense. We'll watch you for twenty-four hours, and then, if you're still good, you can be on your way." Dr. Waller put his glasses back on and his eyes got huge again. "You almost had to die to get cured," he said. "How's that for irony?" I didn't want him to go. He'd figured something out that none of the other doctors had, not even Ryder.

"So, your scan is clean," Ryder said after Dr. Waller's clogs made a squishy exit on the floor. "Which means no tumor." Jamie kissed my father again, and he beamed. "But we should do one more zap with the radiation as planned, just to be sure, and you're going to need some PT. You've been lying in bed so long, your muscles will be weak."

"As long as I can go home soon." My dad blew Jamie a kiss. "And, Whobaby, you can finally go back to your life." He winked at me, and I winked back, but since he'd been in the hospital, I hadn't been thinking about going back to Santa Fe. With Nic out of communication and all my energy focused on my dad, it'd been easy to pretend Santa Fe didn't exist. I felt Ryder's eyes on me. And then the same black-haired nurse from the hallway saved me by coming in. "Party's over," she said. "We're moving the patient back down to the neuro floor."

Ryder nodded. "I've got to check in at the office anyway."

"You're coming to dinner as soon as I get out of this place." My father was letting the nurse help him up, his legs pale and thin, dangling off the bed. "Luke will cook."

"A feast for the gods," Luke said.

Jamie stood up. "I'll help you get settled," she told my dad.

"I need a shower," I said. "And I have to charge my phone."

"Whobaby," my father said as the nurse helped him into the wheelchair. "I'd like to talk to you."

I thought of him going through that break in the chain-link fence the night of Will's birthday. My belly went weak. "Okay."

He settled into the wheelchair, and I watched him close his eyes.

"You have plenty of time to talk, sweetheart." My mother slid in front of the nurse and took the wheelchair from her. "Now it's time to rest."

But my dad opened his eyes and searched mine. "Don't forget," he said. "Soon." He sounded stern, and he seemed to be speaking only to me.

28

When I got back to Colston, there were a ton of messages from Nic on my cell phone and even more on the home phone. He was arriving in New Haven that afternoon. The wall clock in the kitchen said he'd be landing in an hour. I had only a few minutes to shower, change, and call Mandy back. She'd just returned from France. "Come over," she said when I told her the news about my dad. "We'll celebrate."

"I can't," I said. "Nic's on his way."

She groaned.

"Mandy!"

"Well, it's just that now that your dad's better—I mean, I'm happy and all, of course—but now you'll have to go back to Santa Fe."

This was the first time I'd thought about it. "Yeah," I said. "But we'll see each other a lot before I leave."

"Okay." She sounded disappointed.

I hung up and got in the Lexus. My hair was still dripping wet. I raced up I-95, going about a hundred miles an hour.

Almost as soon as I parked in the arrivals area, I saw Nic coming toward me. He was tan, and the leather strap of his bag was slipping off his shoulder. Before I could say his name, he was squeezing me into a hug. He smelled like salt and fresh air. I ran my hand down his face. I'd never seen him with a beard.

"No time for shaving." He grinned. And then he kissed me full and deep on the mouth. When I drew back for air, he said, "We're moving there, J." He kissed me again, quickly this time, on the forehead. "I got the perfect place. You'll never believe it. A restored monastery with super-high ceilings, the best light, and the most spectacular view of the Ionian Sea."

A hard stone rose into my throat. "Really?"

"Yeah." He opened the driver's door, and I handed him the keys. "Wait until you see the pictures. You're going to love it. I tried to send photos from Crete, but the Internet was too slow. How's your old man?"

I got in on the passenger side. Nic always drove when we were together. I glanced at a new brass thumb ring and noticed that his hair was longer. He had that exotic look people got when they'd been abroad. I felt plain next to him, boring. "He's okay now."

"Now? What happened?"

"It's a long story."

He glanced at me so long, I thought we were going to get in an accident. "Is he still in the hospital? Do you want to go there?"

"Yes, but not now. Jamie texted a few minutes ago. He's sleeping."

"How about I take you to lunch, then? You're too skinny." He reached over, and I felt his fingers find my hand. He squeezed it. "I'm sorry I was MIA, J."

I didn't say anything to this. "We can go to Penny Lane Pub. It's right around the corner."

He held my hand while he drove and didn't let go when he shifted. "You look worn-out."

"I was up all night."

"But you're still beautiful."

I didn't want to hear about how pretty I was, especially when I looked like shit. "My father almost died last night. But one of the doctors figured out he was having a bad reaction to his antiseizure meds."

"But he's okay now?"

"I needed you, Nic." I watched the traffic behind us in the side-view mirror. "I kept trying to call you."

"I know, and I'm sorry." He brought my hand to his lips and kissed it. I felt myself go warm. "I'm sorry, sunshine. I would have come right away if I'd known."

I tried to smile, but something in me felt hard as stone. I kept imagining him and Demetri playing guitar on the beach while I sat in a hospital room getting pale and ugly. It made me want to start a fight and throw things at him. But I kept quiet, and we drove the rest of the way without talking.

Penny Lane Pub used to be a bowling alley. The jukebox was a giant bowling ball and the salt and pepper shakers were little bowl-ing pins. I kept glancing at Nic while we looked at the menu. I didn't know if it was the beard or his tan or how long his hair had gotten, but I felt like I was sitting across from a stranger. He still looked like that sexy sculptor I'd fallen in love with, but something was different.

He folded his menu and reached across the table for my hand. "I missed you, J. Every single day, I'd wake up wishing you were next to me."

Before I could answer, a skinny kid with spiked hair, black eye-liner, and bowling shoes recited the specials. I ordered a Swingshot Greek salad and Nic got a King Pin cheeseburger, fries, and a beer.

"Are you glad you went?" I could barely be civil to my husband, whom I hadn't seen in six weeks.

"Very," he said too easily. "But I missed you like crazy. I'm tell-ing you, Jensen, the view alone will take your breath away."

I kept my hands on my lap and looked out the window. "Glad you had a good time." The maples along College Street were start-ing to turn orange. Summer was ending without my even having realized it.

"Hey," he said. "Earth to my beautiful wife."

"Sorry, but I'm exhausted." The waiter set down our drinks.

He held his beer up to clink it against my water glass. "We'll get you all taken care of when—"

"Did you hear me? He almost died," I snapped. "If you had been here with me instead of sailing around the Greek isles with Demetri, you would have known that."

He swallowed. "I'm sorry. I don't know what else to say."

I wanted to deck him.

The waiter came back with our food. Will had always said they had the fastest service on the planet. Nic's burger was fat and delicious-looking, with juice dripping into the bun. Day after day of sitting vigil had meant eating only the slop in the cafeteria or bags of pretzels from the vending machine. I would have given anything to eat his burger, quickly, greedily, all by myself.

"I would have flown back. I already told you that."

I stabbed at an olive and didn't answer.

"Listen to me. I. Am. Sorry." I raised my eyes and he held my chin. "I'm just so excited and so goddamn happy to see you." He let his hand fall, and I didn't look away. "You won't believe the house I found for us. It has enough studio space for both of us and a garden, and you can even bring Hadley if you'll miss him too much."

I imagined moving six thousand miles away with Nic. A million times we'd talked about living there, but there was something lonely about it, terribly isolated. "I haven't talked to Hadley since he left for Croatia on his quest for photographers." I thought of Hadley's gallery, of the blue Santa Fe sky, and the square on market day, but it felt like a movie set I'd once visited. My whole world had washed away in the red-hot panic of my father's illness.

"What?" he asked. "Why are you looking at me like that?"

I kept studying his face. Something was different about him, and it wasn't the beard or the tan. *Maybe,* I thought, *something is different about me.*

"Look J., you know what I realized while I was away from you?"

I shook my head. "I've been taking you for granted. I want to start over in Greece. We're going to make it a lovers' paradise." He waited for me to speak, and when I didn't, he said, "I love you, Jensen." I couldn't remember how long it'd been since he'd said that to me. "And I'm never going to let you go."

My phone beeped with a text message. "Hurry up and eat. My dad's awake."

We visited with my dad for a few minutes, but he was still exhausted. After he dozed off again, Jamie told me to take Nic to the house. "Get a good night's sleep," she said when she kissed my cheek. "Daddy will be home in the morning."

When we got home, Nic showered after I did and then he came and lay next to me on my bed. I thought he was going to kiss me, but he just watched me. Finally, he spoke. "Do you remember the first time I sculpted you?"

I'd been so nervous. I'd taken my clothes off for plenty of boys since Ryder, but I'd never let any of them really see me. Nic was so intense with his work, choosing the smallest chisel for my cheekbones, sweeping the granite dust with a handmade down brush. I remembered him lifting my arms, tilting my hips, all the while talking to himself about light and shading.

He pushed back my hair. "I chose you because you didn't want to be noticed." It was rumored on campus that girls lined up at his apartment to ask if he would sculpt them. Walking home that day, I knew I should have felt proud—I'd landed the sexy professor, the famous sculptor—but I didn't feel anything except a vicious need to hide behind him. "Do you know why I used granite?" he asked.

I didn't answer.

"Because it's beautiful but impenetrable. Granite is forever. Marble corrodes over time. Granite never does."

I felt his hands under my blouse. He unbuttoned my shorts, slipped his fingers inside of me. All through lunch, I'd wondered if we still had that one thing that had kept us alive all these years: the intensity we got when we made love. But as we started to kiss, I couldn't find it. I didn't feel that hot current that usually went through me. He was hard against my leg, and he flipped me over so I was on my back, and then he ran his tongue down the center of my stomach, stopping at the thin strip of hair between my legs. He took me in his mouth, sliding a finger inside of me. For one instant, it burned, it had been so long. But then it felt familiar, and I found my mind drifting back to the hospital, to my father waking up that morning and Waller saying it was just the medication. The scan was clean. My dad was going to be okay.

"What's wrong?" Nic touched my face; his fingers were rough.

"Nothing."

"I get the feeling you don't really want this."

I couldn't imagine how he knew that. "Why would you think that?"

He came up and lay beside me again. "Knowing what you're thinking is my secret superpower. Everyone has one."

"Oh yeah?" I propped myself up on my elbow. "What's mine?"

He watched me. "Making people love you even when they shouldn't."

"Ouch."

He tucked a few strands of hair behind my ear and then he drew me toward him. His skin was hot. The dark room around me was out of focus. I tried to squint, to make it come back, but it was all shadows. I settled, as best I could, into his chest. "I love you, Nico Ledakis," I said defensively.

He didn't say anything. And before long, he was asleep.

29

The next morning, Nic and I let my mom out at the front entrance of the hospital and parked the car. When we got to my
dad's room, Luke, Jamie, Mandy, Dale, and Ryder were all there.
Ryder glanced up when we came in the room, and I felt my face go
red. My dad was sitting in a wheelchair. Behind him, ready to deliver
him to Jamie's car, was the male nurse who'd told me to eat a burger.

"Obviously, we've taken him off the Keppra," Dale said to Jamie.
She never looked at me anymore. Then to my dad, she said, "I think
one more radiation treatment is all that's necessary, since your scans
are clean. I dare say after that we'll declare you cancer-free and good
to go."

"What about surgery?" I stared at Ryder. "I thought you were
going to resect the tumor once radiation was over."

He grinned at me. It made me want to kiss him. Or kill myself.
"There is no tumor to resect. It's over, Jenny. Your dad is as good as
new."

"Oh my God." I swallowed. "I didn't realize. It's really over?" My
father really was healthy.

"How in the world can we thank you?" Jamie held her hands out
to Dale and Ryder.

"No need to thank me," Dale said, squeezing my dad's shoulder. "It's my job."

Please. I turned my head so she wouldn't see me roll my eyes at Mandy, who rolled her eyes back.

Jamie threw up her hands. "Sterling, you're cured. Can we please go celebrate?"

"Technically," Dale said, "Sterling's not cured." I sucked in my breath. "He's in remission. But that alone is cause for celebration." The room erupted in a cheer, and everyone hugged and clapped and high-fived one another. Ryder and I weren't looking at each other, and I could barely stand to be next to Nic. I just wanted to get the hell out of there.

In the parking garage, my dad's gait was steady, and his cheeks still had that healthy color. He hadn't looked this good since I'd been home. Mandy kissed him good-bye and said she'd stop by later in the week to check on him. "Good to see you, Nic." She gave him a quick, annoyed smile. "How long are you staying?"

"Actually, I'm off to New York in a few days to set up my fall show at the Chelsea Gallery. From there, I'll fly back to Santa Fe and wait for my beautiful wife to get home." He squeezed my hand.

"Yeah," she said. "We'll all hate that, no offense."

My dad opened the passenger door. "Let's charter a boat," he said.

Luke was waiting in the Navigator with the window down. "Now the man's talking."

"Today?" I glanced at Jamie. "Don't you think you should go home and rest?"

"I've been sleeping for ages," my dad told me. "Some fresh air will do me good."

Luke chimed in. "Screw the charter. I want to see if that teak ketch we've been eyeing is still anchored at the River Museum in Essex."

Jamie got in on the driver's side and kissed his arm, gazing at him as though they'd just gotten married. "Your father's thinking of buying a boat," she said to Nic and me as we climbed in the back-seat. She never once took her eyes off my dad.

"Well, can't he do it tomorrow?" I asked. "Shouldn't he take it easy?"

"Yes, Whobaby." My dad strapped his seat belt. "I can."

And then I remembered that we hadn't talked about Will. For once, I was glad Nic had come. I didn't think my father would take me aside and try to talk about it with Nic in the house. As we drove out of the garage, I wondered if my dad realized I'd never even told my husband. The only person on earth I'd told besides Mandy was him.

30

I asked Nic not to talk about Greece in front of my parents. I wasn't ready yet to break the news, and we wouldn't be leaving until after Thanksgiving anyway. A couple days after my dad got out of the hospital, I dropped Nic off at the train station.

He sat in the car with one leg out of the door and one leg in, kissing my hand. "You sure you can't come to New York?" People were heading onto the platform in droves, and for some reason, I didn't want anyone to see us.

"I should spend a little more time with my parents before I head out," I told him. He was wearing his new leather and brass jewelry from Greece and a pair of suede pants.

He kissed my fingertips, which were peeking out of the gauze bandage I'd just changed. We'd spent the day before grinding winches on the new boat, getting splashed by the Connecticut River. I'd been trimming the jib when the wind ripped the sheet through my hand, taking some skin with it. As I wrapped it up, it reminded me of Ryder the night I hit my head on the crash cart. "One week," Nic said now, "and we get our life back. I can't wait for Greece." I didn't want to pick a fight then. But the words were rising up in me like a tidal wave.

"One thing at a time. Let me get out west first. Then we can talk."

I hesitated, watching a young couple kissing by the escalator. "I'm not sure I'm ready for Greece. It's so far away."

He opened his mouth like he was going to speak, but then he pressed his lips to my forehead.

My parents were eating lunch when I got home. I sat across from them at the kitchen table. My dad put the newspaper down. "I went against the rules of sailing and renamed the boat. *Miss Majestic* will from now on be known as *And She Was.*"

"I love it," I told him. "It's so profound, in a Zen sort of way."

Jamie poured lemonade into three glasses and handed one to me. She was wearing white clam diggers, a blue-striped boatneck shirt, and docksiders. Her belt had tiny anchors on it. "Thank you, Mrs. Stubing," I said.

My dad laughed. "Prettiest captain's wife I ever saw." He pushed his chair away and put his arm around her.

"We're taking an afternoon sail. You want to go out with us?"

"I'm good," I told them. "I have to do a few things."

"Ready, darling?" she asked my father. Jamie's eyes were bright.

"I was born ready," my dad said.

I'd wanted to weed the whole garden before they got back, but forty-five minutes into it, I was covered in sweat, and I couldn't pull out any of the stubborn chickweed roots. I needed a trowel to dig them out. I was in the garage, looking for one, when I heard the doorbell ring. Wiping my forehead with the back of my hand, I ran through the kitchen to the front hall and opened the door. And there they were: those red pumps, *the* red pumps.

Dr. Dale Novak was standing on our front steps, as beautiful as if she'd just stepped out of a Talbot's catalog. "I'm so glad you're home," she said. She had perfect posture.

"Dale." I touched my ratty ponytail. "What are you doing here?" I was wearing a hand-me-down Yale T-shirt Ryder had given me when we were teenagers. "My dad's not here." My toenail polish was chipped and I wished I'd gone to the spa with Mandy.

"Actually, I came to see you." Her voice got softer. "May I come in?"

She followed me into the house, stopping at the photographs in the foyer. I felt as if she were eyeing me naked. She paused the longest at one of Will and me sitting on a tree branch. Seconds after it was taken, I'd fallen off, and Will had laughed so hard, he'd peed in his pants.

Dale and I sat on opposite ends of the living room couch. "This is Ryder's favorite song." She pointed at the overhead speakers. I'd forgotten to turn off the iPod before I went outside. "She sits on the porch of her daddy's house / But all her pretty dreams are torn," Springsteen sang. I got up and turned it off, then washed my hands at the kitchen sink.

When I sat back down, she was glancing around the room as though she were deciding whether to buy it. Her hair was pulled back in a low ponytail and twisted through itself. She clasped her hands together and I put mine on my dirty knees. "I had a whole speech planned out," she said. "I even rehearsed it in the car on the way over." The diamond ring was gone from her finger.

"Why don't you just tell me whatever's on your mind," I said.

"Can I have something to drink?"

"I made lemonade this morning."

"Do you have anything stronger?" She touched her wrist, straightening her charm bracelet. "Like whiskey?"

I disliked her a little less at that moment. "Sure, come with me." We went to the dining room, and I pulled down a bottle of good bourbon and two highball glasses from a shelf by the sideboard. Then I walked to the kitchen. "You can sit at the counter if you want to." I took a boiling pan out of the cupboard. "Old-fashioned?"

She nodded hesitantly. I gathered she didn't know what an old-fashioned was. I watched her out of the corner of my eye as I took a couple of oranges, a carton of cherries, and a can of ginger beer out of the fridge. We'd stocked up so we could celebrate. Old-fashioneds were my dad's favorite. I felt sort of sorry for her, sitting there in her catalog outfit with her nails and hair all done up like she was going to a wedding. I dumped a few spoonsful of sugar in the pan, took the grater out of the drawer, and peeled plastic wrap off the cherries.

"Are those gray cherries?" she asked.

I laughed. "Did you think maraschinos are really bright red?" I picked up one. "Here they are, in their natural glory." I dropped it, stem and all, in my mouth and chewed. Seconds later, I held the stem between my teeth. I'd tied it in a knot.

"No wonder Ryder is in love with you," she said.

I choked on the pit. "I'd better make us a pitcher."

I finished making the drinks, handed one to her, then led her through the kitchen door to the deck. When she took a sip, I saw her hands were shaking. She rested her glass on the arm of the glider. I was glad I was on the side where the initials were carved. The Eiffel Tower and the tiny stethoscope on her bracelet dangled off her wrist. "How long have you been sleeping with him?" she asked nonchalantly. I thought for sure bourbon would shoot out of my mouth and I'd cover her perfect white pants with regurgitated alcohol. "You can tell me," she said. "He's not my boyfriend anymore." She rattled ice in her glass. "I got tired of going to bed every night with him, when he so clearly wanted to be with someone else."

My mind flashed back to that night in his driveway when I saw her heels in the living room. Since then, I'd been imagining him picking her underwear off his floor, making her dinner, washing the sheets after they'd made a mess the night before. I couldn't believe anyone would ever leave him.

"Did you know this was our second go-around?" She set her drink down without waiting for me to answer. "Did he tell you why we broke up the first time?"

The girl looked just like you. "Not really." I took another sip.

She sat stock-still. The tips of her ears were red. "That son of a bitch never told me about you," she said evenly. "I knew his best friend died when they were kids, but I had to piece it together from there. He never even told me William had a sister."

"Will," I said. "His name was Will."

"Whatever." She waved me off. Her dismissal made me feel invisible. "My point is, for all the stories I heard about *Will*"—she said his name mockingly—"how the two of them cut off the cat's whiskers to see if it would bump into things, and how they colored mustaches on their faces with blue permanent marker on Halloween, he—"

"It was purple," I said. She looked at me like monkeys might fly out of my ass. "The Sharpie they used—it was purple, and they had to sit for their class pictures with these ridiculous drawn mustaches. Will's was short and full like Hitler's, and Ryder's was a Wild West handlebar."

"Exactly," she said, as if I was her star witness and had just made the case for her. "I've heard every story about the two of them, but he never once mentioned you."

"He must not have thought it was important." Was it the same reason I'd never told Nic about Ryder?

"Oh, that's bullshit, and you know it. Now that I know who you are, I think"—she finished her drink—"that you two would still be together if not for Will." She reached for the pitcher.

So he'd told her. He'd told Dale Novak what we'd done. I swallowed hard to settle my stomach. I watched her fill her empty glass.

"I get it: It must have been terrible for Ryder to come downstairs in the middle of the night to get a drink and see his best friend having a seizure on the floor." *Seizure? There was no seizure.* "But I still don't know why it broke up the two of you. Every time he told me the story, I felt like he was leaving something out." *Okay, so he didn't tell her.* I filled my glass. "Like there was something about that night he didn't want me to know." She glanced at me.

"It was a long time ago," I said.

She shook her head, as if snapping out of a trance. "What was I saying? Oh, when Ryder cheated on me the last time—"

"He didn't cheat on you this time," I said sharply.

"Yeah." She sipped her drink. "Sure. Anyway, he said the girl from the conference reminded him of someone he'd never gotten over. I finally figured out that someone was you." A car door slammed in the distance. "Is that him?" she asked, her voice rising with each word. "Do you two have a date?"

I shook my head. "That didn't come from our driveway."

"Oh, well, I know he's off today." She took a long sip of her drink. When she spoke again, her tone was softer. "Your dad is very sweet."

"Yes, he is."

She stretched out her legs. "I didn't know what to expect when I met him," she said. "I mean, of course I knew who he was; everyone knows him . . . My dad was a garbage man." She cleared her throat. "Sanitation worker. Isn't that funny?" She glanced quickly at me, and I guessed I wasn't supposed to think it was funny at all. She wiped her hand across her nose. "I'm from Nebraska. My father was so . . . angry, like someone had forced him into it and there was nothing he could do." She touched the cherry in her drink. "He could have gone to college, for one." *Dale is from Nebraska?* I pictured her shooting out of the womb a grown woman who had lived all her life at Yale. "I knew from the time I was seven I was going to be a doctor. And marry one." She took the cherry out of her glass and held it up. Her second drink was already half-done. But so was mine. "I used to think Ryder was the whole package. Even after his first . . ." She looked around the yard again, as if a wooden picnic table and old goalposts would fill in the blank. "Mistake."

"He didn't make a mistake this time." I sat up straighter, already tired of defending myself for something I hadn't done. *Might as well fuck him,* I heard Mandy say, *if you're going to get blamed for it anyway.*

Dale glared at me, still holding that gray cherry in her hand. "You don't have to gloat. You won, okay?"

I tucked my knees up and rested my chin on them. "Tell me again why you're here." If she'd already broken up with him, why did I get the feeling she was here to pee a circle around him.

She put the cherry back in her drink and wiped her hand on her linen pants. *Drunk*, I thought, *she's definitely drunk*. Dale grabbed the arm of the glider and started to stand, but she lost her balance and sat heavily. Her cheeks were flushed, and those ironed linen pants were wrinkled. "I should go," she said, but she didn't move. "I shouldn't have had a drink on an empty stomach."

"I don't think you should drive." I was feeling sort of light-headed myself; everything was a little unfocused. I picked up the pitcher and topped off our drinks. "So you might as well have another."

"I'm not used to this," she said, holding up her glass.

"I didn't think you were."

One of the bright orange-and-blue birds Jamie liked landed in a tree in front of us. "I'm so stupid," she said. "I'm just so stupid." She picked up the cherry again and popped it in her mouth. I liked her much better drunk. "I mean, he must have told me a thousand times that Sterling was like a father to him. And then you showed up in my office with your forty-seven color-coded typed questions."

"So?" I said defensively. "I'd think you'd have appreciated that."

"Oh, it wasn't that. I thought it was wonderful you were so prepared. Most people can't even pronounce the names of the diseases I treat. It's just that I knew right away you were the girl Ryder never got over. And God did I hate you."

"I still hate you," I said quickly.

We both started laughing.

"To hatred." I raised my glass, and we drank.

"Seriously." She stretched her arms over her head. "Why on earth would you hate me?"

"Uh, because you look like you were born in a gym, and you went to UPenn, and you're an amazing doctor. And the whole time Ryder was telling us that he worked with the best radiation oncologist ever, he referred to you as Dale Novak. He purposely made me think you were a guy. A fat, balding guy."

"Well, he failed to tell me that there was a little sister, never mind that she was all grown up and beautiful."

I held the bottom of my stained T-shirt. "I look like I should be washing windshields at the corner of Chapel and York."

"You intimidate the shit out of me."

"Me? I didn't even wash my hair today." I pulled at my tangled curls.

"That's my point. You look good without trying."

"Okay," I said. "We've already established that we hate each other." Her glass was empty. "Now what?"

"How about you tell me every annoying habit Ryder has, so I don't miss him so much." When she blinked, sunlight caught her eye. There was a sadness there I hadn't seen before.

"Sometimes he chews with his mouth open."

"Is that the best you can do? I was hoping for a doozy. I mean, I know he steals the covers, but that's really not enough."

I felt my chest tighten. "I haven't slept in the same bed with him since we were teenagers." Her eyes narrowed, like she was deciding something. "I swear." I crossed my heart.

"Really." She said it like a statement.

"Yeah." I felt exhausted, like I did sometimes when I drank during the day with Hadley at gallery parties. "Really." The deck needed painting. All of a sudden, I started to cry. It came out of nowhere. Painting the deck was something my dad would have had done at the beginning of summer. He'd call the right people, and they'd take care of it, and the deck would be brand-new again. "I'm sorry," I said, rubbing my eyes. "I was thinking about my dad. I'm just so relieved he's okay that sometimes I want to bawl."

"Oh, Jenny," she said, and I didn't correct her. "We're a fine fucking pair."

A fuzziness had settled in my stomach. It made the crying seem okay; it made Dale's being there seem like the most normal thing in the world. "I think we'd better eat something," I told her.

"This is not turning out at all like I thought it would." She slipped her heels off, and they lay sort of helter-skelter on the deck.

"What did you think it would be like?"

"I thought I'd leave really hating you," she said. "But now I get it."

She seemed like an entirely different person as I watched her lean back and close her eyes.

"Get what?"

"That you and Ryder are supposed to be together."

"I'm married."

"Yeah, yeah." She rolled her eyes. "Do you ever wish you could have a do-over?"

"All the time. But what's done is done."

She emptied the pitcher into our glasses. "The fuck it is." I startled at her use of a curse word. "I'm still looking for my soul mate. You found yours in high school. Now go get him."

31

When I came downstairs after my drunk midafternoon nap, the house felt stagnant and eerie. Dale's perfume lingered in the foyer. I was just about to go into the kitchen to get something to eat, when through the living room I saw my father sitting in the leather easy chair in his office, still in his boating clothes. He looked like he was waiting for someone. "Hey," I said. I leaned against the doorjamb.

"Come on in here, Whobaby."

I noticed then that his face was serious, and I felt my stomach drop. I sat across from him and couldn't quite meet his eyes. "Where's Jamie?" I asked. I felt hungover and cotton-mouthed from my surreal lunch with Dale.

"She ran out to the garden shop." He fiddled with his glasses for a moment. "Accidents happen, Jensen."

I stared at the trophies along the far wall. They were dusty, and I had an overwhelming urge to clean them. It was an inane thought, but it kept me from thinking about the horrible rush in my ears. Somewhere in the distance, a car alarm was ringing.

He leaned forward. "Why didn't you ever tell us?"

"I tried telling Mommy." My voice sounded withered. "Right after."

He sucked in a breath. "Aw, Whobaby." He folded his hands in his lap. They were so familiar, hands I'd known all my life, with that one crooked knuckle and the square, thick fingers. The alarm stopped.

"You know that kid from Hopkins had a full ride to Notre Dame, like your brother?" He was staring past me, out the window. "Never played ball again." I understood he was telling me this so I would know someone else shared my guilt. "Ended up at Quinnipiac."

And just then, I realized it. "You don't hate me."

"Of course I don't hate you."

I'd told him the truth, and he still loved me. The thought was miraculous.

"I knew something happened." He took his glasses off and put them back on. "A dad knows." His blue eyes were infused with a kind of wisdom I'd never seen before, or maybe I hadn't noticed. "I tried to find ways to ask before you left for Andover. And on the phone all those Sundays. And whenever we went out to Colorado and Santa Fe. I kept thinking the words in my head, Whobaby, but I never could get them out." I stared at him. Of course he'd known. How could he not have? "That's my fault, you see? If I'd only asked what had happened, what had made you so sad, so different, I could have told you what you needed to hear." He leaned toward me again. "Now you listen to me. You didn't take Will from us." My head felt light, strange. "Do you understand? We can't know what happened. Maybe there's a God, like Luke says, who turns that big wheel in the sky, and when our time is up, it's up." He watched me. "So maybe it doesn't matter what happened, Whobaby. Do you understand that?"

I couldn't answer.

"Did you mean to do what you did to Will?" His words seemed to echo in the still room. I thought about the question. At first it seemed to make no sense. And then I shook my head. He put his hand behind his ear. "I can't hear you."

"No," I said. The word sounded tiny.

"No, what?" He was using his coaching voice, the voice he used to motivate a player.

"No, I didn't mean to."

"Didn't mean to what?" I sat there. The words went silent inside me. I couldn't think how to say them aloud. "Because intent is everything," he said.

I nodded mutely. I had never really thought about intent. All those years of guilt and hiding, of shame and self-hatred, I had never stopped to think that it hadn't ever been my intent to hurt my brother.

"Sixteen-year-olds get mad at their older brothers, don't they?"

"I guess."

"You guess?"

"Yes."

He leaned forward and watched me. "Haven't younger sisters been pushing older brothers for centuries?"

"I didn't mean to," I said softly.

"Didn't mean to what?" he asked again, his voice gentler now.

"I didn't mean to . . ." My voice caught. I stumbled over the words, but there was my father, watching me, and I understood that I had to say them out loud. "I didn't mean to, Daddy, please." And then I was across the room, on his lap, burying my face in his chest, in his salt and fresh air smell. "I didn't mean to," I said. "I didn't mean to." I was crying again, but this time it was harder, a different cry than how I'd cried with Dale.

He put his arm around me. "That a girl," he said, nestling me closer. "Get it all out."

I was sobbing so hard, I couldn't see, and he was rocking me, his arms around me. "But I never came home."

"That doesn't matter now."

"I just left you here all alone."

"It's okay. You're here now." I heard him saying my name, heard him telling me it wasn't my fault, and I felt thirteen years of unspoken confessions and wordless apologies escape in my tears.

Sometime after dusk, Jamie came home and sat next to us. I felt her rubbing my back, and I felt my father lift one arm and put it around her. I knew he'd told her, too. And they still loved me.

I had been forgiven.

32

Jamie liked first appointments of the day, so we sped through town at 7:45 A.M. to the Chapel Street Spa. She drove erratically, like she always did, with one foot on the gas and the other on the brake, weaving in and out of traffic as though a victim to it rather than a driver. "You were right," she said suddenly. "I was keeping a secret, but not the one you thought."

I looked over at her. I had a horrible feeling that she was sick and all those secret phone calls were to a doctor. Her silk blouse slipped down, revealing a skinny collarbone that looked almost breakable. "What is it?"

She sat up straighter in the driver's seat. "I'm selling my interest in the agency to Piers. I'm getting out of the modeling industry." Glancing in the rearview mirror, she dived into the next lane. "I'm going to join the staff of A Will to Live." She spoke quickly. "All the news about what modeling does to little girls, the anorexia, and the body-dysmorphic issues." She looked at me. "I'm going to run self-esteem classes. Do you know that sixty percent of girls will quit an activity they love because of the way they look?"

I wouldn't have been more surprised if she'd told me she was going to clown college. "Why now?" I tried to keep my voice level so it wouldn't sound like an accusation.

"I started thinking about it when your father got sick. I wanted to do something that would let me spend more time with him." She cut someone off, and the guy honked and flipped her off. But she didn't notice.

"Is that what all the secret phone calls and random meetings have been about? Selling your business?" She nodded but didn't speak. "But he's in remission now. Are you sure you still want to do it?"

"Oh yes, now more than ever. Think how great it'll be for both Daddy and me to be at the foundation." She put on her blinker but didn't change lanes. "I can't get back those wasted years. But I can make sure I spend the next thirty doing the right thing."

"Really? Are you sure?"

"Oh, Jensen. After Will, I was no mother to you at all. Maybe it's not too late for me to help some other little girl."

"Help her, or turn her into what I never was?"

"What does that even mean?" She watched me so long, I thought she was going to drive off the road.

I shrugged. "Forget it."

She stopped at the end of an exit ramp. "No, tell me."

I picked at a ragged fingernail. Behind us, someone revved their engine and Jamie accelerated. But she never took her eyes off me. "I guess I never felt pretty enough for you. Good enough."

"Is that what you think?" Her voice was faint. "I could have signed you in a heartbeat; of course I could have. You were a beautiful child, you photographed so well, but, you were . . . too good to be like me. You were so smart. Your father and I used to marvel that you were our child. There you were, playing Bach at eight. I'd never heard Bach before, and you were offered all these gifted programs."

"Then why'd you let me live my entire life feeling like I was too fat, too ugly, too much of a nobody to be one of your girls?" I turned to her, and this close, I could finally see the beginning of silver hairs in her part.

"You always acted like you wanted nothing to do with modeling." She turned left onto State Street. "I felt like it was all so stupid to you, so . . . provincial, or . . ." Her eyes had filled with tears. "I'm so sorry, Jensen. I never meant to make you feel that way."

"How could you have known? I never told you. I just trotted around with Will and Ryder, pretending I didn't care."

She wiped her eyes. I thought of her sitting in board meetings with my dad and Sid and all the others at the foundation. She'd had me at twenty-three, she was only fifty-two. She could do this. "You'll be great at A Will to Live," I told her.

"Do you think so?" She dabbed at her eyes with her sleeve.

She was smiling. It wasn't the smile she used for models and photographers and her friends at the agency. It was a true Jamie smile, one I'd seen in pictures of her as a little girl, when the world hadn't shown her yet that she needed smoke and mirrors and her beauty to get by.

The spa was nearly empty except for Mandy, who was waiting for us in the reception area. As soon as we got in the door, Jamie took off to the facial rooms. Mandy and I sat in the pedicure chairs. I wanted to tell her right away about Jamie and A Will to Live. But she'd been overly giggly on the phone, and it wasn't because I told her about my afternoon with Dale.

"Okay," I said. "Spill it."

"Let's play the guessing game." She unzipped her ankle boots. "I'm thinking of a boy."

"Did you kiss him?"

"Of course."

Mandy kissed everybody. "Is he from Hamilton?" There were two glasses of seltzer with cucumber slices floating in them on the table between our chairs. And our footbaths were filled with hot water and lavender oil.

"Kind of."

"Did you sleep with him?" My manicurist picked up my foot and began scrubbing it with a loofah; it felt so good, I wanted to cry.

"Nope."

Of all the people Mandy had kissed in high school, I remembered only two she hadn't slept with: One was a hot bad boy senior who sold pot, but Will and Ryder threatened to kill him if he touched her. The second was her physics tutor senior year. He went to Yale, and Mandy had said he was tall, skinny, and walked like a colt that hadn't grown into its legs. He'd kissed her once and then told her he just wanted to be friends. "He says I'm too young," she'd said, sobbing into the phone after he left every Tuesday night. When he went off to Japan for a semester abroad, she never heard from him again, and she about had a nervous breakdown. It was so weird that she'd fallen for the geeky science tutor. But Mandy was into brains.

"Where on earth did you find Freddie Frederickson after all these years?"

She stared at me, her mouth hanging open. "How the hell did you know?"

I smiled. "I can read your mind."

"He saw my Andes layout in *National Geographic* and Googled me."

"Let me guess. He grew out of his gangliness, ditched his glasses, and has the body of a linebacker?"

She leaned back and closed her eyes. "He's a professor at Wesleyan, writing a book on how air travel could be improved if planes were shaped more like birds."

"That sounds about right for Freddie." The lady's hands on my feet felt like little miracles.

"He goes by Fred now," she said defensively. "And teaching is the last of the noble professions, in case you've forgotten."

Was Mandy going goody goody on me? "I thought that was prostitution," I said, trying to lighten her up.

"That's the oldest." She smiled. "Anyway, he's already coauthor of a book about"—she pursed her lips like she was bragging, which she was—"how ancient cave drawings prove the wheel, or at least the concept of it, was invented about half a million years before anyone thought."

"Oh my God, Mandy." I sipped the sparkling water. "You like him."

"He smelled exactly the same and still has that adorable little stutter. And want to hear the best part?" She reached across and grabbed my fingers. "He wants kids."

I tried to swallow back my bite of jealousy. In all the years we'd been friends, I'd never seen her like this. "You still haven't slept with him?"

"Nope." Mandy slept with everyone on the first date, even if it wasn't a date. "But I kissed him, and it was delicious."

"Huh," I said, holding up the darkest of the three polishes I'd picked out.

"He wears rimless glasses now, very understated. And he *is* broader. He does martial arts, some kind of sword fighting or fencing."

"That is so dorky," I said.

"Okay, he's still pretty dorky. But he's so freaking sweet." And then her cell rang. "It Had to Be You" played. She squealed, holding up her phone so I could see Freddie with his slicked-back hair and V-necked sweater. I thought about Nic, waiting for me in Santa Fe, and the babies I'd never have.

"That's his custom ringtone?" I asked. "Oh sister, you're a goner."

"Hey there," she said in a voice I'd never heard her use before.

I flipped open a fashion magazine. The taste of jealousy was acidic in my mouth. Mandy wouldn't miss me at all when I went back to Santa Fe, because soon she'd be fucking Freddie and getting pregnant. I glanced at her. She was smiling like she was in a great daydream. I'd felt like that before, so many years ago that it was becoming less like a memory and more like a dream. Ryder had made me feel that way.

Jamie came out with green stuff all over her face.

"Mandy has a boyfriend," I told her. "And she's bringing him to my going away dinner."

Mandy tossed her phone in her bag. "I am?"

"You're talking about having babies with this guy. Don't you think we need to vet him first?"

"Oh, absolutely," my mother said. "Jensen has to meet him before she leaves."

Mandy clapped her hands excitedly. "You'll love him." She frowned. "But I hate that you're leaving. I'm just going to pretend you are NOT going anywhere."

I held two bottles of polish up to the light. I'd been pretending the same thing. But I was scheduled to start modeling again for three studios the following week, and Nic was planning a welcome-home party for me at the loft. I thought of my birthday party the night before I'd left; it felt like a lifetime ago.

"Brazilian?" A hunky man with an accent came from behind the curtain. "Someone wanted a Brazilian."

Mandy waved her hand in the air. "I'll come back for the polish," she told the woman doing her pedicure. "Isn't he hot?" she whispered to me.

We watched her disappear to the back. Only Mandy would let a guy do her Brazilian. Jamie watched the woman filling her footbath with water. "Oh, sweetheart." She drew in a quick, hard breath. "I hope I'm making the right decision about selling the agency." I saw some cream had gotten on the collar of the robe they'd given her. Without makeup, her eyes were tiny and vulnerable. She watched the woman putting lavender oil in the water. "Anyway, we're all going to miss you. I've gotten so used to having you here. But you'll only be a short plane ride away."

I hadn't told my parents about Greece. "By Christmas," Nic kept saying on the phone. "We'll be there by Christmas." And then: "Why so quiet, J.?" I kept telling him, "I'm tired. Really, really tired."

"Even still, New Mexico feels so far away," Jamie said. "And to think I used to worry that you'd wind up with Ryder."

A flutter spread through my stomach. "You worried about that?"

"Well . . ." She hesitated. She had on what she called her "mommy clothes," a velour zip-up and matching yoga pants. I would have looked like a Wal-Mart ad. She was glamorous without trying. "I used to worry you wouldn't get out and see the world. All those years you followed your brother and Ryder around, and they just adored you. I'd watch you climbing trees and making forts with them and then"—the tiny dark-haired woman scrubbed her feet hard—"you got beautiful, that long hair and those sapphire eyes. I saw the way Ryder looked at you. He couldn't help it." Her smile was faint, apologetic. "You'd come through the kitchen door, claiming you'd been at the library, but I could see it in your eyes, those flushed cheeks. I knew what was happening. Your father and I used to talk about it and—"

"Daddy knew?" I asked, stunned.

"Oh, sweetheart, we all knew. Except Will. Will didn't want to know. And I was so worried Ryder would never let you see the world. He'd just snatch you up and marry you." Her hand came over and touched my chin, and I flinched involuntarily, but she smiled. "A mother wants things for her daughter. You were so talented with the piano and your grades." She laughed breezily. "I actually fantasized that you would meet someone just like Nico, an artist, European, a little older." She flexed her ankle a few times, the one she'd broken on location in Spain the year Will died. I could see the faint scar along her Achilles tendon. "Nico's lovely, don't get me wrong. He takes care of you in a way you'd never let Daddy or me. But Santa Fe is so far away, and after losing Will, well . . . you've been different since you've been home. Happier."

"Nic makes me happy." I could hear the defensiveness in my voice. "I'm happy."

She adjusted the towel on her head. "Sometimes I wish I hadn't wanted that for you so badly. I mean really"—she licked her lips and leaned back—"what's so wrong with staying close to home?"

And then I saw Jamie as an old woman, white hair and wrinkles, all of it, living in the big house on North Parker Drive, her son dead and her daughter all the way over in Greece. I'd never bothered to ask what it was like for her after Will died. Had my father still touched her? Had they been able to talk about it? Or had he turned away from her like I'd done to Ryder? *Maybe that's why she left,* I thought now. *Maybe it wasn't all her fault.*

She leaned back in her chair and closed her eyes. "Sometimes I look at Nic, and"—she sounded nervous—"I mean, I just wonder, does he really *see* you?" She opened her eyes and reached over to pat my hand. "When you do leave, I just hope we get to visit with you more, now that we've had this summer together."

It hit me all at once that I was going. Santa Fe, with all its space and earth colors, used to feel like the perfect place to fall into, but now I couldn't imagine leaving the closeness of New England, the ocean and the green. There was no way I could go to Greece. "Mom." I felt a tightness in my chest.

"Yes, sweetheart?" She handed her polish to the lady.

"I don't know if I want to be married anymore," I blurted out and instantly wished I could take it back. "I love Nico. I do. But, I'm scared," I told her. "I'm scared I'm nothing without him."

She took her foot out of the water, and the lady scrubbing her heel backed up. She came stumbling over to me. "You are something without him, you know that?" She held my face in her hands. "You're perfect," she said. "You're absolutely amazing. You always have been, and I'm sorry I couldn't tell you that after Will."

I let her hug me. Her robe opened and my cheek was pressed against the bare skin of her chest. She got green face goop all over my cheek and neck, and I felt a huge surge of energy, like I was going to break into a run or sing loudly.

Mandy came around the corner. "What's all the hugging about?"

"Jensen's getting a divorce," Jamie said.

"Mom." I laughed. Tears were running down my cheeks. "I did not say that!"

Mandy was hugging me, too. "Oh, J.J., I knew you'd stay."

"I'm not staying," I said. "I still have to go back to Santa Fe." They were on either side of me, smooshing me with their lovely perfumed bodies. "It's my home," I told them, though I wasn't quite sure where my home was anymore.

My mother kissed my cheek. "Home will always be here in Colston, won't it, Mandy?"

Mandy kissed my other cheek. "Of course," she said.

And I kept my mouth shut. It was useless to argue with them.

33

I spent the afternoon working on my self-portraits in the attic. Holding the paintbrush in the air, I stood in front of the four pictures I'd almost completed, so similar to one another, and yet they weren't me. I squinted at the one on the easel with the red mark down its face. I could hear a leaf blower going outside, the kids on the cul-de-sac playing a game of capture the flag and calling out clues. The face I'd painted was stronger than mine, bolder. I traced my brush lightly around the hairline, trying to add a feathery, feminine feel. "Just take photographs instead," Hadley had told me before I'd left Santa Fe. "They are so *not* ambiguous."

I'd told myself all summer that I was dodging the attic because it was hot or I was too busy with my dad, with piano, with . . . but it was these eyes I was avoiding. They seemed to be trying to tell me something. And it made me feel watched.

After I showered, I went downstairs, dressed in a shimmery silk top and black jeans. I felt sexy and happy. "Let's rock," I said, peeking in the kitchen. "Dad? You down here?"

"Over here." He was lying on the living room couch with his arm over his eyes.

I rushed over to him. "Are you okay?"

He sat up slowly. "I'm fine, Whobaby. Just a little tired." He rubbed his temples before putting his glasses on, a sure sign of a headache. I sat on the arm of the couch. "Why don't you rest before everyone gets here? I'll get the appetizers ready."

"No way am I missing a moment with you before you leave." He put his arm around me; then I helped him up. He smelled like the house: cedar and furniture polish.

"Can I ask you something, Daddy?"

He kissed the top of my head. "Sure, anything."

"How happy I feel. Do you think I'll lose it after I get back to Santa Fe?"

Wrinkles appeared on the sides of his eyes when he smiled.

"Ah, Whobaby, that's why we come home. We fill the well so we can go out into the world again. You might get back there and fall in love with that dry desert air and your modeling jobs, and that café with the funny name." He rustled my hair like he used to when I was a little girl. "It might just feel that way today, and then tomorrow you'll get back and see that's where your life is and everything will be okay." He squeezed me, and I could feel his breath in my hair. "Everyone here loves you. That's not going to go away."

In the kitchen, he watched as I took pears and prosciutto out of the fridge "All I want before I die is for you to be happy."

I handed him a knife and the pears. "Cut these in half," I told him. "And you're not dying." It felt so good to say that and know it was true.

"I meant in the grand scheme of things." He took the pears and put them on the cutting board.

"Yoo hoo," Jamie called from the foyer.

"We're in here," I called back. She was talking to someone, and it took me a minute to recognize the voice. "Ryder's coming?" I whispered to my dad. "I thought he had to work."

He knocked on my head. "Do you think he'd miss your going-away party?"

Jamie came through the archway, wearing an off-the-shoulder

brocade wrap. "Our favorite doctor brought two kinds of wine, always the perfect guest." She held them up.

Ryder rounded the corner, wearing a linen button-down shirt and jeans. He smelled like he'd just stepped out of the shower.

My father clapped him on the back. "What's the good word?" I watched them hug.

Ryder kissed me on the cheek. "The disappearing woman," he said. He went into the foyer and returned a moment later with his hands behind his back. "Right or left?" I patted his left arm, and he brought forward about four dozen red roses. "Christ." My father rinsed his hands. "We'll need a hell of a vase for those."

"Oh but darling"—Jamie took them from him and started for the dining room—"we have just the thing. Get my wrap, will you?"

I watched Ryder fold her wrap into a neat square and drape it over a chair.

"Thank you," I said. I remembered reading somewhere that in olden times people believed the smell of roses took away fear.

The front door opened, and I heard Luke call out, "Hey, folks."

My father went out to meet him. I could hear Jamie still rummaging around in the dining room, and I felt awkward, like I didn't know where to put my hands. I unwrapped the prosciutto.

Ryder leaned on the counter. "You ever coming home again?" he asked.

I felt a lump in my throat.

"I've got a cake the size of Rhode Island in the car," I heard Luke say. "And about seven gallons of ice cream and a Balthazar of champagne."

"Ryder," my dad yelled. "I think we need a hand."

"Coming," Ryder replied. He didn't take his eyes off me.

"The cake looks so good," I heard Luke say, "Starflower almost ate it in the car."

I quit unwrapping the prosciutto. "I'll miss you," I said.

Ryder moved toward the door. "When do you fly out?"

"Friday."

"You want to have drinks with me tomorrow night?" he asked.

My mouth went dry. "I'd love that," I told him. And then he disappeared to help Luke and my dad.

While Starflower and my mom went out to the deck to set the table, I lined Ryder, Luke, and my dad up in a row in the kitchen and pointed the knife I'd been using at them. "Mandy really likes this guy," I told them. "So behave yourselves tonight."

The three of them raised their palms, declaring their innocence. "We're always good," Luke said.

"Tell that to the guy from Uruguay you cornered at the tumor party." I shook the knife at them. "Remember that night?"

"How could we forget?" Ryder asked. "That was an awesome playlist. 'In My Time of Dying' and 'Spirit in the Sky.' "

"We were very nice to Ricardo," my dad said.

"Antonio," I said, correcting him, "just about ran out of this house when he finally figured out why you guys kept telling him he was one in a million."

"We just wanted Eduardo to know that Mandy's"—Luke looked to Ryder for help—"a fun girl."

"Mandy is a fun girl, but she's also my best friend. And when I tell you she really likes this guy, I mean it. So please." The three of them were trying hard not to laugh, and so was I. "Don't fuck it up."

Luke held up two manicured fingers. "Scout's honor."

Ryder slapped him on the back. "Dude, that's a peace symbol. You need three fingers for Scout's honor." He put up his middle finger on his other hand, and the three of them cracked up.

The doorbell rang. I flicked a dish towel at them. "Promise me." I eyed each one. They clicked their heels together and saluted me. "One more thing. His name is Fred. Not Freddie. Not Frederick. Fred."

"But it's Fred Fredrickson," I heard Ryder tell my dad and Luke, and a new wave of laughter came from the kitchen.

When I opened the door, I was surprised to see Mandy's shoes were neither strappy nor slutty. They were pretty sandals with an open toe. She wore black linen pants and a white blouse. With just lip gloss on, she was stunning in a girl-next-door kind of way. When she kissed me on the side of my mouth, she smelled like cherry. "J.J.," she said, her voice springy and light, "I want you to meet Fred Fredrickson."

He wasn't so much handsome as the kind of guy you meet at a party and think what a great husband he would make, solid, kind. He was holding a bouquet of sunflowers, and he offered his hand. It was a soft, warm hand that seemed to describe the word *safe*.

Jamie came in from the kitchen. "Mandy," she said, not taking her eyes off Fred, "darling, we are all so pleased you could come. And who is this handsome man?" He held out the flowers. My mother loved sunflowers. "My goodness," she said. She kissed him on both cheeks. "You *are* a keeper."

He blushed a deep crimson. Mandy grabbed his hand. "Let's go meet Sterling."

Jamie took my arm, and we watched them walk down the hall to the kitchen. "He's so . . ." She searched for the word. "Appropriate," she finally said.

A bottle of Cakebread Cabernet was already breathing on the counter when we walked in. Next to it, a Chardonnay was chilling in a bucket. I pulled down eight wineglasses while Mandy introduced Fred all around. She looked insanely happy.

"We both like red," she told me when I asked what they wanted to drink.

"So Fre-ed," my dad said, as if he'd been going to call him Freddie and then thought better of it. "Mandy tells us you're a physics professor."

"Yes, sir, I am, used to tutor high school kids, but a precocious senior a long time ago made me switch gears." Mandy was smiling up at him like he'd just been elected president. Fred continued: "I find college students easier to handle."

Luke coughed. "No one has ever accused our Mandy of being easy to handle."

Starflower poked him in the ribs. She was wearing a peasant blouse and dangly earrings and her dark hair was loose down her back. There was something very comforting about her.

My mother held up her glass. "To new friends," she said. Fred gently pulled a piece of hair away from Mandy's face. She nuzzled her nose against him.

I caught Ryder watching me watching them. "And to old friends," he said.

My dad raised his glass to Luke. "And to old goats."

They made bleating noises and touched their glasses together.

"And to having people to love," Mandy added.

The timer rang. "I hate to interrupt the lovefest," Luke said. "But dinner is served."

Jamie had hung lanterns off the branches above the deck and put early fall flowers on every available space, and white linen, crystal, and sterling silver on the table. She'd set Ryder's flowers in the middle, and it was more beautiful than a wedding. I sat between Ryder and Mandy. Mandy rubbed her foot on Fred's under the table the whole time and fed him cherry tomatoes from the salad. My father sat on one end of the table, and Luke at the other. Luke kept breaking into song, "Do I Ever Cross Your Mind" and "Tupelo Honey." Starflower, exotic in the candlelight, promised to read everyone's palms after dessert. Ryder and I touched fingers and knees about forty times, until finally, after I'd finished my second glass of wine, I let my hand rest on his thigh. He put his hand on top of mine. There was still that electricity, and I realized with a calm acceptance that it would always be there.

All the way through dinner, I focused on the grilled steak and sweet potatoes, on Mandy's laugh, on how my father held my mother's fingers in his and kissed them every so often, on Luke's superwhite teeth and his dreads and how happy I was to be there. I tried not to think about Santa Fe, the loft, and modeling. I tried not to think about Greece.

It wasn't even eleven when my dad said he was going to bed. I squeezed Ryder's hand and glanced at my father. I thought I'd been discreet, but my dad set his napkin on the table and said, "Jensen, I saw that." He sounded annoyed and amused at the same time. "Your old man is allowed to be tired. I promise I'll still be breathing in the morning."

Jamie swatted his butt with her napkin. "Not funny, Sterling."

Fred sprang up and shook his hand. "Thank you so much for having me, Mr. Reilly. It's an honor to be a guest in your home."

My dad put his arm around him and walked him across the deck to the door. He stood with his back to us. "If you're with Mandy, you're never a guest. You're family. Now let me tell you something."

We all got quiet so that we could listen.

"I've known Mandy since she was a girl. And I love her like my own."

"Aw, J.J.," Mandy whispered. "Your dad's going to make me cry." I put up my finger up to shush her.

"Take care of her," my dad told him in a tone that was both warm and threatening. Fred didn't answer, and I thought maybe he was about to pass out or pee in his pants. My father turned around and winked at us. "We're done now," he said. "You can go back to chatting."

We all cracked up.

"Thanks, Sterling," Mandy called out. "I love you, too."

Jamie stood. "I'll walk you to the bedroom, darling." I watched my parents disappear into the house. Before Fred made it back to the table, Starflower reached over and took Mandy's hand, holding it against her heart. "Yes," she said with her eyes closed. "I believe you're going to marry that one."

Mandy laughed. "Oh, I want to marry him. But I'm in no hurry."

Starflower picked up her tea with both hands and took a sip. "You will be once the baby comes."

Fred came back to the table, and I noticed his cowlick and those long, dark eyelashes. Here he was, the first man Mandy had ever loved.

"So, Jensen." Luke swirled his cognac around in his glass. "You got a piano out there in Santa Fe?"

"Yeah." I thought of the old Steinway my father had insisted on getting for me when he came to visit one Thanksgiving. I wondered vaguely if I would play it when I got back.

"Not like that one at Woolsey Hall, I bet." He winked at me.

I felt Ryder breathing next to me.

"No," I said. "Not quite like that one."

"A piano is a piano is a piano." Luke lifted his glass. "Doesn't actually matter much what kind."

"We're going miss you, J.J.," Mandy told me.

"You know I'll be back," I said.

Starflower was watching me, blinking those brown eyes expectantly, as if she knew something I didn't.

"Well." Luke took a sip of his drink. "We're counting on it, baby girl. If you don't, there's more than one heart that's going to break."

34

I can't come," Ryder said into the phone the next night. I'd been to see my father's attorney, then met my parents for dinner. I was in the living room, watching Jamie pull out of the driveway to go sign papers at A Will to Live. "I'm sorry. I just got a call from the hospital and—"

"You're scared." I sat on the couch.

He was quiet on the other end. I could hear my father turning on the shower upstairs. "Let's say good-bye right this time," I told him. "Please." He didn't say anything. "I'll wait all night for you."

"All right," he finally said. "I'll be over as soon as I can."

In the attic, I put on Furtwängler's rendition of Beethoven's Ninth. It had been recorded in Berlin and had a sort of Old Testament, fire-and-brimstone feel. I liked to play it when I painted. The self-portraits I'd tried to finish over the summer were still hanging on the walls, staring at me from their dark backgrounds. They were the only things left to pack, and I'd been putting it off.

I didn't hear my dad come up the stairs, but suddenly he was there in the doorway in a bathrobe, his hair wet. "Aren't you supposed to go out for drinks with Ryder?" he yelled over the music.

"Don't come in here." I heard the snap in my voice, but I couldn't help it; I didn't want him to see these paintings. They seemed like testimony to all the ways I'd failed in my life.

He took a step forward and cupped his hand behind his ear. "What?" he yelled. He'd already noticed them.

"Nothing." I turned down the stereo. "Ryder got called to the hospital. He's coming by later." The room seemed oddly quiet without the music.

"Well, I like wine." He was studying the paintings. "If you don't mind hanging out with your old man, we can have a glass on the deck."

I gathered the brushes. "That sounds great, Daddy."

He leaned into the painting that had the red mark across its face. "We have that good Chilean stuff Luke left last night. I'll uncork it." But he kept staring at my work. He went from one to another, moving his glasses down his nose and then stepping back and pushing them up again. In Santa Fe, this was the moment I hated, when Nic came into the studio without warning and made some offhand remark about contours, depth, or color. I gathered the remainder of the brushes and piled them next to the wooden paint box and leftover canvases.

"You capture the best part of him in these," my father finally said.

It took a minute to sink in.

"All this time, I had no idea this was what you'd been doing here." He was standing in the middle of the room, his face shot through with light from the yard lamps outside. "I understand now why you came up here." His eyes had a faraway look. "It's how you see him again."

I got up slowly and stood next to him. The paintings looked completely different now. We stood there with all those faces gazing back at us.

"You did good, Whobaby." He put his palm on my shoulder. "You brought him home." We both stood there until my dad, as if coming out of a dream, said, "Well, I better go get some real clothes on." Before he turned to go, he said, "Jenny?" I hadn't heard him call me that since before Will. "You know why I loved football?"

I shook my head. "No."

"Running," he told me. "Believe it or not, I was a skinny thing. And I grew up in a hard part of South Philly. The neighborhood kids were tough as hell on me and I was too scared to fight back." He laughed a little, his mouth turned into a smile, his eyes far away. "I was a runner. You understand me? When the going got tough, I ran. I ran away from the bullies. Away from my crappy neighborhood. Eventually, I made a good living out of running. But Whobaby, that's a hell of a way to live, running. You got to stop sometime. You got to turn around and face what you think's been coming at you. And damn it, you did." His voice was hoarse but strong. "That's better than any award or fancy accolade. You understand me? That's something to be proud of." He smoothed back his hair with his big bear-paw hand. "I'll never forget that day when I turned around and fought back." He laughed. "I got a black eye and a fat lip. But you know what?"

"No," I said quietly. "What?"

"That's the best goddamn thing I ever did. Finally, I wasn't afraid the bigger kids were coming after me anymore." He kissed my head. "I haven't been the same since." He looked around the room, his focus landing on my paintings. "Good work," he said softly. "Beautiful, beautiful work, my Whobaby, my shining star."

I listened to his footsteps fade as he went down the narrow attic stairs. I was still staring at the painting with the red mark. After a moment, I squatted down and opened my paint palette, took out one of the midsize brushes, and stuck it in water before dipping it in the white paint. Using wide horizontal strokes, I covered the suggestion of long, dark curls. I took the top off the yellow, wet another brush, and dipped it in, mixing it with the base and making a sun-blasted blond color. I painted this around the contours of the face. Then I closed my eyes and listened to the stillness in the attic, the quiet there. It's what I did before I viewed a painting. I closed my eyes and counted to one hundred.

Finally, I opened my eyes. I could see his cheekbones, the regal line of his nose, the heaviness of his brows, that gentle sloping forehead. The change in color had made him absolutely real. Staring back at me with the cut he'd gotten on his face the day he flipped his bicycle when he was nine was not my portrait, but Will's.

All those days I'd come up here and listened to Beethoven's Ninth, trying to find myself, he had been here the whole time, watching me, waiting for me to recognize him. Now that I saw him, I couldn't unsee him. He was everywhere.

I stood in the attic room, where he and I used to play with the dollhouse, where for hours at a time it had just been us, and where I had come on hot, sticky afternoons this summer, trying to find myself, and I saw that my brother had been with me all along. Nic was wrong. "Before you do anything else, you have to paint your self-portrait," he used to say. Before I did anything else, I had to bring Will back, or maybe, I thought standing in the middle of the room, I had to let him come back to me.

It came to me slowly but very clearly; there was no mistaking it. On Will's face I saw the one thing I'd wanted most from him. I saw forgiveness.

I don't know how long I stayed there, seeing that, but when I finally left the paintings hanging there and headed downstairs, I felt washed through. Walking down the steps, everything seemed brighter. I had been in this house for years, and yet I'd never seen it quite like I saw it now. The knots in the wood were beautiful. The bright yellow in the hallway had a celestial feel. I was feeling something I hadn't felt in a long time: I was excited. I thought maybe I'd leave a message on Ryder's cell and tell him to meet us at The Wharf. My dad and I could get the convertible out and drive to the shore. I'd have a Maker's Mark on the rocks and a piece of chocolate cake. Maybe Jamie would be home by then and she'd want to come, too.

"Dad," I called. In the hall, I didn't turn away from the picture of Will and me on a Ferris wheel; I let myself stop at the photo of us riding inner tubes on Martha's Vineyard the summer I was twelve.

Will had forgiven me. I had seen it. I knew it like I knew my own name, my telephone number. "Dad," I said again.

When I passed his room, I caught a glimpse of him lying across his bed, his glasses still on, both hands pressed to his heart. I pushed the door open wider. "Daddy." I crossed the room. I didn't know what I would tell him, how I would explain the happiness he had given me by seeing what he had, but I thought for now I could just kiss him on the cheek and take him out for a drink.

I stood over the bed, almost not wanting to wake him. Since he'd recovered from the Keppra fever, he could fall asleep anywhere, and I was envious of that peace. He looked calm, his mouth slightly open, his palms resting on his chest. I sat next to him. "Daddy?" I reached out to touch his arm. And then I stopped. Later, I couldn't say what it was. A stillness, or a feeling that something had left the room. I knew at once I was completely alone. Drawing my hand back, I saw then that his belly wasn't rising and falling. I put my fingers to his neck for a pulse. A panic rose from my thighs into my throat. There wasn't one.

And then I was grabbing the phone off its cradle and dialing numbers. "The nature of your emergency," a voice said, and I saw that my father had been in the midst of putting on his shoes. One loafer was on the floor near him, and the other was still on his foot, waiting to drop.

35

The morning of my father's funeral, I was sitting on the living room couch, wearing a pair of Ryder's old sweatpants and a Steelers T-shirt my father had given me as a teenager. "Nic's here," Mandy said. She was standing at the window, barefoot and wearing a black dress.

"Can you let him in?" I asked.

I kept my eyes closed as I listened to her open the door. "Where is she?" Nic asked. Then I heard his boots on the floor, and when I opened my eyes, he was looking down at me. He was wearing a black collarless button-down. He'd shaved and didn't smell like pot. I put my arms up and he sat next to me. "Hey, sweet lady."

"Hey," I said. As if no time had passed, as if we were still happy and in Santa Fe, I leaned into him and fit myself into the crook of his arm. He smelled like the homemade soap we used to buy at the farmers' market.

"Have you eaten anything?"

I shook my head. "I can't."

He checked his watch. "How about a shower, then?"

Mandy sat on the other side of me. "Good idea."

"No," I said too loudly. "If I shower, you'll make me get dressed. And if I get dressed—"

"You'll have to go to the funeral," Nic said. "Where is everyone?"

I thought about my dad in the funeral home, pumped up with embalming fluid, dressed in the same suit he'd worn to Luke's birthday party the night he found out he had a brain tumor. I closed my eyes again. My exhaustion felt palpable, cement running through my blood.

"Jamie and Luke went for a drive," Mandy told him. She was staring at the ceiling, probably trying to think of what to say next. "To the cemetery," she whispered.

"I can hear you," I said, and we all laughed a little.

"What about . . . Ryder?" he asked.

"He went home to get his suit. He'll be back in a little while," Mandy told him.

The coroner had told us my father hadn't suffered. I wondered if she told everyone that. She said the disease and radiation had weakened his heart, and that it'd given out. But he'd gone quickly and without pain. "I feel sick," I said now.

"Let's get you in the shower," Nic said.

"Can I just sit here for a few more minutes?"

"Unfortunately," Mandy said, taking my arm, "we don't really have a few more minutes."

They hoisted me up, and together the three of us shuffled to the hallway. I think they knew that if they quit holding on to me, I'd fall down.

We'd made it to the stairs, when the doorbell rang. "Can you take her?" Mandy asked.

"Easy does it," Nic told me, guiding me up the staircase.

"Sid," Mandy said below us. "Please come in."

"Quick," Nic whispered, "before he tells us he's in line behind Walt Disney for the cryogenic machine."

"How do you remember that?"

We got to my room and he sat on my bed. "Sunshine," he said, and I saw the corners of his mouth fall a little, "I remember everything about you."

"Nico," I held on to his arm, "I can't do this."

He kissed my fingers. "Wait here." He went across the hall and into the bathroom. And I looked down at my bedside table, where the legal papers were spread out. I'd sat in Attorney Doherty's office hours before my dad died. It had only been three days ago, but it seemed like months, and he'd told me that in legal terms a divorce was actually called a "petition of dissolution." It had sounded so benign, so affable and doable.

I heard Nic turn on the shower in the bathroom. He was so good in a crisis. If the world fell apart, Nic would have it under control. "It's that white church," Mandy told someone on the phone downstairs, probably Freddie, "on the green."

The lawyer was an older man and his bow tie had been slightly crooked. He had drawn up the papers for me, and I had felt elated, a little empty, but light. I'd bought myself a silver bracelet from a sidewalk stand on my way home, but then I had given it to a homeless woman on Chapel Street.

But now, panic had set in. I wanted to get in the car with Nic, or on a plane, and I wanted him to take me back out west, to the loft on Iron Works Road.

I picked up a Mickey Mouse pen from the bedside table. My dad had given it to me with a matching diary when I was ten. The diary had a lock and key. The memory of it brought a rush of grief. When Nic came back into my room, I was curled up on my bed, holding Bear to my chest. "Hey," he sat next to me, "you all right?"

"I really can't do this."

"I found a clean towel, and the shower's running."

I touched the hard line of his jaw. "I'm so sorry."

He watched me, that half smile playing on his face. "For what?"

"Everything. This summer. Greece."

But Nico touched his fingers to my lips. "No sorrys. We've got to get you showered and dressed. We'll talk about everything else later."

But I think I already know, I wanted to tell him. *I sat across from a little man in a bow tie.* Nico took my hands and pulled me to sitting. "Arms up," he said. Like a parent, he slipped off my T-shirt, and I sat there, bare-chested. As he slipped off my shorts, I thought how he was like an eclipse; he had the power to erase everything. He was a hole I could fall into. I wanted him to look at me; I wanted him to put his hands on my breasts. I wanted him to kiss me. It would take away the funeral. None of this would exist. He slipped his arms under mine and eased me up so that I was standing, naked, in front of him. "Okay." His voice was hoarse. "Let's get you in the shower."

But neither of us moved. His eyes had that lazy look, and next to the black shirt, they appeared navy blue, and I saw him taking me to bed that first night so many years ago in Boulder, how I'd let myself be led as a shadow is led. I hadn't needed to think. This, I remembered thinking as he'd kissed my neck, my shoulders, is what power looks like. This black-haired man.

"Nic," I whispered. His breath was coming hard. I could hear Mandy downstairs talking to Sid. Jamie and Luke were probably putting Hershey's Kisses on Will's headstone so he'd know they'd been there. Ryder would be back soon with his clothes. I touched Nic's lips with my fingertips. When he kissed me, I could feel that drowning sensation starting to take over. Memory fell back. His mouth was on my neck, his hands on the small of my back. And then I heard Will's voice, as if he were in the room. *All ye, all ye! Come home, be free!* Something he used to yell out when we were playing hide-and-seek as kids and he couldn't find me. I opened my eyes. I saw again my childhood room, the piano awards on the walls, Bear. And the grief about my father arrived suddenly and acutely, like a breaking wave out on Ocean View Beach, where Will, Ryder, and I used to try to surf. "If you hold sadness off," Luke had told me when we were practicing piano one afternoon, "it comes back a thousandfold and eats you up inside. You got to feel it, put it in those ivory keys." I quit kissing Nic and held my hand to his chest. He was watching me, waiting.

Behind us, the sun was bathing the goalposts in light. And I stepped back, away from him. Then I turned and walked across the hall. Nic followed me. He sat waiting for me on the closed toilet seat with a fresh towel while I showered behind the wavy glass.

36

When we stepped into the church's foyer, the organ started playing Mendelssohn's "On Wings of Song." Hazy sunlight filtered through the church's windows, and as we neared the parish hall door, I saw that the congregation was packed to standing room only. It smelled of heat and perfume, and across the nave, the casket shined. "I want to go home," I told Jamie, but she must not have heard me. She just kept walking forward on those high, high heels, her updo flawless and her perfectly tailored black suit belying her unending grief.

As we walked, people made way for us, I felt Nic's hand on my back, and I kept my fingers on Jamie's arm, trying not to look at anyone. But, my eyes kept traveling to familiar faces: staff members from A Will to Live, coaches my dad had been buddies with, ESPN commentators, a whole pew of his brothers, Mandy's parents, all our neighbors from North Parker, and a few boys from Hamilton who had played football with Will. They were all dressed up now and had receding hairlines. I wondered for the millionth time what Will would have looked like if he'd lived.

Before I turned into the pew, I glanced back. I thought maybe somehow I'd see Hadley, miraculously back from Europe. Instead,

I saw Dr. Griffith, and this time I was almost positive it was him, that sickle-shaped scar bright in the church light. Then he ducked into a row and I lost sight of him.

Starflower, Fred, Mandy, and Ryder were in the second pew already. I felt solitary and small, sitting on that long wooden bench between Nic and Jamie. Her hand was fragile in mine.

The organ finished "On Wings of Song," and I looked at that solid-cherry casket Luke and my mother had picked out a few days before. The program read, *Sterling Will Reilly: Father of Jensen Reilly Ledakis and Will James Reilly, deceased.* I folded it in half. I hadn't slept, and I had that wavy, disassociated feeling that I might pass out.

Just when the silence became deafening, Luke came from behind the altar and stood at the pulpit dressed in a simple white robe. "It's often said that when someone dies from cancer," he began, "they've lost the battle. In my friend Sterling Reilly's case, I disagree." A honey-colored Steinway sat behind him near the choir stalls. "He fought the good fight for four months." The piano was on wheels. It seemed odd for a church to have a piano when there was already an organ. "And when he went gently into the night last Thursday, it wasn't because he'd been beaten, but because he had done what he needed to do in this world: He enriched lives; he taught us and encouraged us; he showed us how to love unconditionally." Luke stared out at the congregation. "Perhaps you feel you have lost a friend, a colleague, a coach, a mentor." He caught my eye. "Perhaps you have lost the one person who said you could do anything. Who never doubted you, but gave you wings to go anywhere and do anything." The congregation shifted. I heard people crying. "You have not lost," he said. "You have gained by knowing him. He is with us still."

And then he began singing "Amazing Grace." He sang it a cappella and the words rang out, filling the church. Jamie collapsed beside me. I slipped my fingers through hers and she put her head on my shoulder and cried.

The rest of the service was a blur. I was there, but I wasn't. Sid told stories about A Will to Live and how many kids' lives my dad had touched. My father's old Steelers coach talked about his sportsmanship and the positive psychology of his game; someone who worked with him at ESPN read a tribute he'd started writing when he found out my dad was sick. I knew later I would want to remember everything they said; I would want to go over and over it. Here were the people who had known my father best, talking about what kind of man he was, but my mind was slipping around. And then no one else was speaking. Luke was stepping back to the pulpit to talk about the reception at the foundation following the burial. Before he was finished, I felt myself rise. "Jensen," Jamie said. "What on earth—" We had agreed not to speak, that it was too emotional, but without knowing quite what I was doing, I went past her and into the aisle. Luke and I locked eyes. "I had it rolled in for you, baby girl," he said when I reached the altar, "just for you."

I sat at the piano, running my fingers over the keys. The church fell silent, and I pretended Luke and I were alone in Woolsey Hall. My fingers found the notes. I felt my feet move to the pedals. And then I began to play, slowly at first, hesitantly, until, after the first few notes, I was playing with my eyes closed, the song flowing through my fingers as though for thirteen years I'd never stopped playing. I played the song I hadn't been able to play at Will's funeral: "Reverie." It lasted five and a half minutes. And for 330 seconds, I was absolutely positive my father was with me.

37

I woke to thunder rumbling over the house. Lying in bed with my eyes closed, it took a minute to remember the endless stream of people at the reception at A Will to Live. At some point during the evening, I'd realized Jamie wasn't next to me, and I'd found her in the rec room, shoes kicked off, suit jacket flung over a rocking horse, playing Ping-Pong with some kids from the foundation.

Outside my window, storm clouds were moving across a nickel-colored sky. And I wondered how long Nic had been out of bed; it was rare for him to get up first. And then I saw those papers on my bedside table, spread out in a fan—the petition of dissolution. I knew, in the same way I knew when the phone was going to ring or that rain was coming, that he had seen them.

The world felt drained of color. I threw a sweatshirt over my tank top and wandered downstairs. Luke was at the sink, washing dishes. My mom was drinking coffee at the kitchen table, her pale yellow robe pulled tightly around her, her hair back in a messy po-nytail. Grief had stripped her face of color, and in shades of alabas-ter, she was more beautiful than I'd ever seen her.

"Hi, sleepyhead," she said.

I sat across from her, and she reached over to squeeze my fingers.

Her hands felt more substantial today, and she managed a little smile.

"Beautiful playing yesterday," Luke said. He set an espresso in front of me.

"Oh, sweetheart." My mother's eyes filled with tears. "I wish your father could have seen you. He always loved watching you play the piano." Luke went back to washing dishes. "You know, I always thought he'd live forever."

Luke laughed a little. "He had that way about him, didn't he?"

"I remember when we met, he seemed too good to be true." Jamie let go of my hand and pushed a stray hair out of her eyes. "And when it lasted day after day, it just seemed like a miracle to me."

"We were lucky we had him for as long as we did." Luke turned off the water and started drying.

The coffee tasted good. Everything Luke made tasted two hundred times better than whatever anyone else made.

Jamie was still looking at me. "It's official. The agency is all Piers's."

I was about to take another sip of my coffee, but I stopped. "Wow, I guess you were serious."

Luke was grinning.

"It was time." My mother smiled. "Farewell to the anorexics."

"And to crazy cameramen," Luke added. "Your mother's quite the businesswoman. A Will to Live won't know what hit them."

I realized this was true.

Nic had slipped in and was standing in the doorway in his jeans and a rumpled T-shirt. My mother glanced at him. "Darling, you're not going to steal her away too soon, are you?"

He watched me, his expression unreadable. And I knew. He must have seen the papers. They were right there on the table. He couldn't have missed them.

"I need to shower," I said quietly.

I stood in the hot water, trying to think of what to say to Nic, but instead I found myself thinking back to those moments after we'd all filed out of the church.

"Mand," I'd said on our way out. "Can you grab the guest book, please?"

She'd been signaling to the driver, trying to get him to clear a path for us. "Don't worry about it, J.J. I'm sure someone will bring it over to the house later."

"No." I had touched her arm. "I need it now. Please."

She was gone and back before we'd reached the limo. "I got it."

We'd sat in the backseat, with Nic, Ryder, Luke, and my mother across from us. The book had been cool in my hands. I flipped through the pages while we moved slowly behind the hearse.

"Is she okay?" I heard my mother say.

I kept going through the pages, but there were so many names.

"Who are you looking for?" Nic asked.

"The guy who ran down the steps as we were leaving. I saw him when we first got there. It was creepy, like he was waiting for me."

Mandy poked me in the side. "We *were* all waiting for you." I ignored her and kept searching. "Do you know him?" Her words were slow and measured, as if she were talking to a child.

"Yeah, I think so."

A few minutes later, we pulled through the gates of the cemetery. The driver opened the door and bright sunlight poured in, but I kept flipping through the guest book.

"Jensen." I barely heard Nic's voice. "We're here. You have to get out."

He slipped out of the limo and everyone followed. Ryder was about to slide out, when I finally found what I was looking for. "It *was* him," I said.

Ryder was still sitting there. "Who?"

"Ron Griffith. I thought that's who it was."

"The doctor?" His face had gone white. We walked to the grave site in silence.

I shut off the shower now, toweled off and threw on the same jeans and sweater I'd changed into after everyone left the night before.

When I got downstairs, Jamie and Luke were sitting close to each other on the couch, not speaking. It reminded me of when Will died, when we didn't talk for an entire day after his funeral. Luke had told me later that the Yupik Eskimo culture didn't allow people to speak of their dead. I wondered, vaguely, if we'd created our own society of grief. "Your husband went outside." Luke motioned to the front door. "Sounds like he's on his way out of town soon." He raised his eyebrows.

Nic was sitting on the front steps, holding an empty coffee mug. I sat next to him. "Hey, you," I said. Out on the road, a boy and a girl were riding their bikes, circling around and around, the streamers on the handlebars standing straight out in the wind. I slipped my hand through Nic's and leaned against him.

"I'm not stupid, J.," he said quietly. "I knew it before you did." His face was like stone, but I saw that quick twitch in his jaw. He wouldn't yell. It was one of the things I loved and hated about him.

After a while, I said, "I was painting Will." The girl stood up on her bike and her blond hair flew out behind her. "Those self-portraits were really Will. That's why they sucked so bad."

"They didn't suck." He kept watching the kids. Eventually, he said, "I told myself when I met you that you'd break my heart."

I watched the kids ride off, leaving the street empty. It started to drizzle, but we kept sitting there. "I wish I'd known him better," Nic said.

"My dad?"

He nodded. "I'm an asshole."

I buried my face in his shoulder. No matter how many times we washed his shirts, they still smelled like glaze. I knew that later it might come, the yelling, the fights over the separation, the horrible words between us, but right now there was a certain peace. In a way, I felt closer to him than I had since we'd met. I pressed my shoulder against him. "You're not an asshole. You're a big shot. You're so big, I could stand on your shoulders and see the whole world."

"My world." He gazed down at me. "I never really let you see your own."

38

Nico left the next morning. I stood in the window and watched the black town car pull out. He hadn't wanted me to drive him to the airport. He'd slept in the guest room, and I saw now that this was how he would be. That was Nic's way, his defense. He'd grieve alone. That's one of the reasons I'd been drawn to him in the first place. I understood the way he hid his vulnerability. He'd cut me off. His pride would make me nonexistent. Some other girl would worship him and together they'd go to Greece. The thought brought a sting of jealousy, a helpless urgency to run after him. But beneath that, I felt something deeper: relief, reprieve.

"I'm going out for a little while," I told Jamie and Luke when I got downstairs. They were sitting on the couch together, like they'd been doing for two days.

"Out?" She looked startled. She'd been clinging to me since my dad died. "Out where?"

I saw Luke take her hand. "That's fine," he told me. "We'll be here when you get back."

. . .

"Excuse me," I said to the triage nurse. Her long dark hair wasn't tied back and I thought that must be some kind of health code violation. "Can you tell me where I might find Dr. Griffith?"

"You're in luck." My eyes followed her pencil. "He's right there." She was pointing across the hall, where he was leaning on a counter, talking on the phone. I walked over to him, and he startled, mumbled something into the receiver, then hung up. He was wearing wire-rimmed glasses, and deep wrinkles spread out from those piercing blue eyes like a road map. His hair, which had been thinning and black so many years before, was a faint ring. He still had that curved scar. When he spoke, it was as if he'd been expecting me.

"Jensen. Let's go to my office."

I followed him down a brightly lit hallway to a small room. He waited for me to enter, then closed the door. I had the strange, sudden thought that he might kill me. He motioned to a straight-backed chair with a brocade cushion, and I sat. I watched him take a seat on the other side of his desk, leaving a thick mahogany barrier between us.

"I kept thinking I saw you over the summer while my dad was sick, but I wasn't sure. And then I did see you . . . at his funeral." I waited for him to say something, to give me an explanation or offer his condolences, but he just tapped his pen on the desk. "Thanks for coming," I said.

"I had a feeling when you saw me at your father's service that you'd come here. I guess, in a way, I've been waiting thirteen years for this moment." He tapped the pen one last time before putting it down. "The night your brother died, this place was a madhouse." His voice sounded loud in the tiny room, and my stomach tightened at the mention of Will. He made a temple of his hands and rested his chin on his index fingers. "When he came in the first time, we had an MVA involving a bus of senior citizens going to the casino." A thin line of sweat stood out on his top lip. "We were up to our ears in broken hips and concussions. Radiology was backed up for hours."

The burning feeling in my stomach felt like it would eat through me. There was something about this man. I remembered how he hadn't looked at anyone when he'd told us about Will thirteen years ago. Now he leaned back in his chair, putting his hands behind his head, his gaze fixed on the middle distance between us. "Because Will suffered a head trauma on the football field, I ordered an MRI of his brain, then did a full neurological workup. Other than a mild headache, he seemed to have no residual effects from the impact. His balance was excellent, he wasn't dizzy, and his pupils were working properly. He had no signs of impairment." I thought it was odd that after such a long time, he remembered so much about my brother.

And then I realized he was going to confront me. I heard Luke's voice telling me the only way to freedom was to confess your lies. "Listen," I said.

But Dr. Griffith put his hand up to stop me. "I'm going to say this once." His eyes nailed me to my seat. "I could lose my medical license for telling you this, my reputation. . . ." He took a sharp breath in. "The fact is"—he blinked—"I never saw your brother's scan that night. The film and report were misplaced somehow." He spoke quickly, defensively. "Radiology was backed up, so we couldn't do another. And he seemed fine. So I released him. Then he died, and I couldn't understand it, because he'd presented with a normal neuro exam. That's why I asked about a second trauma."

My head felt like a balloon as I listened, and I didn't know if I was hearing him correctly.

"A few days later, Will's scans showed up on my desk. Apparently they'd been filed under the wrong name." He held his pen again and his lip twitched. Finally, he looked right at me. "Your brother had sustained a subdural hematoma during the game."

I didn't understand what he was saying. "What does that mean?"

"Will had a brain bleed on the football field. That's what killed him."

"No," I said, loudly enough to startle us both.

"Yes," Ron Griffith said. "The injury on the field caused a slow bleed at the base of his skull, which is what killed him. I would have seen it if I'd been able to check his MRI, but he seemed okay, and I didn't want to keep him here for hours while I waited for someone to redo the scan. We didn't even have enough beds." I watched his eyelid twitch. "I read about your father in the paper and went to his funeral because all these years, I'd wanted to tell your parents that I'd misdiagnosed their son." His forehead was wet with sweat. "I wanted to tell them I was wrong and that I was sorry. I should have made Will stay here until I read his scan. But it wouldn't have made any difference. We can't, of course, reverse something like that, which is why I never told your parents." His face had turned an odd pale color. "To have hope that your child is okay and then . . ." He cleared his throat.

"But he was fine when we got home. His head didn't even hurt that much."

He massaged his temples with his pointer fingers. "That's the thing about brain injuries. It's rare, but sometimes there are no symptoms at all. The only way to diagnose them is with a scan."

The room was so quiet, I could hear the ticking of his watch. He took his glasses off and placed them on his desk as if they were made of eggshells.

"It was me." I could barely hear my own voice. "I pushed Will later that night and he hit his head." I felt suffocated in that tiny space. "It was my fault."

He shook his head. "It had nothing to do with that."

"Yes, it did." My tone was accusatory. "You said so. You kept asking if he'd had another accident." I sat on my hands. "I pushed him, and he hit his head on the hearth. And then he died. Right there."

"The hematoma was so massive that it was only a matter of time," Ron Griffith told me. "If he fell when you pushed him, it was probably because the pressure in his brain affected his balance. You need to understand this, Jensen. Will would have collapsed and died even if you hadn't pushed him." He paused, waiting for me to understand. "Nothing, not even surgery, could have saved him. Basically, your brother was dead as soon as he got hit on the field."

I stared at him, at his scar and the odd, shifty way his eyes slipped from mine. For the first time, I remembered that Will had wavered when he came at Ryder; he'd faltered, as though off balance, as though drunk. His words had been a little slurred, and I remembered thinking it was the anger, the rage. I could see the weave of Dr. Griffith's shirt, a small rip starting in the corner of his pocket. It dawned on me in his antiseptic office that my father had been right; it wasn't my fault. It. Wasn't. My. Fault.

"I would have told the truth had I known you thought you were responsible. But you were so adamant that nothing else had happened." He put his elbows on the desk and leaned forward. "If it would help, I'll talk to your mother."

"That's not necessary." I stood; I couldn't look at him any longer. I went to the door and stared at the pattern in the wood grain. I was about to tell him how his mistake had ruined my life, but then he spoke up. "Miss Reilly," he said. "I'm sorry. I'm so, so sorry."

39

When I got back to the parking garage, it was like I'd never been there before. I couldn't remember which floor I'd parked on. *Basically, your brother was dead,* Dr. Griffith's voice chanted in my head, *as soon as he got hit on the field.*

Tires squealed on the floor above me, echoing against the concrete walls. I walked until I saw an elevator, got on, and went up a floor. The doors opened. Three giggling teenagers got in.

"Ma'am?" the tallest one said.

I was standing with one foot on the pavement and one foot still in the elevator. I could hear the soft clicking of the doors trying to close. "Sorry." I stepped out, feeling dizzy, drugged. My car was under a spray-painted number, which was a faded daffodil color: R4. It took me three tries to turn the key in the ignition. My hands were slippery with sweat. Backing out of the parking space, I saw myself in the rearview mirror; my skin was colorless as parchment.

I thought about how I woke up screaming from the image of Will's head hitting the stone. I'd spent so long feeling haunted by what Ryder and I had done, hunted even, that I couldn't reconcile this new information. I used to think if I could take it back, if I could have made it so it wasn't my fault, everything would fall into place. I circled down the exit ramp, the steering wheel almost unmanageable in my hands.

"How's your dad?" a skinny kid asked when I gave him the parking stub and a five-dollar bill.

"I'm sorry, what?"

"Your dad?" He rested his hand on the edge of the booth and smiled. He was missing a bottom tooth. He was the one who'd let me go without my ticket the first time my father was in the hospital in June.

"He died," I said, my voice flat and stiff.

"Jesus." He stood up like he'd been struck. "Sorry."

The striped lever rose, and I drove through, turning right on Howard Avenue. Stoplights blended together, and it wasn't until a horn screamed that I realized I'd run a red light. It had all been a waste: running away from my parents, leaving Ryder, my missed ride to Juilliard, Nic. And what had I been running from? Nothing. Above me, the tree line was a brown blur of branches, and the sun was trying to poke through a heavy film of clouds.

His car was in the driveway, parked in front of the garage. I pulled in behind it and got out. I was on my way across the lawn when Ryder opened the front door. He was in jeans and wasn't wearing a shirt. I saw the number 18 on his bicep, and it made a hard lump rise in my throat.

"I was just on my way over. Are you okay?"

"I have something to tell you," I said.

He opened the door wider. I walked into the living room. It was the first time I'd been inside his house since I'd been back. He wasn't kidding when he said he'd gutted the place. The southwest wall was now a set of French doors and floor-to-ceiling windows. He must have cut down thirty trees, because the view of the harbor was spectacular. "Sit down and let me get you a sweater." He stared at me. "You're shivering."

"I'm not cold," I told him, but still he started for the stairs. I reached up and grabbed his arm. "It wasn't our fault," I said.

He turned back and squinted at me.

"I just saw him."

"Ron Griffith?"

I nodded. Ryder backed up. "He never saw Will's MRI the night of the accident. Someone misplaced it and radiology was backed up. Will looked and felt okay, so Griffith let him go." Ryder's eyes went very dark. "A few days later, someone found the scans and put them on his desk." I could hear my voice trembling, my insides shaking. "Will had a brain bleed from getting hit on the football field. Griffith said it was so big that he would have died anyway. It was just a matter of time."

Ryder had gotten angry very rarely when we were younger. But if people cheated at a game, called points that weren't theirs, or when the neighborhood kids used to bully the autistic boy on North Parker, he'd get mad fast and as thoroughly as if he were infused with some explosive. Now the blood rushed to his face, and it turned bright red. "That fucking bastard." He backed away from me. "That squirrelly fucking asshole." He was running his hand through his hair. "How does a doctor lose a scan? What the fuck does that mean? Radiology was backed up?" He was facing me, but I could tell he wasn't really seeing me. "You don't lose scans, Jensen. You stay all night until you find them. Do you understand me? Do you know what this means? Do you? All that fucking time, I felt like a murderer. I went through medical school trying to prove myself." His chest was splotched from anger. "All those fucking late nights, trying to save people who couldn't be saved. And that asshole never saw the fucking scans? Never saw them? Never called us back when he found them?" I thought he was going to break something. Or cry. "I'll strangle him." He picked up a shirt from the back of the sofa. "I'm going to kill him." He started for the front door.

"Ryder," I said. I caught his arm, but he swiped it away. "Ryder!" I yelled at him. For one terrifying moment, I thought he might hit me. "Ryder," I said again, softer this time. "It's me." He didn't look away. His eyes started to clear. "It's me, Jenny." Stepping into him, I felt him relax.

And then he collapsed against me. I felt him bury his face in my neck. "Don't you know what this means?" he asked again. "We could have been together. We could have . . ."

"I'm here now," I told him. "We can't go back." I kissed his neck, kissed his earlobe, his jaw. His hands had been at his sides, but slowly he moved them up my back, tangling his fingers in my hair. A cloud must have moved away from the sun, because the room lightened slightly.

"Jesus," he whispered. "I can't fucking lose you again." He kissed my collarbone, felt my rib cage with his hands. "I can't."

"Nic left yesterday."

"He did? Why?" He kissed my earlobe. "You know what, I don't care. You can stay married forever and have me on the side."

"Do you know what a petition of dissolution is?" I tasted his lips, his sweet Ryder taste. He groaned.

"No, what?" He kissed me again.

"It means I filed for divorce." I put my mouth to his ear and whispered, "We're free."

He quit kissing me. Then he took hold of my waist and set me in front of him. And in that moment, Ryder became Ryder again, that boy I had known as a child, the one with those trusting dark eyes, the boy who was so sure of the goodness life had to offer him. Then he started laughing. He picked me up and twirled me around and around, kissing me and kissing me and kissing me.

And finally there was nothing else in the world except for Ryder and me, undressing each other as we fumbled up the stairs, down the hall, into his old room with that same antique bed, that bed I'd dreamed of so often, all those years, when I was lost and alone, wanting for all the world to come home.

Epilogue

After dinner, Ryder holds the door open and we sneak out onto the back deck. The night is crisp; it smells of hickory smoke. Leaves litter the grass.

He lifts me into his old macramé hammock, frayed and stained, but sturdy between two oaks, and climbs up next to me, smelling of the apple pie he made for Thanksgiving dinner. I can hear them in the living room, the twins' high-pitched giggles, Luke's baritone voice, Jamie in the kitchen, rinsing the dessert dishes. Ryder squeezes my thumbnail between his fingers, something I find strangely erotic, and that warmth rises from the bottom of my belly.

A warm breeze blows chimney smoke our way. "You think this Indian summer will last?" he asks.

I don't answer, just lie back and weave my fingers through his. When I am an old woman, these are the days I'll remember: Luke giving me away when Ryder and I got married during a blizzard; the morning our twins, Piper and Will, were born; the night my dad was posthumously inducted into the NFL Hall of Fame.

Ryder puts his hand over his heart. He points at me with two fingers in the shape of a peace sign. It's our code, our silent love song. I put my hand over my heart, too, and do the same sign back.

And we keep wordlessly signing like that, back and forth, under the bright November stars.

It all seems so long ago. Will's death, the first thing that fractioned my life, feels far away. And my father's death is less constant, if not less painful. I finally realized the things that split me open, then halved me again and again never really broke me. Seventh grade pre-algebra taught me you could divide a number forever and never reach zero. Perhaps the same holds true for a person.

My night blindness is gone. I noticed it that first fall I was back in Colston. I could see clearly again in the dark. I went to a specialist, who said the same thing as the doctor who'd diagnosed me. Malnutrition can cause nyctalopia. And proper nutrition can help reverse its effects. Now it's the past that's out of focus, hazy and fading. I'm beginning to forget the time before Will and my dad died. I see that part of my life as if I still had night blindness. I can make out faint images but not specific memories. There is no before. Nor is there an after. It's only here. It's only now.

Still, there are times I want to see Will riding that yellow horse around the carousel, run with him up Heartbreak Hill. I want to be standing at Caller's Island, talking with my dad about his childhood, picnicking on the teak ketch he and Luke bought on a whim, racing down the Merritt in the car from *The Graduate,* or just sitting with him in the kitchen, reading the Sunday paper. But when I think back on those times, I can't quite remember if that car was candy-apple red or maroon, or what songs we sang to on the radio. When nostalgia hits hard, sometimes I wish I could bring my night blindness into focus and see everything, even the hard parts, clearly again.

Acknowledgments

I was not born a writer; I was made. When I was little, my family spent a lot of time fishing. Because I was neither a lover of fish nor of water, my mother would bring along a notebook and tell me to write stories about our adventures. So, my first thank-you is to my lovely mom, Nancy Moroso, who, although she probably didn't know it at the time, started the fire that would turn into my career as a novelist. Mom, for your boundless support and love, I thank you and I love you.

Suzanne Kingsbury deserves as much credit for this book as I do. I brought her a crumpled, neglected first draft that had been transferred from one computer to another. Never did I think it would go anywhere. For two years, Suzanne worked with me scene by scene, chapter by chapter. Through characters that I loved but couldn't fit into the book, seven different beginnings, more than that many endings, and figuring out how to do away with Will, Suzanne talked me off the ledge, sat on my living room floor taping scenes together, and made me laugh throughout the entire experience. Jenny, Ryder, Will, and all the others are as much her babies as they are mine. For her creative genius and beautiful style that regularly brought me to tears, I am humbled and honored to work with her and to call her my friend.

Sasha Weiss Sanford gets a huge shout-out for two reasons. First, she introduced me to Suzanne. And as I said, undoubtedly without her, *Night Blindness* would still be in a forgotten file in an old, cracked computer in my basement where old, cracked computers go to die. Second, Sasha has been my best friend, the sharer of our brain, the keeper of my secrets, and the source of my best times since we were nine years old. That's a privilege few people have. Sash—you are my family and I love you for that.

This book most certainly never would have been published without my agent, the incomparable Lisa Gallagher of the Sanford J. Greenburger Agency. A year before Lisa signed me, she personally wrote to me, providing detailed edits she thought would make *Night Blindness* the best it could be. At that point, we'd never met. She had no obligation or commitment to me, but she took the time to help an unknown writer and I am thankful every day that she did. I worked on her edits for months and emerged with a book that felt like home. The first time we spoke on the phone, it was as easy and comfortable as if I were talking to a close friend I'd known for years. Ten days later, she sold the book to St. Martin's Press. Ten days! Are you thinking what I'm thinking? This woman is nothing short of brilliant. Having never done this before, I wondered if after Lisa sold *Night Blindness*, her job would be done. How wrong I was. Lisa continues to be my biggest advocate, the giver of endless support and a constant source of amazing feedback and input. She sends me funny e-mails that have nothing to do with work, always asks about my family, and nudges me forward when I stall. Lisa—for your friendship, your belief in my writing, and your stand-back-and-get-out-of-my-way attitude, I am grateful beyond words. Every day I wonder why you chose me, but I am so thankful that you did.

Lisa's awesomeness led me to the fantastic team at St. Martin's Press. Publishers Tom Dunne of Thomas Dunne Books and Sally Richardson of St. Martin's Press made all this happen. Assistant editor Melanie Fried holds the flashlight that illuminates this magical journey. Thank you, Melanie, for being so wonderful and for answering my endless questions. Lisa Senz and Angelique Giammarino, the marketing and social media gurus, have helped me become a little less tragically unhip when it comes to the online world of getting my name out there. Lisa and Angelique, along with production manager Cheryl Mamaril, designer Kathryn Parise, team leader Dori Weintraub, production editor Lisa Davis, and publicist Katie Bassel have worked tirelessly to bring this book to readers. A thank-you to jacket designer Steve Snider for a terrific jacket. Thanks to Katie Gilligan for being the force behind acquiring *Night Blindness*. And a special high-five to Pete Wolverton, editor in chief and rescuer of all things that could have gone south. He kept me laughing while I was trying to write in a house full of kids in the middle of a snowstorm. To the entire St. Martin's Press and Thomas Dunne Books team, thank you isn't nearly enough. You all are the superstars.

My two closest friends from graduate school, Cindi Williams and Sallie Spignesi, were my original early readers. They both came back with such honest reviews that it was a little hard to hear, but their input helped produce a better book. To my two best Gestalt girls, thank you and I love you.

On to the multitalented Dr. Patrick Doherty. Not only is he a neurosurgeon extraordinaire, but he was one of the fabulous physicians who cared for my dad as if he were his own. For that, I am eternally grateful. Pat was also my own personal medical consultant, who strapped on his seat belt and rode this bumpy ride with me while I was writing *Night Blindness*. He responded to no fewer than two thousand e-mails and phone calls and explained his answers both patiently and in terms I could understand. He also spelled all the big words. And not even a month after I was done figuring out Sterling's fate, I decided the old chap needed a new diagnosis. Rather than changing his name and all his contact information, Pat sat with me while I asked him another two thousand questions (I'm not kidding here) and once again responded to each and every inquiry like the consummate professional that he is. Pat— for your friendship, wisdom, knowledge, and e-mails that made me laugh out loud while I was writing in crowded coffeehouses, thank you doesn't begin to cover it. I hope you know how much you mean to me. Pat is a genius. Any medical mistakes are mine and mine alone.

My father, Dick Moroso, and Clarence Clemons had a friendship unlike any other I've ever known. They loved each other more than brothers, more than best friends. Had they possessed any physical resemblance, I might have believed they were separated at birth. Their bond taught me so much about life and love. The two of them shared much the same kind of kindred connection that Sterling and Luke had. For giving me that story and for how much they both loved me, I will never forget how lucky I was to have them for as long as I did. Although they are gone, I love them still and miss them every day.

My brother, Rob Moroso, really did cut off my cat's whiskers. While I didn't see the humor in it at the time, it did make for a funny chapter. Rob was a lot like Will—a rock star who was taken from us long before his time should have been up. I wish that I could have grown old with him, but he will stay with me forever in pictures, memories, and in hints of Will.

A thank-you to my closest high school friends, Helen Chandler Smith and Andy Cober. You made high school more fun than it should have been. I'm so lucky that twenty-five years later you're still in my life. And to my nearby friends, Erika Celentano, Paulette Rider, Sarah Rector, Sarah Waterhouse, Rae Wyrebek, Sarah Whitney, and Marta Collins who always ask about my books, thank you! A thank-you to John McDonough for your knowledge of flowers. And to Howard Paris, my Sunshine Man, thank you for keeping me from losing my mind during the years when I was sure that was a given. I hope that my eighth-grade English teacher, Mr. Hershnik, knows that I still have a copy of his Hernickian Rules of Writing. To my riding trainer, Peter Leone, who has given me a haven for the last fifteen years that has kept me sane enough to write, thank you. And to Alison Finger, Brittain Ezzes and all my other Lionshare girls, thank you for sharing the magic of the horse world with me.

And now for one of the three great loves of my life—my husband, Kurt Strecker. When Kurt and I met, I was just a girl in a bar (isn't that how all great love stories begin?) working on my master's degree. I was three careers and a lifetime away from becoming a novelist. Throughout the years spent working on this book, Kurt hunkered down with a glass of wine for each of us and answered endless questions about football and head trauma. He gave his opinion on which phrase, word, or sentence sounded best. By the way, he was always right. The list of what Kurt has given me is limitless, one of his greatest gifts being confidence. He has this amazing ability to never be surprised by my accomplishments, but to expect them. Kurtie—thank you for being my sounding board and the best part of my life. I love you now and forever.

Finally, my two other great loves: my children, Cooper and Ainsley. These awesome kids went through all thirty-two NFL team rosters while we were thinking of a name for Jenny's hometown. Coop also shared his love of *Star Wars* when he named Luke. Ainsley gave me the idea for Ryder's name. They regularly ask when they can read *Night Blindness*, and I truly believe they want to. My kids are the light and love of my life. They are patient when I burn dinner because I'm writing, they bring me snacks when I haven't come out of my office for a while, and they ask me all the time how my new book is going. Cooper and Ainsley—you make me proud every day to be your mom and I love you more than life.

1. *Night Blindness* begins with Jensen, the narrator, talking about her medical condition, nyctalopia, that began shortly after her brother's death and prevents her from driving after dark. In what other ways do you think Jensen's life has been restricted since Will died?

2. Jensen keeps a secret from her parents that quite possibly alters the course of her life. How do you think her life could have been different if she'd told her parents the truth about Will's accident? Have you ever kept a secret that could have profoundly changed your life if others knew it?

3. Throughout the book, Jensen believes her mother is keeping a secret from her. It turns out it was a good secret, so why do you think Jamie didn't tell Jensen that she was selling her business?

4. It's been thirteen years since Ryder and Jensen have seen each other. Jensen is taken aback by how much Ryder has changed. He no longer appears to be that long-haired, easygoing teenager that she knew. Now he wears stiff penny loafers, monogrammed shirts and has very short hair. Through flashbacks, we see Ryder as the laid-back boy that he was. Which version do you think is the real Ryder? And why do you think he changed so much?

5. Jensen has always been very close to her father. But, until he got sick, she rarely came home. What do you think kept Jensen from one of the people she loved the most? And do you think it was difficult for her to stay away?

6. Jensen's best friend, Mandy, has a reputation for being wild and carefree. She's never had a serious relationship. What is it about Fred that made her settle down?

St. Martin's
Griffin

7. Near the end of the book, Jensen finally confesses to her father what really happened to Will. He dies having forgiven her. What would it have been like if he hadn't been able to forgive her?

8. After Sterling dies, Jensen learns that what she thought was the truth about Will's death, isn't what really happened. How do you think it weighs on her knowing her father died thinking she was responsible for her brother's death?

9. The entire book takes place in the fictional Connecticut shoreline town of Colston. How do you think the book would be different if it had been set in a different location?

10. Jensen has been angry with her mother for her infidelity since Will died. But throughout the book, she learns from Luke and Jamie that her parents' relationship was more complicated than she had believed it to be when she was in high school. Why do you think Jamie never corrected Jensen's belief about the marriage?

11. Was it fair for Jensen to be so angry at her mother when Jensen had never gotten over Ryder and still found herself being attracted to him even though she'd been with Nic for more than a decade?

12. Throughout the book, Jensen is torn between her first love and her husband. What are your thoughts on her thinking about Ryder while she's still married to Nic?

13. Nic is painted as not always being kind to Jensen. Is it ironic that he seems to have finally given Jensen what she needed by divorcing her?

Turn the page for a sneak peek at
Susan Strecker's next novel

NOWHERE
GIRL

Available March 2016

1

The day Savannah was killed, she was fifteen minutes late to meet me. I was cold, standing in the November wind outside our school. Because she'd told me to wait for her, I'd missed the bus, and now I'd have to walk home in the dark. Mrs. Wilcox's red Honda was the only car in the front parking lot. It was just me and a stone cherub above the entrance, giving me the creeps. Finally, I pushed back through the glass doors and plopped down in a leather recliner, furniture meant to make Kingswood Academy's waiting area feel like a living room rather than a school.

I knew I should have been out looking for Savannah, but I'd been a little pissed at her lately, coming home smelling like the cigarettes she'd smoked behind the carved oak trees out back with the upperclassmen girls. She was the one with the older, cooler friends; the secret boy crushes. She was the one who'd been getting high and having sex since we were fourteen. Somehow, she was also where she was supposed to be all the time. Which is how she fooled our parents, never giving them reason to suspect that their identical twin daughters were only the same on the outside.

Kingswood had been renovated the year before, thanks to a generous and wealthy alum. The skylights above me brought a constant brightness like the manufactured cheerfulness of a hospital's children's ward. Somewhere in the office, I heard Mrs. Wilcox typing on her computer. When I closed my eyes, I felt a vague sensual pleasure, as though someone had his warm hands all over me—a feeling rather than a thought. I'd only kissed one boy, barely touched our lips together, so I understood it was Savannah's experience I was feeling. As different as we were, I knew her the way a newborn knows to nurse and birds know to fly in a V.

That morning while she was flat-ironing her hair, INXS turned up too loud on the CD player in the bathroom, she told me to cover for her at the dance planning meeting after school.

"I'll ride the late bus home with you, and we'll just tell Mom and Dad I went."

I'd stood in the doorway of the bathroom watching her, wondering what had been making her smile so much lately.

"Where are you going?" I'd asked. But our brother, David, called us for breakfast, and she disappeared down the stairs.

She was probably off with Scarlet and Camilla, securing her place in that coveted inner circle of senior girls where no other underclassmen were allowed. Maybe my friend Gabby was right. Savannah was too cool for us; she only wanted to hang out with older girls now. There were so many days she'd asked me to take her backpack home and do her homework. Afterward, she'd come traipsing in the front door as I was setting the table for dinner, making up a lie about being at some school meeting that would look good on the college applications we wouldn't be writing for another two years. As I listened to Mrs. Wilcox type, I thought about something I'd been asking myself lately whenever resentment about Savannah began to creep in: *What if I said no? What if I walked home alone and told my mother I didn't know where she was?*

Of course, I knew from the second she didn't meet me outside the glass doors for the late bus that something was wrong. Still, when that hazy sensuality gave way to anxiety, I fought it. Panic crept into my stomach, my throat. If I'd allowed myself to hear Savannah, to listen to the message she was trying to send me, I would have known that, not more than a thousand yards away, she was dying.

I tried to tell myself that I was having an asthma attack, but it didn't feel like they usually did. It was more of a choking feeling in my throat than a tightness in my chest. When it got so bad I could barely breathe, I fumbled in my backpack for the cell phone my parents had given me for emergencies only. I'd never used it before.

"It's my sister," I told the 911 dispatcher frantically. "She's hurt."

"The nature of her injuries, please," the operator said in a robotic voice.

"I don't know. I think she can't breathe."

"Is the victim with you?"

"No, no. I don't know where she is, but she's hurt."

"Miss." The operator's monotone turned to impatience. "If you don't know where she is, how do you know she's injured? Did she call you?"

"She's my twin." I was sobbing, not from the pain in my throat but because I knew even as I was on the phone with the police that it was too late.

I could tell the dispatcher didn't believe me, but she asked where I was and my name, and then she clicked off.

By the time I hung up, I felt weak, so weak I thought my knees might give if I got up. Somewhere far off, I heard sirens. And then suddenly, something left me. I felt washed out, empty. The wind could have blown right through me. Something ineffable and bright, a ball of light I'd been carrying since birth, exited my body.

All my life, I'd remember that moment. But it was only in my thirty-third year that Savannah decided to finally return to save my life by leading me to her killer.

2

2015

It was Valentine's Day, and as usual, Greg and I were lying in bed, working. "How can you not like this holiday?" I asked him. He handed me a stack of letters three inches thick bound by a wide, green rubber band. "It celebrates love."

"It perpetuates mental illness and loneliness"—Greg pushed his glasses up his nose—"and its only purpose is to sell cheesy cards and chocolate." He put the letters on my lap and then picked up a case file. "Anyhow, if you're going to respond to all your fan mail, like your website says you will, you'd better get going."

I held up the elastic. "Is this from the broccoli?"

He gave me a half smile. "I had to use something. The ones in the junk drawer kept breaking."

I aimed it at his face. "Maybe someone in this stack will ask me to be his Valentine." I swerved at the last minute, and the rubber band headed toward our wedding photo. That picture could turn my mood nostalgic. We'd been so happy.

"Really, Cady." He set his file aside, got out of bed, and retrieved the elastic. "Grow up."

I watched him walk to the bathroom and shut the door. I listened for him to lift the toilet seat. The name on the file he'd been reading, gibberish to anyone else, was clear to me. Greg took his HIPAA laws seriously, but it hadn't taken me long to crack his code. Each letter was the one to the right of the actual letter on the keyboard. I'd spent so many years deciphering his files that I could do it almost instantly now.

I glanced at it while I slid the letter opener across the first envelope. What was this patient's problem? With the metal tip, I flipped open the file and got as far as "PP: Complains . . ." before Greg came back in the room.

"Hey." He grabbed the file.

PP—presenting problem. Complains about what? His wife? Thoughts of doing unspeakable things to children? Not being able to get a hard-on?

"If you need material for the new book, you could just ask. You don't have to snoop." He climbed in bed again.

"I might." I sighed. "My new friends at the pokey aren't cooperating."

"I really wish you wouldn't go there alone."

"Why?" The envelope in my hands was smudged with greasy fingerprints and smelled faintly of hot dogs. This one probably wasn't fan mail, but I opened it, anyway.

"It's not safe," Greg said.

"There are security cameras and guards everywhere."

"Can't you just Google whatever you need to know?"

He held his hand between us, palm up, an offering. And I knew I should take it, but instead, I unfolded the letter.

"No, this novel is set in a prison. I have to go there and feel it out." I pulled out my elastic and ran my hand through my hair. "But I haven't been able to find an inmate to talk to yet, so it could be a no-go."

He said something that I didn't hear because I was reading. *Ms. Bernard: You have no imagination. You keep writing about the same thing over and over.* "My website says I'll read and answer adoring fan mail." I handed him the angry scrawl. "Do I have to respond to this?"

He scanned the bottom of the letter. "Maybe Joe Mama is right. Scrap the prison drama and write something uplifting. You don't always have to be so dark."

"Have you met me?" I snatched the letter back. "Dark is all I know." Joe Mama didn't leave his contact information, so I tossed the letter on the floor. "I don't do cheery. Puppies and rainbows are not interesting. Besides, I must be doing something right. A lot of people love my books."

He opened the file. "Except your mother."

This was true. Every time I sent her a bound galley, she'd call, make small talk about how gorgeous Saint Augustine was, and tell me that the book was beautiful but upsetting.

"Let's leave my mom out of this. I don't blame her for not wanting to read about dead children and murderers."

"It wouldn't kill your family to talk about Savannah every now and again."

I winced at his choice of words. "I see my parents twice a year. I don't think that's what we want to discuss at Christmas dinner." I could feel another fight coming on. "Besides, you know why we don't talk about her."

"I know your reasons. I just don't agree with them."

I reminded myself that I chose to marry a shrink. And that once upon a time, we had loved each other. "I don't talk about my sister because I don't want to. It fucking hurts too much, okay?"

He patted my hand. "I'm sorry. I didn't mean to upset you."

I didn't feel like fighting. "It's fine."

"You are a strong writer, you know."

"But?" There was never a compliment without a *but*.

"But your work is disturbing, hard to read."

"No shit. My life is disturbing."

He slid his hand over and set it on top of mine. Greg's hands were big and boney. "It is not disturbing." He said it in the way you might talk to a child. Or a patient. "You live in a beautiful house." After my first book was published, the same year we got married, Greg found this place. It was much too big for us, but we bought it, anyway. The day we moved in, I stood in the foyer with its echoey, sterile feel and cried. "You're happily married." *To a man who wanted to fix me and hated Valentine's Day,* I thought. "Nothing about your life is disturbing. You're happy." No. I wasn't. He leaned over and gave me a dry peck on the cheek. "Right?" Quick kisses were all I seemed to get anymore. I didn't know if I was disappointed or relieved. I just wanted things to be the way they were before the money fights and miscarriages.

"Yes." I had at least seventy-five letters to read and didn't want to waste time arguing about something we were never going to agree on. "Life is good."

I thought he might kiss me again and then switch off the light, but we hadn't had sex since December after the last miscarriage the month before. I'd been inconsolable for weeks, and there was probably nothing else he could think to do to comfort me. Now, though, he went back to his file, and I sifted through the mail until I found one I wanted to answer.

I woke the next morning with the letters spilling off my chest onto the floor. Greg's side of the bed was neatly made, his reading glasses against his bedside table light. The weight of my dream pushed against me, and I sat up, careful not to disturb the duvet. I heard the shower shut off. Greg knew about my Savannah dreams, but I hadn't told him how real they were. He didn't know that every time she came to me, I woke with a slight depression on my side of the bed, as if someone had been sitting next to me. It was there now. An indent where a person might sit if they were watching you sleep. Or trying to wake you. I could feel that warm, melting feeling pouring out of me, leaving me cold in the room. It'd been months since Savannah had been in my dreams, but after New Year's, she'd come back. Usually, she appeared in bright colors, ringing out her singsongy voice, her eyes full of mischief. I'd wake up smelling her honey shampoo. But when she came back a few days into January, it'd been in memory and feeling. I couldn't recall the specifics, just a strange sadness as though she were reluctant to do what she had to do. The only thing I remembered from the initial dream was the prison.

Before those dreams began, I'd been planning to call Deanna and tell her I was quitting, that there would be no fifth book. I was stumped and stuck beyond recovery, but when I'd woken from that first one with that strange sensation in my body—as though I'd not only seen Savannah but I'd actually *been* her walking toward a prison in weak sunlight—I'd gotten up groggily and Googled directions to the South Jersey Penitentiary. I didn't know why she wanted me to go. But I had one small hope: maybe the son of a bitch who killed her had landed there, and I was finally supposed to find him.

Because I hadn't known who to call about an interview and it was only twenty minutes from my house, I'd driven there, hoping to charm someone into talking to me. It was a long shot. Skinny girls with flirty smiles were charming. Awkward, fat girls got sent away. But they hadn't denied me. And now I'd been there three times already under the guise of research and had spoken to the head warden, two psychologists, the continuing education teacher, and a public defender. But when I asked about the prisoners, I got shut down. "Inmates don't give interviews," the warden had told me. "They're convicts, not movie stars."

Now I ran my hand over the depression on the bed. Through the bathroom door, I could hear Greg humming. He turned on the sink. I closed my eyes and entered again the blurred world of razor wire and armed guards. Deep in me, I knew what Savannah was really doing. She was telling me there was a reason to go back to the prison. She'd find someone to help me. Behind the guards, metal detectors, and bulletproof glass, I might come one step closer to finally knowing what happened to her.

. . .

It was Thursday, so after I made a cake for my weekly dinner at my brother's house, I got in the car and headed south on the Jersey Turnpike toward the prison. It was a nickel-colored day of spitting snow, and the forecast was for nothing but that and freezing temperatures for the next week. I was in a down parka and a ridiculous hat, and because the Volvo Greg had bought me had heated leather seats, halfway there, I was sweating my ass off.

A blond guy with handcuffs dangling from his utility belt handed me a plastic box from a visitor's locker so I could stick my purse in it. His left eyelid was limp, and it made him look sneaky and a little terrifying. His good eye stared at me as if he'd never before seen a porky girl with a notebook and a voice recorder. "Here to see?"

"Please," I said, glancing behind him at the glassed-in office where other employees were doing paperwork. "I don't actually know any of the inmates. I've been here before and have interviewed some staff members. Everyone has been super helpful, but I'm trying to write a book, and now I really need to speak to a prisoner." I was talking quickly. "Preferably someone with a life sentence, because—"

But the guy put up his hand.

"Please?" I asked him, leaning across the counter. "I only need one inmate."

"No can do, ma'am." His limp eye scanned my body from one end to the other. "Rules are rules."

He staked both hands on the counter, and I tried to focus on his good eye. It was hard and steadfast, and I knew I wasn't getting anywhere. Having no one else to see and feeling foolish, I thanked him and hurried down the metal stairs, pushed the heavy door open, and stepped out into a gray landscape. Savannah, I thought, had steered me wrong.

I was unlocking my car door when someone in a blue DOC jacket came down the front steps. He was rough in a sexy kind of way, strong cheekbones, full lips. And as he got closer, I saw it was Brady Irons, the boy from high school who I had loved from the moment he'd transferred in as a junior at the end of my and Savannah's freshman year. He was a military kid whose father was stationed at Fort Dix, and I used to watch him as he walked through the halls with his head down, a white T-shirt on, and cigarettes rolled in the sleeve like James Dean, but I could never make myself speak to him. I did, however, talk about him endlessly to Gabby and Savannah. He seemed older, more experienced than all of us; he'd lived all over the country and in Panama and the Philippines, and I was just a stupid freshman. I was pretty sure Brady Irons never even knew I existed, and still I found myself shutting my car door and calling out his name.

"Brady!" I yelled.

He turned toward me, and I walked quickly to him. I could feel my thighs rubbing together as I went.

"Hey." I was out of breath. "Brady, right?" He nodded, and there was no doubt it was him. He still had the same slicked-back hair and slightly uneven gait. Now he stood staring at me, not speaking. I could only imagine what he was thinking. It probably wasn't every day a fat girl charged him in a prison parking lot.

"I'm Cady Martino. Well, Cady Bernard now."

He shifted his keys from hand to hand. I couldn't tell if he was nervous, late, or had no idea who I was.

"David Martino's sister. From Kingswood?" I knew if I'd said something about Savannah, he'd recognize me right away, but I didn't want to talk about her. It had been 5,914 days since she'd been gone, and it was still hard to speak her name.

"That's right." He looked profoundly uncomfortable. "How're you doing?" He was holding the door handle of a baby-blue antique Ford pickup. "I was just leaving." The prison took up the landscape behind him.

"Yeah," I said, checking the time on my phone. I had forty minutes to get to David's house. "Me too. I don't mean to hold you up, but do you work here?" It was a ridiculous question given his attire, but I was a little desperate to keep the conversation going.

"Sure do." He jiggled his keys. "Everything good?"

How was I supposed to answer that? "Um, sure." And then I got it. What he really wanted to know was who I was visiting in prison. "Oh, I'm here on business."

He let his eyes travel up and down my body, maybe trying to figure out what I might be pedaling.

"I'm a writer, doing research for my next book." I'd forgotten how startlingly blue his eyes were.

He cracked a beautiful white-toothed smile. "I thought you called yourself a novelist." That Brady Irons would know this shocked the hell out of me. The word *writer* made me think of a red-faced, sweaty reporter with a cigar hanging out of his mouth, pounding out stories for *The Post* about why the Jets hadn't had a winning season in forever. But for some reason, I couldn't say *novelist* to him.

"You're on Facebook?" I asked, thinking of the *About* section of my page.

"Nope. I don't need to know when the guy next door buys new underwear. But I've been following your career." He said this shyly, ducking his head as if unsure of himself. "It's not every day a friend from high school becomes famous."

Friend. If only he knew that I'd spent more than a year signing my name in cursive as *Cady Irons*.

"Is your new book set in a prison?"

"It was going to be, which is why I'm here, but I need interviews with guards and inmates. There's only so much information the front desk clerk or the guy who runs the metal detector can give me." I was rambling, but I couldn't stop. Seeing Brady Irons again after all these years made me nervous. It was like the crush had come rushing back in, or the feeling had never gone away. "Are you a guard?" *Please, please, please be a guard.*

"Corrections officer." He said it with the same disdain I did when I corrected people on my job title. *Right, you didn't call them guards.* But at least he wasn't a lunch lady.

"I really need some help." I felt myself stepping toward him. "Can I pick your brain sometime? My agent is going to kill me if I don't get a move on." I was doing it again. Babbling.

He spun his watch around on his wrist but didn't answer.

"Might you have time tonight? I'm going to David's house for dinner. He'd love to see you."

I thought of my brother cooking Indian in the new fat clothes I'd bought him. He'd eaten his way out of his monogrammed oxfords and pleated pants since Emma had left him.

"That sounds great, but I volunteer at Hope's Place on Tuesday and Thursday evenings."

"The women's shelter?"

"They have kids there, too. But yes."

"Wow. That's so nice of you." Every year in December, I'd donate a couple of thousand dollars to the ASPCA when my accountants told me I needed to make some charitable contributions. I thought of how good that made me feel and imagined it was nothing compared to what Brady Irons did.

He shrugged off the compliment. "They feel safer with me there. I teach them self-defense and give them all my cell number in case their boyfriends and husbands find them."

"Wow," I said again, feeling shallow and stupid. "Can I give you my number?" As if Brady Irons, the do-gooder, were really going to call the chubby novelist from Kingswood, but I told it to him, anyway.

He winked at me. "Okay," he said. "How about next Tuesday? I'm off on Tuesdays."

Twenty minutes later, I parked behind David's side of the garage. Now that Emma had left him, I guessed both sides were his.

"The cake's here." I stepped into the kitchen, and there were the people I loved most in the world: Gabby, David, David's best friend, Chandler, and Chandler's boyfriend, Odion. Chandler was standing at the stove, stirring a pot. Odion was at the sink washing what must have been a month's worth of dishes. It smelled like curry and dirty laundry. Gabby was sitting amid piles of socks and undershirts on David's kitchen table, pouring a thick, orangish drink into five glasses.

Emma was a bitch, and I was glad she'd run home to her police chief father and overprotective mother, but she'd kept a clean house. Through the doorway, I could see my brother building one of his model cars.

I set the cake on the counter. "Smells good," I said.

"Hope you like it spicy." Chandler was wearing a half-dozen rings and a chunky bracelet Odion had brought back for him from his last import trip to Cameroon.

I picked a piece of chicken out of the hot skillet and popped it in my mouth.

"What's with the stupid grin?" Gabby asked, putting Chandler's glass on the counter. She was wearing a heavy leather jacket with a fur collar, which explained the Harley sitting outside, even though it hadn't been above freezing for weeks. She'd changed her nose ring to a silver star, and it twinkled as she brought me a drink.

"You will never guess who I ran into at the prison." I peeked in the living room, where David's head was bobbing to music on his iPod, all those little Mustang parts spread out in front of him. "Is he still at it?" I asked.

"He's moping," Chandler said, turning off the stove.

"He's heartbroken," Odion told Chandler. "Give the poor boy a break. It was Saint Valentine's Day yesterday, and he was alone."

"Did you see Emma?" Gabby guessed. "Is she an inmate?" She gave Odion his drink, and he sniffed it before taking a sip. "Chief Fisher would have a hell of a time explaining that his perfect daughter got arrested for being a cow."

I laughed. "No, I did not see Emma, and let me get David. He needs to hear this."

We walked into the dining room with our drinks. David had on dorky magnifying glasses, because everything in a model car kit was about an eighth of an inch long. I handed him his drink.

He pulled out an earbud. "Is dinner done already?"

"Guess who I saw at the South Jersey Pen today?"

Even though his eyes were gigantic behind the magnifying lenses, David was handsome in that messy, absentminded professor way that sometimes made me wonder if he knew how to shower. "What the hell were you doing there?"

I waved my hand at him. "Research for the new book, but that's not important now." I couldn't wait to tell them. "Brady Irons." I took a sip of my cocktail—which, from the taste of it, was mostly rum.

David raised his eyebrows. "Brady Irons is in jail?"

I balled up my napkin and threw it at him. "Of course not. He works there. Isn't it amazing that after all these years I found him?"

Odion disappeared into the kitchen and came back with five plates. "Who is this Brady Irons? I missed so much not going to high school with all of you."

Gabby took them from him and set the table as she talked. "Cady loved him in high school."

"You did?" Chandler and David asked at the same time. Jesus, boys were so dense.

Gabby peered up and saw my flushed cheeks. "And apparently she still does."

I picked up the napkins and silver I'd brought in and followed her around the table, setting each place. "I do not." I could feel my face getting even hotter. "It was just really nice to see him again."

David finished his drink in one long gulp and then let out a loud burp. "I don't think a married woman should be this excited about seeing an ex-boyfriend."

"Hardly," I said. "I don't think I ever spoke a word to him in high school."

"Just because you were too shy back then doesn't mean you're too shy now," Gabby said, puckering her lips.

David reached in his pocket and handed me his cell phone. "Call Lover Boy up," he said. "Invite him for dinner next week. We won't tell Greg."

"I'm not inviting him anywhere near here until it gets a little less sty-like." I swept a pile of crumbs off the dining room table into my hand. "You know, sometimes I miss Emma."

"Fuck you," David said pleasantly. "I'll clean . . . eventually."

"We can argue about Cady's crappy marriage later," Chandler told us, bringing the chicken vindaloo in on a platter. "It's time to eat."

"My marriage isn't that crappy," I told them. But the whole way through dinner, I couldn't get Brady Irons out of my mind.